No Fear

S.J. Frost

mlrpress

MLR Press Authors

Featuring a roll call of some of the best writers of gay erotica and mysteries today!

M. Jules Aedin

Maura Anderson

Victor J. Banis

Jeanne Barrack

Laura Baumbach

Alex Beecroft

Sarah Black

Ally Blue

J.P. Bowie

Michael Breyette

P..A. Brown

Brenda Bryce

Jade Buchanan

James Buchanan

Charlie Cochrane

Gary Cramer

Kirby Crow

Dick D.

Ethan Day

Jason Edding

Angela Fiddler

Dakota Flint

S.J. Frost

Kimberly Gardner

Storm Grant

Amber Green

LB Gregg

Drewey Wayne Gunn

Samantha Kane

Kiernan Kelly

J.L. Langley

Josh Lanyon

Clare London

William Maltese

Gary Martine

Z.A. Maxfield

Patric Michael

Jet Mykles

Willa Okati

L. Picaro

Neil Plakcy

Jordan Castillo Price

Luisa Prieto

Rick R. Reed

A.M. Riley

George Seaton

Jardonn Smith

Caro Soles

JoAnne Soper-Cook

Richard Stevenson

Clare Thompson

Lex Valentine

Stevie Woods

Check out titles, both available and forthcoming, at
www.mlrpress.com

No Fear

S.J. Frost

mlrpress

Copyright 2010 by S.J. Frost

Published by
MLR Press, LLC
3052 Gaines Waterport Rd.
Albion, NY 14411

Visit ManLoveRomance Press, LLC on the Internet:
www.mlrpress.com

Editing by Kris Jacen
Cover art by Deana Jamroz
Printed in the United States of America.

ISBN# 978-1-60820-136-5

First Edition 2010

Unable to contain his excitement, Jesse paced quick strides back and forth across his dressing room. For more than a year, it'd become routine to go out on stage night after night, performing for thousands of raucous people. He woke to a new city nearly every morning, and often slept in one different than he'd awoken. But tomorrow, he would be back in Chicago, and tomorrow night, he and his love would sleep in each other's arms in their own bed. A smile rose of its own will to Jesse's lips. He stopped pacing. Home. They were going home. A wave of pure joy surged inside him, making him want to dance, sing, sprint around the room.

Through his thoughts, Jesse caught the voice of his guitarist and lifelong friend, Kenny Cooper. "He's left us again. He's back in Jesse's Happy La La Land."

"It's the Frappuccino he finished a little bit ago. He's always like a gerbil on speed when he drinks those things."

Jesse faced the two. His older brother, Brandon, met his gaze with a smirk. Of all the people in his life, there were only three he knew he could always depend on, and one was Brandon. Together, they had survived their father, from his fits of rage when they were young to his prejudice against them both for being gay. Brandon stood up to their father to protect him, but in all aspects of his life, Brandon always took care of him. The colorful names they used to address each other were more like pet names, their bickering more an act of play than seriousness.

While Jesse trotted around the world announcing himself as the next greatest singer to hit the scene, Brandon became one of the most popular stage actors in Chicago. Brandon wore his black hair long enough to sport a short, sleek ponytail, perfect for his role as the Phantom in *The Phantom of the Opera*, which would be putting on its final performance just after the New Year, and he already had his next role lined up playing Billy Flynn in a large scale production of *Chicago*. Throughout their mutual success, they always sought to support each other, which was why Brandon flew out to New York for no other reason than to see him perform for this last concert.

Beside Brandon was the second person he knew he could always depend on. Jesse met Kenny's honey-brown eyes. Halfway through Conquest's tour, Kenny traded in his longish, shaggy dark blond hair for a cut shorter all around and spiky on top, claiming it wasn't as hot on stage and the fan girls liked the new style better, which he knew was Kenny's main motivation.

"You back with us now?" Kenny asked.

Jesse's smile widened. "No. My mind's already home."

Julian jumped into the conversation. "Just so long as your body and voice are still here. No one's interested in your mind, anyway."

Jesse's gaze turned to his keyboardist and pianist, Julian Forrester. Julian looked at him with a grin that reached his light blue eyes. The Julliard-trained classical pianist completely shocked him a few months ago when he traded in his perfectly groomed ponytail for a cut that made his pale blond hair look wild and messy. But no matter how rock-starred out Julian tried to get, he never could shake his distinguished air.

"There's one person who values my mind just as much as my body," Jesse retorted.

Julian, Kenny, and Brandon all burst out laughing.

"That's highly debatable," Julian said.

Jesse allowed a good-humored glare to settle on him. "You know, Jules, I'm starting to miss the quiet, polite, formal boy you were when we first met."

"Well you have no one to blame but yourself. After spending so much time with you, I came to realize it was a matter of sheer survival, both professionally and for my sanity, to become a smart ass."

As everyone laughed again, Jesse didn't catch the high laugh he was so familiar with from the other person in the room. He turned toward his drummer, Trish O'Connell. She sat at a small table with her back to them all, the fingers of her left hand expertly twirling a drumstick. Her dark red hair cascaded down her back in a braid. A white tank top patterned with pink roses revealed her toned arms.

"Hey, Trish," Jesse called. "Don't you want to join in on picking on me?"

"Sorry. I've got my mind on other things at the moment."

"Are you still mad at me for hiding your birth control pills? Because you know it was just a joke, and it was pretty funny. Well, I thought it was funny."

From the others chuckling, they seemed to agree with Jesse.

Trish smiled at him. "It was funny. And I can never be mad at you, Jess."

At the sound of the door opening, Jesse turned his attention away from her. His smile returned brighter than earlier as his gaze locked with the brilliant azure eyes of the third, and most important, person he knew he could always depend on, Evan Arden.

For Jesse, when Conquest headlined their own sold-out tour it was a dream achieved. Then to be Evan's opening act on his *Addiction World Tour* surpassed it. Nothing compared to his joy at being with Evan every day, every night, watching him perform, learning from him, loving him. Evan's music, his voice, his gift, was a source of unending inspiration.

Labeled as a musical and vocal genius, Evan brought elegance to rock music and his concerts themselves were a work of art, with pyrotechnics, light shows, perfectly choreographed routines with professional dancers, and a mini symphony. Evan could match moves with the best dancers, change between playing guitar, piano, violin, and drums with the ease of breathing, and still hadn't tapped out all the instruments he was skilled in. He'd sprint across the stage, then blast out his baritone not the slightest bit winded. He could lift an audience up; he could bring them back down. During his time on stage, thousands of people became Evan's willing captives.

Jesse's gaze coasted down Evan's body. A light blue shirt of fine silk formed around Evan's lean torso. With half the buttons undone, he admired Evan's smooth chest, the curves of his solid pectorals. Black leather pants hugged Evan's narrow hips and cloaked his legs down to a pair of black snakeskin boots. He returned his gaze to Evan's face, his refined cheekbones, his slender jaw. At twenty-eight years old, the superstar vocalist hardly looked twenty-three. His dark chestnut hair shone with highlights of gold and copper, the layers lightly touched with styling wax to have a slight wave, the length falling to the middle of his neck in back.

For all their days together, Evan still managed to take his breath away.

"Hey," Jesse said, his voice soft.

A smile shone across Evan's lips. "Hey, gorgeous."

Evan closed the door, muting the sounds of the audience chanting for entertainment. He walked toward Jesse, his gaze moving over him. Jesse wore a pair of stylishly faded Diesel jeans that fell off the tops of his slender hips, and the tight, V-neck, dark purple T-shirt gave his indigo eyes a violet tint. His Jesse, his savior, his shining warrior. The only person who knew all his secrets, who had seen all his flaws, who he trusted completely and fully.

Jesse moved to meet him. The distance between them closed as Evan slipped his arms around Jesse's waist.

Jesse embraced Evan's neck. "You appreciate my mind just as much as my body, don't you?"

A thoughtful expression crossed Evan's face. "That's a difficult question. I guess it depends on the situation."

"Point proven!" Julian called out, Kenny and Brandon laughing with him.

"That's not what you were supposed to say!" Jesse said over their snickering.

"Well, you have to set the scenario up better." Evan dipped his head down and laid a gentle kiss on Jesse's neck. He drifted one hand lower on Jesse's back, his fingers tracing the curves of his ass. "Like how long has it been since we've had sex? Or what are you using your mind for when I'm supposed to appreciate it?" He raised his head to meet Jesse's eyes. "Are you using your brilliance to create beautiful music, or are you babbling about old gods and ancient people? Because if it's the first, we could not have had sex for months and I would still appreciate your mind. But if it's the latter and we haven't had sex within twenty-four hours, then I might be forced to put something thick, long, and hard in your mouth to express my appreciation for your other qualities."

Jesse's attempt to maintain a serious countenance withered as a chuckle slipped from his throat.

Julian and Brandon broke into hysterics. Even Kenny snickered. Trish stood up and headed toward the door.

Jesse looked over Evan's shoulder at her. "Don't go too far. We're hitting the stage in twenty."

Trish flicked her hand in acknowledgment and opened the door, nearly running into Conquest and Evan's mutual producer, Greg Hansen.

Greg glanced back at her in confusion over her hasty retreat, then aimed a scowl at Jesse and Evan while closing the door behind him. "Roadies, groupies, security, performers, and countless other people running all over here and you two can't keep from wrapping around each other."

Evan dropped his arms from around Jesse's waist. "The door was closed."

"And doors don't accidentally get opened with this many people trying to find their way around a new venue every night? You could at least lock it."

Evan sat on the tan leather couch. "If only I had remembered."

From the glare Evan gave Greg, Jesse caught his meaning, and from how Greg's scowl deepened, he saw Greg did as well. Greg hadn't traveled with them on the tour except for meeting them at special events and award shows. His role at Phoenix Records was steadily shifting to his taking on more administrative duties, and Jesse felt it was just as well.

A little more than a year had passed since rumors erupted in tabloids alluding to just how intimate Jesse's relationship with Evan was. The rumors forced Evan to leave him, believing he needed to let Jesse go to protect him. And he walked away from Evan for fear his presence would hurt Evan's comeback. But the devastation their break-up caused made them realize their hearts, their spirits, their minds, their bodies, no longer belonged to themselves. They were no longer whole without the other. Though the innuendo in the media calmed with them not giving the paparazzi further fodder, they had enough stress watching their actions in public without Greg yelling at them every time they sat too close in a private situation.

Jesse lowered his gaze, his bright mood sobering. For as perfect as their relationship was, the one black spot of having to keep it silent from the public hung over it. At times it seemed like a void that threatened to swallow all happiness that neared it.

He understood, or at least understood in part, the need to stay silent until his career grew stronger, and Evan was the main advocate as he didn't want to affect Conquest's success, but Jesse yearned for the day when he would have Evan's full support in coming out together. He didn't blame Evan for their secrecy; there were other obstacles too, such as convincing his band their coming out wouldn't destroy Conquest and making sure they had Phoenix backing them, but he felt if he had Evan's support, no obstacle could hinder them. It really was rather funny how they both cared more for each other's careers than they did for their own. Soon though, he wouldn't have Evan's career to worry about.

Jesse met Evan's gaze. He saw in Evan's eyes that he knew his thoughts as if he'd spoken them aloud. Evan raised his left hand to him. Jesse went to him and took it. On Evan's left ring finger was the gift Jesse gave him for his twenty-seventh birthday, a ring of white gold holding a finely faceted, round cut alexandrite stone, its color a rich burgundy at the moment, but would change naturally to deep bluish-green in the sunlight. Eight diamonds, four on each side, embraced it. On the inside of the band, hidden from all eyes but always touching Evan's skin, was the inscription, *Forever Yours, Jesse.*

Of all the rings Evan had a penchant for wearing, only two were ever-present on his fingers; the alexandrite, and on his right index finger a ring that had belonged to his father, also made of white gold and featuring an eagle in flight atop a square cut onyx, gripping a blood-red, marquise cut ruby in its talons.

Evan took Jesse's left hand so he held them both. His gaze went to the ring he gave Jesse on the Christmas night they reunited, white gold trimmed in yellow gold, shining with a square cut diamond of a size that always brought attention. Nestled in the yellow gold trim were diamond chips, and the Greek meander wrapped around the band. The inside of the band bore the inscription, *All My Love Forever, Evan.*

He had watched Jesse in many interviews where he was asked about the ring, and always Jesse answered the same. With a sad smile on his lips, he'd say it was a gift from the person he loved most in the world. Jesse may have bent slightly in upholding the wishes of everyone to keep their relationship on the down low, but he refused to yield fully. If Jesse were single or dating a regular guy, his sexuality might not be as much of an issue, but Evan being Jesse's partner made things more complicated. Evan feared because of his place in music and the straight persona he'd put up during his career, his fans would react with hostility toward Jesse.

But even with the suspicion floating around, twenty-two year old Jesse had conquered a large portion of the world with his music and beautiful tenor voice, and he knew Jesse wouldn't stop until he claimed the entire world. Jesse's inner strength, his confidence, his pride, were just a few of the characteristics Evan loved so dearly about him, and it broke his heart that he couldn't give him the one thing Jesse wanted most. Only reminding himself it wouldn't be this way forever eased the pain.

Evan felt Jesse squeeze his hands. He looked up. Jesse gazed at him with a warm smile. He returned Jesse's smile, then with a hard tug, yanked him forward so Jesse fell half on him, half on the couch, laughing. He silenced Jesse's laughter by covering his mouth in a deep kiss.

Greg exhaled a loud sigh and dropped into a chair. "I don't know why I bother."

Evan drew back from the kiss, looking into Jesse's eyes.

Jesse saw from the playfulness in Evan's gaze, the kiss was his way of telling Greg to back off.

"I don't know why either," Jesse said, shifting on the couch to sit beside Evan. "We've done pretty damn good this past year without having you being our watchdog."

"And this is the last concert," Evan added. "It's a little late for you to start criticizing us now."

"Plus, I thought you came to New York on Phoenix business that had nothing to do with us. You shouldn't add to your workload by nagging at us."

Greg ran a hand through his dark brown hair, more peppered with gray than the previous year. "You guys can stop the double team routine. I get it."

Evan laid his arm across the back of the couch. His fingers sank into Jesse's hair, absentmindedly toying with it. "You never did say what your *official* business was."

"That's because it's being kept quiet for now."

"Come on!" Jesse said. "What do you think we're going to do if you tell us? Go running to the media? And since Phoenix would've gone under if it wasn't for Conquest, I think I have a right to know more than anyone else."

Evan cleared his throat.

Jesse grinned at him. "Your album sales and tour helped a little too, I guess."

Evan laughed softly and shook his head at him, then looked to Greg. "But he does have a point. Phoenix wouldn't be here right now if Conquest and I hadn't shoved the label into the black."

Greg stared at them for a moment. He glanced at Kenny, Julian, and Brandon. "I guess it really doesn't matter. It won't be a secret once the contracts are signed, anyway. I'm here to help finalize bringing Black Heart Down under Phoenix. They were having some major issues at their label and turned their attorneys loose to get out of their contract. Their agent called us expressing BHD's desire to come under Phoenix, and we weren't about to say no to a band who's been as successful as they have for the past seven years."

Jesse took a long, deep breath in an effort to maintain his composure. Black Heart Down had been one step behind Conquest all year. Admittedly, they were a hell of a rock band, and he had nothing against the majority of them. He thought their lead guitarist, Robbie Russo, was awesome, both as a musician and as a person. Their drummer, Adam Hunter, and bass player, Kevin Moore, seemed like great guys, but when it came to Kyler Christenson, the lead singer, there were some issues.

The first issue: it disgusted Jesse how Kyler sold-out on their last album and used a songwriter to write all their material. Yes, it was a common practice, and maybe Jesse was of an old school mentality in believing musicians should create their own original music, but it bothered him all the more with Kyler because he knew Kyler had the talent in him. For Black Heart Down's first four albums, Kyler and Robbie wrote all the material. Jesse didn't know why Kyler went with a songwriter for the last one; whether he hit a mental block, became too lazy to do it himself, or thought he could make more cash by having someone else write songs for him, none of the excuses were valid enough for Jesse personally.

The second issue: Kyler knew what Evan looked like naked, and especially a certain choice part of Evan since Kyler had wrapped his lips around it. Evan had told him about the incident. It happened back when Evan was traveling the world on his own. He returned to the States for his mother's wedding, but throughout the ceremony he couldn't shake his anger in believing she was betraying the memory of his father by remarrying, and what was more, his new step-relatives sickened him.

After the ceremony and five glasses of champagne at the reception, Evan left, deciding he needed to let his frustration out. He knew Black Heart Down was in New York, and his name got him in the door and backstage without a ticket. Kyler took Evan to his apartment, but when Kyler grew uncomfortable with the things they were doing, Evan stopped and left.

Jesse looked at Evan. "So Kyler will be signed under Phoenix. Isn't that a special little treat?"

"It was a long time ago," Evan said softly. "And just because Black Heart's under Phoenix doesn't mean we have to associate with them. Chances are they'll record in New York where they all live and we'll never see them."

"And if they end up recording in Chicago, then what? Even though he doesn't officially know we're a couple, I'm pretty sure he suspects it and still has a thing for you since at award shows he always looks at me like he's picturing me under the wheels of his Range Rover."

"He wouldn't dare touch you," Evan said, his voice carrying a protective edge.

Brandon chimed in, "Maybe you guys could introduce him to me. He's painfully hot."

Jesse scowled at him.

"You're not my enemy, so I wouldn't do that to you," Evan replied.

"And what about the waiter at the little café up the street from your apartment you've been telling me about?" Jesse said. "That Christopher guy. You don't like him anymore?"

"No, I do, I just haven't made a move on him yet." Brandon laughed under his breath. "He's so cute. Every morning when I go in to grab my usual bagel and mocha, even if he's not working the counter, he always comes up to take my order and make small talk. He's been trying so hard to get my attention, he really deserves a reward."

Jesse looked away to hide the concern on his face. Brandon, always desperate to please the men in his life, had been taken advantage of more than once. He knew he didn't have any reason to not trust this Christopher guy, but with how Brandon's bank account had swelled with the success of his career, and he now lived in a very nice neighborhood on the North Side, Jesse wanted to meet the guy as soon as possible to make sure he wasn't out for Brandon's cash and status.

Greg's talking brought him back to the moment.

"Well, don't get yourself too wound up over BHD, Jess. It seems you'll have some other competition from a group out of L.A. called Swiller. They're new, but they show a lot of promise from what I've been told. I'm not sure when they're supposed to come in, or if they even will. They may end up staying in L.A. to record because apparently the guitarist is on probation for a DUI. I guess the court hit him pretty hard since he's underage and his license was already suspended. I've known their manager, Jon Kurtz, for a long time. He called me the other day and said he thinks this group is a 'Conquest killer.'"

Jesse's right hand balled into a fist. "No band can take us down."

Kenny leaned toward Greg, speaking in a pleading voice. "Greg, c'mon man. Don't get him riled up, or he'll drag us straight from the airport to the studio. I need a break!"

"I'm not trying to fire him up." Greg looked at Jesse. "Actually, I hear the lead singer is quite a fan of yours."

Evan flung his arms around Jesse and rocked him. "Awe! You see? You *do* have a fan!"

Jesse let out a couple chuckles, though there wasn't much humor in them.

Evan kept his arms around him and looked at Greg. "I think that's enough business talk. He needs to finish getting ready so he can hype up the crowd for me, and if you keep talking, you're going to completely ruin his mood."

Greg held up his hands innocently as he stood. "Sorry. I didn't mean to break your concentration for the stage, but you wanted to know."

Brandon, Kenny, and Julian all rose to follow Greg's lead out. Silence filled the room in their wake.

"Have you warmed up your voice yet?" Evan asked.

"No," Jesse grumbled.

He moved to stand up. Evan caught him by the back of the shirt and pulled. Jesse flopped heavily back down, then felt Evan's hand drift under his shirt. The single touch was all it took to shift his mood from irritated into an opposite direction.

Evan leaned close to him. "Then I'll help you." He licked down the outside edge of Jesse's right ear to the two small silver hoop earrings in the earlobe.

Jesse closed his eyes. A hushed moan hummed in his throat. He tipped his head away from Evan, offering his neck.

Evan moved his lips from Jesse's ear to his neck, placing a line of tender kisses down to the curve. "I'll make you hit every note you're capable of." He pushed his hand between Jesse's legs, and at the same time, took the skin near the curve of his neck between his teeth in a firm bite. A high groan broke from Jesse's throat. Evan grinned and lifted his head. "And some you didn't know you could hit."

"I'm pretty sure you've discovered my whole range a thousand times at this point in our relationship."

With a light push, Evan directed him to lie on his back. "I still think you have more talent hidden away and I'm determined to find it." He eased on top of him, softly stroking Jesse's hair near his temple. "Have I put you in a better mood?"

"Almost." Jesse placed his hand behind Evan's head and guided him to his lips.

Evan's tongue glided into his mouth. Jesse massaged it with his own and tightened his hold around Evan's back. A dizzying rush spun through him at the strength he met, Evan's body, so firm, so warm.

Evan passed a pleased sigh into his mouth as Jesse worked his tongue. He shifted his hips, pressing their erections together through their clothes, and pushed Jesse's shirt up. Evan kissed down Jesse's throat. His lips moved over the two black leather cords of the choker around Jesse's neck, from which dangled a gold pendant of the sixteen-rayed Vergina Sun. He moved lower to Jesse's chest, licking and sucking at one nipple. Jesse groaned and pushed Evan's head to his chest. Evan smiled and gave him a light bite.

Jesse sucked in a sharp breath, then laughed. "That's the second time you've bitten me. You're in one of those moods, aren't you?"

Evan tugged the button loose on Jesse's jeans and lowered the zipper. "Maybe."

Jesse glanced at a clock on the wall. "It's too bad we don't have enough time to get into playing like that. I have to hit the stage in ten."

"If you're late going on, it'd just keep to the pattern of half the other nights on this tour."

"True, or you could always let me unleash my youthful impatience. That is, if you think you could keep up, geezer."

Evan paused in reaching inside Jesse's boxers. "I guess my mind must be going with old age, because I seem to have this memory of a certain someone crying out a few nights ago, 'Ev, please! I'll die if you keep doing that! I can't take it!'"

Jesse pointed an accusing finger at him. "I said it that night and I'll say it now, next time, we're going to see how long *you* can take being tied down while I'm teasing you with my mouth and shoving a vibrator up your—"

Evan silenced him with an index finger to Jesse's lips. "Shhh, you shouldn't let talking ruin how pretty you are."

Jesse laughed and pushed on Evan's shoulders. "You're so denied!"

A knowing grin curved Evan's lips. "Is that so?"

A mischievous smirk graced Jesse's lips as he wrapped his arms around him. "Well, maybe not."

CHAPTER TWO

Jesse gazed out the dark tinted window of the limousine, his hand on Evan's thigh, Evan's hand resting atop his. The streets of Evanston were quiet despite it being late afternoon. With only two weeks until Christmas, snow was piled along the edges of the road; ice coated the tree branches in a crystalline sheen. The grayish-white sky threatened more snow for the evening.

Jesse watched the town slip by. It seemed surreal to him, how different it all looked covered in winter's cloak. He wondered why his heart was beating a nervous cadence, why it felt like he was going home with Evan for the first time. Maybe, because in a way, he was. They hadn't returned home since being reunited. Whenever they had time off on the road, they always stayed in the town they were in or went ahead to the next destination and relaxed in the hotel or explored the area. Coming home together solidified things were truly as they were meant to be.

Evan squeezed Jesse's hand. "You okay?"

Jesse turned a soft smile on him. "Yeah. It just feels weird to be back. Good too, but..." he trailed off, uncertain how to end his thought. His last time there, he drove away from the mansion, away from Evan, and with each mile he traveled his heart felt like it ripped more and more as tears poured down his cheeks.

Evan wrapped an arm around Jesse's shoulders, pulling him closer.

The limo wound down quiet roads toward Lake Michigan. It came upon a private road on the right where no tire tracks marred the snow from the previous evening. It swung in and pulled up to a set of ten-foot tall steel gates. Two white brick pillars supported the gates, and mounted on each, the eyes of security cameras watched them. Posted on the gates, signs declared Private Property and No Trespassing.

Evan climbed out and walked to the keypad. He entered the code to manually override the gates, then climbed back in, stomping snow off his shoes.

Jesse smiled, watching him. "Remember when I was telling you we need to buy a winter home?"

Evan gave him a teasing grin. "But there's nowhere to ride snowmobiles in Maui."

"We don't have snowmobiles."

"We will before the week is over."

Jesse chuckled and shook his head.

The limo continued its trek through the gates. As it entered a small cluster of woods, Jesse brought the window down a third of the way. The fresh water scent of Lake Michigan drifted in with the chilly breeze. The air felt damp, a soft wind clacked the skeletal branches of the trees together, and other than the distant sloshing of the waves, created the only sound. Serenity and solitude pervaded.

The limo came through the trees to expansive fields on both sides of the road. To the left, the empty field continued on with no building in sight. To the right, the ground sloped, then dropped to the beach and Lake Michigan beyond. All of it belonged to Evan, and soon, to him as well since Evan planned to put him on the deed.

Jesse looked ahead to their destination. Built in the 1920s and styled to replicate an English Victorian manor, the white brick mansion with gray stone accents rose up from the snow. The long front stretched on to the attached three-car garage on the right hand side, and on the opposite end, a castle-like tower pierced the sky, its stained glass windows splashing the stark whiteness with brilliant color.

The limo slowed as the private road came to an end and made a right turn into the driveway. A ten-foot high white brick wall topped with sharp, upward pointing gray stones and security cameras enclosed the estate proper. To continue to the mansion,

Evan once again climbed out to manually override the twelve-foot steel gates closing off the driveway.

No one could ever say Evan didn't value his privacy.

When Evan got in, the limo coasted up the long drive toward the mansion. The driveway could be taken to the left, where it circled before the double oak front doors, or to the right, where off to the side stood a twelve-car garage resembling a Victorian coach house. Jesse knew inside that garage was his Ferrari F430 with a custom paint job of midnight blue kissed with metallic, a gift from Evan.

The limo drew to a halt at the front doors. Jesse let his dog, Achilles, bound out. A year and a half old, the Collie/German Shepherd mix had grown into seventy-five pounds of fur and energy. His long Collie coat was patterned in three colors, white on his chest, legs, and belly, tan on his head and sides, and black tips on his pointed ears along with a black saddle patch on his back.

Jesse followed Achilles, smiling as the dog dove into a drift of snow and flipped white crystals into the air with his nose. Jesse walked around to the trunk and pulled out two of their bags while Evan jogged up the steps to the porch and unlocked the front doors. Evan turned back to help with the bags. As they passed each other, they exchanged knowing smiles.

Jesse stepped over the threshold. He stopped in the entrance room, feeling a weight lift from his heart he hadn't realized was there. He took a tentative step forward, then another. Beneath him, the dark hardwood floor was polished so it reflected his shoes. The walls paneled in large wooden rectangles of rich brown traveled up to the vaulted ceiling. Across from him, the broad flight of wooden stairs were the same brown as the panels and the woodwork that edged the Gothic peaked open doorways; one to the right of the stairs leading into the kitchen, and further to the right another went to the family room, and the dining room to the left.

Jesse walked to the stairs and rested his hand on the banister, the wood smooth and cool. He heard the door shut and turned to see their bags piled inside, Evan standing at the security system keypad watching the limo on the monitor so he could close the gates behind it. Achilles, claws clicking on the wood, walked past him with his nose to the floor in an exploration of the house. Jesse looked back to the stairs, his gaze drifting up where he knew the master bedroom was.

Evan moved behind him and embraced him around the waist. He touched his lips to the back of Jesse's neck in a whisper soft kiss. "Welcome home, gorgeous."

At Evan's words, joy erupted through Jesse. He faced him and covered Evan's mouth with smiling lips. He brought the long kiss to a slow end, but kept his lips on Evan's. "I didn't think I would feel like this, but now it's like things are more true, more solid. Does that make sense?"

"It does. Being together on the road isn't the same as being together in our own home. I've been counting the days until I could bring you back here."

"Then let's go upstairs. Welcome me home by making love to me."

Evan dipped his head down and kissed the soft skin of Jesse's neck. He took Jesse's hand, and Jesse held Evan's in both of his, following him to the master bedroom, where they both halted.

A comforter of royal blue covered the four-poster king-sized bed. It was folded down, revealing new white satin sheets. A bottle of chocolate syrup and a note was nestled against the pillows cased in white satin. They moved to the bedside, and Jesse picked the note up, reading aloud,

"Welcome home, boys. Enjoy yourselves, but try not to trash the sheets too much, they weren't cheap. Love, Brandon.

P.S. Sorry, Evan, I just couldn't take the poster down like you asked me to. It's too funny and he had to see it."

Jesse chuckled as he finished. "I can't believe he did this." He held up the syrup. "And you've been telling stories about our sex life again, haven't you?"

Evan tried to summon an innocent smile. "Well, it was when we were all in Tokyo and Brandon had caught up with us for a few days. You and Kenny were in the arcade across the street from the bar where Brandon, Julian, and I were hitting the *sake* and the tales started flying."

"I remember that night. When you came to get me, you were so damn horny I could sense it without having to look at you. We almost killed each other from screwing so hard for so long." Jesse looked down at the note in confusion. "What's this poster he's talking about?" He raised his head, his gaze moved beyond Evan to the low dresser across from the foot of the bed. His mouth dropped open with a shocked cough. "You built a shrine to me."

"One poster doesn't make a shrine," Evan mumbled.

"It does when it's framed and directly across from the bed."

Evan glanced away from Jesse. "I asked Brandon to take it down. I forgot before I left for the road."

Jesse gazed at the poster of himself, one of many regular pieces of Conquest merchandise. This one featured him solo and was their best seller. In it, he stood with his legs wide apart wearing black leather pants and a white silk button down shirt hanging open to show his smooth, toned chest and abdomen. He had his usual three small silver hoop earrings in his left earlobe with a fourth up in the cartilage, and two more dangled from his right earlobe. His ever-present sixteen-rayed golden sun pendant rested in the hollow of his throat. A black leather guitar strap was across his chest, and slung behind his back was his sunburst Fender Stratocaster. The head of the guitar pointed toward the ground, and he was reaching back with his right hand grasping the neck. His left hand was strategically placed near his groin, his thumb hooked over the top of his pants, pulling the unbuttoned top provocatively low. His layered black hair had a tousled look, his indigo eyes penetrated through the photograph, and a confident smirk rested on his lips.

Jesse turned his real life smirk on Evan. "Well, at least I know you're not a solo artist with just your music."

"Could you not?" Evan pleaded. "This is embarrassing enough."

"What's so embarrassing about it? I look wicked hot in this one. And you found all those magazines I had with you in them in my suitcase, Mr. Sexiest Man Alive according to People Magazine."

A grin dimmed some of Evan's embarrassment. "Yeah, but the pages were all stuck together, so I couldn't look at the pictures."

"Cute." Jesse chuckled, giving him a light shove.

Evan wavered from the push, but rebounded to embrace him and looked at the poster. "I used this to be my motivation, to remind me every night before I fell asleep and every morning when I woke up of what I had lost and what I was determined to get back." He strengthened his hold on Jesse. "I love you so much, Jess. I'll never push you away again."

Jesse buried the fingers of one hand in Evan's hair. "I'll never let you push me away again. I love you, and I'm sorry, but I'm going to cling to you for the rest of my life. You'll never be able to shake me."

"I'll never try to."

Jesse met Evan's lips in a soft, chaste kiss. At the same moment, each opened his mouth and passed his breath into the other before their tongues slid together. Jesse twisted his fingers in Evan's hair and pressed against him more. He savored Evan's tongue, soft and slick, gliding against his own. He sucked it deep into his mouth and stretched his over it to feel and taste every fraction. Jesse leaned heavily against Evan, his muscles loosening as his body surrendered to him. Refusing to take his lips from Evan's, he shook off his coat and pushed Evan's from his shoulders.

Evan kicked his coat away and turned Jesse toward the bed. Jesse could feel Evan's hunger growing as his breathing shifted to more shallow and quick; the pressure of his guidance increased the slightest bit. His own body responded. His heart drummed a rapid rhythm of anticipation. Yearning spread through him to feel Evan's weight pinning him to the mattress, to be filled with Evan's cock that he knew so well.

The yearning fed his desire until it had full control over him. Jesse broke their kiss to tear Evan's shirt over his head. Before Evan could reach for his, he removed it himself. He grabbed the top of Evan's jeans and yanked the button so hard Evan's hips swayed forward.

Jesse brought both Evan's jeans and boxer-briefs down. The instant Evan's cock sprung free, Jesse focused his eyes on it in an admiring gaze. He touched his fingertips reverently to the glistening tip and caressed down the thick vein on the underside. Same as him, Evan kept himself immaculately groomed with only a small patch of dark silken curls above the base.

The wetness on the tip caused Jesse's mouth to water for want of a taste and he went to his knees before him. Wrapping his fingers around the base, he took Evan deep into his throat. Evan groaned and rubbed one hand through Jesse's hair. Jesse let Evan's taste dance over his tongue before releasing him. He nosed between Evan's legs to the smoothly shaven sac and breathed in deeply, his masculine scent tinted with the flowers and spice of Chanel's Platinum Egoist cologne. He licked and gently sucked at the delicate skin, then before they reached an unstoppable point, slowly rose to his feet.

Evan gave Jesse a hard shove, knocking him to his back on the bed. Evan went down with him, bracing himself over Jesse on both arms as he brought their lips together again.

Jesse kicked his shoes off, each one falling with a soft thump to the floor. He undid his jeans and wiggled them and his boxers down. Once they passed over his hips, Evan pressed their bare cocks together. As Evan's silken flesh slid against his own, Jesse moaned loudly. He rubbed his hands down Evan's back to his ass and clenched onto the cheeks. A hard groan sounded in Evan's throat, and he thrust on Jesse. Jesse clamped Evan's hips in place with his thighs and rocked up against him.

Evan lifted himself up and climbed off the bed. He grabbed the bottoms of Jesse's jeans to pull them off, with Jesse helping by sliding back to lie in the center of the bed. Evan walked to the nightstand on his side where they kept their lube and toys. He opened the drawer to the bottle on top of dildos and vibrators, cock rings and plugs, silk bondage straps and anal beads. He picked up the lube, giving it a couple shakes.

"I know Brandon said he was using one of the guest rooms as his bedroom, but I wonder if he did any snooping in here."

Jesse smirked at him. "Well, I did tell him where to find our toys in case the nights were getting long and lonely."

A wicked grin graced Evan's lips. "Did you?"

"No!" Jesse laughed. "So quit picturing him sprawled across one of the beds with a pile of plastic cocks at his side."

Evan gazed at Jesse. "How could I picture anyone else with you lying before me as gorgeous as you are now?"

His flattery earned him a bright smile. He moved his gaze down Jesse's graceful body, drinking in the lean muscle. Pre-cum was smeared across the lines of Jesse's abdomen, his cock jutted up from his body in a vision of readiness.

As Evan admired him, Jesse did the same to Evan. At only an inch taller than himself, Evan's frame bordered on the small end of medium, his musculature toned to perfection. If his beautiful body wasn't enough to make him appear like a celestial being, his azure eyes and face of soft, refined features were. To him, Evan was nothing less than his own private god.

Jesse held his hand out to him. Evan took it, putting one knee on the bed, and before he brought his second knee up, Jesse's legs were bent back, in offering. Evan settled over him. His lips hovering near Jesse's, he drifted his slick fingers to Jesse's hole and eased one into him.

As Evan's touch entered him, Jesse exhaled a long breath that took his needful tension with it. He closed his eyes and rolled his head to the side. Evan rubbed his soft internal flesh, and with an upward curl in his finger, found his gland. Jesse gasped at the shock of pleasure. Evan added his index finger with his middle and gently massaged Jesse's prostate. Jesse's breath came faster, his cock leaking fresh drops on his stomach. He took it in his hand and pumped the shaft.

Evan withdrew his fingers and caught Jesse's wrist, forcing him to release his cock. Jesse whimpered, but didn't resist when Evan laid his wrist on the bed. Evan delivered a deep kiss as he took his own cock and pressed the head to Jesse's hole.

Jesse's breathing quickened. Evan thrust and pushed past his rim. Jesse broke their kiss with a loud moan. His arms went around Evan; his fingers clung to his back. His body trembled with a euphoric rush at each inch Evan sank into him. During their time together, he had grown so he craved Evan's cock pushing into him, forcing him open, the slickness of it gliding in and out of him. He loved the sensations it gave him, but even more, he loved that it was Evan doing it to him. In sharing their bodies, they found a salvation the outside world couldn't touch.

Evan eased into him a little more than halfway and stopped. He opened his eyes and gazed at Jesse. Jesse met his gaze and touched his hand to Evan's cheek. Evan turned his head, placing a warm kiss in his palm as he pulled his hips back and pushed in again, expelling a low groan.

With the next thrust, Jesse wrapped his legs over Evan's hips and rested his calves on his lower back, applying force. Understanding their silent language, Evan lowered himself down to his elbows and thrust as deep as he could. Jesse sucked in a sharp breath and arched to take in all of him.

Jesse fell into a trance of pleasure as Evan rocked him in fluid, steady motions. Nothing existed but the hard rod of flesh inside him, Evan's breath on his lips, the ridges of Evan's abdomen slick with pre-cum and sweat bumping over his cock. He could feel the warm wave building. As if recognizing the burgeoning climax added to its strength, it spiraled closer to the surface. Every thrust pushed him nearer to the edge. Just a few more.

Jesse cried out. His body shuddered, his cum slicked their skin. In that instant, Evan slammed into him with a low groan, his cock spilling his climax into him. Through the aftershocks of his orgasm, Jesse felt Evan's cock pulsing inside him. He pushed up against him, wanting to claim every drop of Evan's ecstasy. After a long moment, Evan relaxed on him, though still didn't pull out, and laid his head in the curve of Jesse's neck. Jesse rested one hand in Evan's hair and stroked his back with the other. He felt Evan's lips smile against his neck.

"I'd say welcome home again, but I have a feeling I'm going to be welcoming you for the rest of the night," Evan said.

Jesse kissed Evan's temple. "And I have a feeling it's going to continue on forever."

Evan raised his head and put his smiling lips to Jesse's.

CHAPTER THREE

Evan slammed the heel of his hand to the steering wheel, sounding the Porsche Cayenne's horn, then shouted over it, "If you can't parallel park, don't try it!"

Jesse sat in the passenger seat, fighting down laughter. "I know you have a hell of a voice, sweetheart, but I'm pretty sure no one can hear you with the windows closed."

Evan glowered at the white Chevy Suburban trying to wiggle into a parking spot two feet too small, and grumbled, "Three days before Christmas and you decide you want to go shopping again."

"It's not like I wanted to, but I haven't been able to find anything for Trish yet. I got Kenny that guitar autographed by Brian May from Queen. And I got Julian that sweet leather duster."

"It is a sexy ass coat. I'm still trying to picture Jules in it, though."

"That's why I got the chocolate brown leather instead of the black. It's cool enough to feed the rocker side of him, but not too hardcore so as to scare away the sophisticated piano boy side. He's going to totally rock it. Maybe it'll even get him a man. But back to Trish, I keep drawing a blank on what to get her."

Evan tapped a rapid beat of irritation on the top of the steering wheel. "She'd be happy with a piece of shit in a jar if it came from you."

Jesse looked at him. He'd witnessed firsthand tension between Evan and Trish when they toured together in how they not only avoided speaking, they didn't even look at each other. When he went in search of answers to the cause, Evan told him he believed Trish wanted him as something more than her friend and lead singer.

True, she was flirty with him when they first met, but that was ages ago, and besides, she knew he loved Evan. So finding Evan's answer unreasonable, he went to Trish. She merely said her and Evan's personalities clashed. Many people who didn't know Evan well, which was pretty much all people, tended to think him cold and aloof, and he tried telling her to give Evan time, he'd warm up to her eventually, and even though she agreed, nothing changed between them. He came to the conclusion not all people were destined to be great friends, and so long as their tension didn't affect the band, they could all live with it.

Jesse turned his thoughts back to Evan's statement. "If this is more of your jealousy—"

"It's not jealousy, it's fact."

Jesse took a breath to retort to Evan's comment, but before the words could form, Evan smashed the throttle to the floor, shot the Cayenne around the Suburban into the oncoming lane, then brought it smoothly back into the proper lane.

"Just get her something sparkly," Evan continued. "That should make her happy. But nothing with diamonds. Diamonds are a lover's gift."

Jesse glanced down at his left hand joined with Evan's right and the large diamond on his ring finger. When he looked up again, he realized with all the turns and shortcuts Evan had taken, they were coming up on the studio.

A twinge of motivation rose in him, but he battled it back. He refused to think about music and recording…for the most part. He could still work at home. He just couldn't record, though Evan had mentioned building a mini-studio in the mansion. The familiar gray building and glass doors of Phoenix Records studios came into view, but the sight of who stood outside made Jesse grip Evan's hand with blood stopping force.

Evan tried to flex his hand, then saw what caused Jesse's sudden tension. "Isn't that Kyler?"

"You would know," Jesse replied between clenched teeth.

Evan lifted Jesse's hand and kissed his knuckles with smiling lips. "I like you all possessive and feisty. It's making me hot."

Jesse chuckled softly, then looked at Kyler as they drew closer. Kyler leaned back on the building, one leg cocked up with his foot on the wall while he smoked a cigarette, his jeans tight enough to hint at what was beneath, but not enough to fully flaunt it. Despite the cold, he wore only a thin brown leather jacket, the front open to show a white shirt with the top few buttons undone, revealing his sleek chest.

Kyler's slender face had features sharp and lovely, his thin lips beautifully shaped, and Kyler stood taller than Jesse by a good four inches. But two things always captured his attention about Kyler; his eyes and his hair. His eyes were very light hazel, but when looked at closely, flecks of green dotted the irises like chips of emerald. He wore his hair long to the tops of his shoulders, though today he had half of it pulled back, a few strands loose about his face, and its golden blond color captured the winter sun.

Jesse hated to admit Kyler was hot, but he couldn't deny it either, and truthfully, he couldn't blame Evan for wanting to hook up with him all those years ago. If he wasn't with Evan, he could see himself being attracted to Kyler. Though, other than what Evan had told him and what he saw in the media, he really didn't know much about him. Not that he really cared to know, but he did have some curiosity toward the other singer.

Evan slowed the Cayenne as he brought it next to the curb.

Jesse snapped his head toward him. "What're you doing?"

"Stopping to talk to him."

"Why?"

Evan threw the Cayenne in park and turned in his seat to Jesse. "Because there's something I want to tell him."

Before Jesse could protest, Evan hit the button to roll Jesse's window down and called, "Hey! How much you asking for a blowjob, honey? Twenty-five...fifty cents?" He chuckled, then saw the lethal glare Jesse gave him, and stopped his laughter short by clearing his throat.

Jesse brought his gaze back to Kyler when he heard a deep laugh. Like Evan, he was a baritone, but a couple octaves lower, and he didn't have the range either of them had, though that wasn't to say he couldn't sing. His voice was wicked powerful, and he truly did sing his lyrics rather than scream them, which was another reason why Jesse respected Kyler as a musician. When Kyler made his own music, he excelled at it.

Kyler pushed off the building and put his cigarette out in the ashtray by the door. He advanced toward the SUV, his long strides saturated with grace. With his head tipped slightly down, he raised his eyes in a look that Jesse wasn't sure was meant to be sensual, but managed to be regardless. The crooked smirk lifting one corner of Kyler's lips gave Jesse's heart a fluttering of unease over the thoughts Kyler could be thinking about Evan thanks to his joke; but it also fired his protective spirit that he wouldn't stand for Kyler trying to move in on Evan.

Kyler folded his forearms on the open window edge, his gaze looking past Jesse to Evan. "Well, since I normally charge my clients by how long they can last, that should be about right for you."

"You know, Kyler," Jesse cut in, "maybe in New York you look cool dressing like that when it's fifteen degrees out, but around here, you just look stupid."

Kyler slowly brought his gaze to him. "Hey, Jesse, it's great to see you."

Jesse let out a doubtful snort. "Yeah, I'm sure that's the first thing you thought when you saw me in here with him."

"It wasn't much of a surprise. The whole world knows how *tight* you two are."

Evan interrupted. "Kyler, jump in the back so we can talk and I can put his window up before he freezes."

Kyler moved to the rear door.

Jesse made a disgusted face as he got in. "You reek of cigarette smoke."

Kyler tipped his head back and inhaled deeply. "And this car smells delicious. What's that cologne you wear again, Evan?"

"None of your fucking business!" Jesse snapped.

His smirk still in place, Kyler leaned toward Jesse's seat. "I never realized what a sharp little tongue you have. Whenever I've seen you, you've always been such a pretty sweet thing. I like this new nasty side."

"Kyler, cool it," Evan said.

Despite Evan's even tone, Jesse caught the sharpness edging it. Jesse glanced at Kyler, who maintained his position sitting forward, his gaze on Evan. Evan turned in his seat, locking his gaze into Kyler's. If the warning in Evan's voice was subtle, the threat in his eyes wasn't. Evan's beautiful eyes were the physical feature Jesse loved most about him, but as much as they enchanted him, he also knew how disarming they could be when Evan turned them on a person in anger. When pushed, or sometimes barely provoked, Evan's temper could be explosive. He never unleashed it on him, but Jesse had seen its effects when aimed at others, the results at their worst ending in what looked to be a great deal of pain for Evan's opponent.

But it shocked him how Kyler didn't back down. He steadily held Evan's gaze. Jesse glanced back and forth between them. Where before he could understand why Evan wanted to hook up with Kyler, now he saw how they couldn't make it through one night together. They looked like their foreplay would be sparring with swords and spears and whoever drew first blood got to be on top.

Kyler let out a single soft laugh and sat back in the seat. "I figured you two were screwing when those rumors hit last year. For how long?"

Evan laid his hand on Jesse's upper thigh. "This May, it'll be two years we've been together."

Kyler shook his head and clicked his tongue in disapproval. "I can't believe the paparazzi hit on the truth for once. You've become reckless, Evan."

"Love will do that to a person."

"Love, huh?" Kyler's gaze traveled over every portion of Jesse's body. He offered his hand to him. "Well, congratulations on bagging one of the sexiest men in music. You're a stronger man than me to be able to tolerate his attitude."

Jesse looked at Kyler's hand, then slowly took it.

Evan watched their interaction, his temper igniting. He wanted Kyler's eyes off Jesse and spoke through teeth nearly clenched. "What're you doing here, Kyler?"

"Checking things out," Kyler said, his gaze still on Jesse. Slowly, he turned to Evan.

In his gaze and the smirk on his lips, Evan saw Kyler knew he'd gotten to him. He mentally chastised himself for falling into Kyler's game and berated himself further for letting it be so obvious.

Kyler reclined back against the seat. "We wanted to get a look at our soon-to-be home away from home. As it is, Robbie and I are going to be hanging here over the holidays to visit our families in Michigan and to keep hunting for somewhere to live. Adam and Kevin are heading back to New York, then they'll be back after Christmas." He looked to Jesse. "You're a native Chicago boy. We should have you show us around so we can figure out where we want to buy our places."

Looking as if he disbelieved he'd heard Kyler correctly, Jesse said, "You're moving here?"

"For a few months, at least. Maybe permanently, I'm not sure yet. I love New York, but I'm a Midwest boy at heart. I grew up in Indy, then finished high school up in Ann Arbor, Michigan when my family moved there. Robbie lived his whole life in Ann Arbor until I dragged him out to the East Coast so we could seek our fame and fortune. But we both felt like we were coming home again when we came out here. Robbie's never liked living in New York, but he's been really happy here these past couple weeks, so if he decides to stay after we finish this album, then I will, too. Though, I kind of want to move back to Indy, but hey, it's practically next door, so that works for me."

"When are you hitting the studio?" Jesse asked.

"Not sure. We want to get settled first, but probably in a couple months."

"Right when we're planning on recording," Jesse mumbled.

A grin slid over Kyler's lips. "How fun. We can bounce ideas off each other."

"Yeah, unless you're using a songwriter again." At Kyler's slight flinch, Jesse realized how deep his words stung.

Kyler averted his gaze to Evan. "What about you? When are you going in?"

"I'm still working my next one out in my head. It'll be my last, so I want to make it good."

Kyler stared at Evan. "What do you mean, *it'll be your last?*"

"I'm done after this one."

The thick silence filling the Cayenne seemed impenetrable by sound. For all the times Jesse heard Evan say he was going to make one more album to be his finale, to hear Evan say it so bluntly and for the first time to someone other than himself, made a needle of pain twist in his heart. From the stunned expression on Kyler's face, he knew he felt close to the same thing.

"You can't stop making music," Kyler said.

"I'll keep making music. It just won't be for the world's ears. It'll be private."

"You finally came back. You can't leave again now."

"I'm not going anywhere. I'm just not going to record and perform any longer."

"But why?"

"I don't want to do it anymore."

Kyler turned his gaze out the window and sat quiet for several seconds. "I should get back in there before Robbie thinks I ran off on him."

"Alright," Evan said. "Tell the six-string master we said hey."

"Yeah." Kyler put his hand on the door handle and looked back to them with a smile that seemed forced. "Have a good Christmas."

"You too," Jesse said.

Kyler nodded and climbed out.

Jesse watched him disappear into the studio, then turned to Evan. "The whole reason you wanted to stop was to tell him about us, wasn't it?"

Evan put the Cayenne in gear. "I wanted to make sure he knows where the boundary lines are."

"He didn't seem real pleased with your news of retiring."

"He's just pissed because he never got a chance to challenge me until last year and that wasn't even his music since they used a songwriter."

"I guess," Jesse said softly, though he wondered if it was more than that. For him, Evan's music had kept him strong when he was living on only the dream of becoming a great performer and singer. Maybe it was the same for Kyler. He knew Kyler was only a year younger than Evan, but by the time Black Heart Down hit the scene, Evan was already an established artist having recorded his first album at seventeen, and hit the road when barely eighteen.

Jesse gripped Evan's hand tighter. Regardless of what Evan's music meant to Kyler, his decision to no longer record would be felt in the hearts of all who admired his musical gift.

CHAPTER FOUR

Among pillows and cushions, Jesse sat on the plush blanket spread on the floor in front of the fireplace. He gazed around the family room transformed to a den of holiday spirit with garland lying over the mantel and entertainment center, and mistletoe hanging from the doorways, which he and Evan caught each other under at every opportunity. In the corner, a live Douglas fir tree glowed with multi-colored lights, adding the only light to the room other than the fire. Under the tree were gifts for everyone, who they would entertain the following day on Christmas Day, but tonight they decided to hold their own private celebration.

Jesse looked back as Evan entered the room carrying two glasses of red wine. The ends of Evan's hair were still damp from his recent shower, one that Jesse noticed lasted a little longer than usual, telling him what Evan wanted from him that night.

Evan handed him a glass filled with pinot noir and ran his fingers through Jesse's hair after he took it. He raised his own glass of cabernet sauvignon to his lips and looked toward the mantel, where, along with the pictures of them together, were photos of Evan's father.

Jesse followed Evan's gaze to the pictures of the handsome man who gave Evan his stunning blue eyes, his beautiful features, and his musical genius. If there was one impossible thing he could have, it would be to meet Ethan Arden. Evan carried Ethan's name as his middle name and also the grief of losing him even though ten years had passed. Jesse noticed as the holiday drew closer, he'd see the familiar sorrow in Evan's eyes that told him his thoughts were on his father, the same expression he held now.

Jesse gently took Evan's hand. "We could've gone to New York." For some reason, whether it was a fear of hurting Evan or because he didn't want to say it himself, he couldn't bring himself to say "visit his grave."

Evan slowly moved his gaze from the photos to Jesse. "I think he's closer here." He sat down on the blanket across from him. He touched his fingertips to the side of Jesse's face and caressed down his cheek. "So, do you want your present now?"

Jesse jumped on Evan's attempt to lighten the mood. "Of course I do! I've been waiting all day!"

Evan chuckled and stood up. "I'll go get it from its hiding place."

Jesse watched Evan walk toward the entrance room. As immature as it was, he had searched the house for his present from Evan, but never found it. He returned the favor by stashing Evan's away and hopped up to retrieve it from behind the couch. He carried the long slender package back to the blanket and sat cross-legged with it over his lap. His eyes widened when Evan returned carrying a massive, thin rectangular package he could barely see around.

Evan laughed when he saw Jesse sitting with the gift. "So you had it hidden somewhere down here, huh? Behind the couch, perhaps?"

Jesse let out a disappointed huff. "You already found it."

Evan carefully set his gift on the floor, the top of it coming to his chest. "No, but now I know where to look next year." Before passing the gift to Jesse, he bent around it and kissed him lightly on the lips. "Merry Christmas, gorgeous."

"Merry Christmas." Jesse held Evan's present up to him with both hands. "Open yours first."

Evan leaned his gift to Jesse against a recliner and took Jesse's offered present. He sat beside him, examining the length of the package, how narrow and heavy it was, before tearing the silver and blue wrapping paper free to reveal a long wooden box. A faded gold-leaf emblem of an eagle in flight adorned the top of the battered box. Evan carefully flipped open the front latches; the hinges whined a soft creak as he lifted the lid. A gasp passed over his lips.

An authentic English long sword lay inside on blue velvet. The edges of the steel blade still looked sharp, the blade remarkably clean with no dents or wear. The cross-guard swept in graceful downward arches, the grip wrapped in supple black leather. Beside it was a black leather scabbard trimmed in silver. Other than the masterfully crafted beauty of the sword, what made him fall instantly in love with it was the image carved on the circular medallion pommel of an eagle in flight, the same emblem as on the box, and which so resembled his father's ring.

"It's beautiful." He looked up at Jesse. "When did you get it?"

"When we were touring in England. I saw it in a little antique shop when I was walking Achilles one morning while you were still in bed. The old woman working the shop was really nice, she let me bring 'Chilles in with me to look at it, and when I saw the eagle on it, I knew I had to get it for you. It reminded me of your dad's ring, and I know he was from England. Maybe it belonged to one of your long lost ancestors and now it's back with its rightful family again."

Evan moved the case to the floor and pulled Jesse into his arms. "Simply saying thank you seems such a weak way of expressing how much I love it."

"Then I'll give you a chance to express yourself without words in a little while."

Evan laughed softly. He flicked his head toward Jesse's gift. "Open yours."

Jesse spun on his knees and gazed at the present in gold wrapping. From the size and shape, he already guessed it was a framed picture of some sort. He moved the package around to undo the tape on the back, separating each piece from the paper with great care. The wrapping fell away, and as he turned it around to see the image, his breath caught in his throat.

Oils applied expertly to canvas in the Neoclassical style of the eighteenth century blended together to create the mythical image of the Greek god Apollo and his young lover, Hyacinthus.

The heartbreaking tale of Apollo and Hyacinthus was among his favorites, and no matter how many times he read it, it always brought tears to his eyes. So many paintings depicted Apollo cradling the body of his dying lover, but this one featured them sharing a peaceful moment together. Both were nude, lying in a forested glen. Apollo embraced Hyacinthus with one arm, and the young man was resting his head of curly black hair on the god's chest. A circlet of laurel was nestled among Apollo's golden hair, his bow and lyre at his side. The frame of the painting was deep red mahogany, gilt on the inner edges in gold. He saw the artist's signature in the bottom right corner, but couldn't make out the name. Whoever they had been, they were a master.

Jesse wrapped his arms around Evan. "I love it. How did you get this without me knowing?"

"I found it when we were in Rome on the tour and we were hitting all those galleries and shops. Remember that one we were in and I suddenly had to pee really bad?"

"Yeah. You dragged me out of there so we could go find a restroom."

"I dragged you out of there because I saw this and wanted to buy it for you. I gave Julian the cash and he got it for me, then I had it shipped home to Brandon." Evan took both of Jesse's hands. "Actually, I almost didn't get it because I don't like how their story ends, but at least this image isn't one of the sadder ones."

"I always thought I bored you when I talked about stuff like this."

Evan laughed. "You do. It's like having a commentator from the History Channel follow me everywhere I go, but I still pay attention."

Jesse gave Evan a playful push. Evan came back from the shove to put one hand behind Jesse's head and bring him to his lips. Jesse slid his hands up the back of Evan's shirt, caressing the smooth skin of his back. He brought his touch higher, breaking the kiss to lift Evan's shirt off. He returned his lips to Evan's, and giving him a gentle nudge, Evan went easily to his back.

Jesse followed him, and drifted one hand down Evan's chest, across his abdomen. He opened Evan's jeans and rubbed his solid cock. Evan's boxer-briefs posed as a soft barrier, heightening their desire to feel skin touch skin. Jesse dipped his hand inside them, taking the thick shaft in a firm grip as his lips found Evan's neck. He traveled lower on Evan's body, tracing one pectoral with his tongue, then moving up to the nipple. It perked and hardened under his sensual assault.

Jesse licked across Evan's chest to the other side and applied devotions in the same way. In his jeans, his own cock ached with the demand for attention. He pulled his hand from Evan's boxer-briefs and guided them down with Evan's jeans as he made his descent on him. Jesse brushed his lips over Evan's cock as it became exposed and kissed Evan's muscled legs. With Evan's clothes removed, he stood to shed his own.

Evan's anticipation grew as he watched Jesse strip. He felt it deep inside, the need to have Jesse enter him, to have him climax again and again, filling him with his cum. He flipped onto his stomach and slid the lube back from where he'd placed it among the cushions near his hip, in easy reach for Jesse.

Fully unclothed, Jesse took a moment to gaze at Evan's firm ass, beautifully rounded and muscled, covered by soft ivory skin. He went to his knees between Evan's legs, and as his did, Evan brought his elbows under his torso and lifted his ass off the floor, raising it higher than his shoulders.

Jesse stared at Evan's hole, the back of his sac that hung heavy between his legs. He ran his hands up the backs of Evan's thighs, feeling the powerful cords of his hamstrings. He bowed his head and licked the curve of one ass cheek, going from the outside to the strip of skin leading to his sac. Jesse followed it down and lapped at the delicate skin of Evan's balls from behind, then moved up and traced the other cheek. When he reached the outside of Evan's leg, he returned along the path, and this time when he reached the strip of skin, he followed it up rather than down and licked Evan's hole.

Evan's breath shook in his throat. Jesse's wet and warm tongue moved over his hole in long, slow licks, sparking to life every pleasure-tipped nerve. He dropped his head between his arms, breathing deep and fast, twisting the blanket in his fingers. His cock felt so stiff it couldn't move, though it leaked white drops on the blanket. Jesse's hand moved around his hip, and when it gripped his shaft, the shock of pleasure incapacitated him for an instant. He rocked back toward Jesse's mouth with a deep groan.

Jesse knew Evan's desire was peaking from the slick moisture on his tip. He pulled back and reached for the lube. Holding it above Evan's hole, Jesse squeezed the clear fluid over it. Since it wasn't far from the fire, the liquid was warm, but Evan's body still trembled with a shiver. Jesse massaged the generous amount over Evan's entrance and pressed his middle finger inside him. Evan pushed back, taking the full length of it.

Jesse placed his other hand on Evan's back and pressed down lightly. Following his command, Evan lowered his hips until he rested fully on the floor. Jesse moved over him, kissing the backs of his shoulders, and eased his index finger in with his middle. He licked up the outside edge of Evan's left ear and back down, sucking the two small gold hoop earrings into his mouth, all while his fingers stretched him.

Evan shifted his ass to get Jesse's fingers deeper, already feeling they weren't enough. As if knowing his thoughts, Jesse slowly withdrew his fingers. A moment later, the broad head of Jesse's slick cock pressed against his hole for entrance. Evan relaxed his hips fully to the floor once again, taking a sharp breath as Jesse penetrated him.

Jesse pressed until their bodies were flush, and Evan relished in how perfectly their bodies were molded to each other, how warm and comforting it felt to have Jesse holding him so tightly. Jesse set a slow pace, but Evan knew it wouldn't last. They both wanted to give the other ultimate pleasure.

Evan brought his hips up to meet Jesse. As he did, Jesse's pace increased; more strength entered his thrusts. Jesse's weight held him in place, his thrusts making Evan's cock rub against the soft blanket. Evan shuddered at the sweet friction; a deep moan left his throat.

Jesse answered him with a high groan and moved faster, harder. On each exhale of his rapid breathing, his hips pumped forward. Jesse felt Evan's back expanding in quick breaths; his internal muscles squeezed his cock. Evan jerked back toward him, his passion sounding itself by moaning Jesse's name as his orgasm took him. Feeling Evan's release through his body, Jesse's control broke, and his cock emptied cum into him. Evan relaxed fully under him, his breathing already evening out.

Jesse rested more of his weight on him and buried his nose in Evan's thick hair, placing a kiss on his head. "I want to be inside you until the sunlight separates us."

Evan looked back at him. "Then we both want the same thing."

Jesse squeezed Evan to him, silently telling him that he would make love to him throughout the night.

CHAPTER FIVE

Jesse scowled at the Phoenix Records studios as Evan coasted the black Cayenne into the private parking garage across the street. Where before he felt motivation to start recording, now resentment filled him since it would take away from his time with Evan. He knew he should be grateful. Conquest's fans were already starving for new material, but telling himself that didn't help his motivation much.

Not to mention he hadn't even seen his band members since Christmas. Everyone was off doing their own thing, building stability back into their lives and working on whittling down their plush bank accounts. He supposed it was to be expected. They spent every day for over a year in each other's company, but it didn't mean they should all vanish as soon as they got the chance.

It was the same story with Brandon since he made his move on his new man three weeks ago, the waiter guy, Christopher. Jesse understood besides having a new man, Brandon was also working like crazy after joining the cast of *Chicago* late when *Phantom* added encore performances, but Brandon should still make time for him. He felt a slight touch of irony at the reversals of their roles. Before, he had neglected Brandon for Evan, but at least Brandon met Evan within the first week of their relationship. He hadn't even seen a picture of this Chris guy.

Evan threw the Cayenne in park and switched it off. "Ready?"

Jesse answered with an indiscernible grunt and sank lower into his thick black leather coat.

Evan took in his sour expression. "What's wrong? You're going back to work. You should be bouncing off the walls."

"I'm lacking motivation."

Evan leaned toward him. "It's because you've gotten spoiled by laying around the house all day getting sex whenever you want it."

Jesse turned to him. "I'll still get sex whenever I want it."

"Except for when you're in the studio, since we're still playing it straight and it'd probably be bad if I got caught bending you over the piano."

Jesse chuckled. "I can't think of a better way for us to come out!" His moment of good humor fled and he took a deep breath. "I guess we better get in there."

Exhaling a heavy sigh, he opened the door with what seemed tremendous effort. Evan at his side, he walked through the parking garage, spying Kenny's red Yukon Denali and Julian's light silver Audi Q7, but Trish's white Lexus SUV was nowhere in sight.

Evan glanced at the vehicles. "We really need to get a second truck for the winter. I was thinking about another Escalade. We could pick one up this week."

"That's fine." Jesse stepped from the shelter of the garage to a blast of early March wind. He yanked his dark blue cashmere scarf out of his coat and up to cover his neck. "Shouldn't it be getting warmer, not colder as the year progresses?"

"You tell me. This is my first full winter in this town."

Jesse looked at Evan strolling along with his dark brown leather coat unzipped, no gloves or scarf. "How are you not freezing?"

Evan gave him a sidelong glance and grin. "Because I'm walking beside you. I'm always hot when you're nearby."

Jesse reached for one of the glass doors to the studio. "I think your painfully bad sense of humor is starting to taint your charm."

"I thought that was a pretty good line!"

Jesse grinned and continued into the studio. He stepped in the lobby, unchanged since his last time there with dark maroon carpet patterned in small blue heraldic crests. On his left hung a large tapestry of a phoenix in flight, its beak parted in song, its wings of flaming feathers stitched in gold, red, and orange. Above it hung a wooden plaque, its Old English letters reading,

Phoenix Records
Always Soaring

To Jesse's right sat the blonde receptionist, Tammy, behind her massive desk. A security guard, who either recognized them or was too lazy to challenge their entrance, leaned on the desk. Tammy waved and chimed out a bubbly hello to them. After returning her greeting, they headed toward the hall and the depths of the studio.

They passed the vocal booth with its control room on the right, then came upon Studio A on the left where Evan recorded his last album. The three separate studios in the building, Studios A, B, and C, were all identical, having a live room stocked with a piano, keyboards, full drum set, various models of basses, electric and acoustic guitars. Each also had individual control rooms for recording and adjusting the slightest nuance of sound; whether tone, speed, pitch, volume, it could all be engineered to perfection.

Jesse had great pride that Conquest didn't need such studio tricks. They had the talent to sound awesome in the studio, then reproduce it live. Only one song, "Vanish," posed problems. He had no problems with it, after all he wrote it, and Kenny and Julian managed their roles perfectly, but the fast rhythms for the drums were too much for Trish, leaving them with no choice but to have their sound engineer, Jeremy Kane, adjust her playing during editing and they slowed it down when playing live.

As they neared Studio B on the right, Jesse's strides slowed. He peered inside Conquest's studio. He had all but lived in it when recording. Now with the lights turned off, the silence inside seemed charged with the need to be broken by driving drums and wailing guitar.

They continued up the hall.   Deeper in the building was Studio C and the drum room, where he had spent a good number of hours when attempting to help Trish master "Vanish." Soon they would be coming up on the chill-out room. Many hours were spent there retreating from the music.

From around a corner at the end of the hall a familiar figure stomped into view, sound engineer Jeremy Kane, but he looked like he was in a mood Jesse had never seen him in—frustrated. His wavy black hair was bound in a ponytail, and with his head cast downward, he didn't seem to see them. In his right hand remained the near permanent fixture of a white coffee mug featuring a yellow smiley face winking, sticking out its tongue, and brandishing the middle finger of its little yellow hand.

Hoping to brighten Jeremy's mood, Jesse called out, "I always feared I'd be here on the day the studio ran out of coffee. See, Ev, this is one more reason we should be recording in Maui rather than freezing our asses off here. Look how scary he is."

Jeremy's head snapped up. His scowl disappeared with a wide smile. "Hey! The golden god of music has finally returned!"

"That's right! I'm back!"

Jeremy flung one arm around Jesse, the other around Evan, and squeezed them both. "Next time you guys go on the road, take me with you. I know I've never done engineering for live gigs, but I can learn. Put me with a senior engineer, cut my pay, I don't care. Just don't leave me to work with the shit that's been coming through these doors."

"Has it been that bad?" Evan asked.

Jeremy released them. "I'm arrogant enough that I've always considered myself a damn good sound engineer, but there are some truths all the technology in the world can't change. You can't make a turd smell like a rose, and I can't give talent to someone who ain't got none. I do my best to fudge it on their albums, but beyond that, it's out of my hands. I guess it doesn't really matter. Who sings live these days, anyway? Well, besides you two. If you guys ever start lip-synching, I swear that's when I quit this business.

"And either my hearing's going or I just got spoiled working with you guys, but everyone keeps saying this new band Jon Kurtz brought in, Swiller, has got a hot sound and I'm not hearing it. They sound like every other rough-edged modern rock band out there. But I guess that's not so bad. They might sell a few albums just on sheer confusion of people not being able to tell the difference between them and other bands. They'd be a hell of a lot easier to work with though, if they didn't already think they were The Rolling Stones."

Jesse's competitive spirit stirred at the mention of Swiller. "Are they here now?"

"Yeah, they came in last week. Between them and Black Heart Down, it's been pretty hectic around here. Of course, BHD isn't getting shit done. If Kyler's not showing up two hours late, he's not showing up at all. What the hell am I supposed to do? I can't tweak music when there's no music to be tweaked." Jeremy exhaled a hard breath and gave them an apologetic smile. "Sorry. I didn't mean to dump all that on you guys. I should've just ended it at I'm glad you're back. Are you both going to start laying down some new material?"

"Just me," Jesse said.

Jeremy looked to Evan. "And what're you going to do? Take five years off again to make another dramatic comeback?"

"I'll start recording soon, but I don't think much of it will be done here."

Jeremy's eyes widened. "You're not leaving Phoenix, are you?"

"No, not exactly." From behind Jeremy, Evan saw three guys rounding the corner. "I'll explain later."

One of the younger members of the trio stopped. He pointed at Jesse and shouted, "Holy fuck! It's really you! You're Jesse Alexander!"

Evan leaned slightly toward Jesse and whispered, "And this must be your fan."

Jesse glanced at him out the corner of his eye, then was forced to turn his attention back to the group as they came forward. The oldest, who he assumed must be Jon Kurtz, appeared in his early thirties with gelled back blond hair a few shades lighter than natural and a bad fake tan. Jesse recoiled inwardly from only a glimpse of the other two before the one who had yelled bumped Jeremy aside to extend his hand to him.

"Dude, it's awesome as hell to meet you. Your voice is killer! You rock hardcore!"

"Jesse, Evan," Jeremy said with as much zest in his voice as he seemed able to muster, which left it monotone, "this is Trent Cohen, the lead singer of the band I was just telling you about, Swiller. And this is Matt Wilkes, guitarist, and Jon Kurtz, their manager."

Jesse fought down his reluctance to take Trent's offered hand and accepted it, scrutinizing him at the same moment. Though Trent slouched while he stood, the guy was still taller than him, but so bony he looked like he weighed less. The bitter smell lingering on Trent hinted his thinness could be due to taking more time to smoke pot than to eat. His hair hung in limp strands past his shoulders, the color most likely dark blond when clean.

He couldn't quite discern if the guy's jeans were meant to be rough and dingy looking, or if they actually hadn't seen a washing machine in a month. Judging from the rest of Trent's appearance, he figured it was the latter. He moved his gaze down and stared in disbelief at the pair of bare feet in sandals, the toenails long and yellowed. Who the hell wore sandals in Chicago in March? And who let their toenails get that fangly looking?

Swallowing his disgust, Jesse retrieved his hand from Trent's grip. He glanced at the guitarist, Matt, and hoped he didn't want to shake his hand, also. The guy looked as greasy as Trent with his dark brown hair flipped to one side and the spotty stubble on his face. All in all, they took the definition of grungy rocker boys to a whole new level.

Jesse glanced at Evan and saw his arms folded across his chest, his stance announcing he had no intention of shaking anyone's hand. Now that his hand felt like some strange organisms crawled on it, he wished such an idea had struck him quicker. He brought his gaze back to Trent, and taking a deep breath, decided to be polite since chances were he wouldn't have to see him much.

"Thanks, man. I've heard a lot of good things about you guys, too. Jeremy was just saying you've shown a lot of talent since you came in."

Trent turned a harsh glare on Jeremy. "That's a surprise." His expression lightened as he turned back to Jesse. "But fuck yeah, we're a kick ass band! You totally have to come check us out! You're the whole reason we're recording here. We were going to stay in L.A., then Jon heard you were going to be hitting the studio around the same time, and I was like, no way! We gotta go to Chicago so we can work with him! And it turned out perfect 'cause Matt just finished his bullshit probation. Man, it's totally fate that we work in the same studio! 'Course, I'll admit I kinda want to go back to L.A. Nobody told us this city was a frozen hell at this time of year."

Trent's gaze flicked to Evan. He smiled at him as if noticing him for the first time. "Hey, I like some of your music, too. Not all of it, though. I hate to say this, man, but I felt pretty gypped when I bought your last album and like two whole songs were nothing but instrumentals. People dish out their cash to hear you sing, you know? Not dink around on a piano. But my mom loved it, so I gave it to her. She thinks you're totally hot."

Despite being agitated at Trent's ignorance about Evan's music, and everything else he'd brought up so far, Jesse couldn't help but find some humor in Evan's unenthused expression.

A serious tone came into Trent's voice and his gaze went to Jesse. "I couldn't believe it when those tabloid bastards were calling you queer. I was like, no way, that dude is way too cool to be a fag, but I guess that's the danger with being famous, huh? Man, if ever someone tries to say shit like that about me, I'll sue their asses. That's what you should've done."

Jesse stood in shock for a split second before his anger erupted. "Fuck you! Why is it the people with the smallest minds always have the biggest mouths?"

His grayish-green eyes round, Trent swayed back from Jesse. "Dude, I'm sorry. I shouldn't have brought it up. It'd be a sore spot if it had happened to me, too."

"You think I want your worthless apology? What I want is for you to get your nasty, stinking ass out of my face!"

Jon stepped forward. "Who the hell do you think you are talking to my singer like that?" He snatched the sleeve of Jesse's coat.

With reflexes faster than anyone's eye could catch, Evan grabbed Jon's arm below the wrist, digging his fingers into the tendons to force Jon to loosen his hold on Jesse, and ripped his hand from Jesse's coat. Keeping hold of his wrist, Evan yanked Jon to him, caught Jon's other arm, and flung him to the side. Jon flew into the wall.

Knowing the danger of Evan's temper when it snapped, Jesse leaped around Evan to get between him and Jon. "Ev, it's fine. It's not worth getting upset about."

"The fuck it isn't," Evan growled.

Jesse was startled that his words hadn't cooled Evan's rage. Normally all it took was a reassuring touch or look to pass between them, but Evan's eyes were still focused in fury on Jon. From behind, two voices erupted in hysterics. Jesse looked to Trent and Matt.

Trent wheezed between laughs and pointed at Jon. "Dude, you look like you just shit yourself! He totally kicked your ass!"

Beyond them, Jesse saw Kenny and Julian hanging out the doorway to the chill-out room, their stunned faces showing no humor. Further past them at the end of the hall stood Kyler with his guitarist Robbie Russo, drummer Adam Hunter, and bass player Kevin Moore. Of the four of them, three wore expressions akin to Kenny and Julian, but Kyler's smirk reached his entertained hazel eyes. Jesse couldn't believe it. They were in the studio for less than ten minutes and already the pissing matches had begun.

"I can't believe the rumors about you are true!" Jon bellowed.

Jesse winced, knowing the accusations about to fly.

"You really are a psychopath!" Jon looked at Evan with a loathsome glare.

Jesse let a sigh of relief pass through him. Certainly not the kindest accusation, but also not the expected one. He brought his gaze to Evan and saw his expression had changed from lethal to amused. Evan turned around and walked toward Trent. Jesse watched as Evan paused in front of Trent. Though Trent was taller than him, whether it was Trent's slouch or Evan's confident presence, Evan seemed to tower over him. Trent's laughter shriveled into silence under Evan's cold stare.

"Little boys who don't understand how the world works should learn to keep quiet lest the world comes up and slaps them in the mouth." Without waiting for a reply, Evan walked past Trent with the air of a nobleman dismissing a lowly vassal from sight.

Caught between being shocked and turned on, Jesse stared at Evan's back as he disappeared into the chill-out room. The grin pulling at his lips told him to which side he was leaning.

"Damn," Trent said. "I guess those rumors were wrong about him, too. Queers don't act like that." His attention returned to Jesse. "Man, I really am sorry for bringing up bad shit. We can still be cool, can't we?"

Jesse answered him with a dirty look and shoved past him. He glanced at Kyler, who acknowledged him with a nod. Jesse continued into the room without returning the greeting. Jeremy hastened to follow him.

"What the hell fired all that up?" Kenny said to Jesse as he walked in.

Jesse quickly relayed the events while he went to the refrigerator. Furnished to be as comfortable as an apartment, the room had a small kitchen to the left of the door and a sitting area to the right with a TV. Across from the doors were two couches with an oval wooden coffee table between. Four plush red chairs, two at either ends of the couches, made for extra seating.

Jesse took a Pepsi from the refrigerator and shrugged out of his coat while walking to Evan, who was sitting on a couch. He stood in front of him, one hand on his hip. "How long are we going to keep doing this?"

Evan glanced up at him. "Getting into fights with dumb-asses? Probably our whole lives."

"Evan."

Jesse's firm voice and use of Evan's full name, instead of his usual "Ev," birthed an uncomfortable silence in the room. Evan stared up at Jesse like a schoolboy being reprimanded by the principal for mouthing off.

"Um…" Kenny started, "you know, Trish isn't here yet. I think I'm going to go call her to make sure she's on her way."

"And I'll call Greg," Julian said. "He's not here either."

"I'll go with you guys," Jeremy added.

"Close the door on your way out," Jesse said, without moving his gaze from Evan.

Kenny, Julian, and Jeremy scurried out the door, shutting it quietly behind them.

Jesse's voice gentled. "I can't keep doing this, Ev. It was hard enough when we were on the road and had cameras shoved in our faces, but at least we didn't have to keep the act up for long. We could get away from it in our hotel rooms and traveling between shows. How am I supposed to hide who I am for hours on end while I'm working? I can't. And not just because it'll be too hard on me, but also because it'll kill my music. I need to be able to put my whole self into it, and how am I supposed to do that when I can't even be myself while I'm working on it?"

"It'll be better for you when I'm not here. Actually, I can stop coming after today."

Hurt filled Jesse's face and voice. "That's your answer for this? To avoid the whole situation?"

"I'm not trying to avoid it. I'm just looking for the easiest solution."

"I know what the easiest solution is."

"We agreed to wait, Jess."

"I'm sick of waiting! Why is it so much harder for me to keep quiet about us than it is for you?"

Evan pushed off the couch and stood up. He laid his hand on Jesse's cheek in an attempt to soothe his pained expression. "It's just as hard on me. Maybe even harder because I don't have anything to lose by coming out, but you have everything. My career is coming to an end. You're the one who's going to take my place in the music world. My heart would break if you lost that because of me."

Jesse wrapped his arms around him and leaned into him, tucking his forehead into the curve of Evan's neck. "My heart will break if I have to keep hiding my love for you."

A knock boomed on the other side of the door. Before either could reply, the door flung open and Greg stormed in. Kenny, Julian, and Jeremy trailed after, and with them Trish.

Greg slammed the door shut behind everyone. "What the hell is going on? I wasn't even through the doors yet when I saw these three standing outside, which was odd enough, then had to listen to Kenny and Julian stammering excuses to cover the ass of their great leader. Then I'm walking up the hall with them on my tail and what do I find? Jon trying to calm his singer down, who was babbling about how bad he screwed up with you." He pointed at Jesse, then his finger aimed next at Evan. "I had Jon shouting in my face that *you* attacked him. And you," his finger went back to Jesse, "insulted the poor kid."

"Poor kid!" Jesse yelled in disbelief. "He's a greasy little freak! He's a shining example of de-evolution!"

"What he is, is eighteen years old and all of a sudden he's got his dream in hand of becoming a famous singer and he's recording in the same studio as the performer he idolizes. Sound familiar?"

"Not unless he wants to suck my cock," Jesse retorted.

Greg's face darkened with more anger than Jesse thought possible. "You're becoming as uncontrollable as Evan, and don't you dare take that as a compliment. There's nothing good about behaving the way he does, throwing temper tantrums and fists when things don't go his way."

"I didn't even throw a punch out there," Evan said.

Jesse smirked at him. "No, but you did throw *him*."

Greg's eyes widened. "You threw Jon?"

Evan flipped his hand nonchalantly. "Not far. The wall caught him."

"I can't do this," Greg said more to himself than anyone else. "I thought it would be better than the last time. For some reason I thought you'd both be able to control yourselves now, but it's worse. You're like two super villains who have joined forces."

Jesse let out an offended huff. "That's not fair. I could be a superhero. My voice alone borders on a superpower, and I always use it for good since my singing makes millions of people happy."

Evan snorted, trying not to laugh. Kenny, Julian, and Jeremy ducked their heads to hide their smiles. Trish stood by the door, her expression flat.

Greg stared at Jesse. "Seriously, do you even live in the same world as the rest of us? And you..." his gaze went to Evan. He shook his head. "Never mind." He moved to one of the red chairs and sank down, running his fingers through his hair. "I'm getting too old for this."

"What're you talking about?" Jesse said. "You're not even fifty."

"You two have me feeling a hundred. It doesn't matter. Jon is less upset about Evan tossing him around than he is about you mouthing off to Trent. The kid won't settle down until you apologize to him, Jess, so—"

"He'll be upset for a very long time."

Greg closed his eyes in a long blink. "Would getting some work going today also be too much to ask?"

"Hell no! I'm completely motivated now!" Jesse shot a fist high into the air. "We're going to bust out our tightest album yet!"

"But, we've only put out one album," Julian said.

"And this one will be even better!"

Jesse's eyes shone with his freshly fired battle spirit. Their first album laid the foundation for his conquering the world with his voice. Now all they needed to do was put out a second album, one to prove their talent was true and not a fluke, then the world would be theirs, but more importantly, once he established his voice and musical skills deep into the hearts of millions, he could come out with Evan and it'd be all the more difficult for his fans to reject him for his sexuality. He would achieve ultimate victory; a successful music career while holding the hand of the man he loved before all the flashing cameras. He could be destined for no other fate.

Jesse's gaze moved over each of his band members as he spoke. "We're going to work harder than before, push ourselves to draw out every bit of talent. On the last album, except for me and Kenny, we didn't know what we were all capable of, but now we do, and we're going to use every skill each of us possesses to create an album so incredible, nothing will come close to it. We'll still use our electric backbeat in some of the songs to put in that extra energy, but I want guitar riffs where once they're heard, they're never forgotten. I want piano and keyboard that as soon as it touches the ear, people drop everything to listen. I want drums with rhythms so powerful, when our song is on, people feel it beating in their heart. And on my end, I'll sing with such emotion people will feel my voice delving into their souls.

"*Conquest* was a success, but it also could have been better. It was a great album to introduce us to the world, and now, we show the world what we're really capable of. I've already written most of the material for this one, but it's all open to improvements based off your opinions. Today, I'm going to play one of the ballads for you and see what you think." A slow smile spread over his lips. "So, let's do this!"

Kenny and Julian shared a look and a grin.

"And there it was," Kenny said.

"The sound of the whip cracking," Julian finished. "Somehow, strangely, I've missed it."

Jesse clapped them each on one shoulder. "You ready for this?"

"As if I haven't been around your hyperactive, loud-mouthed, cocky ass since we were in kindergarten," Kenny said. "I can take anything you got."

Julian patted Jesse's hand on his shoulder. "And we both know there's nothing I'm incapable of playing."

"You'll get a challenge on this one." Jesse looked around them to Trish. "What about you? You ready for this?"

"Sure." She flicked her head toward Evan. "What's his role?"

Jesse went to Evan and slid behind him, his arms around Evan's waist. "That's obvious. He's my muse."

Trish folded her arms across her chest. "Don't you think it looks a little funny for him to be here if he isn't doing anything, like working on his *own* music?"

His sarcasm thick, Evan said, "How kind of you to be concerned for us, Trish. It touches me, truly it does."

Anger flushed Trish's cheeks, her gaze narrowed on him. "All I'm saying is, you being here could cause more damage than good. I think we can all agree when you're around, Jesse tends to be a little distracted."

Jesse's defenses rose at Trish's words. "What's that supposed to mean?"

Trish turned softer eyes on him. "I just mean you can't even sit down to eat without him crawling all over you."

"If either of us *crawls* on the other more, then it's me on him," Jesse said. "He's got a lot more control than I do."

"Can't argue with that," Kenny muttered.

Jesse took a breath to let another retort fly, but Evan spoke up quicker.

"This just goes right back to what Jess and I were talking about before everyone came in. The last thing I want is to cause disruption, so if it's better my presence isn't here—"

"It wouldn't be!" Jesse stepped around Evan and stood between him and his band. "We're here to make an album, not bicker all damn day! Ev's here because I asked him to be here, and he'll continue to be here and offer his advice on our work because it's what I want. If anyone has a problem with it, then I want to hear it now."

With Jesse's gaze settling on her, Trish shrugged. "All I was doing was offering my input. If you want everyone here to find out about your relationship, that's your business."

Jesse ground his teeth to keep his mouth shut before he unleashed his full anger on her. He marched toward the door, whipped it open, and led the way to Studio B. He walked through the control room, paying no heed to the long control desk with its countless knobs and switches, the comfortable black leather chairs and couch, the massive speakers set into the wall, and went straight into the live room paneled in golden oak. With quick steps across the hardwood floor, he made a restless circle around the room. He went past the guitars and basses finished in wood tones and flashy colors, the four keyboards, and drum set. He moved the main mic stand to his favorite spot in the middle of the room, then finally settled at the black grand piano. He stretched out his fingers and flew them over the keys to check the tuning.

The others found a place to sit or stand in the room.

Evan watched Jesse, each quick flick of his fingers revealing his annoyance. Normally when Jesse played the piano or keyboard, his fingers floated over the keys. Now they were tense, their movements abrupt. Evan peered at Trish. She stood as far from him as possible and separate from the others with her arms still folded across her chest, her eyes on Jesse. He understood Trish's tension over his being there better than anyone else; she looked at him as the barricade between her and Jesse.

She was discreet about it, but her eyes betrayed her. Affection lit them when she looked at Jesse. They had an unspoken agreement on the road to ignore each other, but now Jesse wanted him to listen in on this album as it was crafted, and he wondered if he and Trish could hold to that deal.

Jesse started warming up his voice along with his fingers, going from the bottom of his range to sound like a deep baritone, to the top, lifting in a high angelic pitch.

Evan saw how he relaxed with each second he let his voice flow. After a few moments, Jesse stopped playing and fell silent. He set his fingers to the keys once again. Weaving and blending gentle notes in a harmony inspired by Pachelbel's *Canon in D*, their song, Jesse added his tenor to the music,

"Sometimes it feels like the world is falling
All around us.
They're out to bring us down.
And the secret life we live everyday
Presses on us.
Who wants to live this way?

People say our life is wrong
But they don't know us.
Who are they to say?
If they could see how we lay so close
They'd understand,
It's meant to be this way."

Jesse's voice rose higher for the chorus and changed the rhythm of the song by speeding up the lines slightly.

"No fear, anymore.
I know what to do.
No fear, anymore
So long as I'm with you.

You're all that I could ever want,
All I'll ever need.
I'll have no fear
For the rest of my life,
So long as you never leave."

His fingers glided over the piano, keeping up the faster pace of the chorus through the interlude, then slowing it as he moved into the next verse.

"I lost you once,
I'll never lose you again.
All my fears are gone.
And it doesn't matter what they say or do,
We're too strong now,
They can't break us down.

The only thing I could ever fear,
Would be seeing you, walk away.
So hold me close,
Don't let me go,
Let me know you'll always stay.

No fear, anymore.
I know what to do.
No fear, anymore
So long as I'm with you.

You're all that I could ever want,
All I'll ever need.
I'll have no fear
For the rest of my life
Because I know you'll never leave..."

Jesse's fingers moved slower over the piano. He drew the final notes out and brought the ballad to an end. He raised his eyes to the sight of a packed control room, Trent and Matt with Jon, Kyler and Robbie. Irritation touched him that they'd come uninvited, then he calmed. This was only a rough version of "No Fear." The masterpiece version in his head had violins, piano, acoustic and electric guitar, no bass, no drums. It would be a work of beautiful harmonies and soft timbres, something to caress the ear of the listener.

He looked to his band, Evan, Greg, and Jeremy. Expressions of awe were the most dominant, though Greg looked trapped somewhere between awestruck and horrified, and Evan was sitting forward, his head down as if fascinated by his loosely clasped hands dangling between his knees, which wasn't the reaction he hoped to get from him.

"Jess, have I told you how glad I am you're back?" Jeremy said. "If this song is a forecast for the album, it's going to be amazing."

"Your voice always kicks ass in ballads," Kenny added. "It's gonna be even better than 'Shattered.'"

Julian nodded in agreement and winked at Jesse. "And you actually looked like you knew how to play the piano."

"Do you want to have another classical showdown?" Jesse laughed. When bored on the road, he and Julian often battled each other on keyboard or piano trying to outdo the other with complex classical pieces, and since he could hold his own against Julian, he always teased Julian he should pass his Julliard diploma over to him. Jesse moved his gaze to Trish, and despite feeling a touch of vindictiveness for her attack on Evan, he didn't look forward to telling her she wouldn't be needed on this song. "Trish—"

"The song's beautiful," she said quickly.

"Thanks." Jesse paused, then cleared his throat. "The thing is, I'm planning for it to be pretty heavy on the classical side, and I haven't written in drums for it. It's not going to be like a power ballad. It's meant to be more artistic, a stage for my voice, so—"

"I get it. I'm out on this one."

"I wouldn't say you're out. I still want you to be a part of it while we're polishing it. And wait until you hear another one I've written, 'Twisted Destiny.' It rocks hardcore."

"It's fine, Jess. You have to do what's best for the music."

Her tone, her expression, all said it wasn't fine, but he didn't know what to say to make it so. Maybe once she heard the finished product, she'd understand.

The door opened and Trent walked through. The glare Jesse turned on him pinned him in place. Hesitantly, Trent stepped toward him, extending his hand when still more than halfway away.

"The song is sweet. I wish I could write something like that." Trent stopped before Jesse. Jesse looked at Trent's hand and back up to him. Trent shifted his weight from one foot to the other, continuing to hold out his hand. "Dude, I know I messed up back there, but I'm trying here. I just want to be cool with you. I say stupid shit sometimes. I can't help it, I just do."

Kenny snickered. "Sounds like somebody else we know."

Jesse shot him a quick glare. He turned his gaze back to Trent. He didn't care about Trent's apology and he sure as hell didn't want to shake his hand again, but for the sake of professionalism, and practically feeling Greg's will trying to lift his hand and put it in Trent's, he decided to relent outwardly. Mustering his courage against greasy microscopic life forms, he took Trent's hand.

"I appreciate your apology, Trent, but if you ever say something like that to me again, I'll end your singing career by reaching down your throat and ripping out your vocal cords. Cool?"

"Uh…" Trent started chuckling as if he believed Jesse was joking. "Yeah, dude. It's cool."

Jesse stood up. Concern squirmed through him that Evan still hadn't spoken. He wanted to ask him what he thought of the song, to tell him he wrote it for him, but there were too many people around, and if Evan hadn't volunteered his opinion for all ears, then it was meant for his alone. Since it was nearing lunch, he decided it'd be a good excuse to get Evan to himself while driving to a restaurant.

"Well, I don't know about you guys, but my metabolism can't keep up with all that work. I need some food."

Julian laughed. "You sang one song!"

"You should try exerting this much talent and see how hungry it makes you." Jesse looked to Kenny. "Uno's?"

"You know it!"

Jesse headed toward the control room with Trent dogging his steps.

"Jesse, I'd kill to hear what you think of us. Maybe you could give us some tips."

"Yeah well, we'll see." Jesse walked into the control room to Robbie smiling at him. Just a fraction shorter than Kyler, Robbie's lean build carried all muscle and no fat. He wore his black hair short, but long enough to have little spikes with the aid of styling wax. His blue eyes held a perpetual smile, except for when he and Kyler were at odds. His hands, though, were the feature Jesse appreciated most; long, graceful fingers with amazing reach on the neck of a guitar, perfectly manicured nails, thick veins revealing the strength in his grip.

"It's great to see you again, Jesse," Robbie said.

"You too."

They clasped hands, and Robbie pulled him into a hug with their joined fists between their chests. His lips to Jesse's ear, he whispered, "I'm so happy for you both."

Knowing Kyler had revealed his and Evan's relationship to his most trusted companion, Jesse smiled and replied with a hushed "Thank you."

"I guess that was a taste of what your sound's going to be on this one," Kyler said. "It's pretty good."

Jesse drew back from Robbie and looked at Kyler. "So how're things going on yours? You guys recording yet, or still writing?"

"Still writing," Robbie answered for Kyler. He cast a quick glance at Kyler, then his gaze moved to the floor. "It's been a little rough getting going on this one."

Jesse felt Evan's presence next to him.

"You just need to find the right way to boost your creative energy again," Evan said. "You'll be fine."

Jesse locked his jaw at the rush of instant jealously that Evan would offer such encouraging words to Kyler, but hadn't made a single comment on his song. He looked at the open appreciation on Kyler's face and started for the door before he exploded. He heard Kenny inviting Kyler and Robbie to lunch, and Kyler's quick acceptance. Jesse balled his hand into a white knuckled fist to keep from slapping Kenny upside his clueless head and quickened his strides away from them.

Trent sped after him. "We're going to be eating soon, too. We can join you guys."

"Trent!" Jon yelled. "We've got a schedule to keep! Let's go!"

"Asshole," Trent grumbled at Jon's back retreating down the hall in the direction of Studio C. He glanced at Jesse as he reluctantly followed his manager. "Another time."

Jesse stormed to the chill-out room to retrieve his coat. He grabbed Evan's as well and held it out to him. As Evan took it, he winked at him. The subtle gesture of affection eased some of

Jesse's jealousy. Evan walked silently at his side out of the studio, and once in the parking garage, everyone broke to separate vehicles.

Jesse jumped in the Cayenne's passenger seat, and as he reached for the seatbelt, he found himself pinned up against the window, Evan's lips pressed against his. Jesse laughed through the kiss and put his arms around him.

Evan pulled back enough to say, "You're so getting laid tonight."

Jesse laughed harder, making it impossible to continue the kiss. "Does that mean you like the song?"

Evan placed his hand on Jesse's cheek. "I love it."

Jesse took Evan's other hand and entwined their fingers. "I wrote it for you. You had me worried in there when you weren't saying anything."

"I was too emotional to speak or move. If I tried to say something, the only thing to come out would be 'I love you.' If I tried to move," he smirked at Jesse, "I would've done what I threatened before we went into the studio."

"Bending me over the piano? I wouldn't have objected!"

"I know you wouldn't have." Evan sat back in his seat and fired up the SUV. "You're going to take the world with this one, gorgeous. I know it."

Glowing with a bright smile, Jesse kept his hand joined with Evan's, feeling unconquerable with Evan at his side.

Chapter Six

His frustration in control of the throttle, Jesse whipped the Cayenne around a corner of the parking garage attached to Brandon's apartment building. After a bad start in the studio the day before, today began better in there were no confrontations with grungy little rocker wannabes and Trish was in a brighter mood, but Evan hadn't come in with him. Besides that irritating him, he carried over his annoyance with Greg from the previous day.

First, he was dumbstruck that morning when he got out of bed and Evan stayed curled under the warm covers, informing him of his plans to remain home and research SUVs. Yes, they needed another winter truck, and he understood car shopping was one of Evan's favorite hobbies, but he couldn't believe Evan would leave him hanging the day after so much conflict.

Second, Jesse felt if he choked Greg until his eyes bulged, he'd be justified. Greg demanding his kindness to Trent was bad. Greg saying later there was a good chance Swiller could be Conquest's opening act for a few shows was enough of an insulting remark, Julian and Kenny grabbed him when he leaped off the couch in the chill-out room, both thinking he was going to put his hands to Greg's throat. Such action wasn't a thought at the time. His overexcited fury simply made it impossible for him to stay sitting while he roared out his protests, but the idea, in hindsight, sounded pretty good.

Swiller as his opening act. There was no way that could happen. An opening act was supposed to hype the audience up for the main performer, not cause chain-reaction vomiting from their stink. He called Evan to tell him, and at least Evan soothed him by reminding him it was months away and it wasn't set in stone, or even more permanent, in contract.

Adding to the frustration, the night before he tried calling Brandon and the jerk cut him short, saying he had dinner plans with Christopher. He almost threw the phone across the room after that one. He understood Brandon wanted to spend time with his new man, but to ignore him? It angered him, but even more so, it hurt. He felt lost without having him to talk to, which was why he decided to stop by Brandon's apartment while everyone broke for lunch. He thought he'd surprise him by taking him out to eat, and if Brandon wasn't there, he'd head to the theatre and snag him.

Jesse saw Brandon's SUV parked in the garage, a metallic silver Mercedes-Benz ML63 AMG, a gift from him and Evan for house-sitting. Beside it was Brandon's still preferred mode of transportation, a blue and white Suzuki GSX-R1000 motorcycle. Jesse parked and hopped out of the Cayenne, arming the alarm while he walked to the elevator.

When he reached his destination on the eleventh floor, he stepped out to a white hall carpeted in dark blue. Plants and artwork filled the spaces between the dark oak apartment doors. A man who looked to be in his forties walked toward him, his sandy hair lined with gray matched the trimmed stubble on his face. His dress was of classic sophistication in a sweater pulled over a collared shirt and dark khaki pants, but the way his brown eyes moved over him made Jesse's stomach churn in uneasiness. Just as his sense of cleanliness was repelled by Trent, his intuition blasted a warning about this guy.

The other's gaze met his.   Jesse nodded in quick acknowledgement and broke eye contact. As they passed, the man caught his leather coat, saying "Excuse me" at the same moment.

Jesse jerked his arm from the other's grasp.   "Hands off, chief!"

The man startled back a step. "I'm terribly sorry. It's just you look so familiar."

"You're mistaken."   Jesse moved to continue on his way, making a mental note to warn Brandon about the creepy guy who might live on his floor.

A door up the hall opened and Brandon poked his head out. "Christopher, wait! You forgot…" Brandon paused, his gaze on Jesse. He flung the door open and stepped out, smiling wide. "Hey! What're you doing here?"

"I thought I'd take you to lunch." Jesse turned an uncertain eye on the guy. "Christopher?"

Christopher smiled and inclined his head.

Brandon hastened toward them and threw his arms around Jesse, rocking him back and forth in his embrace. "I was just telling Christopher we need to get together with you guys soon."

"Yeah, like continuing our old tradition of going out to dinner on Tuesdays instead of ditching us like you have been."

Brandon released him, but kept one arm around Jesse's shoulders. "Rehearsals have been ridiculous since we're opening next month. As it is, I hardly have time to see him." He pointed his thumb at Christopher. "But I should introduce you guys properly. Jess, this is Christopher Sullivan, who you already know about. Christopher, this is my little brother, Jesse."

"I adore your music." Christopher took Jesse's hand and laid his other over top of it. His gaze once again coasted down Jesse's body. "My goodness, but you're a lovely one, aren't you? You always appeared so in the magazines and on TV, but you hold it up in person even better." He laughed. "It's a shame I didn't meet you before your brother!"

Jesse pulled his hand back, affronted by Christopher's comment and also stunned at Brandon's laughter.

Brandon dug in his front pocket. "Here, you asked to borrow some cash to get cigarettes."

Jesse snapped his head toward his brother. Christopher was a smoker? Brandon couldn't stand cigarette smoke.

"I already grabbed a twenty from your clip when it was on your dresser, babe. But you can give me more if you want." Christopher laughed loudly at his own joke. Brandon chuckled with him. Jesse stood silent.

"Well, I'll let you boys visit while I run down to the store." Christopher laid his hand on Jesse's upper arm. "It's wonderful to finally meet you."

Jesse's body reacted on its own, his arm doing a sharp shake to free it of Christopher's touch. Christopher drew his hand back, his gaze flicked to Brandon. Brandon met his gaze before turning a scowl on Jesse.

Jesse cleared his throat. "Yeah, you too."

Christopher gave a slight smile and turned to leave.

With Brandon's arm still around his shoulders, Jesse felt Brandon's fingers hook under his collarbone and squeeze.

"Let's head in," Brandon said.

Between Brandon's death grip and voice snarling through clenched teeth, Jesse knew he was mad at him. He let Brandon lead him to his apartment and stepped into the spacious living room. Beside the sliding door to the balcony was a set of six-foot tall shelves crammed with DVDs. Next to the wide screen TV sat a large stone sculpture of a meditating Buddha, whose serene presence Brandon faithfully carried to all his homes despite its heavy weight. On a small bamboo table next to it smiled a statue of Hotei, the chubby Japanese deity of good fortune. Having practiced karate from the age of seven until seventeen, Brandon had developed a deep respect and appreciation for Japanese culture that never left him.

Jesse strolled around the room in his best attempt at being oblivious to his brother's angry stare. He paused and pointed to a long silk painting, its beauty held in the delicate simplicity of the image; the branch of a blossoming cherry tree with a small red bird fluttering down to land upon it. "Is this new?"

"Yeah," Brandon said, leaning back against the door. "So, what do you think of Christopher?"

Jesse shrugged. "He's cute, but he's older than my personal preference."

"He's only forty-two. And you and Evan have a pretty decent age gap."

"Our six years is a far shot from sixteen."

"So you have a problem with his age, or is it something else?"

Jesse faced Brandon. "He's a little flirty, don't you think?"

Brandon's barely suppressed anger rose in his voice. "Why do you say that? Because he was attempting to be warm and welcoming to my little brother, who in return disrespected him and treated him like he was beneath him?"

Jesse folded his arms across his chest. "No, because he was looking at me like he wanted to shove his cock up my ass."

Brandon shoved off the door and advanced toward Jesse, stopping hardly a foot from him. "You and your freakin' ego. You've always thought every guy who glanced at you wanted you. But you're wrong about him. He's better to me than anyone's ever been. He cares for me."

Jesse leaned toward Brandon's face. "He's a weasel. I can see it in his eyes. All he wants is your money and your ass, and probably in that order."

Brandon's eyes narrowed. "Well, I suppose you would be good at spotting that type of person."

"What the hell is that supposed to mean?"

Brandon let out a contemptuous snort. "Did it even take you an hour after setting foot in Evan's mansion for the first time before you were shoving your ass at him? You were living in that shit-hole apartment surviving off Ramen Noodles and McDonald's dollar menu until you became his kept boy. The only reason you were so upset when he kicked you out the door was because your days of driving his Ferraris and playing on his private beach were over."

"You know that's not true! Why would you even say something like that?"

"You're so naïve, Jess. You always hold up to what I say about you, all book smarts and no common sense. Everyone knows you're where you are today because of Evan. And even now, you might have a fat bank account, but you're still his kept boy, there to serve him whenever he wants."

Pain closed Jesse's throat to air. Was that what Brandon really thought of him? What everyone thought of him? That he was subservient to Evan? He loved surrendering to Evan's dominance in the bedroom, but was he doing it outside of it now as well and everyone could see it but him? He didn't think Evan controlled him. If Evan made a suggestion to do something, whether it was eating at a certain restaurant or kinky sexual play, if he didn't feel like it, he'd say so, and they wouldn't.

Yes, Evan had a hand in getting him discovered, but he hadn't forced Phoenix to give him a contract. His talent won him his place in the music business. And so what if Evan took care of him early on in their relationship? Evan loved him, and he loved Evan.

Jesse took a step back from Brandon. "Who the hell are you to criticize me? You think your opinion on my relationship means shit to me? It doesn't! And you know why? Because if the roles were reversed, if Evan had met you first, you would've been trying to get his dick in your mouth before he finished saying hello. All this proves is that you're still hard for him and you're jealous because I have him!"

"That's bullshit, and you know it!"

"What I know is that you wouldn't know love if it slapped you in the face, so instead, you'll take having some lowlife loser slapping you with his flaccid cock!"

For an instant, the look that came over Brandon's face made Jesse feel like a practice dummy about to be pummeled by a black belt.

"Get out," Brandon growled.

Jesse stormed around Brandon to the door and yanked it open.

"Jess," Brandon said, his voice quieter. "Not all of us are as lucky as you to have found their soul-mate at twenty years old, but I have as much right to be happy as you do."

"Good luck with that." Jesse slammed the door closed behind him.

CHAPTER SEVEN

Jesse rubbed his temples with the fingertips of both hands, his headache from his fight with Brandon swelling to the limits of his skull with the added frustration of helping Trish master the hard driving rock song, "Twisted Destiny." He forced as much calm into his voice as he could muster. "It's not that difficult, Trish. The rhythms are right in between 'Euphoria' and 'Vanish.' Harder than 'Euphoria,' slower than 'Vanish.'"

Trish glanced at him from her seat behind the drum set. "Are you getting upset with me?"

With only two threads of patience remaining, Jesse replied, "No."

"Because it seems like you are. Are you sure everything's okay?"

"Everything's fine." Jesse heard the opposite in his voice.

After leaving Brandon's, he made himself return to the studio instead of doing what he really wanted, swinging north to home. He denied himself the pleasure of calling Evan while he analyzed Brandon's venomous words, believing he needed the distance to uncover any truth in them, but all it did was make him yearn for Evan more and leave him short-tempered with his band members, with whom he hadn't divulged his argument. All they knew was when he came back from lunch, he was tense, irritable, and distracted.

Trish's voice sounded through his thoughts. "You know if something's wrong, you can talk to me, right?"

"Yeah, I know," Jesse answered abruptly, one thread of his patience breaking. "Let's just finish working on this. I don't want to be here all night."

Kenny, Julian, and Trish all shared a look at his uncharacteristic statement.

Jesse slid behind Trish. He bent over her shoulder and took her hands in his. "Alright, you're not catching it when I play it, so we'll do it this way. This is how Ev shows me during our violin lessons when I'm not getting it, he guides my hands for me."

Thinking of the lessons, Jesse swallowed the desire to feel Evan's arms around him. Maybe Brandon was right. He couldn't even go a day without wanting to be with Evan. But was that a case of being controlled by him, or simply loving him? Or being wicked horny?

Jesse gave his mind a mental shake to clear it from all the ricocheting thoughts. He moved Trish's hands in exaggerated movements, slowly pounding out every beat and vocalizing each one. "Right, right, left. Foot pedal, foot pedal. Right, right, left. Foot pedal…you're not hitting the bass. Foot pedal, Trish. Concentrate."

"R-right," Trish stammered. "Sorry."

Jesse shook his head and lifted her right hand. "Right…"

The drumstick slipped from her grasp and clattered to the floor.

"Are you kidding me?" Jesse huffed in disbelief, his final thread of patience snapping. He straightened and walked toward the door.

"Jess, wait," Trish called. "My palms are sweaty. I just need a break to dry them."

"Yeah well, I need a longer break than that." Jesse marched through the control room, throwing a glance at Jeremy. "Still glad Conquest is back in the studio?"

Jeremy saluted him with his coffee mug. "Hell yeah!"

It was enough to make Jesse's lips break into a grin, but not enough to break his bad mood. He stomped down to the chill-out room and aimed directly for one of the couches. Jesse collapsed to his back, flung his forearm over his eyes, and turned his head away from the door. When he heard footsteps coming up the hall, he tried to tuck himself further into the cushions in an attempt to become invisible. The footsteps paused in the doorway.

"Well, well, well. I came down to grab something to drink, and instead I find a pretty boy all laid out and tempting."

Jesse gnashed his teeth together. "There's no temptation going on here, Kyler. Just a guy trying to settle his pounding headache."

Kyler sighed loudly and continued to the refrigerator. "Should've known it was too good to be true." He pulled out a bottle of water, a can of Pepsi, and headed toward Jesse. "If you want, I'll massage your neck and back to help you relax."

"Even if I went stupid and let you do that, it still wouldn't mean you'd get me to suck your cock."

"Can't blame me for trying." Kyler held the Pepsi toward him. "Here. This is your favorite, right?"

Jesse peeked from under his forearm at the offered drink. He reached out tentatively as if it were a trap and the can could either explode, or Kyler could bite him. When he touched the can and neither happened, he took it and sat up. "Thanks."

Kyler flopped down beside him. "Let me ask you something. Is the only thing keeping you from liking me the fact that I know how Evan's hung?"

Jesse popped open the soda with a violent forward snap of the ring. "No. It's because you'd like to see if he's *still* hung the same way."

"Actually, no, not really."

Jesse shot him a doubtful look.

Kyler shrugged. "Believe me or don't, but I'm telling you the truth. He's not worth the effort or the attitude." He leaned toward Jesse, his voice deepened to a husky timbre. "Now you, on the other hand, the first time I heard you sing was over the radio. I had no idea what you looked like, but just your beautiful voice got me hard. And when I first saw you, I thought I was going to erupt." He brushed the backs of his fingers down Jesse's arm.

Jesse knocked Kyler's hand away. "Are you this much of an ass on purpose, or can you not control yourself?"

Kyler laughed under his breath and scooted further down the couch to give him more space. "Robbie's asked me something similar to that before, too."

"So why don't you go bother him with your sweet self instead of making me suffer?"

Kyler sighed and rested his cheek on his fist. "He's mad at me right now."

Jesse let out a soft snort as he raised the can to his lips. "Forgive me if I don't seem surprised."

An indiscernible grumble of agreement rumbled in Kyler's throat. He looked toward Jesse. "So seriously, why is Evan quitting?"

"He doesn't want to do it anymore."

"Other than that's just damn selfish, there has to be more to it."

Jesse stared down at the can in his hands. The truth of it was Evan had never enjoyed fame. His whole reason for entering the music business was to earn a large amount of money with the hope he could then afford to take his father to better cancer specialists and save him. When his father passed, Evan continued with music because he felt he needed to uphold his father's dream of being a great musician. Had his father never gotten sick, he doubted Evan would have become the performer he did. It simply didn't bring him happiness. Evan loved making music, he enjoyed being around it, but all the frustrations his celebrity status brought him didn't make it worthwhile in his opinion. But Jesse wasn't about to get into those personal details with Kyler.

"First off, he's not selfish. And second, he's tired of it all. He's at a point where he can live like an emperor for a dozen lifetimes and doesn't feel he needs to keep driving himself into the ground making albums and touring."

"He doesn't even care what his work has meant to others," Kyler said, his voice holding quiet anger. "Don't you think that makes him selfish?"

Jesse glanced at Kyler, his suspicions confirmed that Evan's music was important to him as well. "No, I don't. He gave his music to people for years. He's touched countless lives through it, and has given more to the world than most people. If he feels it's time to stop, then it is."

"Will he still make music through you? Will he write songs you'll perform?"

"His music is his, and mine is mine. He would never push his opinion on me or ask me to take on material of his. Well, maybe he would if he wrote a song with the intention of wanting me to sing it, but he's never done that. I'll keep writing all of Conquest's material myself."

Kyler sat quiet for a long moment. "Do you…" he stopped and shook his head. "Forget it."

Jesse looked at him. Kyler averted his gaze out the door. From his tense demeanor, he could tell Kyler wanted to ask something that made him uncomfortable. With Kyler's bold personality, he couldn't imagine what that could be, but it stirred his curiosity. "What is it?"

Kyler slowly filled his lungs and held his breath for a second before he spoke, hesitation lingering on each word. "It's just, I was wondering, do you ever have moments when the music goes silent."

"No," Jesse said, then laughed. "Well, expect for when Ev's working me really good. Then I can hardly remember my own name, let alone think of music."

Kyler chuckled and gave him a sidelong glance.

The warmth in Kyler's laugh, the charm in his crooked smirk, and the humor that made the green flecks dance in his hazel eyes, was almost enough to make Jesse believe that buried somewhere beneath all the testosterone and arrogance, Kyler might actually have a good person inside him. His mind caught up to what

Kyler asked him. "You're having trouble writing material for this one, aren't you?"

The humor retreated from Kyler's expression.

"Well, it's not such a big deal," Jesse said, startled by his burst of sympathy for him. "You just need to find some inspiration."

"That's easier said than done. I think I've made myself a little gun shy. I'm afraid nothing I write will be as good as what that songwriter put out. What if my material isn't as true to our talent as what some stranger's was?"

Jesse stared at Kyler, shocked by the confession. He didn't know what had brought on this sudden camaraderie, if Kyler was desperate for someone to talk to, or if he wanted the opinion of someone not as close to his music, and part of him wasn't sure he could even trust this odd moment of comfort between them, but it did make him want to help him. After all, what good was having competition if the competition was down on themselves?

"I wouldn't worry about it. The songwriter you used wasn't that good. Black Heart Down always hit the Number One spot before, but on your last album, the highest you got was third." Jesse winked at him. "That songwriter couldn't even write material good enough to beat some guy releasing his first album in five years and a rookie band with their debut."

A slight smile lifted to Kyler's lips. "It was still our best-selling album, though. What does that tell you?"

"In the gap between albums, new fans discovered your material for the first time. I bet BHD is on a lot of people's favorites list on YouTube. Especially since I hear the ladies think you're pretty sexy."

Kyler laughed. "Strange, I've heard the same thing about you."

"Yeah, but at least with you, they've got a shot. With me, it's nothing but an exercise in futility."

Kyler laughed harder.

Jesse smiled at him. "Seriously, Kyler. You don't need to do anything fancy or special on this album. Just go back to the basics and be what Black Heart always was before that songwriter came in, an ass kicking rock band."

Kyler nodded slowly. He slapped Jesse on the thigh and pushed off it to stand up. "Thanks, man."

"Sure."

Kyler headed toward the door, then paused and turned around. "Hey, what had you lying in here with a headache?"

"I had a fight with my brother earlier today." Jesse suffered another hard shock at sharing the information with Kyler.

"He's that stage actor, isn't he?"

"Yeah."

"He's hot. I've seen you guys together in photos and at some award shows. You should bring him by and introduce him to me."

"Since I'm pretty pissed at him right now, I might. You'd be a good punishment for him."

His smile unwavering, Kyler spun around to leave.

Jesse sank back into the couch and closed his eyes, allowing his fatigue to show now that he was alone again.

CHAPTER EIGHT

Jesse let the Cayenne coast down the private road. He looked up through the sunroof. The bare branches of the trees hung motionless against the clear black sky. He could feel his tension ebbing away and wondered why he had thought it best to punish himself by not coming home to Evan earlier. Being away hadn't helped him sort out his thoughts any better. It hindered him. Now that he was almost home, his mind felt as clear as the night sky.

He came from the trees to the sight of the mansion ahead, the front illuminated in a soft golden glow from the outside lights. Along the driveway, the ground lights guided his way home. The gesture was small, Evan probably didn't even think he was doing anything special in turning the lights on, but Evan's thoughtfulness in wanting him to see his way home deeply touched Jesse's heart. Evan loved him, he cared for him. He didn't try to control or dominate him. He wasn't Evan's kept boy. He was his partner, his equal.

Jesse tapped the remote for the gates to the driveway and hit the throttle to hurry through. He checked the rearview mirror to make sure they closed, then aimed for the three-car garage. Once the garage door closed, he jumped out, bounded up the steps to the access door, and stepped into the house.

Achilles danced in place, tail wagging. Jesse went down to his knees, and the dog pushed into his arms, trying to lick his face. Jesse chuckled softly and hugged him.

"I missed you too, 'Chilles. I'll take you with me tomorrow, I promise."

Hearing music, Jesse looked up. He listened for a moment and recognized the first allegro movement of Mozart's Salzburg Symphony No. 3. The fluttering quick notes of the violins sounded in the mansion at a subtle volume through the house stereo system, and he smelled alfredo sauce and garlic bread.

Not only had Evan put in a CD of his favorite composer to welcome him home, but he also made dinner for him. After all he'd gone through that day between Brandon, Kyler, and Trish, he just managed to swallow tears of gratitude.

Jesse stood to remove his coat and kicked off his shoes, then with Achilles at his side, headed into the kitchen. Evan sat at the breakfast counter with his laptop in front of him. The light blue sweater he wore outlined his fit torso. At the sight of Evan's black leather pants, Jesse nearly swooned. When bumming around the house, Evan never wore leather pants. Evan put them on for him, knowing how much he loved seeing him in them.

Evan moved his gaze from the computer to Jesse, a smile curved his lips. "Hey, gorgeous. How was your day?"

Jesse stared at him, his heart pumping fast to supply the desire growing between his legs. If this was what a kept boy came home to every night, then he'd gladly be one for the rest of his life. "Fine. How was yours?"

Evan tipped his head, concern sobering his expression. He stood up. "You look stressed. What's wrong?"

Jesse stepped forward, wrapped his arms around him, and fell against him. Evan always knew what he was feeling. He never could hide anything from him. He snuggled against Evan's neck, breathing in his cologne. "It was a really bad day."

Evan rubbed one hand up and down Jesse's back. "What happened? More problems with stink boy?"

"No, I had problems with just about everyone except Trent." Jesse hesitated before continuing. He tightened his hold around Evan. "Do you look at me as being your kept boy?"

"What? You mean like a kept man? Don't only rich old women have those? Well, I suppose some rich old men have them, too." Evan paused. "Hey, if you're trying to say I'm old, I'll have you know I'm not thrilled about turning twenty-nine this year either, but even that makes me a far shot from those sixty-year-old hags running around with a twenty-year-old humping their leg to hear the coins jingle in their pocket."

Jesse pulled back enough to give him an exasperated look. "Twenty-nine isn't old."

"Then why are you asking if you're my kept man?"

"Because that's what Brandon said I was. He said everything I have is because of you. I went over to his place today to take him out to lunch and I met his new man, Christopher," Jesse spit out the name with disgust and launched into an oratory of what happened between him and Brandon.

While he relayed the events, the food demanded Evan's attention, but throughout the final preparation of it, Jesse could tell by his concentrated visage that Evan's focus was on his every word. By the time he finished, Evan was sliding a plate of fettuccini drenched in alfredo and mushroom sauce with two large slices of garlic bread across the breakfast counter to him.

Evan poured them both a glass of pinot noir and sat on the stool beside him with his own plate in front of him. "Well, as far as the whole *kept boy* thing goes, I think we both know that's not true. Of course, Brandon is right that you didn't have anything before me. But if you just wanted my cash, which is the motivation for all kept men, then after you earned your own, you wouldn't have come back to me." A warm smile graced his lips, and he brushed his hand over Jesse's hair. "But you did."

"I just wish I knew why he said those things. Do you think he really believes that about me?"

Evan shook his head. "No, he was just trying to hurt you because you had hurt him by attacking his man. One of the things with loving and trusting someone so much is they also know your every weakness and insecurity. I know there's no one in the world who could bring me down like you could. But on the other side, that love and trust can allow you to forgive almost anything. You guys will get it worked out. What else had you upset today?"

"Trish, mostly. She was having issues with 'Twisted Destiny,' which blows my freakin' mind, but other than that, there really wasn't much else. I had a run-in with Kyler, and at first that annoyed me, but then we started talking and he was confiding his concerns about his album with me."

Evan lowered his fork, loaded with pasta, to his plate. "Was he flirting with you?"

"He started to, but it was stupid flirting."

"Did he touch you?"

"He just touched my arm, then pushed off me when he went to stand up."

"He was sitting beside you," Evan said more than asked.

Jesse winced at Evan's deductive abilities. From Evan's sharpening tone, he started to get the feeling he maybe should've left out the Kyler part of his day. "Yeah, but not close."

"Clearly close enough to touch you." Evan turned his gaze on him in a piercing glare. "Were *you* flirting with him?"

"Of course not! Is that what you think of me? That I can't spend five minutes alone with a hot guy without trying to coax his dick out?"

Evan looked away from him, the muscles in his jaw clenched. "So you do think he's hot."

Jesse gaped at him, unable to decide if he was more pissed at himself for letting that little tidbit slip, or irritated at Evan for being so damn astute. "Well, he is, Ev. That's just a fact."

Evan turned to him. "Really? Thanks so much for enlightening me to that profound piece of knowledge."

Jesse pushed his plate away and faced Evan fully, forcing his voice not to tremble with underlying hurt and anger. "Considering your history with him, I don't think you have much right to be talking to me like this. Not to mention, just the other day you were the one being so sweet and supportive to him. It looked to me like you were flirting with him, right in front of me! So let's drop the jealous psycho act, okay?"

Evan shoved his plate away. It shot across the counter and came to a halt with a third hanging over the edge. He stood up.

"Since you think I'm such a jealous psycho, let me tell you a few things about your new little friend. He's a manipulator and a deceiver. He's a master at making people believe what he wants and getting them to do what he wants."

Jesse slid off the stool to stand on an equal level with Evan, his eyes and voice accusatory. "It sounds to me like you know him a lot better than what you could've gotten out of one night. Is there anything else you want to tell me about you and him?"

"There's nothing else to tell, but you want to know why I know him so well? Because he and I aren't that different. We've both played the same song in different versions to get who we want in our bed. And you want to know the truth of why he freaked out on me when we tried to hook up? It was because before he knew what hit him, I had already come once in his mouth, and he realized he had met someone slicker than himself."

Jesse choked out a pained breath and stepped back. When their relationship first started, Evan revealed much of his promiscuous past to him so nothing would surprise him down the road. But to hear Evan speak of it so bluntly now stabbed straight into his heart."You were right." Jesse stormed around Evan. "No one can hurt you like the person you love and trust the most."

"Jess." Evan reached for him.

Jesse jerked his arm forward and evaded Evan's grasp. He marched through the entrance room to the sound of Evan's footsteps hastening to catch up.

"Jess, wait! I'm sorry! I didn't mean to say it like that."

Jesse leaped up the bottom three stairs and sprinted up the rest of the flight. "Just leave me alone. I don't want to talk anymore."

"Well I do!"

Jesse hit the second floor and darted for the bedroom. Without looking behind, he whipped the door to slam it closed and heard it thump against something, followed by a calmly spoken "Ow." He whirled around, panicked he had accidentally hurt Evan. "Are you alright?"

Evan grinned and nodded. "I caught it with my hand. But I knew you'd stop if you thought I was hurt."

Jesse frowned at him. "You're not funny."

Evan took a quick step forward and trapped him with his arms around Jesse's waist, his hands clasped behind Jesse's back. "We're not done talking."

"We weren't exactly talking to begin with, but regardless, yes, we are. This bullshit has resurrected my headache from earlier. All day long, the only thing I wanted was to come home to you, and when I do, we end up in a fight. Now all I want is to sit in the whirlpool, then crawl into bed and wait for tomorrow with the hope that it'll be a better day." Jesse reached behind with both hands to pull Evan's grip apart, only to feel the muscles in Evan's forearms and biceps constrict in resistance. Exhaling a sigh of battle fatigue, his tired eyes met Evan's. "Ev, let go."

"Not until we've finished talking. Will you listen to me?"

"Maybe if you let me go," Jesse growled between clenched teeth.

Evan gazed at him for a moment, then reluctantly loosened his hold on him. Before he had finished unlocking his fingers, Jesse stepped back and broke his grip.

Evan nearly gasped at the pain he felt that Jesse wanted to move away from him. His heart fluttered with anxiety. He lowered his gaze to the floor, insecurity silencing him. A moment ago, words to comfort Jesse filled his mind, now it was a blank void. He risked a glance at him. Jesse stood with his arms folded across his chest, his head away from him. Evan studied his profile. Not since their time apart had he seen Jesse look so upset. He felt like a fool for letting jealously control his words, for questioning Jesse's faithfulness when never in all their time together had Jesse given him reason for such lack of trust.

His gaze dropped again. "I'm so stupid."

Jesse mumbled, "You're not stupid."

Evan snapped his gaze up. Jesse still wasn't looking at him, but he couldn't believe he'd come to his defense. He took a halting step toward him. "Jess, I'm so sorry."

Jesse flicked a quick glance at him.

Evan took another step forward. Jesse's stance wavered slightly, and for an instant, he thought he was going to retreat a step, but Jesse remained in place. "How I spoke to you was inexcusable."

Slowly, Jesse turned his head toward him, though he kept his eyes cast downward.

Encouraged by the movement, Evan took the final step and stood half an arm's length from him. "I don't know why I said those things. I know you don't have any interest in Kyler, I just…" he paused and sighed, "maybe I'm the one who's been made insecure by having him around because he brings that part of my past closer than I'd like. What I need to do is never forget my present and future are stronger." He reached out and gently touched Jesse's hand.

Jesse raised his eyes. Evan's heartbeat quickened at the tenderness in his dark blue gaze. Jesse lifted his arms and wrapped him in a soft embrace. Relief washed through Evan and swept his strength away. He clung to Jesse, needing to lean against him for fear his legs couldn't hold him. Beneath the relief, he felt an undercurrent of his old reproach that he didn't deserve to have someone so kind and forgiving. He pushed the feeling down and let it drown under gratitude for the unconditional love Jesse gave him.

"I'll never talk to you that way again, Jess. I promise. You were right when you called me a jealous psycho, but it's because the only thing in this world that scares me is the thought of losing you."

"You're never going to lose me. You have to know that deep down."

Evan nodded, but kept his fear silent about how there were some things in life beyond even Jesse's control. He had witnessed it as he watched his father fight in vain against death's undefeatable grip.

"Ev, you're squishing me," Jesse said, his voice strained.

Having not realized he had tightened his hold, Evan instantly relaxed his arms and muttered a barely audible, "Sorry."

Jesse laid his hand on Evan's cheek. "Don't take all the blame for this on yourself. I'm sorry, too. It's probably more my fault, anyway. I can't be around anyone anymore without pissing them off."

"That's not true."

Skepticism made Jesse's eyes roll. "Come with me to the studio tomorrow and see for yourself." His gaze lowered. "It was wrong of me to call you a jealous psycho. If either of us is, then it's me. This whole thing exploded because even after all our time together, I can't handle the thought that there's anyone else out there who knows your body."

"Jess," Evan took Jesse's hands and pulled them behind his own back, making Jesse embrace him, "there may be others who have experienced it, but you're the only one who truly knows it. My body belongs to you. It's yours to master and have serve you, to love or to harm, to cherish or to throw away. I'd never refuse anything you wanted to do to it."

Jesse strengthened his embrace around Evan. His mischievous smirk curved his lips. "What if I wanted to play with and torture you for hours, then walk away without letting you come? Would you let me do that?"

"Yeah, I would. Even though you're not that sadistic and I'd probably have more willpower against coming than you would against not letting me."

"What if I wanted you to get a tattoo across your lower back with an arrow pointing down your tailbone that says, Jesse's Private Entrance?"

Evan laughed. "Just take me to the nearest tattoo parlor."

Jesse kissed him lightly on the lips. "I'd never do anything to mar your perfection." With peace between them again, his headache claimed his full attention with throbs making it feel as though his brain was swelling from the inside and pushing outward. Jesse closed his eyes against the pain, his brow creased in the middle with strain.

At seeing the physical pain on Jesse's face, guilt for pushing him when he knew Jesse didn't feel well overrode Evan's emotions. He brushed Jesse's hair from his forehead with the backs of his fingers. "Do you want me to get you some aspirin?"

Jesse shook his head. "No, I just want to get into a hot bath and zone out for a while. If it's still bothering me when we're getting ready to go to bed, then I'll take something." He turned around and walked toward the bathroom.

Evan trailed after him. "Do you want me to put in a different CD? You get hyped up when you listen to Mozart. I can put in Bach or Chopin. Or maybe silence would be better."

Jesse climbed the two stairs to the raised tub and sat on the edge as he turned the water on. "It's fine. I love this disc."

"Then what about dinner? You didn't finish eating. I'll bring your plate up and you can eat in the bath."

Jesse looked at Evan, taking in his desperation to make him feel better. He rose and descended one step. He pulled him into his arms, resting Evan's head against his chest. "I never knew my brother could be so wrong about anything."

Evan stood silent, holding Jesse around the waist.

Jesse kissed the top of his head, then cupped Evan's face in both hands. "You know what I want you to do for me? Get undressed and climb in the tub with me."

Evan's countenance brightened with a smile. "I can do that."

The rising water in the bathtub forced Jesse to turn away to shut it off. When he faced around again, it was to the sight of

Evan lifting his sweater over his head. The memory of their argument floated to the back of his mind and, as Evan opened his leather pants, revealing he wore no underwear, the memory dissipated completely.

Bared of his clothing, Evan climbed the steps to the tub. He slipped both hands under Jesse's shirt and rubbed up his sides as he lifted it off. Evan moved his hands to Jesse's jeans and jerked him forward. His voice deepened to a sensual timbre. "Maybe I can make your headache go away by putting your body's attention on something more pleasurable."

Jesse brushed his lips over Evan's. "It's worth a try."

Evan dipped his head and licked a slow line up the side of Jesse's neck. He slid down Jesse's body as he guided his jeans to the floor. With Jesse fully unclothed, Evan stood and stepped into the tub, holding his hand out to him. Jesse took it, and together they sank into the churning whirlpool of hot water, Evan reclining against the tub wall, Jesse sitting between his legs and using Evan's chest as a backrest.

Evan set his fingertips against Jesse's temples and massaged them in gentle circles. Jesse closed his eyes. Cords of tension snapped with each rotation of Evan's fingers. After a few moments, Evan moved his touch to the back of Jesse's neck, rubbing from the base of his skull to the tops of his shoulders. Jesse bent forward to give him more room, and was rewarded by Evan kneading his shoulders and pressing the heels of his hands down his back along his spine. His hands came back up, across Jesse's shoulders and down his arms, untying the knots in Jesse's biceps, his forearms, to his hands where he worked each finger. He returned up Jesse's arms and slipped under them to loosen his wiry chest muscles.

Jesse collapsed on Evan's chest, quiet moans purring from his throat. Evan's touch brought comfort wherever his fingers drifted. Jesse felt like Evan was massaging him into a trance.

"Feeling a little better?" Evan whispered.

Jesse rolled his head on Evan's shoulder and nuzzled into his neck. "A lot."

Evan floated his fingertips down Jesse's abdomen to his hard cock and tickled up the underside. Jesse groaned louder, his hips rising to follow Evan's fleeing touch.

Evan enclosed the tip in his hand, then brought his grip down the shaft. "You can't fully relax when you're in such a state, can you?"

Jesse shook his head. "No, I can't."

Evan performed a painstakingly slow pump. He pushed his other hand between Jesse's legs, fondling his sac while stroking him. "Let's see if I can't put every part of you at ease."

Jesse parted his thighs wider and allowed himself to succumb to the slow pleasuring. He concentrated on each stroke of Evan's hand, how his fingers toyed with his sac. Everything around him, all the events from that day, vanished. Only pleasure and the firm body behind him remained. His head felt light, freed from the weight of his headache.

Jesse placed one hand over Evan's as it pumped his shaft. He lifted his hips to meet the next downward stroke, lowered them on the upward return, raised them again, and once more went back down. His hips thrusting in harmony with Evan's hand, he felt the deep swirling warmth of his rising climax. A hushed groan left him. The sensation intensified still more. He clutched Evan's thighs. It'd break from him in seconds. One more stroke. It hit the surface.

He moaned high and loud, and writhed against Evan as he came. When his climax finally subsided, the aftershocks throbbed through him to continue the pleasure. As the last of those faded, he laid unmoving, feeling exhausted, relaxed, and utterly spent.

Evan kissed him softly on the temple. "Still have a headache?"

"I don't even remember what a headache feels like right now."

Evan hugged him around the chest. "Good."

Jesse felt Evan's hard cock pressed against his lower back. He turned to look at him. "You didn't get there?"

"I wasn't really working at it, but I'm fine." Evan rose from the tub and stepped out. "Though I'll warn you now, come morning, I'm going to ravish you."

Jesse chuckled softly. "I'll be ready for it."

Evan grabbed a towel and held it open to wrap him in it. Jesse climbed out of the water and let Evan enclose him in the plush fabric.

"Now," Evan said, guiding Jesse to the bedroom, "are you ready to finish your dinner?"

"I'm starving."

Evan flipped down the comforter and top sheet on Jesse's side of the bed. "Then get in bed and I'll bring it up to you."

Jesse dropped the towel and crawled into bed. He caught Evan's hand and looked up at him. "I love you."

Evan caressed Jesse's cheek. "I love you too, gorgeous."

As Evan walked away, Jesse slid lower under the covers, his eyes closing.

CHAPTER NINE

Jesse pulled against the black silk scarves and groaned between clenched teeth. Evan had the restraints perfect, as he always did. Their length from the headboard long enough where he could bring his arms down to be comfortable, but couldn't move his hands any lower than his head. Around his wrists, they were loose enough to not hurt, yet he couldn't slip his hands free. Jesse sucked in a sharp breath as Evan eased another anal bead into him. He pressed his head back on the bed, panting each breath.

Jesse's head snapped forward as the moist heat of Evan's mouth engulfed his cock. As Evan moved up and down it, he pushed the last bead into him. Tugging harder at the restraints, Jesse's breath left him in a stuttering groan. He felt the tingling warmth of his soon to be climax, making him anxious for it. He jerked his hips up to Evan's mouth.

Evan sat back.

Jesse let out a short cry of protest. The air chilled his wet cock. He craned his neck to look at Evan. "Don't stop. I'm right there."

Evan took Jesse's cock and gave it a few slow strokes. "I know you are. That's why I stopped."

Dropping his head back, Jesse whimpered. "You're so mean."

Evan pulled on the anal beads until one left Jesse. "You had yours last night. And you like it when I'm mean, don't you?"

A grin slipped onto Jesse's lips.

Evan withdrew a second bead.

Jesse groaned hard, his moment of humor dissipating as stronger desires took over. "Please, Ev…"

Evan slid up Jesse's body, keeping one hand on the beads. He licked Jesse's lips. "Do you want it as I suck you and pull these out, or do you want me to drive you there with my cock?"

Jesse's mind froze at having to choose between the two options. How could he pick? Of course, there was no wrong choice either. "How close are you?"

"Very."

"Then come with me."

Evan smiled and lightly nipped Jesse's bottom lip. "You're so good to me to still think of my needs even after how mean I've been."

Jesse chuckled. "Yeah well, hurry up before I change my mind and make you just get me off."

Evan dipped his head to deliver a quick bite to Jesse's neck, making him twitch and laugh, then sat back to remove the beads. He slowly drew them out, watching as each one left Jesse's body.

Jesse rolled his hips; the emptiness of the beads being gone increased his need to have Evan fill him. He felt Evan grab his legs, slinging one over each shoulder. He opened his eyes in time to see Evan bringing his cock to his hole, then on his next heartbeat, Evan pushed inside him. A high moan burst from Jesse. He loved playing with their toys, but none could ever give him the same pleasure as having Evan buried inside him.

Evan sank into him hard, thrusting quick.

"Faster, Ev," Jesse panted.

Evan instantly picked up his pace and took Jesse's cock in a tight fist. Jesse yanked down on the scarves so hard the headboard shook. Evan hugged Jesse's thighs with one arm. Jesse's body tightened. He bucked against Evan, yelling Evan's name in his passion. Evan watched the fluid burst from Jesse's cock to splatter across his abdomen. The sight finished him. He groaned loud; his head fell back on his shoulders as he came.

Both ceased all movement other than their chests rising and falling as they fought to catch their breath. After his breathing steadied, Evan grudgingly eased out of him. He crawled up the bed and freed Jesse, then fell over to his back and sprawled out. Jesse willed his exhausted muscles to flip him over to his side and snuggled against him.

"So did I give you enough warning last night when I said I was going to ravish you?" Evan asked.

A couple relaxed chuckles left Jesse's throat. "Even with a warning, I wasn't ready for that. You were incredible."

Evan wiggled his right arm under him, pulled him closer, and kissed the top of his head. "I've made you late, though. There's no way you'll make the studio by ten."

Jesse peeked over Evan's chest at the alarm clock and the time of a quarter till nine. He closed his eyes. "I'll call everyone and tell them not to come in until later." Working in delay, his mind caught a particular word Evan used. "You're not coming with me again?"

Evan gently stroked Jesse's arm. "Yesterday I did some research on the Aston Martin DBS V12 and found a dealer in Skokie, so I thought I'd go there today and get one ordered. Then after that, I might go over to the Cadillac dealer and see about getting us an Escalade."

"How're you going to get there? Planning on seeing how the Enzo handles snow?"

Evan toyed with Jesse's fingers lying on his chest. "I thought I'd call JJ and see what he's up to." When silence greeted him for a response, he glanced at Jesse. "That would be bad, wouldn't it?"

Jesse sat up and kissed him lightly on the lips. "It wouldn't be bad, but I'd like to go car shopping, too."

Evan exhaled an exaggerated sigh. "If making me wait to put my order in for a DBS is my continued punishment for being a dick last night, it's just too cruel."

"It's not, and we'll go tonight." Jesse's mood took a quick sour turn. "And instead of buying a new Escalade, I know where we can pick up a free Mercedes SUV. We even have a spare set of keys to it in case the dumb-ass owner ever lost his."

"In a week you and Brandon will be back to normal again."

"I doubt it," Jesse grumbled, then lifted his voice higher. "So you're coming with me, right?"

Evan took his turn to grumble. "I guess. There're some things I need to talk to Greg about, anyway."

"Your album?"

"Yeah. Tomorrow the people from the orchestra are taking me out to lunch to finalize everything, so it's probably about time I let him know what I'm up to."

"I don't think he's going to take it well."

"Neither do I."

"Are you going to let it out about retiring, too?"

"I guess it's about time I did, isn't it?" Evan met Jesse's eyes, a strained smile on his lips.

"Yeah," Jesse said softly. "But it'll be okay. I'll stay by you through every word."

"I know you will."

Jesse kissed the tension from Evan's mouth and curled against him, closing his eyes for a quick rest.

CHAPTER TEN

Jesse headed through the parking garage, Achilles prancing on his right side, Evan dragging along slightly behind on his left. Part of him felt guilty for making Evan come to the studio with him, but after the previous day, he needed Evan's calming presence to combat negativity. Plus, if Trish was still acting like it was her first week on the skins, Evan might know a trick or have a suggestion to help her. After all, Evan had guided countless musicians in the past and helped them improve their craft. Why not Trish as well?

Jesse looked toward the studio doors as he crossed the street and claimed Evan's poor mood for himself. Trent, his guitarist Matt, and two other young guys who he assumed must the other members of Swiller strutted out the door.

Trent waved wildly to him. "Hey, it's about time you got here! Your people have been chillin' for the past half hour waiting for you."

They reached the other side of the street and Jesse noticed Trent's dark blond hair had some shine to it that appeared to be shampoo induced, and while the smell of pot still lingered to Trent's coat and clothes, it was under the scent of spicy body spray. He appreciated Trent's consideration in taking a shower; he didn't, however, appreciate being reminded he was thirty minutes late after he called everyone and told them not to come in until eleven, only to have him and Evan tangle their bodies together once again.

"Car trouble," Jesse said, feeling proud he managed such a short, simple lie and actually made it sound convincing.

Trent burst out laughing. "Car trouble? Dude, how does a millionaire rock star have car trouble?" He flicked his chin toward Evan. "You guys must live pretty close if he was able to pick you up."

Jesse stared at Trent in disbelief over how his lie not only backfired, but also the impression Trent got from it. Did Trent really believe they weren't a couple, or was he acting naïve hoping he'd confess it? But what would be Trent's goal in getting him to confess it? Would he blow it off? Doubtful. Use it against him? Probable. His mind racing, Jesse realized Trent was still talking.

"…so how sweet is that! We're totally going to be touring together!"

Though he hadn't caught all Trent said, Jesse got enough to make his heart clench in horror. "Say that again."

"That's what I said when Jon told me, I was so stoked! Him and your manager, Greg, are working out the details so we'll be opening for you guys! Well, for a few shows at least. We're going to headline our own tour after we get a boost from taggin' along with you guys. But how sweet is that? Dude, you totally have to come down to hear us play now."

His *manager*, Greg? It was true Greg handled most of the managing for Conquest, but he never officially made him their manager. Technically, Jesse considered himself their manager. Greg didn't make a move on anything without consulting him first, so even if he didn't handle the actual bookings, he had the final say in everything Conquest participated in. Jesse glanced at Evan. He stood looking at the door as if he wished it would open and suck him inside. Trent's continued chatter forced Jesse's gaze back to him.

Trent pulled a pack of cigarettes from his coat pocket and casually smacked it against the underside of his wrist. "But I guess I should introduce you to the rest of these losers if we're all going to be working together." He nodded toward the tallest of the group. "This is Eric Burmann, bass player."

Eric flicked his head in acknowledgement, but made no further attempt at greeting him. Jesse did the same, sizing up the lanky bass player with shoulder length, light brown hair.

"And this is Joey Roberts, drummer," Trent finished.

Joey glowered at Jesse, not bothering even the weak greeting Eric gave. Jesse's defenses went up. He didn't like the look or feel of the short, stoutly built drummer.

Trent snapped his fingers and pointed at Evan. "Hey! Before you leave today, I totally need to get your autograph for my mom. When I called her and told her I met you, she got all girly asking what you were like and if you were as hot in person. I was like, how the hell should I know? He's a guy! But she wasn't listening. And if I could get a picture of us together too, that'd be sweet."

The glare Evan gave Trent made the outside temperature feel like summer. He whipped open the studio door and stormed inside.

Jesse gaped at the closing door, then Trent's voice called him back.

"Dude, he's not very friendly, is he?"

Jesse snapped his head toward Trent, his voice coming sharp. "He is to people who aren't rude to him. You insulted him just as much as you did me the other day, and did you even think to apologize to him? Then you have to nerve to ask him for an autograph and a picture?"

"I guess I didn't think of that."

Jesse ripped the door open with more force than Evan had.

"Are you still coming down to hear us this afternoon?" Trent called after him.

Jesse shook his head in disbelief and stomped inside.

The heat in the lobby washed over him, giving him instant relief from the cold, but what gave him even more relief was the sight of Evan leaning against the wall, his arms folded across his chest as he waited for him and, he knew, also staying close to watch over him. His relief waned when he saw the tense scowl on Evan's lips. Jesse stopped in front of him and flashed a bright smile.

"You know what you should do? Go outside, whip it out, and sign your name in the snow with a steaming yellow stream, then tell him to figure out how to get that autograph to his mom."

His comment earned him half a grin from Evan. "Do you really want your new boyfriend to see what your old one's packing?"

Jesse gasped in pretending offense. "I knew your sense of humor was demented, but I never realized how twisted it really is."

Evan's half-grin turned into a full smirk. "Think about it. You wouldn't even have to use any lube on his greasy ass."

Laughing, Jesse whirled around and walked up the hall. "That's disgusting!"

A true smile graced Evan's lips. He put his arm around Jesse's shoulders. "I was just trying to elevate your mood to lower the chances of you choking Greg the instant you see him."

Jesse let out an indignant snort. "I'd still say those chances are pretty good."

"Then you know what we should do?" Evan dropped his arm off Jesse's shoulders, drifted his hand down his back, and let his fingers caress over his ass. "We should go home and spend the day elevating each other's moods together."

Jesse grinned at him. "As much as I'd like to do that, I have a little bit of work to do. You can keep groping me, though. I like it."

Evan returned his arm to Jesse's shoulders. "Then I'll do my best to sneak it in every chance I get."

Jesse peeked into Studio B, finding it dark and empty. He ground his teeth; his pace increased to a purposeful march that forced Evan to keep up and sent Achilles into a trot. Just because he was late didn't mean all work should stop. Trish alone could've been working on the rhythms for "Twisted Destiny." He entered the laughter filled chill-out room and took in the scene of Kenny sitting with Kyler and Robbie on one couch, Julian and Greg on the opposite one, Trish and Jeremy in the red chairs beside them. At the same moment, he felt Evan's arm over his shoulders tense.

Kyler slowly lifted his gaze to them. "Well, good morning, boys. Or, is it afternoon now? And I thought I was the only one here who had a reputation for showing up late. Of course, when I show up, I'm usually looking hung-over. Not like you two, who both look so," a smirk curved his lips, "satisfied."

Evan's arm fell from Jesse's shoulder. He stepped toward Kyler. "Keep it up, Kyler. Please push me one step farther."

Jesse snatched the back of Evan's coat, his touch enough to stop him from advancing on Kyler.

Kyler smiled at Evan. "Since when are you such a prude, Evan? It was just a joke."

"Evan," Greg called sharply, "if all you're going to do is make trouble with the people who are here to work, then I think you should leave, especially since you can't seem to control your mouth and temper lately. You're doing nothing but distracting everyone."

"Seriously," Trish muttered in agreement.

The past days of frustration, hurt, and disappointment surged through Jesse. The news on Swiller becoming Conquest's opening act had pushed him to the edge, Evan being attacked on three sides shoved him over.

"I've had enough!" Jesse roared.

Everyone in the room shrank at the sound of his booming voice. Evan winced since he received the brunt of the bellow in his ear.

"Sorry," Jesse mumbled to him, then stormed to the door and slammed it closed. He moved toward everyone. "Right now, I'm cool with the majority of people in this room, but three of you have pushed me too goddamn far lately." He stopped at Kyler. "You want to be friendly with me, and that's fine. It'll make life a whole lot easier if we can be in the same room and not want to rip each other's dicks off. But let me tell you something, if you keep provoking him, you're going to have to deal with me, and if you think he's a bad ass, you've never seen me pissed. Now do you want to get along with us, or do you want to start a war? And I'll warn you now, you will *not* win a war against me."

"All we've wanted since day one is to get along with everyone." Kyler looked to Robbie. "Right?"

Robbie turned his head in the opposite direction from Kyler. "I don't know why you're looking at me. I'm pretty sure I'm not one of the three people who've pissed him off."

Kyler frowned at him. He looked back to Jesse and smiled. "Fine, I'll quit trying to get a rise out of Evan."

Jesse continued to glare at him. Kyler acquiesced far too easily for his words to feel genuine, but at least he admitted to antagonizing Evan. "Thanks, but now I have to ask if we can have a little privacy. The rest of what I have to say is between me and my crew."

Robbie hopped up and dragged Kyler to his feet by the shirtsleeve. As Robbie passed Jesse, he threw him a covert smirk telling him he thoroughly enjoyed his scolding Kyler.

After they left the room with the door closed behind them, Jesse turned his attention to his next target and met her green eyes. "You agreed with Greg that Evan distracted everyone. Why?"

Trish shifted in her chair. "I didn't…I mean, it's just, I think he influences the music too much."

"How so? Because I ask him his opinion? Which by the way, half of the time I have to practically break his arm to get out of him. Or is it that you disagree with the advice he gives? Because if that's the issue, then you should start speaking up when it occurs. I, for one, highly value the opinion of a man who the rest of the musical world looks at as a genius, and I would feel that way whether he was my partner or not. But that's just *my* opinion, so what's yours?"

Trish shook her head slightly, as if trying to catch up to all he said. "I'm just saying maybe you could concentrate better if you weren't so worried about what he thinks of your work."

Jesse folded his arms across his chest, his voice cynical. "I'm the one with the concentration problem? I wasn't aware of that, considering I can play everyone's parts in all our songs, old and new, without a single misstep. So if I'm the problem, not Ev, then we've got a major issue here."

"You're not the problem," Trish said.

"Then you're sticking to Evan being the problem?"

"No."

"Then what exactly is the problem?"

"There isn't one."

"I hope that's true, Trish. I really do, because if I find out later it's not, there *is* going to be a problem, and it'll be between me and you, because you know above all things, I appreciate honesty. Even if you think what you have to say will upset me, if you're honest about it, I'll always listen and do my best to understand."

She nodded, but kept her eyes directed at the floor.

Jesse swallowed down his sigh of frustration. Two down, one to go, and so far he felt like he accomplished nothing. He faced his biggest and most obstinate obstacle. "And then there's you."

Greg leaned back in his chair, seeming not the least fazed by Jesse's scrutinizing gaze. "You can be as upset as you want with me for my comments, but I call it like I see it. And yes, I'll agree that on the last album, when there was no one else recording here, Evan's presence was valuable. But now, there're just too many cocks in the henhouse and something's got to give. If he's not here to record, then he doesn't need to be here."

"Except for the fact that I've asked him to be here."

"Well, kiddo, you don't get everything you want in this world, and it's about time you learned that."

"Like getting a say in who our opening act is going to be when we tour?"

Greg gazed at him in silence.

"Now you have nothing to say? From what I heard, you've been quite busy making the arrangements for Swiller to hit the road with us. You had no right to make such a decision without consulting me."

"What?" Kenny said, looking between Greg and Jesse. His gaze stopped on Greg. "Is that true?"

Greg's gaze flicked to Kenny, then back to Jesse. "Yes, it is, but it's for the good of both bands. I listened to them yesterday and while they could still use some polish, they're going to be a hot group. And as far as my *right* goes, I had every right to make the arrangements. It's what I do. It's what I've been doing for you for the past two years."

"No, it isn't," Jesse said. "You're supposed to set up tentative events, then clear them with me. I'm our manager, not you."

"If that's what you want to believe."

Jesse's anger built a wall in his mind to all thought. He had wanted to come to Evan's rescue and now he felt like the cornered one.

"Did you sign a contract to be their manager?" Evan said calmly to Greg.

Greg shook his head in confused frustration. "No, but I'm contracted as their producer—"

"That doesn't make you their manager," Evan interrupted. "All that gives you is license to work with them on recording material for the album. As far as managing and promoting goes, you took those responsibilities on yourself, and they've been content to let you handle that aspect of their career. If they're no longer happy to let you continue those responsibilities, then you need to relinquish them back."

Greg glowered at Evan. "Yes, but in their contract, it states Phoenix is handling all the promotion for them."

"For their first album and tour, yes, but now they're free to seek outside representation, at least that's how I read it. The wording was something along the lines of, 'promotion for the first full album release of the band Conquest is to be under the authority of those persons employed within the Phoenix Records organization…' etcetera, etcetera. It was a flaw in the contract you didn't catch. Also, in their contract, Jesse is acknowledged as the manager of Conquest."

Greg's mouth opened to speak; only a shocked breath came out. He cleared his throat and tried a second time. "You've read his contract?"

The smallest of smirks tipped one corner of Evan's lips. "He asked me to."

As Jesse watched Evan and Greg battle, a thought lit his mind so brilliantly he had to force himself not to blurt it out. Jesse saw Greg was incapable of speaking further, Evan looked content with his comments, and decided it was his turn to talk again. "And there you have it. I'm Conquest's manager, *officially*."

Greg snapped his gaze toward him. "Then I guess you can start handling all the bookings, income, promotion, endorsements, and ten thousand other things that go into managing an act like what Conquest has become."

Jesse gave a nonchalant flip of his hand. "I'd never have the time to work on music if I did all that. I'm going to get us a new manager, one who you won't even think to push around."

"Oh really? And where will you find this all-mighty manager?"

Jesse pointed at Evan. "Right there. He's the most omnipotent person I've ever met."

Surprise flashed over Evan's face, but only for an instant before he reined it back in and managed to look as though he expected the declaration.

"That's perfect," Julian said. "If Evan's our manager, no one would dare say no to him on anything."

"Hell yeah!" Kenny chimed in. "He's got more weight than damn near anybody in this business."

Trish refused to look at anyone.

"*And*, then he has every right to be here and everywhere we go," Jesse added triumphantly.

"You're forgetting one thing," Greg broke in. "Evan has a career of his own."

"Actually, I'm retiring after this one."

Jesse winced at Evan's blunt announcement. He knew it was coming, but Evan could've sugarcoated it a little. He glanced at the others, who all wore the same wide-eyed stare, save for Greg's irritated expression.

"Here we go again," Greg said. "You can't keep doing this, Evan. Saying you're going to retire, then coming back and expecting to have just as many fans as before. You got away with it once, but how many comebacks do you think you can do before people get sick of it?"

"When I left a few years ago, I never said I was retiring. I simply walked away. Now I'm saying I'm retiring."

"This is ridiculous. You're not even thirty years old. What're you going to do with the rest of your life?"

"Whatever I want."

Greg rubbed both hands over his face so hard the skin alternated between being stretched and wrinkled. "For someone who's so good at coming up with fresh material, you sure do sing the same damn song a lot. That's all it's ever been with you. Getting and doing whatever you want. You don't give a shit about anything else but seeing that your own needs and wants are met. When are you going to grow up?"

"I stopped growing the day my father died."

Heavy silence dropped over the room. Jesse's heart ached at Evan's harsh, but painfully honest words. He took Evan's hand, squeezing it tight. He glanced at Greg and the pained expression on his face.

Evan looked at Jesse; his countenance softened with affection as he gently cupped Jesse's cheek with his free hand. "But I started again when this man next to me gave me his love." He looked to Greg. "You know my reasons behind entering music in the first place and you also know I failed in the one goal I set for myself when I did. So continuing to make music I'm not passionate about isn't good for me, my fans, or anyone else. This next album will be my masterpiece, and I don't think I'll ever be able to top it. After this one, anything else I produce would sound shallow."

His voice softer, Greg said, "*One More Time* was a brilliant album. You'll be hard pressed to top that."

"I'll be recording with the Chicago Symphony Orchestra. It'll be an album that demonstrates my full potential. Each song will feature a full orchestra and my vocals."

Greg shook his head. "A symphonic rock CD? I know you've always been a classicist at heart, but to go this far? The spatterings of classical touches you've used before have been great, but a whole album of it? And it's been done before. Metallica did it in the '90s with their *S&M* album with the San Francisco Symphony."

"You're not listening to me. I'm not making a greatest hits album with orchestral accompaniment. I've written new songs for an orchestra to play that will have traditional classical instruments with electric guitar accompaniment and my vocals. Not fully operatic, but more showy than traditional pop/rock singing."

"You've written scores for an orchestra?" Greg stammered.

"Yes."

"For each section? Strings, brass, woodwinds, percussion?"

"Yes. As well as pieces with piano, harp, bass, and electric guitars. It's my farewell. It'll be called *Finale* and there will be no comebacks after this one. If this makes the news easier for you, the album will be released under Phoenix since in the discussions I've already had with the orchestra representatives, they agree Phoenix has more marketing power than their label to get the album noticed and sold to mass audiences."

"You've already started a dialogue without me?"

"I felt it was best because I anticipated resistance from you. And let's face it, Greg, classical music isn't your strongest point. Whenever I'd make those divergences in my material, you always let me have full control."

"I still could've helped with the negotiations."

"You still can. But this is going to be a very personal album, so I want to be in on every detail of it. And since this is going to be beyond your musical expertise, I'll be acting as my own producer as well." At Greg's wounded expression, Evan added, "It really is business, Greg, not personal. And when it comes to business, you and I are both ruthless. Personally, I think this is going to be great for us. We can be better friends without business coming between us."

Greg sat silent for a long moment. "I don't know what to say. I'm in shock. I'm not even fully grasping or believing what you're saying."

"Well, when you do, I hope I'll have your support."

Greg nodded. "Yeah, of course."

Confusion and disbelief dominated everyone's mood. Jesse glanced at his watch. It was already twelve-thirty, which meant there wasn't much point in attempting to start work only to stop in half an hour to eat lunch. Deciding everyone needed a break and some food to get their moods balanced again, he cleared his throat to pull their attention back to him. "Well, I don't know about you guys, but I can't concentrate unless I get some food."

Julian walked over to Jesse. "I'll never know how you stay so thin when all you do is eat."

"Sex," Jesse said simply. "Lots and lots of sex."

Trish passed him and he gently touched her shoulder. She kept walking without looking at him. Greg trailed behind her. At the accusatory look he threw him, Jesse realized Greg blamed him for Evan's early retirement, then wondered if that's what everyone else believed as well. He didn't want to have the blame put on him, not when he hadn't done anything to deserve it. He was the one who encouraged Evan to comeback in the first place, and it was because of Jesse that he had.

With everyone except Evan cleared from the room, Jesse allowed his fatigue and frustration to show. He closed his eyes tight and pressed his fingers to his forehead. Evan stepped behind him and massaged his neck. Jesse groaned; his arms fell limp to his sides, his body swayed slightly under the pressure of Evan's fingers.

"Getting another headache?" Evan asked.

"It's never ending."

Evan leaned over Jesse's shoulder to be close to his ear. "I'll relax you again when we get home tonight."

"I was thinking more along the lines of a vigorous beating away of the frustration."

"We can do that." Evan licked up the outside edge of Jesse's left ear to the silver hoop earring in the cartilage. He slipped his hand down Jesse's back, over his ass, between his legs, and rubbed his sac. "Watching you be so aggressive against Kyler got me really hot. Thanks for coming to my defense."

"I always will. Thanks for coming to mine against Greg."

"Well, that's what a good manager does."

Jesse faced him with a tentative smile. "Was it bad to say that?"

Evan chuckled softly. "No. A little warning would've been nice, but it's alright. We just have to figure out what to do as far as finding you a real manager."

"You don't want to be my manager?"

"You were serious?"

"Well yeah. There's no one who knows my music better than you, and there wouldn't be anyone who would be more concerned about what's in Conquest's best interest."

"But what about the others? You haven't even talked to them about it."

"You heard them. They're all hyped at the idea of you managing us."

Evan kept silent that there was one Conquest member who hadn't looked exactly thrilled. "I'm not opposed to the idea of being your manager, but there're a lot of things we need to discuss before we make a final decision on going through with it."

Jesse headed toward the kitchen area to one of the cabinets, retrieved a water bowl he had stashed there for Achilles, and began filling it at the sink. "As far as I'm concerned, it's a done deal. I can only see positives that could come out of it. There aren't any negatives."

Jesse carried the bowl of water out of the room with Achilles and Evan following him, and swung into Studio B. He flicked on all the lights and opened the door between the control room and live room to give Achilles full run. Achilles stood in front of Jesse, looking up at him expectantly. Jesse dug in his coat pocket and came out with three dog treats. He set them on the floor and stroked Achilles' head while the dog crunched away.

"Be a good boy while I go to lunch and I promise to bring you back a steak. If Trent or his jerk-asses try to come in, bite 'em." Jesse walked out to the hall, closing the door behind him, and looked into Evan's eyes. "So will you do it? Will you be my manager?"

Evan smiled and nodded. "Yeah, I will."

Chapter Eleven

Jesse paced from the family room to the kitchen, around the breakfast counter, and back out to the family room with the cordless phone pressed to his ear so tight it pinched his earrings. On the fifth ring, Brandon's voicemail answered. He sighed loud listening to Brandon's recorded voice for the third time that day and decided this time he'd leave a message.

"Hey, it's me. I haven't heard from you since our fight and I was just wondering how you're doing and what's been going on." Jesse paused, gathering his pride in preparation to swallow it. "I wanted to say too, I'm sorry for the things I said. I had no right to talk about your relationship like I did. It's like I told Ev, I've been pissing off everybody lately. Even we got into an argument the same night as ours."

Jesse dropped down to the couch. "There's been so much bullshit going on lately. Trish, I don't know what's wrong with her, but it's like she doesn't care about the music anymore. This disgusting new band is probably going to be our opening act when we hit the road. Kyler Christenson has been all over Ev every time he sees him, more trying to piss him off than flirt with him. Kyler did tell me he thinks you're hot, so that should be an ego boost for you. Oh, and Ev's going to be our manager now."

It hit him he was having an entire conversation with Brandon's voicemail. He missed his brother so much he got carried away in knowing Brandon would get the message and it would be almost like talking to him.

"So anyway, I'm babbling. I really just wanted to see how you've been. I know *Chicago* is going to be opening soon, and I'd love to come on opening night. You're going to be awesome, I know it. I'd like to see you before then, too. Maybe we could get together for lunch. If you want to, give me a call, or stop off here, or at the studio. I'll talk to you later." He cleared his throat to push out the words he and Brandon never said to each other because they knew it inherently, though now, he felt he had to say them. "I love you, Brandon. Take care."

Jesse hit the "End" button and flung the phone to the side. It bounced over the couch cushions, and he hunched forward, his head bowed and held in his hands. His heart felt like a twisted knot of anxiety. What if Brandon didn't call back? He didn't know what he'd do next. Go to his apartment to confront him in person? That could turn ugly real fast, especially if Christopher was there. Or should he write Brandon off, forget about him and move on? That thought made his stomach churn with distress. He could never do that. But if Brandon really didn't want him in his life anymore, if their fight had caused such deep damage, what else could he do? But Brandon had always been there for him, he always protected and took care of him. He wouldn't discard him because of one fight...would he?

His anxiety turned into panic. His knotted heart pounded. What if he had screwed up that bad by insulting Christopher? If the roles were reversed and Brandon said horrible things about Evan, he'd have punched Brandon the instant the words left his mouth. But it was more than just what he said about Christopher. He said hateful things about Brandon as well. The argument replayed in his head. He cringed outwardly and inwardly at his remembered words. Brandon had every right to not want to speak to him ever again.

Jesse peeked at the phone lying a couch cushion away. How pathetic would he look if he called and apologized again?

From the music room came the high, fluttering notes of the first movement in Vivaldi's "Spring" from the Four Seasons. One violin in particular sounded louder, clearer, and more beautiful. He recognized the violin's voice as Evan's Stradivarius and realized he was playing along with a CD.

Jesse stood up. He wouldn't force himself on Brandon. He'd wait for him to make the next move...until tomorrow, at least. If Brandon didn't call him by tomorrow afternoon, then he'd swing by his apartment. He could pick him up a cheesecake, a chocolate one. Brandon loved those. Jesse's shoulders sagged. A cheesecake? How lame. It wasn't like when he scolded Achilles, then felt guilty about it and gave him a dog cookie to make amends.

Jesse entered the music room. Evan stood in the center, his eyes closed, his chin resting on the end of the violin. The golden-brown finish of the Stradivarius captured the setting sun streaming through the tall windows lining the back of the room, running from floor to vaulted ceiling with white columns topped in Corinthian capitals between.

Evan's bowing arm swept the bow over the strings in short, sharp movements to produce the high notes mimicking the bird calls of spring, then extended to long, graceful strokes with the next movement. The concentration on his face eased, and he opened his eyes, his gaze going directly to Jesse. He stopped playing and picked up the remote for the stereo to turn off the music. "Did you get hold of Brandon?"

Jesse sat on the piano bench for the ebony Steinway grand. "No, but I left a message. He hates me."

"He doesn't hate you. You know how busy he is on the weekends when he's getting ready for a play."

"He'd still always call me. He's avoiding me."

Evan laid the violin and bow in its case and went to him. He squatted down in front of him, rubbing his hands over Jesse's thighs. "I don't like you two fighting. Is there anything I can do to help?"

Jesse gave him a weak smile. "You can start playing again. That'll cheer me up."

"I don't know about that. I've always thought I was pretty good, but after watching the people in the strings section of the orchestra, I feel like my fingering is horribly sloppy."

Jesse brought his lips close to Evan's. "I thought your fingering was brilliant last night."

Evan lightly brushed his lips over Jesse's. "Does that mean you'll want an encore?"

"Maybe even two or three." Jesse pressed his lips to Evan's in a tender kiss.

The kiss drew to a slow end. Evan stood and combed his fingers through Jesse's hair. "What do you want me to play?"

"How about the second movement of Mozart's Violin Concerto No. 3, the adagio. I know you know it."

"Yeah, but it's been forever since I've played it. I might make a mistake or two. Do you want to grab the CD so I can balance against the rest of the ensemble?"

"You don't need it. You'll be perfect."

Evan closed his eyes to summon the notes and harmony he needed. Memorizing music had never been a problem for him. Most pieces he could learn by ear, and when he had the sheet music, he could master a work quickly. But there was a big difference between learning to master the mechanics of a piece and actually playing it with the heart and passion it was meant to have.

The difference could be heard when two musicians played the same song. The one who mastered the mechanics could easily make their audience nod in approval over the pretty sound. The one who played with the true emotion of the piece could surround their audience in the essence of the music; the first note played would resonate in the audience's hearts. His father had been such a musician. Jesse was also. He, personally, felt he rarely hit the emotion in music. But on this next album, on *Finale*, he would reach that level. First, though, he needed to get his own classical skills back up to par.

The adagio sounded through his mental ear. He positioned the Strad on his shoulder, put his fingers to the board, the bow to the strings, and went straight to playing the first lovely long note of the main theme established in the first movement of the concerto. He pondered the piece as he played, how it reminded him of love and the way it could leave a person feeling weightless and joyous, making the world a place of beauty beyond what Heaven could possess. How it could descend to the opposite and leaden a person to the ground, ready to sacrifice their life for it. The contradictions it evoked made it mysterious and wonderful.

Evan smiled as he played. Perhaps his interpretation was clichéd, and certainly playing the piece specifically for his beloved partner affected it, but that was the beauty of music, no interpretation was wrong. His mood bright and spirits high, he brought the adagio to its conclusion and opened his eyes.

Jesse gazed at him, his indigo eyes shining with emotion. "You're playing with more energy than usual."

Evan lowered the violin and bow. "Am I?"

"Yeah, you're really feeling it tonight. Sometimes…" Jesse paused, tentative to continue.

"Tell me."

"Sometimes, you seem guarded against music, like you don't want to let it in. But not all the time." Jesse smiled brightly. "On our first night together, it was pure emotion when you played Pachelbel for me, same as when you sang 'Shattered' with me when we did our duet."

Evan moved the bow to his left hand, holding it and the violin, and placed his right on Jesse's cheek. "You know what both those examples prove?"

Jesse shook his head.

"That you're the source of all my inspiration, all my passion, all my emotion."

Jesse's smile widened. He took the violin and bow from Evan's hand.

Evan laughed softly. "But I guess I must not have played that well if you're taking my instrument away."

Jesse laid the violin and bow to rest in the case. He turned back to Evan and took both his hands in his, walking backward to the doorway leading out of the music room. "I took your instrument away because good boys who play Mozart so beautifully get rewarded."

"Then it's a good thing I found you before you decided to give up trying to be a rock star and set your sights on being a conductor. You'd be leading a whole lot of very happy musicians if that's your mentality."

Having reached the entrance room, Jesse released Evan's hands and gave him a light shove toward the stairs. "Get that cute ass and horrible sense of humor upstairs."

Evan jogged up the flight with Jesse close behind. In the bedroom, Jesse grabbed him around the waist and tackled him on the bed. Laughing, Evan pushed across the bed on his back to get more toward the center. Jesse crawled with him, then stopped him by sitting on his hips and working the buttons open on Evan's shirt.

Evan watched him. "Your mood is better from earlier."

"You made it better." Jesse reached the last button and flung Evan's shirt open. He tore his own shirt over his head and tossed it.

His mind still light and resonating with sound, Evan said, "Mozart's harder for me than for you, but I think I'm finally starting to appreciate him more now."

Jesse pulled Evan's zipper down. "He understood life better than some composers, the fun parts of it at least. Others took things too seriously. Like Beethoven, don't get me wrong, he was brilliant, but you can tell from the weightiness of some of his music, the guy had to be a total buzzkill to hang out with."

"You love Fur Elise, though."

Jesse tugged at Evan's jeans in an attempt to get them down. "Yeah."

"And Moonlight Sonata."

"Yep."

"And Symphony No. 3."

"Right, like I said, good music, moody guy." Jesse gave him a light slap on the hip. "Now less talking, more naked."

Evan gasped in mock offense, though lifted his hips so Jesse could get his jeans off. "Oversexed brat! I'm trying to have a conversation with you!"

Jesse yanked Evan's jeans and boxer-briefs away. "Yeah, but it's kind of an old geezer conversation and since you're letting me take your pants off, I'm guessing you're not that into it either."

Evan bolted up, knocked Jesse onto his back, and climbed on top of him. "I swear I'm going to deny you one of these days."

Jesse smirked at him as he reached between Evan's legs. "But not today."

Too late Evan noticed the wickedness in his smile. Jesse grabbed him where his leg met his body, his most ticklish spot, and worked his fingers into it. Thrown into an instant fit of hysterics, Evan scurried off him, trying to catch Jesse's hand. Jesse rolled over with him and pinned him to his back, refusing to end the torment.

"Stop!" Evan choked out between laughs. He writhed and heaved under him in a desperate attempt to knock Jesse off. "You're going to kill me!"

"Well, since I'm not into that, I guess I'll stop." Jesse moved his hand from Evan's weak spot, only to slip it under Evan's leg and sling it over his own shoulder. "Watching you play really turned me on."

"I'm glad," Evan said, breathless and still laughing softly. "But what the hell are you going to do about it when you still have your jeans on?"

Jesse squinted at him in a playful glare. He stood on the bed and wiggled his jeans down.

Evan's eyes settled on Jesse's cock, its fully filled length curving up toward his navel from the groomed patch of black curls above the base, the head already glistening with eager dampness, his full sac hanging down. Evan wet his lips. Jesse truly possessed the most beautiful package he'd ever seen.

Jesse dropped to his knees, making the bed bounce, and brought his body over him. Evan welcomed him by spreading his thighs further apart.

"Eager?" Jesse teased.

"Very."

Jesse bowed his head to him. Both their mouths opened, their tongues swept over each other before their lips met. Evan twisted Jesse's hair around his fingers. He squeezed him with his thighs and raised his hips, sliding their cocks together and sending a deep groan from his throat down Jesse's.

Jesse sucked Evan's bottom lip briefly. "There're so many things I want to do to you, I can't decide where to begin." He kissed down Evan's throat and inched lower to his chest. His mouth covered one nipple, his tongue circled and flicked until it hardened.

Evan arched his chest up. "That's a good start."

Jesse caressed Evan's chest. His fingers found the other nipple. Evan moaned softly and rubbed his hands over every part of Jesse he could reach; his smooth back, his sinewy arms, his slender shoulders, and through his soft black hair. Jesse switched to devote his mouth to the other nipple. Evan sucked in a sharp breath, his hips started moving on their own, grinding his cock against Jesse's taut abdomen.

When he felt warm wetness smear on his skin, Jesse drifted further down Evan's body. He stopped as he felt Evan grip his upper arm.

"You can't do that without sharing," Evan said.

Jesse flipped around to put them in a sixty-nine. Evan instantly rolled toward him, his left arm draped over Jesse's hip to hold him closer. Jesse nuzzled between Evan's legs, his tongue licking over the smooth sac as he savored the masculine scent underlying Platinum Egoist.

He felt Evan's warm tongue trace up the thick vein on the underside of his shaft, following it to the head. The tip of Evan's tongue lapped and probed at Jesse's slit. Jesse pulled in a deep breath, then engulfed Evan's length as his exhale left him. At the same moment, Evan shoved Jesse's cock to the back of his throat.

Jesse pushed every inch he could take into his mouth, then pressed in a little bit more, swallowing the cock head down his throat. Evan's sac lay near his nose. He slid his hand around Evan's leg to fondle it from behind, allowing his middle finger to caress between Evan's ass cheeks. He felt Evan's breath shudder. Jesse released Evan's cock from his mouth, put one finger in to coat it in saliva, then sheathed Evan's organ in his mouth again. He rubbed the outside of Evan's hole, each rotation causing Evan's stomach muscles to clench and release. He heard a desperate whimper from Evan and shoved his finger into him.

A hard groan came from Evan, and his internal muscles clamped around Jesse's fingers. He followed Jesse's lead, slathering one finger with saliva, and penetrated him while sucking him deep at the same moment.

Both rocked toward the other, their movements becoming more fervent the closer they drove each other to climax. Dizzying pleasure surged from Jesse's groin to fill his body. He couldn't hold back. Jesse moaned as high and loud as he could with Evan's cock in his mouth, his orgasm throbbing out of him in a heat filled wave. The first pulse of it wasn't over before Evan's salty taste flooded his mouth.

They continued to lave gentle attention on each other. After a few minutes, Jesse eased away and turned on the bed to lie at the head beside him. Evan found his lips in a lazy kiss. Each sucked their mingled tastes from the other's tongue.

Jesse grinned through the kiss. "I was going to ask what you wanted to do for dinner, but since we just took care of that, how do you want to spend the rest of the night?"

Evan laughed. "Your jokes are no better than mine!"

Jesse gave him a light kiss with smiling lips, then laid his head on Evan's chest, exhaling a contented sigh.

Evan toyed with Jesse's hair. "I think we should spend the rest of the evening in bed. We can bring up some food and throw in a DVD."

Jesse drifted his fingertips over Evan's stomach. "A naughty DVD?"

Evan kissed the top of Jesse's head and moved his fingers from playing with his hair to softly stroking his back. "If you want."

Warm and relaxed, Jesse felt sleep beginning to cover him. Through his lightly slumbering mind, he heard the phone ring on the nightstand and felt Evan gently nudge him.

"Do you want to answer it? It might be Brandon."

"You answer it," Jesse said, his voice deep and drowsy. "I'll talk if it's Brandon."

Evan stretched for the phone, doing his best not to disturb Jesse, and lifted it from the nightstand, answering with a hello that was mostly a yawn.

"Hey, Evan. How's it goin'?"

Evan recognized Kenny's voice. "Fine. What's going on?"

"Not much, but I really need to talk to Jesse. Is he around?"

"Yeah, but he's taking a nap. I'll have him call you when he gets up."

Kenny paused on the other end of the phone. "Is he feeling okay?"

"Yeah, he's just a little worn out."

"Then can you wake him up for me? It's really important and I don't think it can wait."

"Is it anything I can help you with?"

Kenny's voice softened with hesitation in his tone. "I...I don't think so."

Hearing the uncharacteristic stress in Kenny's voice, Evan relented. "Hold on." He hit the mute button on the phone.

"It's Kenny. He's says he's got something really important to talk to you about."

Jesse sat up and took the phone. "If this is something like his last couldn't wait conversation of, 'I've got a rash in a bad place and I don't know what to do,' I'm going to his place and kicking his ass."

"How did that ever end, by the way?"

"It turned out to be a reaction to the detergent one of the hotels was using when he had his clothes laundered." Jesse pressed the mute button a second time and put the phone to his ear. "Hey, what's up?"

"Nothing good. This afternoon, Trish called me and Jules asking if we wanted to go out this evening for a drink. At first I told her no because I've got a date, but she sounded pretty down, so I pushed my date back and just got home from meeting her. When Jules and I got to the bar, we were surprised you weren't there, but she said she hadn't invited you. We thought that was kind of weird, but we blew it off thinking maybe she wanted to have a quiet drink without The Mouth around."

"Cute. You're going to get to the point soon, right?"

"I'm working on it. You think I really want to be on the phone with you when I got a woman waiting on me?"

"Is she hot?"

"Good enough."

"You really should think about setting your standards a touch higher. But anyway, continue."

"Well, Trish started asking us all these strange questions, like if we really thought it was a good idea for Evan to be our manager, didn't we think he was going to change our sound to be his through influencing you, and how we'd never get any work done because if Evan doesn't even care about his own music, why would he care about ours. The questions were kind of all over the place, but she did bring up one good point."

"And that was?" Jesse asked, his teeth clenched.

"That if Evan's our manager, the three of us are going to be supporting you guys since it'd be pretty redundant for you to pay your own partner just to get the money right back into your joint accounts."

Jesse sat silent.

"Are you still there?"

"Yeah, I am," Jesse said, his voice sharp. "Let me address the last thing first. Do you want to know how much Ev's asking to be our manager? Nothing! He doesn't want any money to help us! He's doing this because he cares about our music. Because he wants to help us succeed. The only thing he wants is good head once in a while, and I'm pretty sure I've got that under control unless you want to help out!"

"Why are you yelling at me? All I'm doing is telling you what went down tonight. How were we supposed to know he's going to manage us for free? We haven't talked about it since you announced he's going to be our manager."

Jesse took as deep a breath as he could to calm his voice. "I'm sorry for yelling at you. I'm just not real pleased about this little rebellion going on behind my back."

"It's not a rebellion. Jules and I were only wondering about the money thing. As it is, I feel like shit for snitching on Trish. By the end of the conversation, I don't know if it was the alcohol or what, but she started getting really emotional, and when we left, she said she didn't know what she was going to do if Evan stayed our manager. I think you need to talk to her."

"I'll call her after we hang up."

"No, you need to talk to her in person. She's feeling really insecure right now, and you're the only one who can make her feel better."

"Then I'll talk to her Monday at the studio."

"What you need to do is get off your ass and go see her tonight!"

"I'm not driving back into the city so I can pat her on the head and tell her everything's going to be alright."

"This is our band, our lives, we're talking about! Jules and I are really worried about her! What if she decides to leave us?"

"She's not going to quit." Jesse sighed. "Fine. I'll go see her tonight. It's probably best. I want to put an end to this bullshit once and for all."

"Good. But don't go there being all hard-assed. Be nice to her. She's upset and just worried about where our band's going."

"Right. Thanks for letting me know what happened."

"Sure. Call me tomorrow and let me know what happens."

"I will. Later." Jesse hung up the phone. "Fuck!" He shoved off the bed and snatched his boxers off the floor. "Can't I have two hours go by without some sort of bullshit."

"It sounds like I'm the source of more conflict," Evan said quietly.

"No, you're not." Jesse zipped up his jeans. "Trish is. Apparently she's having issues with you being our manager and she went behind my back to get the others to turn on me. Now I get to go and set her straight."

"It's not you she's trying to get them to turn against, it's me."

Jesse tugged his shirt over his head and returned to the bed. He bent down, looking into Evan's eyes. "By talking against you, she's talking against me, and I'm not going to tolerate that. I'll be back soon."

Evan caught his hand, stopping him from walking away. "Jess, there's more to it than her not liking the idea of me managing you guys. She doesn't like me because I have you."

Jesse gave him an exasperated look. "Not this again. She doesn't have a thing for me, Ev."

"I told you how on your twenty-first birthday all of us walked in on her leaning over you. You were so tanked, you don't remember, but I swear, to me it looked like she was trying to kiss you. And I know she lied about not being able to understand you mumbling in your sleep because when we were alone together, you were surprised to see me since you had asked her if I was there and she had told you no. Just do me a favor. If you get a chance to call her out about that night, do it. And really pay attention to how she is around you, her expressions, her gestures. You'll start to see it if you watch for it."

Jesse nodded, though he still believed Evan was being jealous. He touched his lips to Evan's in a deep kiss. "I love you."

"I love you too, gorgeous. Drive careful."

Jesse headed to the bedroom door and winked at him over his shoulder. "Take a nap and be ready for me when I get back."

"I will."

Jesse spun and walked toward stairs. When he reached the first floor, he swung into the kitchen and grabbed his keys to the Cayenne and cell phone. He glanced at his phone and saw he had one missed call and a message. He took his black leather coat off the hook in the hall by the access door and listened to the message while pulling it on. His heart jumped at the sound of Brandon's voice.

"Hey Jess, it's me. I just wanted to call and say I got your message." Brandon's voice paused, then proceeded hesitantly. "I appreciate your apology, but I don't know if I'm ready to accept it. The things you said were pretty damn low, but I guess mine weren't much higher, and I'm sorry for that. I know you're not Evan's kept boy, but I think the things you said about me you really believe, and I also can't talk to someone who would so horribly disrespect the man I've decided to be with. And about *Chicago*, thanks for your faith in me, but if we don't have things cleared up by then, and I doubt we will, you don't have to worry about coming. Still, I hope you're doing well. I do love you, Jess, I just can't talk to you right now. Take care."

Jesse lowered the phone with a trembling hand. He swallowed growing tears and opened the door with the hope he could at least clear some of the distress in his life before the evening was over.

Chapter Twelve

"It appears we have a problem," Jesse said.

Trish blinked her shocked eyes at him standing outside her apartment door.

Without waiting to be invited inside, Jesse strolled past her and into the living room. The smell of flowery potpourri touched his nose. The white walls were decorated in delicate watercolors of bright blossoms, the small place painstakingly clean.

Trish closed the door and turned toward him. "I can't believe you're here. You haven't come by since I moved in."

"I'm surprised you haven't found some place better. All the others have upgraded. Kenny's got his kickass condo on Lakeshore, and Jules has his sweet penthouse by Millennium Park."

Trish shrugged. "I guess I'm just not that motivated to move into a fancier place since it's only me."

"Maybe you should think about getting a cat."

"Funny," Trish said, her voice revealing her lack of amusement.

Jesse started to take off his coat. Trish moved behind him and gently guided it from his shoulders. Such a simple gesture, kind at heart, and yet it made him feel uncomfortable as Evan's words replayed in his head. Jesse pushed the thoughts to the front corner of his mind to keep them close, but to not allow them to interfere with his purpose for being there.

Trish smoothed his coat over her arm. "Can I get you a drink?"

"No, thanks." Jesse sat on the paisley patterned couch and glanced at the end table. His eyes fell on a framed photo of him and Trish on the tour bus. He vaguely remembered the situation. It was a couple weeks before they joined Evan on the road. Julian was attempting to learn the features of a new digital camera and turned it on him. He had leaped over the seat in front of him and dashed up the aisle, joking that he had cameras in his face enough and Jules wasn't going to do experimental photography on him, which fired Julian's determination to shoot him. The whole thing turned into a game, thanks to the boredom of being on a tour bus for hours, and in this photo, he was using Trish as a shield, laughing as he tried to hide behind her, though Julian ended up getting a nice picture of both of them.

Jesse looked up from the photo to Trish. She quickly glanced away. The soft pink flush in her cheeks betrayed embarrassment, which confused him. They were friends. Her having a picture of them together wasn't anything to be embarrassed about.

"Are you sure you don't want something to drink?" she asked, already hastening toward the kitchen. "Or something to eat?"

"No, I'm fine. I'm not going to be here long."

His words stopped her. She turned back toward him.

Jesse met her gaze. "So do you want to run by me all the things you said to Kenny and Jules?"

Trish sagged back against the wall. "I should've known they'd tell you. Despite everything we've been through together, it's still a boys' club."

"It's not a boys' club. You being a woman doesn't have anything to do with this. I asked you last week if you had a problem with Evan, I practically begged you to be honest with me about it, and you said no. So I'm going to ask you again, do you have a problem with Evan, either as our manager or as a person?"

Trish's eyes focused on the floor, her jaw clenched shut.

Jesse waited in the heavy silence for a reply until he realized none would come. "You can talk to me, Trish. Don't hold back because it's Evan. If anything, let it all out because I might be able to help change whatever's wrong. I'm not going to take his side if he's done something to upset you. I'll talk to him and get it straightened out. I know how his temper can be, I've seen him explode on other people before. Has he ever been mean to you? Said anything that upset you?"

"No," she mumbled.

"Is it about his payment for managing us? Kenny made it sound like that was the main concern, but just so you know, Ev's going to take care of us for free, so it's not like I'll be getting extra money. And honestly, we'll have even more freedom with him managing us. He won't look over our shoulders constantly, or demand we do things we don't want to, and he'll only get us prime gigs."

"That's fine."

"It's fine? So then why did Kenny call me crying that there was a big problem if everything's fine?"

She shrugged and remained quiet.

Jesse gazed at her for a long moment. His heart thumped an anxious rhythm. "Does this have anything to do with what happened on my twenty-first birthday?"

Trish's head jerked up a fraction, her body constricted in tension. She turned her head fully away from him. "He told you. I figured he must of, but you never said anything about it, so I thought you just blew it off."

Jesse's mind spiraled. Maybe Evan wasn't overreacting. "He only told me what he saw when he walked into the bedroom and his interpretation of what was going on."

"I'm sure his *interpretation* had me clawing at you to rip your clothes off, but I only wanted to comfort you."

"By trying to kiss me?"

Trish snapped her head up. "I wasn't trying to kiss you! I..." she stopped, her eyes shone with rising tears. She diverted her gaze from him again, her voice came soft. "I just wanted to tell you I was there for you."

Jesse exhaled his relief. If Trish was leaning over him with sisterly concern to console him over no longer having Evan, he could see where Evan could get the wrong idea, especially considering his delicate mental state at the time.

"You were so upset," Trish continued. "And so lonely. You had thousands of people wanting to be close to you, but there was only one person you'd acknowledge."

Jesse lifted his gaze to her. Anxiety returned to his heart, beating the relief away.

"When you were laying there on the bed, you looked so…" she shook her head, banishing the words before they could be said. "I thought maybe there was a chance I could help you."

"Help me how?"

"It doesn't matter."

"Yes it does."

Trish finally looked at him, the tears in her eyes replaced by anger. "No, it doesn't. You weren't even awake. When I touched you, you must've been dreaming because you said Evan's name, then you started to wake up and asked where he was. I told you he wasn't there because I didn't know he was. You withdrew into your little shell of sorrow over him, then the next thing I knew, he was there."

Jesse rolled her words over in his head. "What do you mean, you *touched* me? Where did you touch me at?"

An annoyance-filled sigh fled from her, defiance sharpened her voice. "You know, I wasn't that much more sober than you. I can't remember everything. Brandon was the only one not drinking. Go drill him on it."

"Brandon wasn't in the room with us. And I'm not drilling you. I'm just asking."

Silence pervaded once again.

Jesse stared down at his hands, working to understand everything Trish said, the messages unspoken. He came to a point where he didn't want to understand and raised his head, flashing a bright smile. "Well, at least we got that cleared up. You were drunk and horny and didn't know what you were doing. I can live with that, and Ev will understand, too. He's told me about a ton of stupid shit he's done when he's been smashed." The dirty look she shot him slapped the smile from his face.

"That night isn't the problem."

"Okay, well, at least now you're admitting there is a problem. Just tell me what it is so we can fix it and move forward."

"I can't work with him."

"Right, we've already established there's an issue between you guys, but I really need you to tell me what it is, because I'm not figuring out why you can't work with him."

Trish shoved off the wall and took a single quick step toward him, her hands flicked and snapped with each word. "I'm sick of watching you two hang all over each other! Day in and day out, night after night on the road, I had to put up with you being kissy-cutesy with him, and I'm not doing it anymore! I can't! You act like he's so goddamn perfect and he's the farthest thing from it!"

Startled by the sudden confession, Jesse quietly contemplated her before speaking softly. "I don't know what to tell you, Trish. He's my partner, the love of my life. I guess I can see your point that I hang on him a lot, but I can't help myself. I love touching him, being close enough to smell his cologne and feel the warmth from his body. His presence calms and excites me at the same time. I'm hopelessly addicted to him, I know that, but I have no desire to change."

She scowled at him. "Then we do have a problem."

Jesse lowered his gaze to the floor, his thoughts a sea of confusion. Each time he tried to grasp one, it floated from reach, making it so he couldn't think of anything to say until one thought drifted closer. "Trish, you knew I was gay the first day we met. I didn't try to hide it. I announced it to everyone in the room. If you had a problem with it, you should've said something back then and not bothered becoming my drummer."

"I don't have a problem with your sexuality."

"You obviously do since you can't stand watching me be close with Evan."

"Evan is the problem, Jesse, not you. It's him I can't stand. He doesn't want to put the effort into making his own music anymore, or more likely, the so-called musical genius's well has run dry, so now he's decided to become our manager and manipulate our music."

Trish's blunt statement sent Jesse's defenses up. He rose slowly from the couch. "As much as I appreciate your critique on Evan, I find it grossly inaccurate. I'll let you in on a little secret that's just between him and me. The first time I brought forward the idea of him becoming our manager was when I announced it to everyone. Believe me, no one was more shocked than him, but being how he is and not wanting me to look stupid, he hid his surprise and followed my lead with it."

He stepped toward her. "He's our manager because I forced him into it, and he's going to stay our manager. I need him to take that role for me. There's no one else I would trust to do it. We're just going to have to find a way to work out the tension between you guys."

"That's not going to happen. I told you, I won't work with him."

"Trish, don't make me choose between you and him. You won't like the outcome."

Her gaze didn't waver from his as she spoke firmly. "Neither will you if you make me choose between working with him or not."

Chapter Thirteen

At the beep of the alarm system disarming, Evan pushed off the couch and walked to the entrance room. Achilles stared at the access door. Evan heard the garage door close, but still Jesse didn't enter. He shifted his weight from one foot to the other in his impatience. The door slowly opened. Jesse walked in, his gaze cast downward as he shuffled to the end of the short hallway. He gave Achilles a few somber strokes on the head.

"It's over," he whispered.

Evan gripped the wood trim of the doorway for support. Jesse couldn't be saying what he thought. "Wh-what do you mean? What's over?"

Jesse lifted his gaze to meet Evan's. "All of it. It's all over."

Evan's stomach churned with a sick flip. His heart choked his throat, breathing seemed beyond his capabilities, then his senses sharpened. He felt like a man in a life or death situation, and his survival instincts took over. He strode across the entrance room to Jesse and grabbed his upper arms, clutching them with desperate force. "No, it's not. I don't know what she said to you, I don't know what brought you to this decision, but it's not over. I'm not going to lose you again."

Jesse stared at him in confusion. Belatedly he realized how his words sounded and leaped to reassure him. "No, Ev, not us. We're not over. We'll never be over. I was talking about my career. *It's* over."

Evan let out a hard breath and quickly took in another. He put one hand to his forehead and staggered toward the stairs. "You'll have to forgive me if I say I'm relieved."

Jesse followed him. "I understand. At least I know you care."

Evan shot him an unappreciative look and dropped down to sit on the second to last step. "What happened?"

Jesse stood between Evan's legs and combed his fingers through Evan's hair. "I'm still confused over a lot of it, but you were right about things not being as innocent as I wanted to believe them to be on my birthday." He recounted to Evan all Trish told him up to her final demand.

"So where do things stand now?" Evan asked.

"When I left her apartment, the last thing I said to her was she'd have to decide what would be best for her, if she could work with you or not, but my decision was final on you being our manager. But I think I already know what her decision is going to be, that's why I was said my career is over. What am I going to do without a drummer?"

Evan's head lowered, his voice hushed. "I've brought nothing but conflict to you since we've come off the road. Brandon won't talk to you, your band is falling apart, you can't work at the studio because of the tension I bring. I'm dragging you down, just like I feared I would. I'm so sorry, Jess."

Jesse cupped Evan's face in both hands, forcing him to lift his head. "You're the only stable thing I have in my life, and I won't tolerate anyone trying to come between us. You belong at my side in everything I do and I want you to stand there proudly and know it's your rightful place. Don't let this, or anything else that's happened, make you doubt where you belong in my life."

Evan stared up at him, enraptured by the intensity of his words, the fierce protectiveness in his voice. This was Jesse in full battle-mode, the warrior inside him stepping forward to meet the challenge that threatened their relationship. When Jesse became like this, nothing could stop him. Even though he said his career was over, he knew Jesse didn't believe it. If he did, he wouldn't insist on him being a manager for a non-existent band. He knew Jesse was already analyzing scenarios that could come to pass in the next few days and strategizing his moves for each one.

Trish underestimated him thinking she could bend Jesse to her desire. She only saw Jesse as he usually was, silly and playful, high-energy and free-spirited. She didn't know the man of brilliance, fortitude, and power underneath. But he did and cherished those traits in him.

Evan wrapped his arms around Jesse's waist and laid the side of his face against him. "I never want to be anywhere but at your side, and I'll do whatever it takes to stay there."

Jesse embraced him with one arm and gently stroked Evan's hair with his other hand.

With each second, Evan felt more and more aroused. He wanted Jesse to take him upstairs and finish what they started earlier. He wanted to feel Jesse press deep inside him, to mark him and claim him. As if sensing his desire, he felt Jesse's cock stir behind his jeans. Evan rubbed one hand up Jesse's thigh. Before reaching his groin, he tilted his head back and looked at him. He saw in Jesse's eyes that his desires would be granted.

Jesse offered his hand. Evan took it and rose to return to their bedroom together.

CHAPTER FOURTEEN

Jesse leaned back against a wall in the chill-out room, his arms folded across his chest, his face concentrated on each word Greg spoke. Evan sat on the arm of the couch beside him, Kenny and Julian on the couch itself. Julian had one hand over his mouth, his shocked expression partially masked. Kenny's head jerked between Greg and Jesse as if to confirm with Jesse the truth of Greg's words.

Seated on the couch across from them, Greg continued. "So, to sum things up, it's been decided that she'll be released from her contract with Phoenix without repercussions, which I can't say enough is very generous, but considering her history with us as a studio drummer, then later with you guys, we thought it was the least we could do. That being said, while she's free to go play wherever and whatever she chooses, that does not include any material by Conquest. She has no ownership rights to any of your songs. She's agreed to pay back in full her portion of the advance for this album and she won't receive royalties off it since when you guys find a new drummer, all the material will be recorded fresh, of which there isn't much to begin with."

Greg sighed and sank against the back cushions. "I knew there was something very wrong when I arrived at my office this morning and she was there waiting for me, but leaving Conquest was the last thing I expected."

Silence followed Greg's words.

After a long moment, Kenny turned on Jesse. "You told me things went fine when you talked to her Saturday. What the hell did you say to her?"

"Not much. Only that she needed to decide what's best for her."

"That's what you said? What's wrong with you? She needed you to comfort her and you go over there and tell her you don't give a shit if she stays or not! You made her feel like she wasn't important to us!"

"That wasn't exactly how it went."

Kenny jumped up and marched a single step toward him. "It never is with you, is it? Whenever anyone left us in the past it was always their attitude that was the problem, or their playing wasn't good enough for you, or they wanted to change a note with *your* music! It was never your fault! If you want to be a solo artist so damn bad, then go be one and quit screwing over everyone who tries to be in a band with you!"

Jesse brought his gaze to Kenny in a sharp glare. "Since I know you're upset right now, I'll forget you said that."

Kenny huffed, flung up one hand, and flopped back down on the couch.

Jesse continued to stare at him. "Do you really think I would let things end like this? Before we were signed, didn't I keep us going through all the hard times? Didn't I keep fighting to get us recognized?"

"Yeah," Kenny muttered.

"I'm not even close to being done yet. We've had a Number One album and singles. We've headlined a sold-out tour and traveled with one of the top musicians in the world. And while all of those things are wonderful, they're just stepping stones for what I want to accomplish. Every album we put out will outsell the one before it. Every tour will be more massive, more incredible, than the one before. These are my goals. Do you really think losing a member of my band is going to stop me from reaching them? Do you really think I'll give up on conquering the world with my music just because one person walks away?

"I know how I am, Kenny. I'm not so narcissistic that I don't know the traits in myself others see as flaws. Am I going to change those traits? Absolutely not. If people want to work with me, they either accept me as I am, or they can go. But you were right about something, it is *my* music. I'm the one who spends hour after hour composing, analyzing, playing, to get a new song perfect. I'm the one who has nights where sleep won't come because the music refuses to be silent. I'm the one who bares everything before thousands of people to be judged and scrutinized. And I'm not going to see it end because one person feels they have more right to it than they do!" Jesse shoved off the wall and walked toward Kenny. "Do you know what she demanded from me?"

Kenny quickly shook his head.

"She demanded I choose between her and Evan. She thought the fear of our band falling apart would force me to get rid of him. She believed keeping the music going was more important to me than having Evan work beside me. What she didn't understand is there are thousands of drummers in the world. I can always find another one to play how I want them to. But there's no one in this world who can equal Ev. The music isn't going to stop because she decided to leave. It'll keep playing on, and on, and on, until I say it stops."

Kenny broke his stare from Jesse with a single blink. "I don't understand." He looked to Evan. "I know you two aren't each other's biggest fans, but why?"

Evan pulled in a long breath. "Well, on my end, I don't care for her because I think she wants Jess. On her end, the best I can guess is she doesn't care for me because I have him."

"But that's ridiculous," Julian said. "No offense, Evan, but if you weren't in his life, it'd be another man, and another after that, with more to follow. The only reason he's been able to hide being gay from the public for as long as he has is because he's with you. If he'd never met you, it'd have been out by our fifth show from the line of boys waiting to be served outside his hotel room door. He'd be the quintessential man-whore."

"Thank you for that lovely, slightly exaggerated monologue, Jules," Jesse said in a flat voice.

Julian looked at him. "Perhaps what I said was exaggerated, but let's be honest, you're not the most modest person about it, and I'm saying this because I find it hard to believe that Trish could maintain any interest in you when we've all watched you trying to coax Evan's clothes off every chance you get."

"I could believe it," Kenny broke in. "Girls have always fallen for him. Back in school, if he was absent, I'd get hounded all day by girls wanting to know where he was. And in clubs, I can't tell you how many fights he almost got in with some chick's boyfriend for her getting flirty with him. They think his cocky ass is cute and funny. But me, the nice one, the *straight* one, I'd get one phone number for every ten slipped to him without his ever asking for them."

"I can agree that when we were on the road, women were always chasing after him, they never picked up he was gay," Julian said. "But Trish *did* know, and she witnessed his being very much so every day."

"You're both getting off the issue," Jesse interrupted. "Her reasons for leaving don't matter. What matters is that she is."

Everyone's mood sobered.

Greg spoke up. "I know from experience, the musicians who've worked with him in the past say Evan isn't the easiest person to get along with." He looked to Evan and bowed his head in apology. "I'm sorry, but it's true."

"I'm sure you have a point," Evan replied.

"Yes, and the point is when she stated problems with you as her reason for leaving, I found it hard to believe. You're difficult when it comes to your own music, because it's your own. I can't see you interfering with Conquest's because no one more than you wants Jesse to have freedom with his creativity. I tried to explain that to her, but she refused to hear me. I felt the matter had to be more personal, and all this talk of her having feelings for Jesse makes it more clear as to why she would walk away. But like Jesse said, her reasons don't matter. Now you guys have to figure out what your next step is going to be."

His thoughts keeping him from being immobile, Jesse paced while he spoke. "That's simple. We find a new drummer. There are a few ways we can go about it. One is we can't get out of talking to the media about this. We'll hold a press conference to announce her quitting, and at that time, we could state some dates when we'll be holding open auditions. That would be the quickest way to get a large number of musicians here. The only problem I see with that is we'll probably hear more crap than quality. Our other options, we could scout the clubs and bars, look for a local drummer who'd want to hook up with us. Or, we could talk to drummers in bigger acts who rumors say may be discontented."

Evan cleared his throat to get Jesse's attention. "I may know someone."

Jesse spun toward him. "Who?"

"Brad Delfini. He drummed for me on my third album."

Jesse's eyes closed as he recalled the songs on Evan's third album to his mind. He nodded slowly. "*Allegro*. I know everyone says *One More Time* was your masterpiece, but I always thought the rhythms on *Allegro* were a touch crisper."

Evan chuckled. "You would catch that."

"Brad was an amazing talent," Greg said. "Before starting work on *Allegro*, Evan saw him drumming in a bar and wouldn't have anyone else on the album. He stole him away from the band he was with, and Brad never let him down with his skill. And he was a real nice guy to work with. Very laidback, like you, Kenny."

Evan cut in, "I don't know if Brad is quite as laidback as Kenny, but it takes a lot to piss him off, which is important if he's going to work with a singer even more high-strung than me."

Jesse narrowed his eyes at him. "And is there anything I should know?"

Evan looked up at him. "If you're asking if I slept with him, the answer is no. He doesn't play our games. But he knows my preferences and he's cool. And he's obviously trustworthy since he never betrayed my sexuality to the media. We could be open about our relationship with him."

"How did he find out about you?"

Evan shifted on the arm of the couch. He glanced around at everyone, then back to Jesse. "Are you going to get upset if I tell you?"

"No, I won't."

Evan gazed at him for a moment. He took a deep breath and sighed. "Here's the thing about Brad, even though he's straight, he's one of those guys who's really comfortable getting and giving attention to other guys, and if you don't know better and you're a little drunk, you'd think he was down with it."

His voice monotone, Jesse said, "And that's what happened to you."

"It was a long time ago, gorgeous. Way, way, *way* before you. It was at least…" Evan looked to Greg for help, "what, seven… eight years ago?"

Greg frowned at Evan. "If you're asking when Brad played for you, yeah, that'd be about right. As to confirming any *incidents* between you two, I'm learning for the first time here as well."

Evan gave Jesse a tentative smile. "See? It was a long time ago and nothing happened. We went out partying with the rest of my band, then when it was time to break and head home, he asked if he could crash at my place since his was all the way down in Brooklyn and my penthouse was just a few blocks away. I mistakenly thought he was opening the door for some fun. We got back to my place, I made some moves, he told me he wasn't into it, and I slunk away to my bedroom alone. But it didn't affect our friendship. We were laughing about it the next day. He's cool like that."

"And what moves did you make?" Jesse pushed.

Evan stared at him. Again, he looked to the others for assistance. Julian gazed at him, rapt by the story and clearly seeking more details. Kenny's expression looked apprehensive, but also curious. Greg continued to scowl at him. He brought his gaze back to Jesse. "He was getting a bottle of water from my refrigerator, and when he straightened to close the door, I stepped behind him, wrapped my arms around his waist, put one hand up his shirt, pulled the button loose on his jeans with the other, and kissed the side of his neck."

Jesse forced his next words out through clenched teeth. "Yeah, I'm familiar with that little move of yours."

Evan took Jesse's hand and brought it to his lips. "But you're the only one I use it on now and you'll be the only one for the rest of my life."

Jesse granted him a half smile. "I take it his reaction wasn't what you usually get out of me."

"Not even close. He yelped like a puppy that got its tail stepped on and dropped the bottle of water, spilling it everywhere. Then he faced me, put both hands on my chest with his arms straight and elbows locked, and apologized for any wrong signals he had sent."

Jesse smiled brightly. "So he rejected you."

Evan pulled Jesse closer and embraced him around the waist. "Yeah, he did."

Greg broke into their conversation. "With that little issue cleared away, now we have a bigger problem. Finding him. I haven't communicated with him in years. Have you, Evan?"

Evan shook his head. "No. The last I knew he was still living in New York, but that was four or five years ago."

"If he's such a talent, why did you lose touch with him?" Jesse asked. "Why didn't you have him play on *One More Time*, or call him in for *Addiction*?"

"I wanted him on *One More Time*, but right before I hit the studio, he got into a bad motorcycle accident. He was driving home at night and a drunk ran a red light and smashed into him. He ended up with a broken leg, arm, collarbone, ribs, and a concussion. He couldn't drum obviously, and I couldn't wait on him to heal, so I started without him."

"Evan," Julian scolded, "that's so cold."

"I paid all his medical bills because I felt so bad about it. And I told him he could catch up to me on the road when he was ready, but he decided to strike out on his own, so we went our separate ways. He ended up with a band called Crimson for a few years. They got a deal and released an album, but it bombed and their label let them go. The last I heard they broke up."

Jesse combed his fingers through Evan's hair. "But you can find him, right?"

"I'm sure I can." Evan cast a hopeful glance at Greg. "With some help."

"I have a few contacts at his previous label I can talk to and some others in New York who might be able to help track him down."

"Perfect!" Jesse threw his arms around Evan, rocking him back and forth in his embrace. "See what a wonderful manager you are? You've already found us a new drummer!"

"Jess," Kenny interrupted. "We don't even know if this Brad guy will be interested. And besides, I can't believe you're already writing Trish off. Just because she said she wanted to walk doesn't mean she actually will. She might just be upset. I think you should talk to her again."

Jesse stopped swaying Evan, but kept his arms around him and looked at Kenny. "Whether she was serious or not doesn't matter. The fact that she would make such a threat proves how much she cares about us and the music."

"I can see your point," Julian said, "but I can also see Kenny's. When people are hurt, they say and do a lot of things they regret later. I'm sorry, Jess, I have to side with Kenny on this one."

Jesse stood quiet, Brandon in the front of his mind. "Alright, I'll go talk to her again, but I think you guys need to come with me to show you value her, too."

"And to keep your mouth in check," Kenny mumbled.

Jesse spun around to get his coat. "Kenny, you know my hearing is superhuman, so there's no point in going sotto voce around me."

"I don't even know what that means, but if it means to not speak quietly, then fine! We'll come along to cover any stupid things you might say in case you have one of your infamous incidents of your brain falling asleep and leaving your mouth in charge."

Jesse looked to Evan and saw he made no move to join them.

Evan shook his head, answering his unasked question. "I think it's better if I stay here with Greg. I want to run some things by him about my album, anyway."

Jesse knew Evan was gracefully bowing out of an already tense situation his presence could worsen. Though he believed the only way to get Trish to come around to Evan would be to force them together, he acquiesced to Evan's will knowing this wasn't the right time for it, and turned to leave with Kenny and Julian.

Chapter Fifteen

"Well, I guess Kenny was wrong when he said you'd be bawling your eyes out over leaving us." Jesse walked into Trish's apartment and scanned the cardboard boxes scattered about, some empty, some already taped shut.

With a sigh, Trish turned from the door and left it open since she couldn't close it with Kenny and Julian standing dumbstruck half in, half out.

Jesse lightly kicked one of the boxes. "What'd you do, go straight from Greg's office to U-Haul? I hope you at least stopped for breakfast and mourned for a minute about the three men you're getting ready to leave behind."

"I'm not leaving you guys behind." Trish hefted one of the boxes off the couch so they could sit down.

Kenny finally made it all the way inside and closed the door behind him and Julian. "Trish, I don't understand. Why are you doing this? If there's tension between you and Evan, there has to be a way you guys can work it out. You don't have to leave the band."

"Absolutely," Julian added. "I can understand how you may be intimidated by him. I know I was when I first met him, with him being who he is, but then I came to realize he's human, just like everyone else, and what's more, once you get to know him he's very kind and generous. If you go to him about your concerns, I know he'll listen to you without bias and do all he can to resolve the issues."

Trish stuffed a throw pillow in a box and picked up a roll of packaging tape. "It's wonderful you all have such confidence in him, but he's not the only reason I'm leaving."

Jesse snatched the tape from her hand. "Do you want to stop packing long enough to enlighten us to the other reasons then?"

Trish shrugged. "It's not that much different from why Evan quit performing. I just don't feel like it anymore."

"But why?" Julian pressed. "Is it something that one of us, all of us, did?"

"I can understand if you're sick of hanging out with us all the time," Kenny said. "And Jess alone is a pain in the ass to deal with, but even if you don't like us anymore, you have to admit, the cash for hanging out with three people you don't like is enough to make you want to work through it."

"It's not anything like that," Trish said. "Leaving really does break my heart, even if it doesn't look like it. And it's not about the money. I'm just tired of the constant media attention and the last tour really burned me out. Even though I always thought I'd want to be part of a big act, I know now I really don't. I want to live a quiet life."

Jesse glowered at her. He didn't believe a word she said. It sounded too rehearsed. If these were her reasons, why didn't she speak them before? He above everyone else could relate to how irritating the paparazzi were, but he also learned a celebrity could maintain a low profile and privacy if they didn't offer them material.

"Those are great excuses. You want to tell us the real reason for leaving?"

She frowned at Jesse. "I just did."

"Sadly, I'm not believing you. Now, if it's something you're too embarrassed to share with everyone, you can tell me in private and I promise I'll keep it a secret, but I'm not letting you walk away until I hear the truth."

"You'd spill it to everyone the second I was out of hearing," she mumbled.

"I wouldn't. Trish, you know me. I take making a promise very seriously and I never make one with the intention of betraying it."

Jesse let silence-filled minutes tick by as he waited for her decision. Trish sat on the couch, her gaze fixed, unblinking, on a patch of carpet. Kenny squirmed in place, his mouth opened to speak. Jesse hushed him with a sharp look.

Trish blinked, an expression of defeat washed over her features. Her shoulders slumped, her back hunched as she leaned forward. Her voice came in a whisper. "You don't know what it's like to be so close to someone you want and know you can never have them. The torture it is to see them every day and watch them love another person and be oblivious to your feelings. I can't do it anymore. It hurts too much to be around you, and that's why I need to leave. I can't even stay in this city. Everything here reminds me of you because you love it so much."

Struck speechless by her words, Jesse stared at her. No coherent thought could form in his mind. It refused to function in comprehending her words.

Julian grabbed Kenny's arm. "I think we should go outside for a moment, get some air." He tugged on Kenny's arm. With his gaze locked on Trish, Kenny showed no sign of having felt Julian's touch. Julian jerked his arm harder.

Kenny jumped, his head snapped back and forth between Julian and Jesse. "Uh, yeah, right, I like air." He hopped to his feet. "Let's go get some."

Jesse watched their hasty retreat. When he looked back to Trish, he saw tears streaming down her flushed face. Gradually, his mind formed words, thoughts, questions, once again.

"So Ev was right," he said softly.

Trish glared at him through her damp eyes. "He always is, isn't he? If he declared the sky was green, then that's what it would be."

Her outburst quieted him for a moment. He took a breath, proceeding as gently as he could. "You can't be in love with me, Trish. You don't even know me as an intimate partner."

"There's more to loving someone than sex, Jess. For as intelligent as you are, I'd think you'd know that."

"I do know that, and I wasn't talking about intimacy in a sexual way. I'm talking about it in every other way. What it is to know the true depth of a person, all their sins and secrets. For as much time as we've spent together, you've only seen the surface of me. If you saw deeper, you may change your mind about how you feel. The only person who knows every ounce of me is Evan, and Brandon is a close second. There are a lot of things Kenny doesn't even know because he's afraid to hear them. And there's intimacy in living with a person, learning their habits and flaws. For as much as I claim that I'm perfection, the truth is, I'm not, and Ev tolerates an awful lot out of me."

Jesse could see from her clenched jaw muscles, the stubbornness in her face, Trish took her turn to not believe his words. He stood looking down at her. "But since you brought it up, sex between us would be a bit on the awkward side considering I'm gay."

"You've been with women before."

"Yeah, when I was fifteen and sixteen, but even then I knew it wasn't right for me. The first chance that came along for me to mess around with a guy, I jumped all over him. Granted I freaked afterward, but I needed to adjust to letting my true self finally take control. Once I got through that, I never looked back."

Trish weaved her fingers together and wrung her hands, still not looking at him. "It's…it's not that much different, though. And, I'd trust you, to do whatever you needed to feel satisfied."

Jesse couldn't help the grin that came to his face. "Wow, you've really thought this through. I have to admit, I'm flattered you'd be willing to go to those lengths to ensure my satisfaction."

Trish's face turned a deeper crimson. She tucked her chin closer to her chest in an attempt to hide her embarrassment.

Jesse sat on the couch beside her, his eyes forward to offer what privacy he could to her. He sighed loudly and set his hand on her knee. "The thing is, no matter what you did, no matter how hard you tried, no matter how good you were at it, you'd never be able to satisfy me. It's hard to explain, but the reason I can be happy with Evan isn't because of *the* sex, it's because of *his* sex. It's because he's a man. I'm attracted to men because they're men. I don't understand it any more than you understand why you're attracted to men and not women. It's just nature, it's ingrained, it's who we are. When you were a little girl, I bet you had a lot of crushes on guys before you realized what a crush and those feelings really meant, didn't you?"

Trish nodded.

"Well, so did I. The only difference is when I was six years old and told my mom I thought Superman was cute, she told me it was wrong to say things like that because boys didn't look at other boys in that way. It didn't change anything, though. I still kept thinking Superman was cute, I just didn't tell anyone about my feelings because I felt they were wrong. Eventually I realized, with a little help from Brandon, there wasn't a damn thing wrong with my feelings. So you see, it's who I am. And if you found a man you wanted to spend the rest of your life with, if something horrible happened to him, an illness or accident, where he couldn't make love to you anymore, you'd still stay by him for the rest of your lives, wouldn't you?"

Taking in a shaky breath, Trish nodded again.

"I'm the same way. Even if we could no longer love each other physically, I'd stay beside Evan beyond the end of eternity. That's how much I love him. Though the sex between us is wonderful and special, it's not what keeps us together."

A strangled sob broke through Trish's defenses. She covered her face in both hands, her shoulders shook as the held in tears flowed freely.

Jesse wrapped both arms around her and pulled her to him. "I'm so sorry, Trish, that I can't love you the way you want me to, the way you deserve to be loved. But I can love you in best way I know how, as a dear friend, as a family member. And I know it'll be hard at first, but please stay with us. If you do, you'll see it'll get easier. You just need to focus on my bad points. Then before you know it, you'll laugh at yourself that you ever thought of me as a potential partner and you'll find a wicked hot guy who'll make me jealous."

Despite his attempt to lighten her mood, Trish adamantly shook her head. "It won't work, Jess. You know I wasn't celibate on the road, but every time I met a guy, I'd look at you and you'd outshine him. I won't be able to move forward in my life if I'm around you. Do you understand?"

Though his mind still spun to comprehend everything, he nodded. He hugged her tightly, then drew back. Tenderly, he brushed the tears from under her eyes, then took both her hands in his. He lifted one to his lips and placed a soft kiss on the back of it, raised the other and did the same.

"I wish you the best of luck and the most happiness one person can possibly have. If ever there's anything you need from me, don't hesitate to call." He laid her hands on her knees and rose to leave.

"Jesse," she cried. "I'm so sorry. I've broken your dream. I've destroyed Conquest."

Jesse stopped at the door and looked at her, a small smile on his lips. "I'm not that easy to conquer, Trish. Trust me, the music will go on." He walked out the door, closing it softly behind him.

CHAPTER SIXTEEN

After sitting at home for a week with nothing to do since Evan had started work with the Chicago Symphony Orchestra, Jesse couldn't take it any longer and decided to head into the studio to listen to the meager bits of recording Conquest had done. The material was all scrap now, they'd record fresh once they settled on a new drummer, but tracking down Brad Delfini was proving more difficult than expected.

He, Kenny, and Julian got together a couple times for dinner and sat with a few drinks pondering how they could've missed Trish's feelings and what they could've done differently. No answers ever came, only memories of events that in hindsight made things seem so obvious, and in turn, made them feel foolish for having not seen the truth, him especially since Evan had told him. He took some solace in that they didn't blame him for her leaving, and it was his only solace since he still hadn't talked to Brandon.

As for Trish, she vanished. From Greg he found out she'd gone back to New York, but she hadn't bothered with a final goodbye, or with giving him, Kenny, or Julian any way to find her. Moments hit him where he became angry at her, then it'd fade as he realized her actions revealed how desperately she needed to get away.

Jesse lifted his Starbucks Mocha Frappuccino to his lips and sighed around the straw before taking a long sip. He pulled open the studio doors, saw neither the guard nor the receptionist, and let out a disgusted snort at Phoenix's stellar security. He slackened his strides at movement down the hall coming toward him.

A woman he didn't recognize rushed for the doors. With her head down, her dark brunette hair shadowed her face and bounced in long waves with each hurried step. In her right hand, she carried a black soft leather briefcase. The air around her vibrated with distress, and he realized he wasn't the only one having problems. He also realized if he didn't move, this woman, for all her slight and slender frame, would plow into him.

A hint of a smirk quirked one corner of his lips, and he slid into her direct line of travel. When she was three strides away, he called loudly, "Whoa! Slow down, girl!"

The woman's head snapped up. She stumbled as she slammed to a short stop, her briefcase fell from her hand to the floor. Jesse hopped forward, catching her by the arm to steady her. His Frappuccino sloshed in the cup, and amazingly, the domed plastic lid kept the icy liquid inside. He looked into her startled gray eyes, his first impression that she was a beautiful woman. He guessed her to be in her mid-twenties, and watched her eyes widened as recognition pushed her startled expression away.

Jesse released her arm and took a step back. "We both almost ended up wearing my Frappuccino."

Her eyes darted to his hand, then met his gaze again. "I'm sorry. I was in a hurry."

"Yeah, I could tell. If that's how you walk, I'd hate to see you drive." Jesse retrieved her briefcase off the floor and offered it to her. "Are you a musician?"

She took her briefcase from him. "Thank you. Yes, I am a musician, but not a recording artist. I'm a songwriter." She extended her hand to him. "Alanna Leonelli."

Jesse grasped her small hand. "Jesse Alexander."

"I know." Her expression lightened as a smile shone over her lips. "The lead singer of Conquest. Vocalist, songwriter, multi-instrumentalist, and front man extraordinaire. But I knew who you were before the rest of the world. I saw you perform a few times in clubs and bars, and even back then, it was so easy to see you were going to break free and take the world by storm some day."

Jesse laughed. "Wow, you're becoming one of my favorite people! So you're a songwriter? What no talent hack can't write their own music now?"

"This one."

Jesse looked around Alanna to see Kyler walking toward them. He glanced at Alanna, back to Kyler, and shook his head in confusion. "But I thought you weren't going to use a songwriter on this one."

"Phoenix is getting antsy over the slow progress we're making and seems to feel we could do with a creative boost." Kyler's hazel eyes flicked to Alanna as he stopped beside her. He put his arm around her shoulders. "Thanks for stopping my girl before she got away."

"I'm not your girl!" Alanna knocked Kyler's arm off her shoulders with a sharp jerk of her upper body.

Kyler leaned toward her. "Al, it's gonna happen sooner or later. There's no point in fighting the inevitable."

Alanna thrust her index finger in his face. "I told you before, I'm not one of your panting groupies, so back off!"

Jesse couldn't help but laugh. "You tell him, girl! Now slap him! Push him down! Beat that testosterone out of him!"

The tense moment broke as Alanna giggled softly and rolled her eyes at him.

Kyler moved next to Jesse and slapped his hand down on his shoulder. "So where's your pup today?"

"Achilles? I won't be here for long, so I left him at home."

"No, I was talking about your other loyal dog, Evan."

Jesse's expression darkened with a glare.

Kyler held both hands up in a gesture of innocence. "I'm kidding!" His countenance shifted to serious, his voice softened to a tone of sympathy. "I heard about Trish leaving. I'm really sorry."

"Thanks," Jesse mumbled.

"Have you started looking for a new drummer yet?"

"Yeah, we have someone in mind, but we're having trouble tracking him down."

"Who?"

"The guy who drummed on Ev's *Allegro* album, Brad Delfini."

Kyler nodded thoughtfully. "You guys would kick some major ass with him laying down your rhythms. So why did Trish leave?"

"It's a long story and most of it's personal."

"Then let's go to lunch and talk about it." Kyler nodded toward Alanna. "She'll go to lunch with me if you come along."

"I already like her too much to do that to her."

A raspy voice cut in, "Jesse, bro! Dude, it's been forever!"

At the sight of Trent heading toward them with the rest of Swiller, Jesse looked up at the ceiling in exasperation and muttered under his breath, "Fuck me."

"Anytime," Kyler whispered.

Jesse glanced at him and took in his smirk.

Trent stopped before Jesse, beaming at him. "Dude, you still haven't come down to listen to us. Don't you want to know what your opening act is going to sound like?"

Jesse grit his teeth. Between working with the orchestra and trying to find Brad, Evan hadn't gotten a chance to tackle that little problem yet. "I've had a lot going on lately."

"I heard. That's some tough shit about your drummer, man. But what do you expect when you got a chick in your band? One bad minute of PMS and off they go." Trent burst out laughing at his joke, his band members joined him.

Before Jesse could retaliate, Alanna's voice blasted over their laughter as she shouted, "Screw you!" less than a foot away from Trent's face.

Trent startled back a step. "Shit. I'm sorry, that was a stupid thing to say. Not all chicks get bitchy around their thing. I'm sure you're cool." He held his hand out to her. "I'm Trent. Lead singer of the best fuckin' rock band ever!"

Alanna looked away from his offered hand. "I doubt that."

Trent shrugged and drew his hand back.

Kyler claimed Alanna's briefcase. "And on that note, we're out of here. Trent, you owe me for taking her away before she kicks your ass, and trust me, she *could* kick your ass." He placed his hand on the small of Alanna's back. "You ready for lunch?"

Alanna sighed. "I suppose." She looked to Jesse. "It was really great meeting you, Jesse."

"You too. I hope to see you around."

Kyler turned Alanna toward the door, his gaze falling on Jesse as he walked by. "Are you sure you don't want to join us?"

Jesse caught the edge of concern in Kyler's tone and knew he was really asking him if he'd be alright alone with Trent and Swiller. It surprised him, but he smiled and nodded. "I'm sure. Another time." He watched them leave, then headed for the hall.

Trent called after him. "Hey, you gonna come listen to us today?"

"It's doubtful. I've got work to do."

Trent looked at his band members. "I'll be out in a minute, and one of you guys save me a smoke 'cause I'm out." He sprinted off after Jesse. "Hey, man! Wait up!"

Jesse kept walking. "I don't have time to talk."

"Yeah, yeah, you're busy. I know. It's just, I was thinking how totally un-cool I was to Evan, you know about the whole queer thing and shit, and I thought maybe I could make it up to him by all of us going to a strip club this Friday. It'd be cool 'cause then you and me could get to know each other better and I know he'll come if you do."

"No, he wouldn't. And besides, I've got plans."

"Plans? C'mon! Who passes up going to a booby bar? You got a date or something?"

"Yeah, I do, and with someone a hell of a lot hotter than you."

"Alright, I get it! I wouldn't pass up getting laid to hang out with a bunch of dudes either. But I bet you don't lack for it. When you guys first came on the scene, all the girls at my school were so hot for you. Everywhere I turned, your picture was hanging in lockers, taped to folders, and shit like that. When you guys would come into town, there'd be no chicks at school 'cause they all went stalking you. You have to tell me, how many girls have you banged?"

Jesse stopped and faced Trent. "Why the hell are you asking me something like that?"

Trent shrugged. "Guy talk, man. I want to know what to expect when we hit it big. I might need to put myself into training now. So how many?"

Jesse continued his trek without answering.

Trent tagged along behind him. "Dude, that's priceless! I never thought you'd be shy about it! So you're busy Friday, how 'bout Saturday?"

"I have plans."

"Damn, you're a hard guy to be friends with, you know? You're always busy."

Jesse pulled in a long, deep breath in an attempt to find a sliver of patience. He could do this. He could be professional. He halted once again and turned to Trent. "I know I'm always busy. You just have to understand I'm dealing with a lot of shit right now. I promise to listen to you guys soon, right after we find a new drummer and things settle down. Is that cool?"

A large smile sprang on Trent's lips. "Yeah, man! That's cool!"

"Good. Now, I really need to get some work done, okay?"

Trent's head bobbed in an enthusiastic nod. "No problem, dude. I'll catch ya later."

"Later, man."

Trent turned back toward the lobby, Jesse to the studio door. He glanced at Trent's departing back. If the worst came to pass and he ended up having to tour with him, at least he was starting to get the hang of handling the boy. Trent might be a grungy little bigot, but at least he was harmless.

Jesse locked the door and went to one of the leather chairs behind the control desk. He dropped down, exhaling a heavy sigh. Still, dealing with Trent was draining. He could manage politeness and professionalism for a few minutes, but would he really be able to keep it up for weeks on the road? The answer burst to the front of his mind. He wondered if he told Greg that him going to jail for kicking Trent's ass could be bad for the tour and profits if it would convince him to not put them together.

His phone rang with his ringtone of Evan singing the chorus of his ballad "One More Time." Jesse retrieved the phone from his pocket, and at Evan's name and cell number glowing on the screen, quickly answered it. "Do you know how happy it makes me to hear your voice?"

Evan chuckled. "Do you know how happy it makes me that it makes you happy? Are you at the studio now?"

"Yeah," Jesse grumbled.

"What's going on?"

"Just more bullshit, as usual."

"Then I guess it's good I called you because I've got some news to cheer you up."

Jesse sat up straighter in the chair. "What?"

"I just got off the phone with Greg, and guess who *he* just got off the phone with."

"He found Brad!"

"That's right. I'm getting ready to call him after we hang up, but Greg already laid the foundation for letting him know what's going on. He's agreed to come into town, this coming Monday. Right now, he's playing with another band. They've got some gigs booked over the weekend and he doesn't want to abandon them without warning, but Greg said he sounded really pumped at the prospect of playing with you guys."

"That's awesome! See what a great manager you are!"

"Well, I don't know if I'd go that far. Greg's the one who found him. There's no one he can't find once he's on their trail, except for me, of course. Sometimes I think he really should have been a detective instead of a music producer. But you have to remember, it's been years since Greg or I have seen or worked with him. Even though Greg said he sounded like the same old Brad on the phone, people can change, so I don't want you to get your hopes up any higher than they already are."

"I know, I'm trying not to. And even though you say to give Greg the credit for finding him, he wouldn't have been looking for him if it wasn't for you, so you still get the credit."

"Thanks. Now why don't you leave whatever you're working on and come get me for lunch. We'll have a mini celebration."

"I'll be there in ten minutes!"

"Fifteen! Drive slowly and carefully."

"I will. I love you."

"I love you too, gorgeous."

Jesse hung up his phone and sprang from the chair, punching the air with his fist as he shouted his elation. "Nothing's going to stop us now!"

CHAPTER SEVENTEEN

From their private balcony seats at the right hand side of the stage, Jesse and Evan rose with the rest of the audience to join in the raucous applause and cheering for Brandon as he bowed to the crowd. The other actors in *Chicago* marched out with glowing smiles, but it was clear who the crowd favorite was. Roses flew on the stage toward Brandon. He stepped to the front and retrieved a bouquet. As he straightened, he looked toward Jesse and Evan. He inclined his head in the slightest nod, then returned to his fellow actors and bowed in unison with all of their hands clasped before leaving the stage.

Jesse gripped the edge of the balcony, his eyes still on the spot where Brandon had stood. "Did you see that? He looked at us! What do you think that means? Do you think he's glad we came? Do you think he's forgiven me? Maybe it was his way of saying we could talk."

"I don't know what it meant other than he knows we're here. It looked like a good sign, though."

Musing on his unanswered questions, Jesse slowly sat down. "I guess he read the cards in the baskets we sent him. He could've refused to accept them after seeing they were from us, so that's good, too."

An hour before the curtain went up, they sent a massive bouquet of flowers wishing him to "break a leg," and since he knew Brandon would get more enjoyment out of it than the flowers, he also sent a junk food basket filled with Brandon's favorite snacks.

"Still," Jesse said softly, "if he had completely forgiven me, he would've sent someone to come get us so we could go backstage and see him."

Evan laid his hand over Jesse's. "We could go backstage, anyway. Everyone would recognize you and know he's your brother. They'd let you back there."

"I know, but I don't want to push him. Maybe after knowing I came to see him even though he didn't want me to, he'll realize how sorry I am and call me."

The curtain separating their box from the hallway rustled. An usher peeked in, his eyes glanced between them and settled on Jesse. "Sirs, Mr. Alexander requests to see you in his dressing room. He sent me to guide you."

Evan smiled at Jesse. "You see? He wants to talk to you already."

Jesse stood and grabbed his suit jacket off the back of his seat. "Yeah, I just hope it's not to slap me in the face."

Jesse and Evan followed the usher backstage. They weaved between pulleys and props, colorfully painted backgrounds and cheerful actors still half dressed in their stage costumes and makeup. The usher stopped before a door with Brandon's name written in gold letters and took his leave. Jesse stared at Brandon's name.

Evan gave him a gentle nudge toward the door. "I'll wait for you out here."

Jesse spun toward him. "You should come in. He'll be less inclined to beat me if you're there."

"When has Brandon ever beaten you?" Evan pushed him a little firmer. "I think you guys need to talk alone. Go on."

Jesse gazed at him for a moment, then faced the door. He took a deep breath and knocked softly.

"It's open," Brandon called.

His voice sounded distant from the other side of the door. Jesse's heart lit into a rapid, nervous rhythm, yet, somehow, his hand moved painstakingly slow in turning the doorknob. He stuck his head in first and saw Brandon on the other side of the dressing room, his back to the door as he sat at a large vanity removing his stage makeup with ritualistic care. Jesse stepped inside and closed the door quietly behind him.

"Hey," he greeted softly.

"Hey," Brandon replied, equally hushed.

Encouraged Brandon hadn't cursed him, Jesse took two quick steps forward. "You were incredible out there! Your rendition of 'Razzle Dazzle' was amazing. You sounded awesome. Your voice was carrying so strong, and the crowd loved you."

Brandon let out a single hard chuckle. "Thanks."

Jesse watched Brandon wipe away the makeup that moments before had made him look older than his almost twenty-seven years. He saw the makeup had hidden a new paleness to his brother's complexion, darkness under his blue eyes. Brandon looked tired, worn down, and thinner than he ever remembered. His black hair, cropped shorter than when he last saw him nearly a month ago, was tousled, some of it sticking up in uneven spikes from Brandon pulling off the gray-haired wig he wore for the show.

Concern for his brother filled him. He wanted to ask why he looked so beaten down, but didn't know how to begin. Instead, he gazed around the dressing room lined with flowers. Jesse looked back at him and saw Brandon contemplating him in the mirror.

"Where's Evan?" Brandon asked.

"Outside. He thought we should have some time to…talk."

Brandon nodded slowly. "How've things been?"

"Oh, okay," Jesse said with forced casualness. "Well, not really. Trish quit the band, and that sucked, but we may already have a new drummer lined up. He's flying in next week, so that's good."

Brandon spun around in his chair. "Trish quit? I can't believe it! What happened?"

Jesse waved his worry away. "It's a long story. A good one, but long. I'd rather hear how things have been with you. How's," he cleared his throat to give himself a second to will the name out, "Christopher doing?"

Brandon averted his gaze to the side. "I wouldn't know. You'd be better off asking one of the other hundred guys he was screwing besides me."

"What?" Jesse gasped and quickly closed the distance between them.

Brandon twisted the cloth used to remove his makeup. "You were right about him. Everything you said was true. He was cheating on me…a lot, apparently." He looked up at Jesse, tears hung on the edges of his eyes. "I tried so hard to make him happy. I bought him clothes, I took him to expensive restaurants. Then I find out that while I was at the theatre trying to make a living, he was out shoving his prick into any guy who'd let him! And do you know how he told me?"

Jesse shook his head.

"I was kissing my way down his body and he stopped me, saying there was something he needed to tell me. Then after he tells me about sleeping around, he informs me he hasn't been the most careful and he was getting tested so I probably should, too."

Fear for his brother overwhelmed Jesse. He grabbed Brandon's shoulders and bent toward his face. "But you're okay, right? Right?"

Brandon laid his hands on Jesse's forearms. "I'm fine. I just got all my test results back this week and everything was clean."

Relief stole Jesse's strength. He sagged forward and wrapped his arms around Brandon's shoulders.

Embracing Jesse around the waist, Brandon laid his head on Jesse's abdomen. "I wanted to call you so many times, but I was afraid you'd turn me away. I don't believe any of the things I said that day. I know you made it big on your own."

"I know," Jesse said softly. "The things I said about you were worse, but I don't believe any of them, either."

"No, the difference between the things I said and the things you said is you were speaking honestly. I wouldn't know love if it slapped me in the face, and I *am* jealous of you and Evan. I don't understand…" Brandon's voice broke as tears and emotion forced their way free, "I don't understand why I can't find someone to love me."

He clung to the back of Jesse's shirt. His sobs came heavy. Jesse held him with one arm around his shoulders, the other buried in his hair, knowing no way to comfort his brother other than to be close to him.

"I wanted to have a relationship like what you have with Evan," Brandon choked out. "I wanted it so badly, in my mind, I created it with that bastard. I made myself see him looking at me the same way Evan looks at you. I made myself hear him whispering lovingly to me the way Evan does to you. But they were all lies! Nothing but mirages! When he whispered to me it was to ask for money. When he looked at me he was only trying to see if I'd figured out what he was doing behind my back. What's wrong with me that all I find are men who want to rip out my soul and wave it around like a victory flag? Why can't I find anyone to love me, Jess?"

Jesse held Brandon tighter. "There's nothing wrong you, Brandon. If you have any flaw, it's you're too nice of a person. You always try to see the good in someone, but some people don't have any good in them. It's not you, it's them.

"But someday, you're going to find another person like you, a man whose heart is just as kind and generous, and when you do, you'll know he's destined to be the love of your life because your heart, your mind, your body, and soul will respond and sing in harmony at the sight of him. You'll have love, Brandon, I know you will. And it'll be a love so deep, you won't be able to breathe without their breath mingling with yours. And they'll love you so much they'd gladly surrender their life for your happiness because their own can't exist without your smile." Jesse leaned back slightly. He smiled down at him. "They'll even sit and watch your cartoons with you, and actually enjoy that time together."

A few rough laughs rasped from Brandon's throat. "That'd be true love, wouldn't it?"

"It couldn't be anything else." Jesse ran his fingers through Brandon's hair. "Your haircut looks good...or, it would if it was combed."

More chuckles came from Brandon. "Thanks." His expression turned somber once again. "Evan must hate me for how I treated you."

"Ev loves you as much as if you were his own brother. You know that."

"He didn't tell you he called me, did he?"

"No. When?"

"The day after you called and left that long message on my phone. I didn't answer because I saw it was him, but he left a message saying the relationship between me and you was too sacred for us to let one fight disrupt it. Then he asked me to come see you because he knew if we could only see each other, we'd be able to get over everything. I called his cell phone at two o'clock in the morning because I was too chicken shit to talk to him and left a message telling him to mind his own business. I thought for sure he was going to show up at my apartment and punch me in the mouth, but he let it go."

"Of course he did." Jesse paused, his voice softened. "I wonder why he didn't tell me."

"He probably didn't want you to get more upset with me than you already were." Brandon caught Jesse's hand and squeezed it. "He's a special person, Jess. He takes good care of you, and I don't mean he lords over you, because he doesn't. I mean it in the way it is, the way it should be. He takes care of you how a man should take care of the one he loves."

"Thank you for saying that." Jesse glanced toward the door. "He's probably going out of his mind with boredom standing out there."

"Bring him in."

Jesse opened the door and peeked out, surprised to find Evan not there. He looked up the hall and saw him in the center of a circle of actors and stagehands, more than a few women and men flirting so blatantly with him Jesse could see it from where he stood. Evan posed for a couple pictures, smiled and chuckled as he signed autographs.

Brandon leaned over Jesse. "Looks like he's made some friends."

"For someone who hates attention, he certainly adapts well when people begin showering it on him." Jesse stepped out to the hall.

Evan caught sight of him and excused himself from the group despite their protests.

As soon as he was within reach, Jesse took him by the jacket sleeve and pulled him into Brandon's dressing room. He closed the door and spun toward him. "We made up! Everything's good again!"

"That's wonderful!" Evan faced Brandon and held his open arms out to him. "I've missed you."

"Thanks." Brandon went meekly into Evan's arms. "I'm so sorry, Evan, for the message I left after you called me and tried to help us work things out."

"I've already forgotten about it. I'm just glad to have you come back to us."

Brandon hid his face against Evan's shoulder, his sorrow breaking him down once again. Evan held him through his muffled tears and glanced questioningly at Jesse. In a hushed voice, Jesse told him what happened. He watched the fury rise in Evan's eyes as Christopher's betrayal was revealed.

"Where is he now?" Evan asked through clenched teeth when Jesse finished.

"I don't know." Brandon pulled away from Evan and sank down in a chair. "I haven't seen or talked to him since I ended it. That was almost two weeks ago."

"Good," Jesse said, glad Evan wouldn't be able to track Christopher down. As much as he wanted to see Christopher get his ass beat, he didn't want Evan to be the person to do it. "Let him leave your life completely."

"Yeah," Brandon mumbled.

Not willing to let Brandon continue to mourn his loss, Jesse perked up his voice. "You know what we should do? Let's all go to Uno's. Then after we eat, we'll swing by your apartment, you can get some things, and come stay with us for the weekend, or longer if you want."

"That's a great idea," Evan added. "I've been thinking about getting a motorcycle, so you can go with me to look at some."

"I don't know," Brandon said softly. "I have to go to the after party in a little bit, then I've got shows tomorrow and Sunday."

Jesse took Brandon's hand in his and swung it back and forth. "So what? We can go out after the party and you can still stay with us. You can drive to the theatre from our place. I'll even let you bring over some of your anime and I'll watch it with you."

Brandon gave him a wry smile. "You must've really missed hanging out with me if you're offering to do that."

Jesse rolled his eyes. "I said I'd watch it with you. I didn't say I wouldn't make fun of it."

Brandon looked up to Evan. "Are you sure it's okay?"

"Of course it is." Evan bent down and placed a tender kiss on his cheek. "Our house is always open to you. The only thing I ask is that I get to sleep in the middle of you two."

"Hey!" Jesse snatched Evan's arm and yanked him back. "We have six extra bedrooms! We're not all sleeping in the same bed!"

"Since I can't get you guys to do a threesome with me, can't you at least give me being snuggled to sleep between you both?"

Jesse raised his chin in defiance. "No."

Brandon's laughter sounded over them. "Alright, I have to get cleaned up. Both of you, out."

They turned for the door and Evan threw a wink at Jesse.

"Jess," Brandon called. "Thanks so much, for everything."

Jesse smiled at him. "Thank you too, for forgiving me."

CHAPTER EIGHTEEN

Jesse leaned back against the black limousine watching the Phoenix Records private jet roll to a halt. This was it. He was finally going to meet Brad Delfini. He glanced at the others, taking in their nervousness. Kenny gnawed on the nub of his thumbnail. Julian had his arms folded across his chest, his fingers flying over his biceps as if playing quick notes on a piano. Jesse looked to his other side at Evan, who stood like a pillar of tranquility, which surprised him since if Evan felt anything like he did, he raged inside with pent up sexual energy.

Having Brandon spend the weekend with them was wonderful, but he and Evan hadn't made love in three days. Out of respect for him, they went quietly to bed each night and behaved themselves, not wanting to take the chance Brandon might overhear them and revive his pain at not having someone to share his body with. Over the weekend, Brandon gained flashes of his old self, but it would take time for him to recover from Christopher's betrayal.

Jesse looked up at the crystalline April sky. His hopes of releasing a summer album were pretty well squashed. The press conference they held the week before, filled with rabid entertainment reporters screeching and pecking at each other, went fairly good when he announced Trish had quit Conquest. But what disgusted him was having to answer "no" to the same question being asked in different ways if he and Trish had been in an intimate relationship and if an ugly breakup led to her departure.

He got so fed up, when one reporter asked it again, he replied by questioning, "Do you have a sister?" The reporter said, "Yes." He then asked, "Have you ever had sex with her?" The reporter lost his cool and yelled how vulgar the question was, to which he answered, "Now you know how it feels. Trish was like a sister to me. Get it through your heads, all of you!" As it turned out, his non-politically correct outburst got more attention in the media than anything else he said.

Their fans freaked out over the news, talking about it in depth on the forum of Conquest's website. He posted a letter on the homepage assuring them it wasn't the end of Conquest, the show would go on, then he logged into the forum under his ID showing him as the real Jesse and chatted with fans personally. The fans went crazy when they saw him online and the posts asking questions popped up faster than he could answer. Now, though, he felt even more anxious to get working on the album.

The door on the jet opened allowing the stairs to descend. A man wearing sunglasses appeared in the opening. Jesse moved his gaze over him, analyzing Brad from his head to his feet.

Brad wore his black hair cut short and spiky. His slender oval face bore a rich olive complexion that made him look as if he'd only just left his ancestral home in the Mediterranean. The strap of his dark blue duffel bag hung over one broad shoulder, his black T-shirt blew tight against him from the gusting wind to reveal a fit, firm torso. His biceps filled the sleeves of the shirt, the musculature of his forearms visible even at a distance. Faded jeans hugged Brad's narrow hips and did little to hide the definition in his thighs.

Beside him, Jesse heard Julian mutter a hushed, "Oh my," and smirked at him. "Remember, Jules, he only likes girls."

"Yes, they always do, don't they?" Julian grumbled.

Brad's head turned in their direction. He smiled wide, showing brilliant white teeth, and flung his arms out to the side. "'ey! If it isn't Prince Pretty himself here to greet me! I'm honored!"

Jesse grinned at Brad's cute Brooklyn accent, then caught what he called Evan and glared at him.

"It's just a nickname, gorgeous," Evan said, and stepped forward to greet Brad. "That's right, boy! And you better show proper respect!"

"A thousand apologies, your majesty!" Brad chuckled, jogging down the steps.

Evan met him halfway between the jet and group. They slammed into a rough hug, laughing while they jostled each other.

When they pulled apart, Evan kept his hands on Brad's upper arms, Brad's hands remained on Evan's waist.

Brad glanced up and down Evan's body. "Damn, look at you. I think all that booze you used to drink is preserving you."

"That's my fountain of youth. Good liquor and a hot lover."

Brad laughed again. "Yeah, you haven't changed."

Jesse watched the interaction. He strained to hear their words, but the wind carried them away and they were angled too far from him to read their lips.

Evan and Brad walked toward the group. They stopped before Julian as Evan introduced them. Jesse fought down a grin. He'd gotten to know Julian's type pretty well in their time together; tall, rugged, athletic, and Brad fit it perfectly, other than the whole straight aspect.

Evan directed Brad next to Kenny. He then stepped to Jesse's side, slid one arm around his waist, and pulled him closer. "And this is the master behind it all, who is also most importantly, my life partner, Jesse Alexander."

Jesse flashed a perfect smile of his own and offered his hand to Brad, meeting his dark brown, almond shaped eyes. "It's great to finally meet you. Ev's talked very highly of you."

Brad took Jesse's hand. "You too. When he called me about this gig, after I got over my shock at him appearing out of nowhere after all these years, he stunned me again by saying, 'Remember those rumors about me and Jesse a while back? They were true and they still are.' Then I think he spent more time talking about how wonderful you are than about the job."

Jesse turned his smile on Evan. "That's my boy."

Evan winked at him and opened the door to the limo. "We should get going. Greg's waiting for us at the studio."

Brad followed the others as they filed in. "I'm surprised he didn't come down here with you guys."

Evan climbed in beside Jesse and laid his arm around his shoulders. "He's been pretty busy these days helping to run the operations of Phoenix. I think it's only a matter of time before he's made VP."

Jesse rested his hand on Evan's thigh. "Which wouldn't necessarily be a bad thing. I mean no offense to him, he knows what he's doing and he loves the music, but sometimes he gets too focused on the business aspect of it over the art. But he's not as hands on with us as he used to be. Not since Ev's become our manager."

Brad stared at Jesse for a moment, then moved his gaze to Evan. "That's a detail you left out."

A smirk slid over Evan's lips. "I didn't want to scare you away."

"You might've too. Here I thought I wasn't going to have to deal with the Mad Genius that much."

"I wouldn't be worrying about working with me just yet. You're here to audition. You haven't been offered the job."

Brad waved his hand, disregarding Evan's words. "Please. I know my skills. This gig's as good as got."

"It's not just skills, it's personality as well," Evan said.

"Oh, well then I *am* screwed."

Kenny leaned toward Brad. "Evan said you were with a band that put out an album. I've been trying to get my hands on it, but it's been tough tracking down."

"That's because it sucked and it's out of print now," Brad replied. "You'd have to go to used music shops and dig through their garbage section to find it."

Evan turned his gaze to Kenny. "I have a copy of it, Kenny. If I'd known you were looking for it, I'd have lent it to you, but Brad's right." He looked back to Brad. "It sucked. But the important thing is you sounded good."

"That's about the only praise we got on it. The critics would say things like 'vocals that sounded worse than a dozen cats in heat,' 'the guitarist should learn the purpose of the frets,' 'the bassist would do well to learn more than one chord.' When it came to me, they'd always start out saying, 'the former drummer for Evan Arden,' then wrap it up saying how sad it was to see how far down the musical ladder I'd fallen. But I couldn't be pissed at them for telling the truth.

"Back when I first joined Crimson, they were an okay group of guys, but after we got the deal, they burned through the advance so frickin' fast, we almost didn't make it through recording. The singer was more excited he could afford prime coke than he was about making an album. The guitar player decided he needed to start consoling the singer's wife since she was pissed about her man's addiction. The bassist really could only play about one chord because it was the only one he could remember since he was always boozed up. And me, I was just wallowing in self-pity that I left playing for Evan. So when the album bombed and our label cut us, I left them. The band was already finished and everyone was breaking their own ways, anyhow."

"You know, Brad," Evan said, "back when you had your accident, I did want you on *One More Time*. I just couldn't wait the months it was going to take you to heal."

"I know, man. Out of everybody, you were the one who came to visit me the most when I was laid up. But lying around doing nothing for so long addled my brain to where I believed I'd be better off striking out with a band of my own. I got greedy and wanted more spotlight than what glanced over me when I was standing in your shadow. Of course now, I have to really think if I want to be with a big act again. I'm feeling a little old to be going on world tours and playing huge stadiums."

"Shut up, you're only twenty-six," Evan said.

"I'm also twenty-six," Julian added. "I certainly don't feel too old."

Jesse jumped into the conversation before it got distracted from the issues he wanted to know. "What's going on with the band you're in now?"

"I've only been with them a few months. After Crimson broke up, I bounced around from band to band, but none I hooked up with ever lasted long. 'Play Hard and Burn Out' was most of their mottos. The band I'm with now, Devil's Claw, are a bunch of metalheads, and I hate playing that shit, but you gotta do something to keep beer in the fridge and macaroni in the cupboard, you know. That and," Brad cleared his throat, his voice dropped to a mumble, "I'm working at a big music store selling cheap guitars to kids with rock star dreams and helping grannies find Frank Sinatra CDs in the Oldies section."

"Why the hell are you doing that?" Evan burst out. "You could've called Phoenix at anytime, asked for Greg, and he would've brought you back as a studio musician in a heartbeat."

Brad shrugged and looked at him. "Pride, man. It's an evil thing. I was too ashamed to call him and say I couldn't make it on my own, so I kept trying. Then I just got to where I figured it wasn't meant to be. I had my shot to play in the big leagues, I blew it, and I had to live with that."

Evan scowled at him. "It wasn't just pride holding you back, it was stupidity. This business is all about connections, I told you that years ago. You form acquaintances and use them to meet your goals. Friendships in this business are only as strong as what the other person can provide for you. That's how it works. Everyone knows it, everyone does it. There's no room for philosophical musings of *it wasn't meant to be*. You arm yourself with everything you've got, you dig in, and you set out to conquer. If you go in with anything less than absolute victory in your mind as the only possible outcome, then you will be beaten back to spend the rest of your days drowning in regrets. I can't believe you didn't listen to me. I can't believe you've been letting yourself live like you are. There's no reason for it!"

In that moment, Jesse fully understood Evan and Brad's relationship. Though it may have started out with intimate intentions on Evan's part, and years had passed since they saw each, the easy, familiar way they communicated and the concern dominating Evan's sharp reprimand made it clear that Evan, whether knowingly or not, treated Brad like a younger brother, and for his part, Brad submitted and accepted the knowledgeable chastising by his "elder brother."

Brad forced a tentative smile. "But hey, I'm here now."

"Let's just hope your skills haven't been ruined with the shit you've been playing," Evan said.

Jesse decided to take some of the heat off Brad. "I'm sure his skills are even better than when he played for you. He's gotten to play with a lot of different musicians over the years, learn from them and their styles. And playing metal isn't easy. It's all about power and speed. So when you look at it, he's made himself incredibly diverse and has pulled out his potential a lot more than if he would have stayed playing for you, because let's face it, Ev, you're not real big on letting your musicians diverge from what you've written."

Evan grinned at him. "Why should there be divergence from perfection?"

"True, but what's perfect for you may not be perfect for another. Just look how perfect I am. But I bet somewhere in this great big world, in some remote place, there's at least one person who'd believe I'd be a horrible match for them."

"There may be more than just one," Kenny said. "There's a whole group of guys out there, I'm sure you've heard of them, they're what's called straight, and this funny group of guys through some weird quirk of nature, enjoy women and have no interest in popping another guy."

Julian patted Kenny's knee. "Yes, I've heard of them! The poor creatures. They have no idea what they're missing."

Evan laughed, looking at Kenny. "You know Kenny, you've been playing in a band with two gay men and a straight woman. With the possibility of Brad joining, I hope you've given some thought to what it'll be like having competition for the women."

"Actually, I have, and I decided it should be okay, because everyone knows the guitar player always gets hotter women than the drummer." Kenny turned to Brad. "Of course, it'd make it a lot easier on me if you're in a relationship. You got a girl?"

"No, man, I'm just playing the field these days. I was seeing a girl for a while, but she broke up with me last month saying I was never going to go anywhere in my life." Brad chuckled. "If I get this gig, I'm going to have to call her and rub it in. I know it's being an ass, but it's okay to hop off the high road to the low one every once in a while, right?"

"Hell yeah," Kenny agreed. "But hey, I'm going to warn you about something now so you know what you're walking into. If Evan's within a mile radius, Jess goes into instant heat."

"And he's not the most subtle about it," Julian added. "Such as all the times he would take Evan to the bunks in the back of the tour bus for one of their *naps*, as if everyone didn't know what was really going on."

Kenny held up his index finger to make another point. "And then there's his Chicago Bears duffel bag that's with him on the road. Even if he says it's okay, never, *never*, go into it for anything. I asked him if I could borrow one of his video games once, and I learned how naïve I was about sex, because he had things in there—"

"Alright!" Jesse interjected. "I think Brad gets it."

Brad spoke through laughter. "Hey, whatever makes your Twinkie cream. I'm no saint when it comes to sex either."

The conversation halted as they pulled up in front of the Phoenix Records studios. Evan slid out, the others followed.

As Brad exited, he stared at the building. "Damn, this looks nice."

Jesse walked through the door, held open by the security guard. "Wait till you see the recording rooms."

The group headed up the hall with Jesse and Evan in the lead. A loud crash came from Studio A, and immediately after it, Alanna burst out into the hall. Kyler appeared next, less than five steps behind her, softly laughing as he reached for her. "Al, c'mon! I didn't mean anything by it. Slow down!"

"Another day in paradise, Alanna," Jesse said to the songwriter.

The rage on Alanna's face retreated against a large smile. "Jesse! Welcome back!"

Evan offered his hand to Alanna. "I haven't had the pleasure of meeting you yet, though Jesse told me about you. I'm Evan Arden."

Alanna gazed at Evan with a star-struck look as she took his hand. "I-I know. I've loved your music for so, so long."

Before Evan could respond, Kyler intervened with an unenthused voice, "I'm sure he's flattered. You know, he eats and shits just like everyone else, so you can quit looking at him like he's some sort of god."

Alanna turned on Kyler, her voice high with anger. "You just love to criticize people, don't you? You want to criticize the stuff I write for you and call it overly romantic melodramatic crap, then how about you take a little of the criticism back? Why don't you try not ending every single line in your new, so-called soon-to-be hit, with the word *babe*? Or do you want to keep sounding like a chauvinistic '80s hair-band when you weren't even playing in the '80s to begin with? Is that what you're shooting for? Trying to bring that little trend back on your own? Why don't you do a cover of 'Cherry Pie' and you'll be all set!"

Nearly every man inched back from Alanna to give her more space. Kyler, unable to move far as the target of her wrath, stared at her as if he feared blinking, because in that split second where his eyelids dropped shut, she could strike and tear out his throat.

Evan chuckled softly. "Well, there's nothing like a fierce woman to teach men the true meaning of fear. I can see why you said she was cool, Jess. She's got Kyler pissing himself."

The others laughed, Alanna included. Kyler scowled at him.

Evan turned toward him. "You really shouldn't agitate her so much. You could use someone like her in your life who isn't afraid to tell you how it is."

"Al and I are great together. We just don't agree on things musically."

"That's not the best marriage for an artist and songwriter, but I wish you both good luck. Now if you'll excuse us, these guys are way overdue for hitting the studio." Evan placed his hand on Jesse's lower back to guide him forward.

Jesse patted Alanna on the shoulder as he passed. "Hang in there."

She smiled at him. "I will."

Jesse swung into the chill-out room. Greg chatted with Jeremy, and at the sight of Brad, jumped up to greet him. After they talked for a few minutes, Jesse herded everyone to the depths of the studio and the drum room. Brad entered the small wood paneled room and paced around the full drum kit, checking it over. Jesse and the others watched him from the control room. Evan, Greg, and Jeremy sat behind the control desk, Kenny and Julian stood on either side of Jesse.

Jeremy looked behind him to Jesse. "Do you want me to record him?"

"Yeah, I think that'd be best. If we're uncertain about him and want to audition other people, we'll have something to compare them to."

"My mind's already made up," Kenny said. "I think he's awesome."

Julian nodded. "I agree. He seems like he'll be a lot of fun to work with."

"And that's wonderful, but it doesn't mean anything if he can't play how we need him to," Jesse said.

Brad took a seat behind the drums and picked up the sticks, testing their weight and rubbing his hands over them. To Jesse, he looked nervous. Brad tapped out a few beats on each drum and the cymbals, then started to warm up by laying down a repetitive beat, getting faster each time around.

Jeremy glanced back to Jesse again. "I'm ready whenever you are."

Jesse leaned around Evan, switched on the PA, and grabbed the mic. "Brad."

Brad stopped and looked up at him.

"When you're done warming up, I want you to play one of our songs for me. Do you know any of them well enough to fake your way through?"

"I know all of them and I'm ready now."

"Then play 'Vanish' for me." Jesse switched off the mic.

Kenny frowned at Jesse and spoke with thick sarcasm. "Why don't you give him something a little more difficult to start out with?"

"If he can play 'Vanish,' then he can play anything we throw at him. There's no reason to start him off with something easy like 'Euphoria.' Let's just get to the point."

Kenny sighed, but nodded in agreement.

Brad held up his drumsticks and tapped them together three times to signal he was getting ready to go, then pounded them down on the skins. Within the first thirty seconds of play, Jesse knew they had their drummer.

CHAPTER NINETEEN

Jesse switched off the drum recordings. He yawned and stretched his arms over his head, looking at his watch. Ten past eight. He wondered what was keeping Evan. He had run home to feed Achilles and let him outside, but he said he'd be back by eight with a change of clothes for him so they could go out with everyone to welcome Brad to the band.

Jesse smiled and let his arms swing down on both sides of the chair. When they told Brad they'd like to make him their drummer, tears of joy overflowed from his eyes and he hugged each of them.

Brad's skill was exceptional. He played "Vanish" without a single misstep and played it the way it was meant to be. As much as it hurt him to admit it, Brad was a better drummer than Trish. He had more power, was smoother, more refined. With Brad, Jesse felt Conquest could come closer to reaching the level he sought to achieve.

At the sound of the door opening, Jesse turned in the chair to see Evan walking in.

"Sorry I'm late." Evan closed the door. "I lost track of time playing with 'Chilles."

"How's he doing? Is he lonely? I've been thinking we need to get him a friend. It's not good for him to be cooped up in that big house all by himself."

Evan set the clothes he'd brought for Jesse on the control desk and leaned back against it. "Yeah, maybe. He was fine when I got there, and I took him for a run on the beach and fed him. He was getting ready to pass out when I was leaving."

"That's…good," Jesse said, distracted as his gaze moved over Evan. "I can't believe you. We haven't had sex in days and look at the way you're dressed."

"Is there a problem with how I'm dressed?" Evan asked with a knowing smirk.

Jesse continued to stare at him. Cut perfectly to his frame, the airy material of the black button down shirt accentuated the V shape of Evan's torso. He had the top three buttons undone, showing the curved lines of his pectorals. Jesse felt the amount of saliva in his mouth increase at the sight of Evan's skin, fed by the mental image of pushing the shirt off his strong shoulders and licking a trail down Evan's chest to the ridges of muscle in his abdomen. As his gaze traveled lower, he saw Evan's black leather pants did a poor job of hiding the large bulge pushing against the front of them. The pants were pulled over a pair of black leather boots. Adorning each of Evan's finger were rings of silver set with onyx, jet, black pearl, and obsidian. Though, he still wore the alexandrite ring on his left ring finger and the eagle on the right index.

Jesse looked again at Evan's face, his azure eyes and soft lips. Two large black diamond studs replaced the usual gold hoops Evan wore in his left earlobe. He had styled his chestnut hair differently, more wild and tousled, but even in the dim lighting, the gold and copper highlights shone. The scent of Platinum Egoist cologne floated in the air around Evan.

Jesse swallowed hard. "We're supposed to meet everyone at nine, and I can't move because I'm so hard at how hot you look."

Evan leaned down toward him, stopping inches from his face, and placed his fingertips under Jesse's chin. "Hotter than Brad?"

"Way hotter."

"Hotter than Kyler?"

"So much hotter."

"It's been too long, hasn't it?"

"Far too long."

Evan tipped Jesse's head back and covered his mouth with his own. A needy whimper sounded in Jesse's throat at the hungriness of Evan's kiss. Evan's tongue delved deep, thrusting over his again and again, then he claimed Evan's tongue, sucking it into his own mouth, savoring and holding it there. Jesse clawed at the buttons on Evan's shirt. He broke the kiss and threw a quick glance at the door as Evan's shirt fell open. He saw it was cracked ajar.

"Ev, the door didn't latch, and the security guard is still here."

Evan put his lips to Jesse's neck. "Old Karl? He's half blind."

"Yeah, but he's not deaf, and for as pent up as I am, I know I'm going to get loud."

Evan walked to the door. "You might want to start by getting naked first."

Jesse kicked off his shoes and stood up while lifting his shirt over his head. "So demanding. I like it." He opened his jeans. "Hey, I've got to ask, are you sure Brad is straight?"

"I've asked him the same question more than once. I saw plenty of women coming and going from his hotel rooms on the road, but he's made me wonder." Evan's eyes focused on Jesse's cock as it rose free from Jesse pushing his jeans and boxers off.

A seductive smile graced Jesse's lips. His hand went to his cock, slowly stroking it up and down. "Where do you want me?"

Evan glanced around the room. He pointed to the black leather couch. "There."

"How?"

"On your back."

Jesse went to the couch and lay on his back, the leather covering the plush cushions cool against his bare skin. He bent his left leg up, resting it against the back cushions, and spread his right leg far to the side and hung it off the couch. He tossed one arm behind his head, his other hand stayed on his cock. His gaze followed Evan as he went to the clothes he brought for him.

Evan flipped the navy blue shirt aside and picked up the lube hidden between the shirt and black leather pants.

Jesse chuckled. "And here I thought this was spur of the moment sex. You came here with naughty intentions."

"I love having Brandon around, but my cock's been feeling a little blocked these past few days." Evan went to Jesse and set his right knee on the couch between Jesse's legs.

"I know. It's not his fault, though. It was my fear of upsetting him if he heard us. He probably wouldn't have even cared."

Evan ran his hand up Jesse's thigh and around his hip. "I could always gag you to keep you quiet. Either that, or we could just invite him to join—"

"Do you want to be denied?"

On one arm, Evan leaned over him. "Do you think you could?"

Jesse answered Evan with a deep kiss. Without breaking the kiss, Evan removed the eagle ring, took Jesse right's hand and slipped it on his finger, then did the same with the black pearl ring from his middle. He coated his fingers with lube and rubbed outside Jesse's hole.

"Sorry," Evan whispered, his lips on Jesse's. "I wish we had time for more foreplay." He shoved two fingers inside him.

Jesse expelled a single hard groan. His breathing stopped for an instant, his muscles constricted, then loosened again. "I don't care about that. I just need you inside me."

Evan responded to Jesse's words with a throaty moan and a firm thrust of his fingers. With Evan's fingers pumping into him, Jesse opened Evan's pants, discovering he wore nothing beneath. He yanked the pants down a little to give Evan's cock more room to work, then grabbed him by the wrist and forced his fingers from him. He took Evan's cock and arched up toward it, ready to insert it himself if Evan didn't.

"A little eager," Evan teased.

Snatching a fistful of Evan's hair, Jesse pulled him down closer to his lips. "Fuck me."

Evan put his left hand behind Jesse's right knee and bent it back, utilizing Jesse's flexibility to pin it to his shoulder. He lined his cock up with Jesse's lube-slick hole and pushed into him.

The intense pleasure drove a high cry from Jesse. He tossed his head back, his fingers hooked into Evan's back though his shirt. He draped his left leg across Evan's lower back, his calf resting on Evan's ass, the black leather warmed by Evan's body beneath it. The silken material of Evan's open shirt brushed over his sides with each of Evan's thrusts, tickling his excited skin. He loved Evan's bare body, but being taken so forcefully that Evan hadn't bothered to undress was also a huge turn on.

Evan increased the pace and the power behind each thrust, driving him into the cushions. Jesse gasped high, short moans between fast breaths. Every thrust from Evan hit his gland, each second intensifying the building sensation of climax. Fluid pooled on his abdomen from his leaking cock. He wrestled his hands under Evan's shirt. His fingertips slipped over the sweat on his back, and he dug his short nails into Evan's skin. Evan sucked in a sharp breath, moving faster, harder. He pressed his weight to the hand that held Jesse's leg back, then grabbed Jesse's cock with the other.

Jesse lurched up against him, his climax rushing to the surface. He yelled Evan's name, the last thing he could coherently think before his body entered the throes of his orgasm. With Jesse shuddering under him, Evan slammed into him a final time, letting out a rumbling groan as he came. He dropped down and rested nearly his full weight on Jesse.

Jesse twisted Evan's hair around his fingers and kissed the top of his head. "I wish we had more time. I don't want to stop."

Evan did a couple gentle thrusts into him. "Neither do I. But we can hold a marathon tonight."

Jesse hugged him tighter. "Sounds like a plan."

Evan raised his left wrist and shook back his sleeve to look at his watch. "We've only got fifteen minutes to clean up and meet everyone. I think we're going to be late." He braced his torso up on his arms, still refusing to pull out of Jesse.

"And you've got another problem." Jesse pointed to the wet spot on Evan's shirt. "When that dries, the black is going to show the white beautifully."

Evan sighed. "I guess I'll have to wear the shirt I brought for you. So much for my dark and dangerous look tonight."

"It already served its purpose. Do you want to call everyone and be the first to get hit with the jokes, or do you want me to?"

"We'll call them in a little while," Evan said, claiming Jesse's mouth once again.

***

Stumbling, Trent's legs seemed incapable of giving him the speed he wanted to get down the hall of the studio and out the doors. At his side, Matt's longer legs carried him faster. The security guard called out a cheery goodnight neither acknowledged as they burst through the doors to the brisk night air.

"I told you!" Matt said, picking his pace up to a jog. "I fucking told you! Thank God you're an idiot and forgot your keys, because now you know the truth!"

"He lied to me. He told me he's been with girls. He lied right to my face!"

"Now you know," Matt repeated, dashing around to the driver's side door of their shared Buick.

Trent climbed in the passenger's seat and slammed the door closed. "Did you hear the shit they were saying to each other? All flirtin' and up on each other?"

Matt reached toward the ashtray, grabbing a joint they hadn't started smoking. He lit it, inhaled deeply, held his breath, and exhaled as he spoke. "Who the fuck cares what they were saying? It's disgusting."

Trent snatched the joint from him. He took a hit and laughed out a cloud of smoke. "Dude, I fucking thought Evan was going to find us when he went to close the door. I can't believe your balls at opening it in the first place."

"I had to prove to you somehow that your hero ain't nothin' but a fairy queen." Matt backed from of the parking space while holding his hand out to take the joint back.

Trent looked at him, his mood turning serious. "We gotta get out of touring with him. I don't even wanna be at the same studio."

CHAPTER TWENTY

Evan laughed under his breath as he watched Jesse from the control room. Jesse was doing more talking than singing in telling Brad about some of his favorite places to frequent in Chicago and making plans with him, Kenny, and Julian to help Brad begin learning the city. A week had passed since Brad became the new member of Conquest, and in that time, not much work got done since Jesse decided the best thing to do would be borrow the Phoenix private jet and get Brad moved right away. He knew Jesse was right, but not much work would be getting done this week, either, what with having scheduled another press conference and photo shoots to introduce Brad.

Evan's good humor wavered. The responsibility of managing Conquest grew by the day. He knew well how to manage the business aspects of a high profile music career from his own, though it was those aspects that made him twitch with annoyance, so while he understood them, he had always allowed Greg to handle things for him. Now, setting up a publicity schedule, going over finances, booking events, photo shoots, interviews, and separate gigs for Jesse since many wanted him one-on-one, he never realized all the work Greg actually did, and this was during down time. When Conquest's album came out and they hit the road, he wondered if he would be able to keep up with it all.

Jesse knew he and Greg were working together, understanding he needed time to get used to his new responsibilities, but more than that, managing Jesse alone would take up all his time where he'd have none left to work on his album. Jesse already told him the last thing he wanted was for him to sacrifice his music. He was grateful for Jesse's patience, and above everything else, it meant more than he could ever express that Jesse trusted him with overseeing his career.

An internal chuckle rose in Evan. Of course, none of it would matter if Jesse didn't quit talking long enough to record a song or two. Evan flipped on the PA. "Hey, singer boy. If by talking so much you think you're warming up your voice, that's a new technique to me."

Jesse whirled around, giving him a playful glare. "We're taking a break, *boss*."

"You're going to *be* broke if you don't start making some music."

Jesse drew in a sharp breath and pointed at him. "You're the meanest manager ever!"

Evan laughed and stood up. "Yeah, I'm horrible. I'll get you some water to dampen your throat since you've talked it dry."

"Grab me a Pepsi instead!" Jesse shouted after him.

"You're getting water," Evan called back.

He heard Jesse huff into the mic and smiled as he walked out the door. He glanced in the direction of Studio A and saw Alanna standing in the hall rubbing her eyes. He moved toward her. "How come you look upset every time I see you?"

Alanna raised her head, her lips lifted in a fatigued smile. "I'm Black Heart's songwriter. Do I need any more reason than that?"

"I guess not. How're things going?"

"Well, other than Kyler and I disagree on just about everything, and right now nothing's getting done because he and Robbie are having a creative dispute, fine."

"Where are they now?"

"Down in the chill-out room. I'm getting ready to head outside and wait for my friend to get here. Hey, is it true you're going to manage Conquest?"

"Yes, it is," Evan said calmly, hiding his surprise at the fact the news had already reached Alanna, when he believed Greg and Jeremy were the only persons outside of Conquest who knew. "Where'd you the news from?"

"Kenny told Robbie, who told Kyler, who told me. It's one big gossiping family around here, you know."

Evan nodded slowly, making a mental note to tell Kenny not all topics were to be shared with others. This was exactly how things meant to be kept private got leaked into the media. It hit him for the first time managing the personalities in Conquest would be as much a part of his job as managing the business. That could definitely cause some tensions, especially if the others came to think he favored Jesse. Things under another manager that may be seen as acceptable, such as Jesse doing solo interviews and photo shoots, could be seen as him taking extra special care of his beloved partner. On the other side, he wondered, would he actually be able to *not* favor Jesse?

The thoughts swirled through Evan's head, building to a headache. Tonight, it would be Jesse's turn to relax him.

"Since you're their manager," Alanna continued, "I guess I should clear this with you. My best friend, Ayame, is stopping by and she's a huge fan of Jesse's. I know he's really busy, but would it be okay if I introduced her to him?"

Evan felt his defenses rise, and when he spoke, heard the tightness in his own voice. "Introduce her to him for what purpose?"

Alanna blinked at him, seeming confused by the shift in his demeanor, then shook her head and waved his implied meaning away. "No, nothing like that! She'd just like to meet him."

"That'd be fine, then." Evan chuckled to make up for his tense moment. "Actually, despite everyone else believing he's very busy, he's not one of them. He's not real focused today, so I'm sure he'd enjoy another distraction from getting work done. Just come down to the studio whenever she gets here."

"Thanks, Evan." Alanna glanced in the direction of the lobby. "I better go wait for her so security doesn't give her any trouble."

"I don't think that's much of a concern with the security around here." Evan jotted down yet another mental note to talk to Greg about getting better security for the studio. He turned to leave, then looked back at her. "Alanna, don't let Kyler beat you down. Greg Hansen told me the other day you're a wonderful songwriter. If he believes that, then it's true. Greg doesn't sugarcoat anything when it comes to artists. So hold your ground and stay strong with your music."

Alanna managed a single nod, her eyes shining over his words.

Evan turned toward the chill-out room. As he approached, he saw the door was closed. He paused outside, hearing the muted voices of Kyler and Robbie. He took the handle, and finding the door wasn't locked, flung it open and strolled inside.

Kyler and Robbie looked up as he walked in. Robbie was reclined on the wall by the door, Kyler standing in front of him, leaning forward with one hand braced on the wall beside Robbie's head.

"Ever hear of knocking?" Kyler snapped.

"Ever hear of a lock?" Evan retorted, heading toward the refrigerator. "You boys should be glad it was me and not some of the other people running around this studio. Otherwise, it'll be you two in the tabloids with articles about you snuggling together."

"He's not really the snuggling type," Robbie said.

"I can be." Kyler brought his gaze to Robbie, his voice hushing. "We'll finish this later."

Robbie put both hands on Kyler's chest and shoved him out of his way. "I'm going back to the studio." He nodded at Evan, then stormed out of the room.

Evan retrieved a bottle of water and a can of Pepsi from the refrigerator. "Trouble in paradise, Kyler?"

Kyler held up his hands in a hopeless gesture. "Story of my life."

"You bring it on yourself. Just how many people are you screwing these days?"

Kyler stopped at Evan's side. "Why? You interested?"

Evan turned a mocking smirk on him. "We tried that once, remember? It didn't work out so well. People only get one shot with me. You had yours and you blew it."

Kyler's crooked smirk quirked one corner of his lips. "Now we both know that's not true. From what I've heard, Jesse's on shot number two."

Evan clenched his teeth. It appeared Kenny had been vocal about a great many things. Kenny probably felt it was safe to tell his new friend Robbie personal details, but what Kenny didn't realize was anything that went into Robbie's ear also went into Kyler's. "You heard wrong. It's me that's on my second shot with him. Not the other way around."

"Then I guess it's a good thing he's a better person than you are."

"I'll never disagree with that."

"Is that why you're giving up music? Because he's better than you and you can't stand the idea of being second to anyone, even him?"

"My reasons for retiring are my own and none of your goddamn business." Evan took a half step toward him, leaving only inches between them, and glared into Kyler's eyes. "Are you done now? I've got work to do."

Kyler held his ground. "Jesse's stronger than you. He'll never quit making music. Nothing will ever stop him or bring him down. He's all confidence and pride. You," he snorted in disgust, "you're not even competition for him. When I first got to see him in public—with that silly little façade he puts up of always being good natured and happy-go-lucky—and knowing how you are, I thought he was nothing more than your plaything to manipulate as you pleased. But now that I've gotten to know him, I've realized you're nothing but his conquest."

"And you think that bothers me? I know better than anyone else how strong Jesse is. Now I'm not going to tell you again, move the fuck out of my way."

Kyler glared at him for another moment, then slid to the side just enough to allow him to pass.

Evan shoved by him, his fingers constricting around the bottle of water as if it were Kyler's throat. He'd never met anyone so adroit at agitating him. It made him wonder what he had been thinking all those years ago when he went after him.

His thoughts broke as he heard Jesse singing the ballad "Shattered." He realized Jesse must be teaching Brad the song. He closed his eyes in a long blink and drew in a deep breath. Jesse's golden tenor soothed his tension and worries. Evan opened his eyes, feeling more at peace, then scolded himself for leaving the door open for anyone to walk in and interrupt Jesse. He stepped inside and stopped at the sight of Alanna sitting behind the control desk with another woman beside her, who he guessed must be her friend, Ayame.

Ayame shook her head of shoulder length black hair. "He's amazing. There're no studio tricks going on with him, are there? I always wondered if his voice was enhanced, but it really is that clear and beautiful. And look at him. He's so...so..."

"Gorgeous," Evan finished.

Both women jumped and spun around.

Evan took in the lovely Japanese features of Ayame, her delicate bone structure, her dark eyes.

Alanna giggled softly and placed her hand over her heart. "You startled us."

"Sorry." Evan closed the door and took a seat at the control desk. "That is what you were going to say, though, wasn't it?"

"Well, you're no slouch in the hottie department either." Ayame offered her hand to him. "I'm Ayame Miyamoto. I've been a fan of yours ever since you first came out, Mr. Arden."

Evan clasped her hand gently in his. "Thank you, but please, just call me Evan."

Alanna cleared her throat, her voice followed hesitantly. "It must be difficult for you, having to share him with the world and not be able to tell anyone."

Evan slowly turned his eyes on her in silent stare.

Alanna shifted nervously. "Am…am I wrong? If I'm wrong, please tell me. I just…I thought I picked up that you two might be…"

"You're not wrong." Evan smiled at her and reclined in his chair. "I knew we hadn't been doing the greatest job at keeping it quiet, but apparently we've been a little sloppier than I thought."

Alanna shook her head. "No, I guessed about you guys on my own. When I saw you together for the first time, I thought I picked up on something between you. You both stood so close to each other. When you moved, he moved, and when he moved, you moved, as if neither of you wanted the space between you to grow. It's small, subtle things, but things that reveal how much you care for each other."

Evan glanced away from her to Jesse. He wasn't sure what to say other than the truth of his feelings or nothing at all, and to say nothing felt like a betrayal *of* his feelings, and even worse, of Jesse. A slight grin came to his lips. Kyler was right. He was Jesse's conquest. He couldn't even deny him when Jesse had no idea what was going on, and if he couldn't deny their relationship to Alanna and Ayame, just how long was he going to be able to keep it up with the rest of the world?

"He's everything to me," Evan said softly. He returned his gaze to Alanna. "And you're right, it is difficult not being able to tell the world he's mine, but I don't really feel that I share him. The Jesse the world sees is such a small part of who he is. All his fans, all the people who gaze upon him, they only get to see him when he's at work, and who he is on stage is a much different person than who he is off it. And no matter how many people scream their love and devotion to him while he's up there, it's my arms he walks into after a show. No matter how creative people are in their suggestions of things they'd like to do with him, it's me he's laying beside every night.

"I'm the one he turns to when he's upset and wants comfort. I'm the one he goes to when he's happy and wants to share it with someone. And I'm the one who gets to see all his flaws. Those little things are mine, a part of him that's so much more intimate than what anyone else ever gets to see."

From the live room, Jesse drew "Shattered" to its soft conclusion. Evan saw him spring up from the piano and head toward the control room. He looked back to Alanna and Ayame. "Plus, I'm the only one who gets to see him naked, so that alone keeps me feeling secure."

Alanna and Ayame burst out laughing.

Jesse walked into the room and stood with his hands on his hips. "What's everybody laughing about?"

Evan looked at him. "I was just talking about you naked."

Jesse choked out a shocked cough.

Evan raised one hand toward him. "Alanna's a sharp woman, gorgeous. She figured it out about us and I confirmed it. You're not mad, are you?"

Jesse went to him, taking his hand before reaching him. He swallowed to stop the tears of joy from tightening his throat. He released Evan's hand to wrap both arms around his shoulders. "How could I ever get angry at you for something like that?" He placed his fingertips under Evan's chin, tipping his head back to look into his eyes. "Though, I'd still like to know what's so funny about me naked."

"Absolutely nothing." Evan handed him the Pepsi. "It's a very serious and beautiful thing."

Jesse smirked as he took the can. "I thought you were going to force me to drink water."

Evan tapped the water bottle. "I am. After you have a drink of Pepsi, chase it with water. It's better for your throat than all that carbonation."

Ayame turned to Alanna. "I'm so glad Shunichi didn't come with me today like he was planning. If he knew these guys were really a couple, he'd be pointing his little I-told-you-so finger in my face."

Jesse glanced over his shoulder to Ayame. "Who's Shunichi?" He turned fully around. "Actually, who are you? I don't know you, do I?"

Alanna quickly introduced Jesse to Ayame, and while she did, the other members of Conquest entered.

After introductions Ayame said, "You can just call me Aya. Everyone does." She settled her gaze on Jesse. "And Shunichi is my older brother. He's the acting Headmaster of our family dojo in Lincoln Park, soon to be full Headmaster once our father retires completely, which won't be long now."

Jesse pulled a chair close to Evan and sat down. "What's he teach?"

"Karate mostly, though Shun is a master in aikido and kendo as well, but he tries to play humble at it. He's also proficient in judo and jujutsu, but he doesn't instruct it. He's won tons of competitions, but he's done with competing now. He says he's getting too old for it, which is ridiculous, since he's only twenty-eight.

"But really, he doesn't have the time for it with all the responsibilities of running the dojo. The number of students has almost doubled since he started. I think the younger people like having a younger sensei, and his looks have all the soccer moms changing their kids after school hobby to karate. He's been living in Japan for the past five years, and probably would have stayed if our father hadn't called him back to start taking over the dojo."

Jesse noticed how clearly Ayame's pride in her brother showed as she spoke. His mind lit on an idea. "You know, my older brother, Brandon, practiced karate for years. He only gave it up because he needed to take more dance lessons for his career as a stage actor, but he may be interested in starting up with it again."

"Then I'll give you Shun's card." Ayame grabbed her purse and pulled out her wallet. "He loves getting new students. I'm sure he'd enjoy bringing karate back to your brother."

She held a white business card out to Jesse. He took it and looked down at the elegant print stating Miyamoto Dojo, Instruction in Shotokan Karate, Aikido, and Kendo, Headmaster Shunichi Miyamoto, and the address, phone number, and website.

"Thanks." Jesse shoved the card in the back pocket of his jeans. "So now I know all about your brother. What about you, Aya? What do you do for a living?"

"Oh, I'm just a secretary at an investment firm. But being a writer is where my heart's at. I've been trying to get my novel published. It's historical fiction about a Japanese-American family struggling to deal with anti-Japanese sentiments and discrimination during WWII."

"Do they get carted off to one of the detention camps that were set up out west?"

"Yes." Ayame's lips curved upward in an amazed smile. "You're one of the first people I've ever met who knows about those."

Evan brushed his fingers through the back of Jesse's hair. "He watches the History Channel for hours."

"It has good shows." Jesse looked back to Ayame. "It sounds like it'd be an interesting story. And don't feel bad that you haven't gotten it picked up yet. Being a writer is a lot like being a musician. You may get told no a thousand times when it comes to getting your work the attention it deserves, but you can never admit defeat. Once you start the battle, never stop until you've conquered. And never lose faith in your dream. On the other side of that, having a few connections doesn't hurt." He looked to Evan. "Don't you know a couple people in the book biz?"

Evan nodded. "I could easily make some phone calls."

Visibly showing her disbelief and gratitude, Ayame shook her head slightly. "I don't know what to say."

Jesse laughed. "I wouldn't say anything yet! We'd have to make sure your book doesn't suck before he calls his contacts. Bring a copy of your manuscript by when you get a chance."

Ayame sank down in the chair behind her as if the shock of being a step closer to her dream had stolen her strength. "You're not anything like I expected you to be."

"What'd you expect?" Jesse asked.

"I thought you'd be arrogant and self-centered, like Kyler."

Jesse smirked at her. "I am arrogant and self-centered, but nothing like Kyler. The sheer beauty of my voice and my incredible talent should've told you that."

As Alanna and Ayame laughed, a knock on the door interrupted them. It opened and Kyler and Robbie walking in, joined by Adam and Kevin. Kenny, Julian, and Brad stood and greeted the Black Heart Down members while Jesse remained at Evan's side.

Robbie looked at Alanna as he nodded toward Adam and Kevin. "I found them. They were talking to the Swiller boys, of all people. Then I got stuck talking to them too since the little freaks wouldn't shut up until he came to rescue us all." He pointed at Kyler with his thumb. "Unlike most people, he has no qualms about being rude to others."

"That's just part of my charm," Kyler said. His gaze rested on Jesse. "Hey, I wanted to ask if I could show you and your boys some of what we're working on and get your opinions. You guys could come down to our studio, if you have time."

Jesse sensed Evan's instant anger at Kyler. He knew what he was about to say could irritate Evan further, but he was also curious to hear what BHD was working on. "Sure, we could do that. But our manager would have to join us."

Kyler's gaze moved to Evan in a look that said he wasn't thrilled with the idea of his presence. His gaze went back to Jesse, and he smiled. "Your manager is more than welcomed."

Jesse stood. "Then let's go."

Kyler led the way down the hall toward Studio A. The other members of Black Heart Down and Conquest mingled in a group. Alanna and Ayame walked behind them, Jesse and Evan trailed further back.

Jesse glanced at Evan and hushed his voice. "How pissed at me are you right now?"

Evan kept his gaze forward. "Not enough where I won't accept a blowjob for an apology later."

Jesse couldn't catch his laughter before it burst out. He got a couple curious looks from the others and managed to quiet his voice again. "Then I guess you're not that mad. But I'll still work hard to give you an amazing apology when we get home."

Evan replied with a smile and a soft bump with his shoulder against Jesse's.

They turned into the studio. Jesse, Evan, and the others all found places to sit in the control room while Kyler, Robbie, and the rest of BHD went into the live room. Jesse watched as Robbie lifted his custom Gibson Les Paul, in a light, natural wood finish, from a stand. He noticed Robbie looked distracted, even a little upset.

Robbie pulled the leather guitar strap over his head, not even noticing it was twisted as it settled across his back. Kyler was instantly behind him. Even from the live room, Jesse saw the gentle way he straightened the strap and, how in a touch so subtle he nearly missed it, Kyler lightly stroked Robbie's lower back. Robbie glanced back at him. Kyler offered him a soft smile.

Robbie continued to gaze at him for a moment more, then with a shake of his head and a smile on his lips, said, "Alright, Ky, let's show them what a real rock band sounds like."

Kyler's smile brightened. He nodded once. "Hell yes."

As Kyler moved to the mic and the others did a quick sound check, Jesse slipped his hand under the control desk to lay it on Evan's thigh. Evan rested his on it.

Kyler raised his left hand, snapping his fingers as he counted down, "One, two, three, rock!" The band blasted to life around him. The drums leading the way with a steady, infectious beat that made Jesse want to tap his fingers along with it. The throaty bass melded with the drums. Then over it all, the smooth, rich sound of Robbie's guitar took over with a hooky riff and deep chords. Jesse watched Robbie play, how fluid his fingers moved up and down the guitar's neck. He could listen to and watch him play all day and never get tired of it, Robbie was such a master.

Jesse's attention went to Kyler as he saw him take the mic in one hand. His voice flowed out in a naturally sensual pitch, as even though Kyler was a baritone, he bordered on being a bass.

> *"Day after day,*
> *Night after night,*
> *Some things never change.*
> *Whenever I need you most,*
> *I see you walking away.*
>
> *Side by side,*
> *Heart to heart,*
> *Is how we've spent our lives.*
> *But every time you speak,*
> *All I hear are lies.*
>
> *It's always been enough,*
> *Surviving on your taste and touch,*
> *Now I need more,*
> *And once again,*
> *You're headed for the door.*
> *This time I'm letting you go,*
> *Because…*

Kyler held the last word as the music built with momentum to enter the chorus, then blasted out,

"You don't hear me,
You don't see me,
You don't care,
About our memories.

You say you want me,
You say you need me,
But this time,
I want to be free."

Kyler bowed his head, silent as the others played on. Robbie's guitar wailed over the drums and bass in a powerful solo. As it came to an end, the tempo slowed to the driving beats from the first half, and Kyler sang again.

"I'm closing the door
Behind you,
And sitting alone
In this empty room.
Tears in my eyes,
Pain in my heart,
Trying to figure out,
How to start a new life.

All those hopes,
All those dreams,
Are slowly fading away.
I'll cry through the night,
And into tomorrow,
But through those tears I'll know,
Harder times would've followed,
Because..."

You don't hear me,
You don't see me,
You don't care,
About our memories.

You say you want me,
You say you need me,
But this time,
I want to be free.

You might think you've left me,
With nothing but sorrow.
It may be true now,
But not forever.
Each day without you,
I'll grow a little stronger."

As the chorus repeated and the song ended, Jesse continued to gaze into the live room. He slowly tapped his index finger on Evan's thigh, though it was more a thoughtful gesture than inspired by the music. That desire had vanished as Kyler finished singing the first verse. Jesse glanced at Alanna. "Did you write this?"

Alanna shook her head. "No, Robbie did."

"That explains a lot," Evan mumbled.

"If you want to know the truth," Alanna continued, "I don't think any of my material is going to be used on this album. Kyler rejects every damn thing I bring to him. He's lifted a few lines and phrases from my songs, but honestly, we clash on just about everything."

Jesse nodded and looked up at Kyler as he and the others entered.

Kyler dropped down in a chair across from Jesse. "So, what do you think?"

Jesse met his gaze. "How honest of an opinion do you want?"

Kyler's smile fell away. "Since you asked that, I'm taking it you didn't like it."

"That's not true. I did like it, but right now, it's a jumbled mess."

Kyler's mouth dropped open. Jesse saw Adam and Kevin looked instantly pissed. He glanced at Robbie, but his eyes were cast downward.

Kyler cleared his throat. "What do you mean it's a jumbled mess?"

"The music doesn't match the lyrics or the emotion of the song. It wants to be a ballad. You're trying to turn it into a rock song."

Kyler stared at Jesse in disbelief.

Robbie softly spoke up. "It was a ballad originally. That's what I wrote it to be, but Kyler thought it'd have more impact if we rocked it out."

Jesse tossed up his hands. "Then there you have it! All you have to do is go back to how it was originally, and it'll be perfect."

Kyler flicked his gaze at Evan. "What do you think?"

Evan let out a huff. "Do you really care?"

"If I didn't, I wouldn't have asked!"

"Fine. My advice? Take it back to what it was. Make it a ballad."

Still holding his drumsticks in one hand, Adam ran the fingers of his other through his copper colored hair. "Well, thanks for your opinions. Sorry I disagree."

Brad turned to Adam. "I can see why you would, man. You laid down some kicking rhythms, but they're just not right for this song. Even I can tell that."

"I don't know how you can," Kevin said. "You don't even know what it sounds like as a ballad."

Julian looked at the dark haired bass player. "It's not necessary to hear the actual music. It's spoken in the lyrics and emotion of the song."

Jesse nodded. "Exactly."

Kyler sat silent for a long moment. He turned his head, glancing back at Robbie out the corner of his eye. "Do you still have the original music?"

"Yeah."

"Do you have it with you?"

"Yeah, but even if I didn't, I've got it memorized."

"Then that's what we'll work on for the rest of the afternoon." Kyler looked at Jesse. "Looks like we've got a lot to get done now."

Jesse stood up. "That's how it goes sometimes. But I've got a feeling once you get this one straightened out, it'll be awesome."

A smile came to Kyler's lips. "Thanks, Jesse. It means a lot to me that not only did you take the time to listen to us, but you gave an honest opinion."

"It's not a problem, but you know, Kyler, I don't think you lack for people who will give you an honest opinion if you take the time to listen to them."

Kyler's smile became more strained. "Right."

Jesse walked past him and glanced at Robbie, who looked like he was doing all he could not to burst with giddiness. Robbie held up his hand to him. Jesse slapped it in a high five.

Robbie wrapped his fingers around Jesse's hand and squeezed. "Thanks for listening to us, Jess."

Jesse smiled at him. "Anytime."

He walked out to the hall with Evan at his side, the rest of his band following. They returned to their studio, and once the door was closed, Kenny, Julian, and Brad began chattering about Black Heart's skill and the song.

Julian looked at Jesse. "You called it perfectly. When I was listening, even though everything sounded good, something didn't seem right. When you brought up how it should be a ballad, instantly I heard softer melodies and a piano for it."

Brad patted Julian on the back. "Maybe you could volunteer your skills."

Julian let out a single, humorless laugh. "I have no desire to be around when that bomb goes off with the way Kyler and Robbie have been toward each other lately."

"What're you talking about?" Kenny asked.

A pitying smile touched Julian's lips. "Poor boy, you really don't see it, do you?"

Kenny shook his head in great bafflement. "See what?"

Jesse stretched his arms over his head. "Alright guys, that was a nice little distraction, but let's get back to work so we can get Brad learning a few more songs."

"He'd learn the songs quicker if you could quit talking long enough about everything but music," Kenny said.

"I haven't heard your guitar trying to drown me out today."

"Now, boys," Julian said. "I guess I have to step in and get everyone focused."

Jesse and Kenny started laughing. They moved toward the live room, snickering at Julian trying to lead them. Jesse held the door open for the other three, then looked at Evan. Evan sat staring at the floor, his expression revealing his thoughts were far from what was going on around him.

"Ev? Are you okay?"

Evan looked at him and forced a smile. "I'm fine."

Jesse walked to him. He caressed Evan's cheek with his fingertips. "I don't like looking at you and knowing you're thinking about another man."

"It's only because he pisses me off, gorgeous."

"I know, but he's not worth it." Jesse bent down, putting his lips a fraction from Evan's, and whispered, "You don't know how happy you made me by telling Alanna and Ayame about us, and tonight, I'm going to work very hard to show you. Whatever you want, however you want. Tonight will be all about you."

"Jess," Evan said softly. He placed one hand on the back of Jesse's head and pulled him to his lips.

Jesse sucked Evan's tongue, and knowing the others couldn't see, pushed his hand between Evan's legs and rubbed his hardening cock. A deep groan vibrated from Evan's throat to his. Evan parted his thighs and pressed against Jesse's hand.

"Hey!" Kenny yelled from the live room. "You want to pull your tongue out of his mouth long enough to sing a couple songs, or you want me to sing?"

Jesse smiled through the kiss. "Now that's something to make us both lose our hard-ons."

Evan chuckled, and Jesse gave him another light kiss, then marched toward the live room, yelling to Kenny, "We're trying to teach Brad our songs! Not make him hide in a corner cowering at your off-key screeching!"

Evan watched Jesse and his band members banter, though slowly, Kyler invaded and with him came the problem of figuring out just why Kyler seemed to want Jesse's friendship.

Chapter Twenty-one

"I can't figure out what his deal is," Jesse said, strolling beside Brandon. In his right hand, he held Achilles' black leash patterned with silver paw prints over crossbones. He allowed Achilles to wander off the trail into the grass, sniffing at the trunks of the elm trees, their green leaves freshly opened. "Kyler acts like he wants to be friends with me, then all he does is antagonize Ev. He has to know he's not going to get my friendship by doing that."

Brandon glanced over the green lawns of Grant Park. "Being nice to you is a more subtle way of antagonizing Evan. Just be careful, Jess. I think it's pretty obvious he's got issues with Evan, whether he's still carrying bad blood from their failed night together, or he's bitter about Evan quitting music, or they simply clash personality wise, he could try hurting Evan by using you."

Brandon stopped walking and faced Jesse. "Remember a few years ago when Kyler was in the media for pummeling that guy at one of their shows? It was apparently self-defense, the guy jumped him backstage thinking Kyler was hitting on his girl, but Kyler beat the shit out of him in the whole thirty seconds it took for security to get to them. I remember seeing the guy on the news when he was using it to get his fifteen minutes of fame. One of his eyes was swollen shut, his nose was broken, his lips were puffed up and split. And if I recall right, that guy wasn't little, either. Kyler's not someone to be taken lightly, and that's probably why Evan hasn't gotten into a physical confrontation with him. He knows he may not come out on the good end."

"Ev's not afraid of him."

"No, but he's cautious around him. And if he is, then you should be, too."

Jesse started walking again. "It just pisses me off how he acts."

Regardless of Brandon's words, there was no way he was going to allow Kyler to keep coming after Evan. He warned him once and Kyler hadn't taken him seriously. The next time he got him alone, he planned on making it unmistakably clear that he needed to quit provoking Evan. As it was, Kyler had Evan so tense he nearly cancelled working with the orchestra that day, saying he would come into the studio with Jesse.

On the plus side, there'd been no encounters with Trent in a couple weeks. On the downside, Greg put it into writing for Swiller to be Conquest's opening act before Evan got a chance to stop it, making it all but official that Swiller would join them on the road. Evan had his attorneys reviewing the agreement, and all he could do was cling to the thin hope they'd find a way out of it.

Jesse glanced at Brandon. Nearly a month had passed since he broke up with Christopher and he had yet to say so much as hello to another man. It took more effort to make him smile than ever before. And he couldn't remember the last time Brandon laughed other than a spiritless chuckle. The physical body walking next to him looked like Brandon, but he was far from the brother he'd always known. Jesse didn't know what to do for him, how to help him find himself again. He wasn't even sure if he was the person who could do it. Brandon needed something in his life he couldn't provide.

Jesse remembered the card for the Miyamoto Dojo he brought with him, knowing he was going to see Brandon at lunch. He dug in his front pocket, pulled out his money clip, and tugged the card loose. "Here. I got this from Alanna's friend who came to the studio. We got talking and she said her family owns a dojo in Lincoln Park. I thought you might be interested in checking it out."

Brandon took the card and stared at it. "Why would I be interested in checking it out?"

"Because you used to practice karate, you're a black belt, you used to love it," Jesse said, as if the answers were obvious.

"I'd just embarrass myself if I tried to start up with it again now." Brandon held the card back to Jesse. "Plus, I don't really have the time."

"Right, because you're so busy sitting on our couch every weekend." Jesse pushed Brandon's hand holding the card back toward him. "What harm would it do to check it out? I'm not saying you have to start taking lessons again. You'd probably have fun just watching other people doing it, and maybe the sensei could direct you to some local competitions. You can become a spectator if not a participant."

"Maybe," Brandon said softly.

They came upon Buckingham Fountain. Jesse dropped down on a bench, looking up at him. "You can't keep doing this to yourself, Brandon. That asshole isn't worth you hiding away from the world."

"I'm not hiding from the world. I'm standing before it six nights a week."

"You're on stage, you're working. I know better than anyone else how that goes. You get hundreds, thousands, of people who say they love and adore you, but none of them really do. And you're not going to find the one who does honestly and truly unless you get back out there and start looking for him."

Brandon sat beside him, his shoulders sagging. "You think I don't know that? But I've gotten to a point where I'm not sure it's something I'm meant to have in life. I used to think it was everybody's inherent right to have a person love them, but now I'm not so sure. This whole thing made me realize I wasn't always the best person to the people I had relationships with. Maybe I've just built up too much bad karma and have blown my chances of finding someone special in this life."

Jesse rolled his eyes. "I think you're over-thinking."

"Maybe I am, but there's one thing I know for certain. I'm tired, Jess. I'm tired of going to clubs and bars trying to meet guys. I'm tired of the games and the one night stands. I don't have the strength to get back out there. I'll admit part of me hasn't given up the hope of finding someone special, but I'm tired of looking for him. If I'm meant for one man, then he's going to have to find me."

They sat silent for a long moment, both watching the water spray high from the fountain, the mist forming faint arching rainbows.

"So are you going to check out the dojo?" Jesse asked.

Brandon sighed. "The play's not running this weekend, so we'll see."

Jesse smiled, accepting Brandon's answer as yes.

CHAPTER TWENTY-TWO

Jesse marched down the hall, Kenny, Julian, and Brad surrounding him as they made their way to Studio C. He had no desire to see, hear, or smell Trent and his boys, but he did promise Trent he would listen to them. Plus, he was overdue for checking out the competition.

Evan told him to stay clear of Swiller, but for a second day in a row, Evan hadn't come to the studio. Things went so well the day before with the orchestra he wanted to keep riding that momentum. Jesse couldn't hold it against him. More than anyone, maybe even more than Evan, he wanted to see his final album crafted into the brilliant masterpiece he knew only Evan was capable of creating. He had Greg and Jeremy to offer their outside advice on his music, and while they weren't quite as sharp on sound as Evan, they were helpful enough.

Jesse stopped outside the closed door to Studio C. From the other side, he heard muffled guitar, bass, drums, and vocals, though couldn't discern enough sound to pass judgment on the music. He saw the recording light wasn't on above the door and figured they were just jamming. He knocked and waited.

The door cracked open with another Phoenix sound engineer, Will, peering out. His green eyes lit with a smile, and he opened the door wider. "Hey, guys. How've things been?"

"Good," Jesse said. "Trent's been hounding us to hear him and his boys. You care if we sit in for a little while?"

"Not at all."

Jesse walked into the control room with the others following. The equipment cloned what was in Studio B, and it appeared the live room was stocked the same as well, though the white grand piano clearly wasn't getting used other than to hold beer and soda cans. Jesse frowned at the disrespect toward the instrument, then looked at Trent and his crew.

Trent stood with his back to the control room and facing Matt, both bobbing their heads while their fingers flew over the frets of their respective guitars. The drummer, Joey, wildly slammed and stretched across the skins, and Jesse wasn't sure how the lanky bass player, Eric, could even see the chords he was playing since his stringy hair covered his face.

Despite their less than elegant playing styles, he had to admit, the sound they created wasn't awful. It had a rough edge to it, not the crisp, sharp sound he sought for in his music. No particular riff or beat came out strong, it all blended in a repetitious circle, but that cycle would be catchy enough to get plenty of airplay. But, he hadn't heard Trent sing and perhaps his voice would be what gave them their unique mark.

As if reading his expression, Will said, "Well, they're not quite as polished as Conquest, but they're not bad."

"No, not at all." Jesse realized he agreed too quickly for his words to sound genuine.

Brad sat behind the control desk. "That drummer's gonna drop dead if he doesn't cool it."

Will took a seat beside him. "It's kinda his style to spaz back there. I've been trying to work with him to get his movements a little smoother, if for no other reason than he'll never make it through an hour and a half concert blowing so much energy, but he won't listen. Everybody's got their own way of doing things, I guess."

"That poor piano," Julian said, his voice holding true pain for the instrument.

"Yeah," Will said. "It's getting more abused than used. Trent took a nap on it the other day. But just because he doesn't play doesn't mean he's not a competent musician. They've all gotten better since they came in, and I really believe they'll keep improving."

Jesse nodded, having heard enough of Will's polite comments. The guitar solo, which was too long in his opinion as it mainly just repeated itself, drew to a close with Trent spinning for the mic and blasting out his voice. It took Jesse's hearing a second to adjust to the raspy, flat sound of it before he could decipher any lyrics, then he caught,

"Girl you drive me nuts,
You make me rage.
The only time I can stand you,
Is when your head's between my legs…"

The line ended with a guttural shout from Trent and hard strumming on the guitars.

Jesse drew in a deep breath and exhaled slowly. He felt a hand rest on his shoulder, then Kenny whispered in his ear, "We can't have them open for us."

Jesse gave him a look that expressed exactly how much he agreed.

The music came to an abrupt halt.

Jesse turned back to the live room to see Trent glaring at him. He then saw Matt flip his hand in the air as if his wrist had gone limp and say something too soft for the mics to catch, though by the outburst of laughter, he didn't have to stretch his mind too far to figure out what kind of joke it was. Trent raised his guitar strap over his head. When he moved toward the door with his band members following, Jesse prepared himself.

Trent flung the door open and stomped into the room, his eyes focused on Jesse. "What the fuck are you doing here?"

"You been hitting the bong a little too hard lately, Trent? You've been asking since day one for me to come down and listen to you."

"Fuck that!" Trent advanced on him. "I don't want your faggot ass anywhere near me and my music!"

Jesse leaped up and into Trent's face. "You need to cool your fucking attitude!"

"What are you gonna do about it?" Trent slammed Jesse on the chest with both hands, making him stumble back a step. "You gonna try to throw a punch with your limp wrists?"

Jesse caught himself from falling. He pushed off his back foot and lunged forward. His right fist sped for Trent's face and connected hard with his left cheek. Jesse leaned into the punch, driving it through with his weight behind it. Trent crashed to the ground, landing on his side.

Matt sprang for Jesse. Brad jumped forward, stopping him by ramming his fist into Matt's stomach. Joey took a quick step forward. Kenny and Julian did the same, their movements stopping his. The gawky Eric stood unmoving with eyes rounded in shock.

"Who's got limp wrists now, asshole!" Jesse yelled at Trent.

Trent shoved off the floor, pushing himself up to make another attack. Seeing Trent move spurred Eric to action. He grabbed his singer to hold him back.

"Let me go!" Trent screamed. "This little fag ain't shit!"

"Let him go!" Jesse roared. "I'm not done with his punk ass!"

Greg, Jeremy, and Jon, burst through the door, all having been gathered when Will, fearing the equipment was about to be destroyed in a band brawl, shot out of the room for help after Jesse threw the first punch.

Greg grabbed Jesse by the arm and dragged him toward the door. "Get out, now!"

Shooting Greg a dirty look, Jesse stormed out, his band members close behind.

Beside him, Brad laughed softly. "I had no idea you could throw down like that."

Jesse gave him a slight grin. "He's had that coming for a long time. Thanks for having my back."

Brad tossed his arm around Jesse's shoulders. "Man, nobody messes with my singer."

Jesse looked back to Kenny and Julian. "I can't believe you two were ready to jump in."

"I can't either." Kenny held up his left hand. "I could've broken a finger defending your skinny ass."

Julian moved to Brad's side. "But Brad, are you alright? You hit him rather hard."

Brad looked at him with a warm smile. "I'm fine. His stomach was all mush. Thanks for worrying about me, though."

Jesse peered around Brad to Julian. "What about me? Aren't you worried about me, too?"

Julian rolled his eyes. "Are you alright also, Jesse?"

Jesse smiled brightly at him. "Why yes, Jules, I am. Thank you for your concern." He swung into the chill-out room. "I wonder what the hell got into him, though."

Brad let out a snort. "Like you said, he's probably been puffing it up so much that his brain's so fried, dude probably doesn't even remember who you are."

"Well, on the good side, there's no way they'll be opening for us now."

"Was that your whole plan?" Everyone turned at the sound of Greg's furious voice coming from the doorway. He surged past the others to stand in front of Jesse. "Because if it was, I hate to break it to you, but this doesn't change anything."

Jesse locked his gaze with Greg's. "The hell it doesn't. And it wasn't my plan, it just happened, and since it happened, that should prove to you it won't work having us on the road together."

Greg glared into Jesse's eyes. "What I know is you're not going to get your way with this. You've hit the ultimate level of uncontrollability and it's got to stop now. What's next, Jess? Are you going to start punching fans when they annoy you?"

"That's different and you know it. He's needed to be humbled from the start."

"And how lucky for him you're the one good enough to do it."

"I don't know why you're blaming me for this! If you think I'm going to stand quietly and take being called a fag and getting pushed around by a dirty little bigot like him, you obviously don't know me very well!"

"What I know is that once things settle down, you're going down there and apologizing to him. If you don't, the resentment will build until you both can't even look at each other when the time comes that you go on the road."

"You don't seem to be getting what I'm telling you. I will *not* go on the road with him."

"You don't have a choice."

Jesse folded his arms across his chest in a stance of defiance. "Is that what you think? Well then, let me tell you what *I* think. I think it's going to be the shortest damn tour in history without me there to sing."

Greg glowered at Jesse.

"Now you realize how serious I am with seeing the dollar signs float away. I won't be forced into anything I don't want to do, not by you, not by anyone. So you better find a way to break the agreement with Swiller."

Greg backed a couple steps away from him. "A friendly warning to you, Jesse. In this business, enemies are made quicker than friends, and grudges last a long time."

Jesse walked around him toward the door. "Just see that the agreement is revoked. I'm heading out for a while to let our manager know what happened. Anyone else coming with me?"

Kenny, Julian, and Brad all moved to follow him.

Greg watched them leave and sank down in a chair, rubbing his tired eyes.

Chapter Twenty-three

With Kenny, Julian, and Brad accompanying him, Jesse walked up South Michigan Ave. to the Symphony Center. When they entered, the security guard nodded to them as if Jesse visited frequently, though it was in actuality his first time there. The guard's reaction told him Evan must have already spoken to security about him, ensuring he would be admitted without difficulty. With the guard acting as guide, Jesse and his band members followed him to the grand rehearsal hall.

Standing at the back of the hall, Jesse swore he could feel the aura of talent circulating around the amassed musicians on the polished wooden stage below, and center and foremost was Evan at a mic stand. The full orchestra behind him looked natural, as though it was Evan's rightful place to lead so many gifted musicians. Along with the orchestra, Jesse saw JJ, Evan's long time guitarist, and four other guitar players armed with Fender Stratocasters, creating their own electric strings section. Slightly off-centered to the right of the stage a pianist sat at a black grand, his gaze focused on Evan.

Jesse knew this album would be the most magnificent Evan had ever done, and Evan told him about it great detail, but he had a way of making even the most phenomenal aspects of his talent sound trivial. Now seeing Evan preparing to lead the orchestra, he realized just how special this album was going to be.

Evan stood motionless, his eyes closed. Slowly, he raised his right hand in the air. Jesse could almost hear the collective intake of breath from the musicians.

Evan held his right hand high, then dropped it a few inches. The small gesture signaled the drums. They came in soft, laying a steady solo beat. Evan swept his hand in a graceful flick toward the strings. They entered gently, creating a rhythm similar to the drums, but higher, a fraction of time quicker. Evan's left hand gestured back to the piano. Deep notes sounded from it, louder than the strings and picking up the same rhythm, the tempo repeating, driving itself into Jesse's mind.

Evan leaned toward the mic, his eyes still closed. He took a breath and allowed his baritone to flow, his voice deeper, throatier than usual.

"My body yearns,
Aching for your touch.
Each heartbeat cries,
Pulsing for your kiss,
My thoughts are gone,
Only passion exists.

The softest caress,
Steals away my strength.
Your lips on mine,
Raises my desire.
My control is gone,
I'm helpless to resist..."

Evan snapped both arms out wide to the sides. The remainder of the orchestra erupted around him in powerful harmony, JJ's guitar and the other electrics leading the way. Evan grabbed the mic and blasted out his voice, singing in his usual, slightly higher range,

"In the twilight of your eyes,
I see my destiny so clear.
And in the darkness of the night,
I press you close, hold you near.

In the twilight of your eyes,
I see my future laid so bare.
And in the darkness of the night,
We're as one, each breath we share.
In the twilight of your eyes..."

After holding the last word of the chorus, Evan stopped singing, letting the orchestra carry out the faster melody, then smoothly it transitioned to a softer pace. The strings, drums, piano, and JJ's guitar stayed slightly louder, a touch faster. Evan deepened his voice to the sensual pitch once again.

"I close my eyes,
Falling in your touch.
I moan so soft,
Begging for your kiss.
And in my mind,
Only you exist…"

The orchestra leaped in full stride with the coming chorus. Evan effortlessly changed his voice from deep and throaty, to high and smooth.

"In the twilight of your eyes,
I see my destiny so clear.
And in the darkness of the night,
I press you close, hold you near.

In the twilight of your eyes,
I see my future laid so bare.
And in the darkness of the night,
We're as one, each breath we share.
In the twilight of your eyes…"

JJ's guitar solo blasted to life, his fingers pulling sharp, high chords from the instrument, keeping the tempo at mid-speed. For the first time during the song, Evan opened his eyes. He focused on Jesse, as if he'd known he was there the entire time. Even across the distance, Jesse found himself entranced by their radiant azure hue.

The tone of the song shifted. All instruments dropped out expect for the drums, pounding a hard, rhythmic beat, and JJ's guitar wailed high, making it sound like the instrument was pleading, panting. His eyes still on Jesse, Evan smiled behind the mic. He raised his voice, singing higher to matching the yearning in the guitar, his voice in the lower ranges of a tenor,

"Oh how I need it.
Don't ever let go.
Oh how I want it.
Just hold me close.
Please don't stop it.
I'm letting it all go…"

Evan held the "o" at the end of the last line, raising it higher and higher. The orchestra lifted with him, all sections exploding as he hit the top of his range. Evan dropped his voice back down, belting out the chorus for the final time.

"In the twilight of your eyes,
I see my destiny so clear.
And in the darkness of the night,
I press you close, hold you near.

"In the twilight of your eyes,
I see my future laid so bare.
And in the darkness of the night,
We're as one, each breath we share.
In the twilight of your eyes…"

The musicians softened their playing, keeping the tempo strong and quick. Evan raised his left hand and dropped it sharply. The music stopped. He faced the orchestra, clapping and smiling. "Perfectly played, ladies and gentlemen."

Some of the musicians let out a few "woo-hoos" and laughter filled in the hall.

Evan looked down at his watch and back up to them. "I believe you've all earned an extra long lunch. Let's meet back at two."

Still in awe at what he just heard, Jesse stood in further amazement at how happy Evan looked. It was as if knowing this would be his last album lifted a great weight from him, and for the first time in his life, he was creating music for himself, not for album sales.

"Well," Julian said, "this has certainly brought back some memories."

Pulled from his thoughts, Jesse glanced at him. "Do you miss it?"

"There's a small part of me that does, but I'm afraid you've turned me into a diehard rocker boy. I don't think I could ever go back now."

Jesse nudged him with his elbow. "I'm glad to hear that, but did you notice the dark-haired hottie behind the black grand stealing glances at you? I think he recognizes you and would like to trade technique secrets. Maybe you should break out of your type and go introduce yourself."

Julian cocked his head and gave the pianist an admiring gaze. "Well, I don't know about breaking out of my type, but there's certainly no harm in two professionals conversing."

"I'll go with you," Brad said. "I'd like to see how that old Aussie's been."

Kenny stepped up to follow them. "Yeah, and married or not, I know he's already scoped out the ladies in this crew and knows who's single, taken, or a lesbian. I'm gonna see if I can get myself a classy woman."

Jesse chuckled. "Yeah, good luck."

He watched his three band members depart down the aisle, passing and greeting Evan who was making his way toward him. Jesse moved to meet him, his head still spinning with sound.

"This is a pleasant surprise," Evan said, a glowing smile on his lips.

"The song… Ev, it's amazing. The way it changes gears, slow to fast and back down, and your voice, you hit every part of your range. It's unbelievable. *You're* unbelievable."

Evan stopped in front of him. He rested his hand on Jesse's cheek. "I'm happy you like it, because it was inspired by your beautiful eyes. I've always thought they were the most perfect blue, like when night is staking a claim to the sky from day. Such a breathtaking, deep royal indigo. But then, you inspired this entire album."

Jesse's fleeing breath parted his lips. "You wrote me a symphony?"

Evan nodded once.

Jesse stared into Evan's eyes, knowing the gazes of the handful of musicians still watched them, how intimate they looked standing so close, Evan touching him. The same thought was reflected in Evan's eyes.

Evan took a half-step closer. "I don't care. Let them all see. At least then they'll know what true love looks like."

"Ev," Jesse whispered.

Evan moved his hand down Jesse's cheek and caressed along his delicate jaw to his chin. He tipped Jesse's head back the slightest bit and leaned toward him. His lips tenderly touched Jesse's. He drew back slowly.

Jesse's eyes remained closed, Evan's warm presence still lingering on his lips. Even though Evan kept the kiss chaste, to him it felt like it was one of their most intimate. He opened his eyes, a soft smile curving his lips. "First you tell Alanna about us, now you're kissing me in front of a crowd. What's gotten into you?"

"I think my will is weakening because it doesn't want to keep fighting my feelings. I know I'm doing the opposite of everything I told you we had to do, but I can't help it. Since we've come off the road, living with you every day in our home, lying beside you every night in our bed, I lose a little more control over staying silent. Is it bad?"

"No, it's not bad." Jesse's smile broadened. "And let me put it this way, if you thought the reward you got for being open about us to Alanna was good, you're going to cry for joy in what you'll get tonight."

Evan laughed and caught Jesse's hand. "I can't wait. Now, do you feel like taking me to lunch and telling me what's bothering you?"

Jesse squeezed Evan's hand. "How do you always know?"

Evan answered him by rolling his eyes as if Jesse should know the answer.

Jesse chuckled softly. "I'll tell you on the way."

They both turned at the sound of laughter and saw Kenny, Brad, Julian, and JJ coming toward them. The senior six-string master, JJ, stood taller and thinner than the others, his short blond hair nearly the same color as Kenny's.

"Jess, how ya been, mate?" JJ said, his Australian accent still strong despite having lived in the States since joining Evan on his previous album.

"I've been great. You?" Jesse asked, as they locked fists and pulled each other into a hug.

"Damn better now that you're here so we can all take a bit of rest from him." JJ held up his left hand, flexing his fingers. "I'm gonna have nothing but nubs left after this one."

Evan smirked at him. "Keep complaining and I'll send you back to play for the kangaroos and crocs."

"Bastard!"

JJ wrestled Evan around his neck. Laughing, Evan ducked out of his hold, hopped out of reach, and taunted JJ to come at him again.

Jesse smiled at their antics, having witnessed them tormenting each other many times on the road, with Evan usually the antagonist, such as when Evan thought it would be funny to take a guitar case identical to the one holding JJ's cherished black Les Paul and super-glue the locks shut. Not realizing the case was a doppelganger, JJ chased Evan around the arena with a mic stand threatening to beat him unless he found a way to get his guitar out. It wasn't until JJ was completely spent and could hardly breathe that Evan trotted up to him and told him the case was a duplicate.

Jesse turned to Evan. "Ready?"

Evan nodded. "Let's go."

They headed out of the Symphony Center and down to where Jesse parked his and Evan's new black Cadillac Escalade. Jesse jumped in to drive, Evan took the front passenger seat, and the others crammed into the back. Jesse swung the Escalade north toward one of Evan's favorite restaurants, figuring taking him to get a good steak may help quell the anger certain to rise in Evan at hearing of his confrontation with Trent. He relayed the events on the way, and by the time he parked near the restaurant, Evan sat glowering out the window.

"I'm sure I made it sound more dramatic than it really was."

"I warned you to stay away from him."

"Yeah well, I was curious about what they sounded like and I promised him I'd listen to them. I didn't expect to be called a fag and jumped."

JJ leaned forward from the backseat. "Jess, if you want my opinion, I think it'd be good for you to lay low for a while. Right now, you're surrounded on all sides by enemies between Kyler and Swiller, and now Greg isn't thrilled with you either. You're running out of allies."

"And that's my fault?"

"No, but JJ's right," Evan interceded. "The studio is turning into a hostile zone rather than a safe one. Maybe it's time to start looking at our options and get you recording somewhere else."

Jesse stared at him in disbelief. Each second that ticked by turned the disbelief to anger. "No, I won't go anywhere else. I'm not going to be driven out of the studio I started in, maybe even out of my city entirely, by a few pathetic losers."

"Jess," Evan said softly, pleadingly.

"There's no changing my mind, Ev. I'm sorry, but I'm not going to retreat before these bastards." Jesse opened the door. "Now let's head in and have a good lunch."

As they neared the entrance to the Victorian brownstone that housed the restaurant, Jesse took in the worry darkening Evan's visage. He laid his hand on Evan's lower back, and when Evan turned to look at him, Jesse gave him a bright smile. "Everything's going to be fine. I won't back down, but I promise I'll keep a lower profile, okay?"

A strained smile touched Evan's lips as he nodded.

CHAPTER TWENTY-FOUR

Jesse paced back and forth in the kitchen, the phone to his ear. As Brandon's recorded voice stopped talking and the beep sounded, he shouted into the phone. "Listen, asshole! I've called you twenty damn times since yesterday! Where the hell are you? I'm starting to freak out! If you don't call me back by this afternoon, I'm calling the cops to look for you!"

Jesse yanked the phone away from his ear and pounded the button to end the call. He leaned both hands on the breakfast counter, all his fingers flying in a rapid, anxious beat. Since the play wasn't running that weekend, he and Brandon had made plans to go shopping. It wasn't like his brother to leave him hanging.

Evan walked into the kitchen and stopped. "Still no word?"

"No. Something has to be wrong." Jesse turned toward the collection of car keys hanging on a rack and grabbed the ones to his Ferrari F430 and Brandon's apartment. "I'm going to his place to see if he's there. If he's not, then I'll check his mail. Getting it is like a religion to him since he's always ordering DVDs and if there's mail in his box, then I'll know he hasn't been home."

"I'll go with you."

The sound of the security system chirping as it was disarmed stopped them both, each knowing there was only one other person who had a code to get by the gates.

Evan went to the keypad by the backdoor and looked at the monitor. "He just passed through the first gates."

Jesse stomped toward the entrance room. "Good! Now I can kick his ass!"

He whipped open one of the front doors and stepped out on the porch, watching Brandon coast down the driveway on his Suzuki. Achilles darted out the door and ran alongside the motorcycle. Brandon turned into the circle before the front doors and brought the bike to a halt.

"Where the hell have you been?" Jesse shouted. "I've been trying to get a hold of you since last night! Do you know how worried I've been?"

Brandon knocked the kickstand down and swung off the bike. "Why do you think I'm here? To show you I'm all in one piece and doing incredible."

Jesse watched Brandon playfully batting at Achilles, which got the dog bouncing and barking around him. He took in Brandon's wide smile and spirited laughter at Achilles' antics.

Evan stepped out of the house to Jesse's side, grinning at Brandon. "You're so perky today, Brandon. You get laid last night?"

Jesse whipped his head toward Evan, then back to his brother.

Brandon bounced up the stairs. He leaned close to Evan as he passed. "A gentleman doesn't speak of such things."

"But you're no gentleman, sweetheart," Evan retorted.

Brandon answered him by throwing a smirk over his shoulder.

Jesse hastened to follow him inside. "Who? When? How? Tell me!"

"You're such a nosey thing," Brandon said, heading toward the family room. He dropped down in one of the dark brown leather recliners, smiling up at both of them. "I really, *really* have to thank you, Jess, for giving me the card to the Miyamoto Dojo."

Jesse took a seat on the corner of the couch closest to him. "Is that where you met this guy whose name you still haven't given?"

"It's Shunichi. Shunichi Miyamoto."

Jesse's eyes widened. "You screwed your sensei!"

Evan laughed. "That's great! Is he hot?"

Brandon reclined in the chair, his eyes getting a dreamy look. "He's the hottest, sexiest guy I've ever seen in my life. And more than that, he's sweet, kind, considerate, honest, and funny. He's amazing. He's just absolutely amazing."

Jesse and Evan both glanced at each other, then back to Brandon as he spoke again.

"The whole way to the dojo I was wondering what the hell I was doing, what the point was in even going. When I got there, I couldn't believe how incredible the place looked. I was expecting just a plain building on a street, but it's in a more residential area. The dojo looks like something transported from seventeenth century Japan, the building is all wood with a wraparound veranda and bamboo growing out front.

"When I walked in, a lesson was going on, but the second I entered, I couldn't take my eyes off Shunichi. He was sparring against one of his students, his uniform crisp and blinding white. During the match, our eyes met for a brief second, then his student struck at him, and in two graceful movements, Shun dropped him to the mats, though he was careful to not hurt him. I swear I could've climaxed just watching him. The lesson finished and after the last student left, we started talking."

Brandon chuckled softly. "He was so cute. He said he wanted to see how much I still remembered and started drilling me on stances, but he was really using it as an excuse to be close to me. I'll admit I started to freak having him so close and was going to leave, but he stopped me. He showed me around the dojo, then took me out back to a garden that's between it and his house. We stood talking by a small pond, and with each minute, I felt a connection growing between us. Then the next thing I knew, he'd put me at such ease, that I kissed him."

"He sounds awesome," Jesse said.

"He is, but I'm not done with my story yet."

"Sorry," Jesse snickered.

"We started making out in the garden, but he had another class coming in. He asked me to stay through the next lesson and I ended up staying all day. When his evening class was coming in, we made dinner plans, then I headed home to get ready. I took him to The Signature Room at the 95th, where we talked more than we ate, then we went back to his place."

Brandon's eyes closed, his smile broadened. "It was like nothing I've ever experienced. All night, clinging to each other, not able to stop. I never knew making love like that was actually possible."

"Oh, it is," Evan said, his hand falling on Jesse's thigh.

Jesse smiled at him, then looked back to Brandon. He couldn't deny the slight trepidation he felt that Brandon could be getting carried away once again.

Brandon's tone became serious. "You know, he admitted right away he was seeing someone, not seriously, well it was on his part, not the other's, but he promised he'd end it with him before we went out to dinner. When I got to his place to pick him up, he was on the phone with the guy and let me tell you, it's over. I couldn't believe it. He did as he said he would, he kept his word. I didn't think there was a man out there who was capable of such a thing anymore."

A soft smile graced Jesse's lips. "Sounds like you might've finally found a good one."

"I know I have." Brandon stood up.

Jesse stood as well. "Wait, you're not leaving, are you? You just got here. What about our plans to go shopping? And when do we get to meet him?"

Brandon walked toward the entrance room. "You don't mind if we go shopping another day, do you? He had classes coming in this morning, and I told him I was just running home to put on fresh clothes, check my mail, and stop by here real quick, then I'd be back to spend the afternoon with him. And we were thinking about going out to dinner with you guys tonight, if you don't have plans."

"That's fine," Jesse said, then added in a mumble, "I really wanted to go shopping, though."

"Well, it's good to be selfless every now and again." Brandon jumped on the motorcycle and grabbed his helmet. "I'll call you later and let you know when and where."

"Alright."

Brandon launched the bike down the drive quicker than he had entered and disappeared through the gates, his speed revealing his desire to return to Shunichi.

"Well," Evan said, "I can't say I'm not curious to meet this superman who in less than twenty-four hours has brought Brandon back."

Jesse sighed. "Yeah. I just hope he's for real."

Chapter Twenty-five

Evan spied an open parking spot next to a newer black Mustang Shelby GT500 with white racing stripes running down the hood, over the roof, to the spoiler. He pulled the black Ferrari 612 beside it. "I think it should be safe parking beside that. A person doesn't trick a car out that nice just to bang its door into the car next to it."

Jesse looked at the Mustang as he climbed out of the Ferrari. "I guess there are other people as obsessive about their cars as you."

"Yeah, unlike you, who only asks your F430 how it's doing and tells it where you're planning to go every time you get in it."

"I'm just being considerate to him."

Evan moved to Jesse's side as they headed toward the restaurant. "I don't know what I'm more excited about, meeting Brandon's new boy or getting to eat sushi."

"I can't believe we've never come here…" Jesse's voice trailed off, his gaze falling on his brother and another man standing outside the restaurant. "Is that him? Holy shit, he's freakin' hot!"

Evan scowled at him. "Say it a little louder so he can hear you."

"Well he is, don't you think?"

"Hell yeah!"

Jesse took his turn to adopt a scowl. "You don't have to be so enthusiastic."

He looked back to Shunichi. Standing about an inch shorter than Brandon, Shunichi wore a pair of black dress pants and a white button down shirt that just covered the tops of his hips. The shirt hugged his slender frame, lines of muscle formed ridges against the thin material. He had the top buttons open, revealing a smooth chest, the pectorals knitted in the center with strength. The black pants covered his long legs, and with how he stood at a slight angle, Jesse caught a glimpse of one of the most perfectly shaped asses he'd ever seen.

Shunichi's black hair was layered and hung to the middle of his neck in back. As they neared, Jesse saw the man was painfully beautiful, his bone structure delicate, his cheekbones sweeping high. Shunichi noticed them before Brandon, and for an instant, Jesse met his dark eyes before Shunichi looked to Brandon and gave his hand a tug. At the movement, Jesse noticed they were holding hands and almost stumbled in shock. His brother never held anyone's hand outside of a gay club.

Brandon turned toward them. "Hey, guys! I can't believe you're actually on time." He hugged Evan as they came up. "What'd you do, Evan? Lock him in the bathroom this afternoon to make sure he'd be ready?"

"Just about. He hasn't realized yet he doesn't need to primp so much to be pretty."

"I don't know if I'd go that far." Brandon smirked at Jesse as he wrapped him in a tight embrace.

"So where is he?" Jesse asked.

Brandon gave him a confused look. "Who?"

"Your new man. I know this isn't him." Jesse nodded toward Shunichi. "He's way too hot for you."

Shunichi laughed. The deep, rich sound of it made Jesse turn his ear toward him to catch more of the melodic timbre.

Brandon shoved Jesse on the shoulder. "This *is* him." He laid his hand on Shunichi's back. "Shun, this is my little brother, Jesse, and his partner, Evan."

His lips lifted in a smile, Shunichi extended his hand to Jesse. "Brandon's talked so much about you both, I'm really glad to meet you. Though, so far, you don't seem at all like the spoiled brat he said you were."

Jesse's mouth dropped open, his hand froze in Shunichi's.

"Shun," Brandon cut in. "I said he was a spoiled *prima donna* brat."

"Whoops, I forgot the prima donna part." Shunichi winked at Jesse. "Sorry."

Jesse patted Shunichi's hand with his other. "Don't worry. I usually try not to throw rock star temper tantrums around people I've known for less than five minutes. Him, on the other hand…"

Evan offered his hand to Shunichi. "I make it a point to throw at least three fits a day regardless of who I'm around. It's great to meet you. When Brandon came by our place today, he couldn't stop talking about you."

Shunichi took Evan's hand and gave Brandon a warm smile. "I'm glad I made such a strong impression on him."

Jesse glanced at his brother, seeing him glow under Shunichi's affectionate gaze.

"My sister, Ayame," Shunichi continued to Evan, "has been in love with you since your first album. She used to have posters of you all over her bedroom and dorm room."

"She played it pretty cool when we met her. But I think she's found a new crush." Evan's gaze moved to Jesse. "I walked in on her and Alanna drooling over him."

"Really? She left that little tidbit out when she told me about meeting you both." Shunichi looked to Jesse. "As she did about telling me she gave you my card. After Brandon told me how he learned of the dojo, I called her to scold her, but she said she hadn't wanted me to get my hopes up that Brandon could be coming in, only to have him not. It would've been nice to know, though, because when he walked in, I thought I recognized him from seeing him on stage, but I was in such disbelief, it took him saying his name to snap me out of it. Then I managed to fail miserably at keeping *my* cool around him."

Brandon slid his arm around Shunichi's waist. "And I'm so glad you did."

Shunichi moved into his touch and kissed him softly on the lips. Brandon brushed one hand down Shunichi's cheek, looking into his eyes as they slowly drew apart.

Evan whispered to Jesse, "I'm so turned on right now."

Jesse grabbed Evan's arm and pulled him toward the restaurant door. "Let's go in, voyeur."

Brandon and Shunichi followed, both chuckling softly. They stepped in to the dimly lit restaurant that broke away from the traditional décor of so many sushi bars with a trendy atmosphere. Techno club music bumped through the space and the hostess led them past the steel trimmed bar with neon blue lights glowing behind panels along the bottom.

Shunichi took a seat at their table. "Have you guys eaten here before?"

Jesse shook his head. "No, we were just saying we couldn't believe we haven't."

"I come here quite a bit with my assistant master, Hiroshi Yoshida. The *sake* cocktails are really good."

Evan scanned the menu. "We'll have to get a round of those. Everything looks so good, I don't even know where to begin." He looked up at Brandon and Shunichi. "You guys order whatever you want, and don't worry about the prices. Dinner's on us."

"You guys don't have to do that," Brandon said.

"Yes we do," Jesse said. "This is a celebration."

"What are we celebrating?" Shunichi asked.

Jesse gazed at Shunichi. "You giving Brandon his smile back."

At the same moment, Shunichi and Brandon reached for each other's hands.

The server stepped up to the table, quickly scrawling their large order of cocktails and a variety of sushi and tempura. When she left, Jesse looked at Shunichi, his voice filled with seriousness. "So I hope I'm right in assuming that you're going to be a one man guy with my brother."

Incensed by Jesse's blunt remark, Brandon snapped, "What the hell!"

Shunichi laid his hand on Brandon's forearm. "It's okay. He's just looking out for you." He turned to Jesse. "Yes, it's not my nature to fool around. Even kissing Brandon before I broke things off with the other person I was seeing goes against my personal philosophy of if you don't respect and care for a person enough to be faithful, then what's the point of being with them at all? And while I'm not making excuses for myself, I'll admit what I felt when I saw Brandon wasn't like anything I've ever experienced before."

He rubbed his fingers over Brandon's hand, speaking as much to him as to Jesse and Evan. "When I'm involved with someone, they get my full devotion." A wry smile touched his lips. "That said, I haven't had many long lasting relationships, so I think sometimes my attentions can be a little too devoted."

"Then you guys should work out perfect." Jesse nodded at Brandon. "He'll practically suffocate you."

Brandon lifted Shunichi's hand and kissed the backs of his fingers. "I'll do my best."

Their server returned with the drinks, and Jesse leaned closer to Evan. "Were we that lovey when we first got together?"

"According to some, we still are. And I think if we weren't always watching our backs for cameras, we'd be even more so, not that anyone who hangs out with us for longer than five minutes in private doesn't figure it out."

They all sat back as three servers carrying trays laden with food stepped up to the table. Once everyone had their plates covered with the food of their choice, Evan looked to Shunichi. "Your sister mentioned you were living in Japan for the past five years."

Shunichi nodded. "That's right. Even though I was born and raised here, I felt more at home when I was living there, but every year when I was younger, we'd fly over to visit my mother's family in Kyoto. I moved there right after I graduated from Northwestern."

Jesse spoke around a mouthful of food. "What'd you study at Northwestern?"

"I have a Bachelor's in Philosophy. I've toyed around with possibly going back for a Master's, but I don't really have time."

Brandon gave him a playful bump on the shoulder with his shoulder. "His being a Wildcat is the only flaw I've found with him."

Shunichi bumped him back. "Same as you being a Boilermaker."

Jesse rolled his eyes. "Please don't tell me that means you're as into anime as Captain Cartoon over there."

"He's got all my favorite series!"

Jesse snickered. "Then it really is a perfect match."

Brandon leaned toward Shunichi, smirking at Jesse as he spoke. "Don't let him fool you. He makes fun of it and teases me about it, but he was completely hooked on Rurouni Kenshin. Trust me, he's a closeted anime fan."

The other three laughed, Jesse not bothering to retort to Brandon's words.

Still chuckling, Shunichi gazed at Jesse. "Aya told me you're reading her book. It's no wonder she's got a crush on you if you bothered listening to her literary babble. I tease her all the time that she wasn't very creative with it since it's loosely based off our grandparents on our father's side when they immigrated to the States before World War II, but if you guys help her to get published, I'd be even more grateful than her. Then I wouldn't have to run from the phone every time I see it's her calling, knowing she's going to be screeching over another rejection letter."

Evan folded his arms on the table, his eyes on Shunichi. "I don't think getting it published will be a problem, if you could do a favor for me."

"If I can, I will. What is it?"

"You see, I've been trying to get these two in a three-way for the past two years, but they keep whining that they're brothers and it's dirty. But now you're in the picture, so maybe we can get some four-way action going on. I just need help convincing them."

Jesse shoved Evan on his shoulder. "I can't believe you!"

Shunichi forced words between hard laughter. "Wow! I don't even know how to respond to that!"

"Saying 'no' is how you should respond!" Brandon said, struggling not to laugh.

Fighting his laughter down, Shunichi nodded. "I guess so, since I refuse to share you with anyone." His gaze went to Evan. "I'm sorry."

"Then how about we just have sex in the same room, you and Brandon, me and Jess, and we could watch each other."

Shunichi paused. "Actually, that's an intriguing suggestion—"

"Don't encourage him!" Jesse said, then shook his head at Evan. "I can't believe someone as beautiful as you has such a bad sense of humor. It's a cruel joke of nature."

Evan pointed at Shunichi. "He thinks I'm funny."

"Yeah, but I have the sense of humor of a twelve-year-old, so I'm not sure that helps," Shunichi said.

The joking and stories continued until the food slowly disappeared. With everyone satiated, Evan signaled for the check and took care of the bill.

Shunichi rose from the table. "It's really sweet of you guys to treat us."

Jesse started toward the exit. "Hopefully we'll be doing it a lot. If Brandon hasn't already told you, the three of us get together every Tuesday to have dinner. Sometimes we go out, sometimes one of us attempts cooking. I hope you know you're more than welcome to join us."

Shunichi's hand found Brandon's as they walked out the door. "I'd like that very much."

The four headed up the sidewalk toward the parking lot, and Evan glanced over his shoulder at them. "Where're you guys parked?"

Shunichi pointed ahead. "I'm the black Mustang next to the beautiful Ferrari which I'm guessing is yours. Brandon said you guys have three. That's really a disgusting display of wealth, you know?"

Evan laughed. "Yeah, but it feels so good. You'll have to come to our place and see them. The Enzo is my baby, though I don't drive it much. The 612 is my usual daily driver when the weather's nice enough where I don't have to pull out the Escalade or the Cayenne. Jesse's F430 is *his* baby. Then there's the Lamborghini Murcielago, and an original '67 Shelby GT500 that had been my father's. And the newest addition, an Aston Martin DBS V12."

"I'm a big car fan too, but my collection stops at the Mustang, then I have a Toyota Tundra that I use for everyday driving. A couple of my friends in Tokyo are drifters, so I got used to hanging around fast cars."

They all drew to a halt at the vehicles.

Jesse turned toward them. "You guys should come over tomorrow."

Brandon stepped in front of Shunichi and wrapped his arms around his waist. "Sorry, Jess. Since tomorrow is his one day off, I'm planning on keeping him locked away to myself all day long."

Shunichi pressed his hips tighter against Brandon's and tipped his smiling lips toward him. "I didn't know about those plans. Sounds like fun."

Brandon brought their lips together, both their mouths opening as they touched.

Jesse laid his hand on Evan's back. "I think we better let these two get home before they start mating in the parking lot."

Evan's gaze remained fixed on them. "Yeah, alright. Let's go home and have sex."

"That wasn't what I said!"

Evan looked at him with a wicked smirk. "But it's what you were thinking."

Jesse returned his smirk with his own mischievous one telling Evan he was right. He faced Brandon and Shunichi. "Okay guys, we're heading out."

Reluctantly pulling apart, Brandon stepped away from Shunichi and threw his arms around Jesse. He put his lips to Jesse's ear, whispering, "He's amazing, isn't he?"

"He's incredible," Jesse said softly. "I knew he was out there waiting for you."

Jesse turned around to see Evan releasing a laughing Shunichi and could only imagine what the joke had been. He stepped toward Shunichi, his arms open to hug him. He hushed his voice as they embraced. "I can't tell you how glad I am my brother found a man like you. I know you'll take good care of him."

"I'll never do anything less and will strive to do even more."

Jesse slowly released him, pausing for a moment with his hands on Shunichi's biceps. He gave them a squeeze. "Damn, boy. You *are* a hard body. Maybe I could get used to the whole four-way idea."

Shunichi laughed again.

Brandon grabbed Jesse's wrists, pulling his hands off Shunichi's arms. "It's time for you to go."

Snickering under his breath, Jesse turned toward the passenger side of the Ferrari. "Call me tomorrow when you guys take a break."

"I will," Brandon yelled, and disappeared into the passenger side of the Mustang.

Evan allowed Shunichi to back out first, then swung the 612 out and followed the Mustang from the parking lot. "All I can say is wow."

"Yeah, me too. He's everything Brandon's ever dreamed of." Jesse took hold of Evan's right hand. "Now both Alexander brothers have perfect men in their lives."

Evan smiled at him and raised Jesse's hand to his lips.

Chapter Twenty-six

Jesse stood at the mic in the live room, his head down, his eyes closed. He lifted his right hand high above him, raising his index finger. A second later, his middle joined the index. He sent his ring finger up with the other two, and on cue, his band erupted around him. He concentrated on the music; Brad's drums pounding steady and hard, setting the heavy rhythm of the rock song, Julian's keystrokes precise and perfect on the keyboard, Kenny's Fender Stratocaster leading the way with a driving, catchy riff. Jesse took a breath, preparing his voice, on three, two, one,

"The first time I saw you
Was like twisted destiny.
Surrendering was so easy.
But you tease me and play,
Pull me close,
Push me away.
I'm stopping the games now.
I'm taking you my way.

Don't try and fight it.
You can't hope to win.
Let yourself become lost,
In my touch against your skin.
Pull me close,
Let me in,
I'll make you tremble,
And take away all your sins.

You know I want you.
You know I need you.
I'll do anything,
Just to have you.

So come here close to me.
Let me take you.
Let yourself fall,
Into this twisted destiny…"

Jesse paused for Kenny's brief guitar solo, backed up by the keyboard. He took a breath, his tenor deepening to match the shift in the song, now thumping in rhythmic beats, filled with a sense of sexual hunger.

"This twisted destiny,
It drives me crazy.
Now that you've come to me
Ohhh, you'll learn to be free."

He smiled, knowing he hit the throaty moan in last line perfect and launched into the next verse, the tempo shifting once again to a hard rock beat,

"The white sheets bind us,
You feel me pressing in.
Our frantic breathing,
Cools our heated skin.
Pull me closer,
Let me fill you,
And we'll trap each other,
In this twisted destiny.

Now that you've felt me,
So deep inside,
The freedom I've granted,
You'll never deny.
Hold on to me,
Let's do it again,
I want to feel you,
Burning against my skin.

"I know you want me.
I know you need me.
You'll do anything,
Just to have me.
So come here close to me.
And I'll take you,
Together we'll fall,
Into this twisted destiny…"

The others played out the song's finish, and as it ended, Jesse sprang into the air and threw a punch. "That was freakin' perfect!"

Through the PA came Jeremy's chuckling voice. "Hey, Jess, you want me to keep that last part or cut it?"

Jesse shot him a good-humored glare, then looked back to the others. "We're really starting to kick some ass now."

Strange as it was, it seemed ever since their fight with Trent and Swiller, things in the studio were going better than ever. Whether it allowed the tension to finally blow or brought them all closer by watching out for each other, he didn't care to question it. Of course, a big part of it was Brad melding flawlessly with them as if he'd been there from the start.

"You know," Brad said, "I wouldn't mind knowing what inspired such wholesome lyrics."

Jesse faced him. "Frustration."

Brad gave him a skeptical look.

"I wrote it when we were touring with Ev," Jesse continued. "When we hit Germany, he got really sick with the flu and he wouldn't let me play doctor with him because he didn't want me to get sick."

"I remember that," Julian said. "He was so sick, but refused to cancel any shows. After one, he had so exhausted himself, he fainted backstage, and almost gave Jess a heart attack when he did."

Jesse's expression sobered as the memory came to the front of his mind. He and a member of the security staff had supported Evan as they tried to get him to his dressing room, when Evan's head rolled forward and his legs failed him. He had caught more of Evan than the security guard, stopping him from hitting the ground, though the guard, a man who stood six foot five and weighed more than him and Evan combined, had scooped Evan up and rushed him to his dressing room.

It was the most frightening moment of his life watching his partner being carried; his body limp in the guard's arms. He stayed at Evan's side while waiting for the staff medic to arrive, gripping his hand until he came to, which even though was just a few short moments after Evan initially passed out, felt like hours to him. During those moments, he swore he would admonish Evan for pushing himself too hard and not listening to him when he told him to take it easy, but when Evan's eyes slowly open and his brilliant blue gaze focused on him, relief made thoughts of reprimand nonexistent.

Brad rose from behind the drums and stretched his arms over his head. "That's Evan. He always put more than he should into his shows. He never passed out when I was on the road with him, but there were a lot of times he looked damn near close to it. 'Course, he was usually drinking before the show, or during it."

"I wouldn't think that'd make him pass out," Kenny said. "He can drink like no one I've ever seen, then walks away like he's been sipping lemonade all night."

"He's worked very hard to build up that tolerance," Brad replied. "The only person I've ever seen who can hang with him when it comes to drinking is JJ."

Jesse shifted in place, all the talk of Evan making him antsy to get home to him. Evan had worked with the orchestra all week, other than making a few quick stops in the studio to hear what they accomplished. Now it was Friday, and he felt like he'd hardly seen him in days.

Jesse glanced down at his watch, prepared to make an excuse for them to head out before wrapping things up, and gasped when he saw the time. "It's nine o'clock!"

Kenny looked at him. "Uh, yeah."

"At night!"

"Well, that would be about right considering we've been here since ten this morning," Kenny said.

Jesse gave him an accusing look. "Why didn't you say it was getting so late?"

"I did. At seven-thirty, I said, 'Dude, it's getting late.' And you said, 'Late! What are you, eighty years old? Let's bust out a couple more songs.'"

Jesse groaned and dug in his front pocket for his cell phone. At the sight of two missed calls, he groaned a second time. Guilt washed through him when he saw they were from Evan. He looked up at his band. "I think we're done for now. There's nothing that can't wait until Monday."

"Hallelujah!" Brad said. "I've been starving for the past half hour."

Julian nodded. "Me too, though it's settled some. I think my stomach gave up asking for food."

Brad moved next to him. "You want to grab something to eat?"

"Yeah." Julian glanced at Jesse and Kenny. "I know you won't join us, but what about you, Kenny?"

"Sorry, can't. Got a woman waiting on me." Kenny hefted up his guitar case and turned to Jesse. "I'll walk out with you."

"Alright. Later, guys." Jesse lifted his hand in a wave to Brad and Julian as the two discussed where to eat.

They both paused in the control room to say goodnight to Jeremy, then headed out of the studio. They crossed the street and stepped into the parking garage, Jesse laughing at Kenny describing his new woman's oral fixation with a certain aspect of his anatomy. He glanced at his midnight blue Ferrari F430, sitting lower to the ground than it should. He looked to the tires and saw sagging rubber on the concrete. One flat tire could've meant he hit something. Four meant his tires were slashed.

Jesse stopped in mid-stride, one hand lashing to the side and landing on Kenny's chest to halt him. He whipped his head around to look behind them at the guard booth. It and the security truck were both empty.

Kenny's voice lifted in nervousness. "What's wrong?"

Jesse remained silent, his ears, his eyes, straining to catch a threat that his sixth sense warned was near.

Kenny's voice pitched higher with burgeoning panic. "You're starting to freak me out."

Jesse took a half-step back and pushed on Kenny's chest. "Turn around. We need to get back to the studio."

Kenny obediently whirled around, the knuckles of his hand holding his guitar case white. "Why? What's going on?"

Jesse moved to follow him. Both came to a short stop.

Three figures slid out from behind other cars in the garage, two wearing black ski masks, the other wearing a dark blue one. Clad in black, they advanced toward Jesse and Kenny like three stalking shadows. In the dim yellow garage lights, Jesse caught a silver flash from the blue masked figure's right hand and knew it was the knife that mutilated his car's tires. Beside him, Jesse heard Kenny softly squeak his name.

"It's alright, Kenny," Jesse said, his voice calm and even. "Put your guitar case down."

Kenny set the long rectangular case between him and Jesse.

With the garage entrance beyond the three, Jesse could watch for help and keep them in sight. Two against three weren't bad odds, minus the fact of the knife and Kenny could hardly hit a punching bag. All they had to do was hold on until someone came, and Brad and Julian should be walking out at any minute. If the worst the three wanted was their money, then it wouldn't be so bad, but considering the malice done to his car, he figured there was more motivation behind their presence than cash. He needed to delay them in whatever they wanted.

Jesse cleared his throat. "If you guys want our money, you can have it, but you're only going to get about fifty bucks out of me. I don't carry much cash and I'll have my credit cards cancelled before you get down the street, so I think you boys would do better to find someone else to play with."

The pace of the three slowed, but not from his words. He heard muttering, saw the blue mask flicking his hand in small gestures. They were planning their strike. Jesse took a quick analysis of their situation. They could try and run, but since the way out was blocked, they'd have to run deeper and higher into the garage, which would do nothing but get them trapped since he doubted they'd be able to outdistance them enough to lose them and hide. Kenny's truck was only three spaces back, and from what he saw, the tires were fine. They could risk a dash to it and hope they could get in before the three closed in on them, but he doubted it. At best, one of them could make it.

Jesse shifted his stance in preparation and whispered, "Kenny, when they make their move, run for your truck. I'll try to slow them down."

Kenny's head twitched in a nod.

Jesse put his full attention on the three. He adopted a demeanor of impatience and let out a loud annoyed sigh. "So do you want our cash or not? I've got plans and I don't want to waste my whole night on you freaks."

Three masked faces focused on him. The blue walked a stride faster than the others, and when just a few steps away, lunged toward Jesse with the other two following his lead.

"Go!" Jesse yelled to Kenny, and at the same moment, ducked to his left and grabbed the guitar case.

Kenny sprinted for his truck.

Gripping the case handle with both hands, Jesse snapped his torso up, swinging the case toward the blue mask. He aimed for the attacker's head, but the heavy case dipped, smashing into the blue's upper right arm. The guy howled in pain, he went down to his left knee. Even though he missed his intended target, his strike dislodged the knife and it slid under one of the cars.

In the split-second after he saw the blue go down, one of the black masks dove at him. The momentum of swinging the unwieldy guitar case left him open. Jesse released the case, spun, and pushed forward, driving his body into his opponent. Both crashed to the ground, Jesse landing on top.

Jesse whipped his head toward Kenny in time to see the second black mask grab him from behind and throw him into the grill of his truck. Kenny crumpled against it, half turning toward his attacker and receiving a punch to the cheek. Kenny slid toward the ground, his fingers clawing at the truck's slick surface to stay on his feet.

Jesse scrambled off his second opponent, running toward Kenny before fully recovering his balance. As he neared, the attacker's knee came up, making hard impact with Kenny's stomach. Jesse reached them, snatched the other black mask by his arm and the back of his shirt, and hauled him away from Kenny. The guy stumbled back a couple steps. Jesse took the moment of weakness and pressed his attack, throwing a straight punch into the other's face. He struck again with a right hook to the other's cheek.

The guy wavered, and as he did, Jesse saw the other two charging. He chanced a quick glance at Kenny, seeing him rolling on the ground. Knowing he didn't have the time to lift Kenny and get him in the truck, he rushed forward to meet their attackers.

The blue mask drew his fist back to strike. Jesse lowered his shoulder and rammed him. His opponent grunted, his body caved and went down. Jesse spun to meet the other black mask and a fist clipped his jaw. His head snapped to the left. He rebounded and drove his fist into the other's stomach. As his opponent's body curled around his fist, he felt another presence behind him. Before he could turn, the blunt force of a knee slammed into his lower back.

Jesse arched in pain. Arms caged him from behind. An impact to his left cheek stunned him. His adrenaline pushed the shock and pain away. He saw another hit coming. He threw his head back and to the side, smashing it into his captor's nose. He surged his full weight backward. Both went down.

Jesse struggled to untangle himself from the other. A blow to the side of his head dazed him. He pushed one arm under himself to rise. A kick on his back stole his strength, and he collapsed. He gritted his teeth against the pain and fought to rise again. A hand grabbed his hair, jerked him up by it, and a fist connected with his left cheek a second time. The instant the strike landed, his opponent released his hair, letting his head fall, crashing against the concrete.

Jesse's vision blackened. He rolled onto his side. For an instant, nothing but pain existed. Then, more pain brought him back to reality. Hard booted toes slammed into his ribs. Another pair connected with his back. A third set of feet kicked and stomped at his legs. Jesse covered his face with his arms. In his mind, he repeated Evan's name for strength.

The kicks stopped. He heard shouting, but it sounded far away, like voices in a fading dream. Racing footsteps receded from him, only to be replaced by more getting closer. Hands touched his shoulder and arm, trying to coax him to roll over. He resisted, then heard Julian frantically calling his name. He allowed his muscles to loosen and for the hands to gently guide him onto his back.

"Jesse! Jesse! Open your eyes! Please, Jesse!"

Jesse struggled to form the words in his mind, to tell Julian he was alright, that he didn't need to be upset, but his grip on consciousness weakened. His mind drifted. Evan. He had to tell Evan he was sorry for not calling him and being late. He attempted a deep breath. Pain in his ribs jarred him alert for a brief moment.

"Ev," Jesse gasped.

Julian gripped Jesse's shoulders tighter. A few feet away, Brad yelled into his cell phone at a 911 operator. Kenny pushed himself up on one arm, his eyes on Jesse.

"Jesse," Julian said. "Do you want to talk to Evan? I'll call him for you. But you have to stay awake so you can talk to him."

Jesse laid still. He wanted to talk to Evan. He wanted it more than anything in the world, but he also wanted to sleep. The latter need wouldn't be denied. He felt it pulling at him. With the last of his strength, he summoned his voice. "Tell him, I'm sorry."

His last word came out in a slur before his mind surrendered to dark oblivion.

CHAPTER TWENTY-SEVEN

Something was wrong.

Evan put his hand to his chest, lightly rubbing over his heart. It was beating so fast. He felt anxious, fearful. It was probably because he was worried about Jesse. He hadn't talked to him since that afternoon. He tried calling him twice with no answer, but that wasn't so unusual. When Jesse got absorbed in his music, he rarely noticed his cell phone vibrating in his pocket. Still, when he came out of his musical trance, Jesse always checked it, and the hour was late for even Jesse to still be working.

Evan pushed off the couch and paced into the kitchen, not sure why he was going in there, but feeling he needed to move. He glanced at the digital clock on the stove. A quarter after nine. Why hadn't Jesse called him? Why wasn't he home by now?

Evan snatched the cordless phone off the cradle. He'd try calling him one more time. If he didn't reach him, he'd start driving to the studio and keep calling him on the way so they wouldn't miss each other.

The phone rang in his hand. He froze. His heart thumped faster. Slowly, he lifted the phone, hit the answer button, and spoke a soft "Hello."

"Evan?" Brad's breathless voice came through the other end. "It's Jesse...he's...he's hurt really bad."

Evan's heart crashed to a stop from its frantic pace.

"He got jumped," Brad continued. "Him and Kenny. But Jesse took the brunt of it because Kenny said he was trying to protect him." His voice cracked. "Goddamn, Evan, they beat the shit out of him. He's in an ambulance now and they're taking him to the hospital. None of us have a clue what's going on. Since the paramedics and cops got here, no one's telling us shit, just pounding us with questions. The last I saw, he was still unconscious. He's beat to hell, Evan. He's really beat to hell."

Evan's body trembled. Standing seemed to take too much strength. He leaned forward on the kitchen counter for support. He started to speak, found his voice lost, and cleared his throat to try again. "W-where…where are they taking him?"

Brad sputtered out the name of the hospital.

Once Evan knew where he could find Jesse, he hung up without saying goodbye, his fear replaced by desperation and panic. He grabbed the keys to the Cayenne and ran from the kitchen. Achilles galloped with him, but Evan didn't notice. He raced into the garage and hit the button to open the doors. He shot out of the garage in reverse, whipped the SUV around, and sped toward the gates, pounding on the remote for them to open. He fishtailed onto the private road and slammed the throttle to the floor. When he passed through the second set of gates, he had just enough presence of mind to close them behind him, then his thoughts turned fully on Jesse.

He had no recollection of the trip. Guided by instinct and driving at breakneck speed, he reached the hospital before he realized it. He swung into the emergency entrance and was confronted with flashing police lights and a massive crowd of media reporters. Police battled the reporters back from the entrance to make way for incoming ambulances. Evan knew the vultures must have heard about the attack on police scanners or maybe even connections in the police. It never took them long to jump on something like this.

He parked close to the entrance. Before the Cayenne's door finished swinging shut from his forceful push, he was sprinting for the entrance. Heads turned in his direction, cameras flashed with blinding brilliance. Police and security rushed to block the paparazzi from reaching him. They formed a circle around him, shouting for the reporters to give them room. Jostled between the bodies of police officers, Evan ignored the voices screaming questions to him, the cameras and mics shoved toward him.

From the moment he hung up with Brad, he had moved at a lightening pace. Now, he moved with painstaking slowness, his progress upheld by those greedy for a scandal. Each second that ticked by was a second he lost with Jesse. His desperation rose, rage took control of him. He lunged forward, breaking through the police line.

"Get the fuck out of my way!" he roared, slamming into one reporter.

The guy reeled back, falling into another paparazzo before landing on the ground. Others stumbled back, stunned by the sudden violence. Evan burst through the doors and into the sterile waiting lobby. His eyes darted around, stopping on a group coming toward him, Julian, Brad, and Kenny, whose left eye had a dark bruise under it. Also with them was Shunichi, his presence letting Evan know Brandon was there as well, though he was nowhere in sight.

"Where is he?" Evan said, his voice shaking as he marched toward them. "Is he alright?"

"We don't know," Julian said. "The doctors have only spoken to Brandon and Greg. They took them back a while ago."

"They moved him to a private room upstairs to get him further away from the paparazzi," Kenny added.

Evan's gaze landed on Kenny. At seeing him standing before him with just a few bruises, his fury erupted. One quick step put him in Kenny's face. "And what the fuck were you doing when he was getting attacked?" He slammed Kenny on the chest with both hands, sending him flying backward three steps before Kenny could catch his balance. "He was trying to protect you, and you did nothing to protect him back!"

Evan moved to push him again. Shunichi caught him under his arms and held him around his chest.

"It's not his fault, Evan," Shunichi said softly.

"Get off me!" Evan fought Shunichi's hold and felt cords of muscle tighten around him.

The elevator doors opened and Brandon stepped out, halting at the sight of Evan trying to break Shunichi's hold on him. Evan saw him and hurled his weight forward. Shunichi released him.

Evan hastened past Brandon and into the elevator. "Take me to him."

Brandon turned to face him. "They're not letting him have visitors right now, Evan."

"Take me to him! Now!"

Brandon sighed and followed him into the elevator. "Why was Shun holding onto you?"

"Because I was going to beat Kenny's ass."

"I know you're really upset, but you can't take it out on Kenny. He didn't come out of it unscathed."

"Yeah, I saw his black eye. Forgive me if I don't give a shit."

"Jesse said he told Kenny to make a run for his truck. He put himself—"

Evan's head snapped toward him. "You heard him say that? He was talking?"

"Yeah, he…" Brandon paused and closed his eyes in a long blink.

Evan gazed at him, noticing for the first time the strain on Brandon's face. He laid his hand on Brandon's arm. "Just tell me he's going to be okay."

Brandon nodded. He swallowed hard and cleared his throat. "He's going to be okay. He's got a mild concussion and three fractured ribs, but he's bruised all to hell. The paramedics said he was a little out of it when he first came to. He kept asking for you and telling them to tell you he was sorry for being late and not calling."

Tears burned behind Evan's eyes, his throat closed to air.

The elevator stopped.

Brandon stepped out with Evan at his side. "At first the medics didn't know who he was asking for, I guess they're not the pop culture type, and asked him, 'Who's Evan?' He said you were his partner." He caught Evan's hand as they walked down a hall. "Don't be mad at him. He was in shock and confused and didn't know what he was saying. One of the medics told me because he wanted to assure me that what Jesse said would be kept confidential, because after he said it, they realized exactly who he was and who he was talking about."

"How could I be mad at him for anything right now, least of all something like that?"

"I just thought you should know since I'm sure you already saw the media out there. Evan, whoever it was, they beat the shit out of him. But," a few forced, humorless chuckles shook free of Brandon's throat, "that vain brat made sure to protect his face after he went down, so he's not too banged up there, at least."

They rounded a corner. Evan saw Greg standing outside one of the rooms. His pace quickened, leaving Brandon behind. Greg slowly raised his head, lines of stress creased by his eyes. Assuming the door Greg stood beside must be Jesse's room, Evan walked past him to go inside.

Greg caught him by both shoulders, forcing him to a halt. "You can't go in right now, Evan. The police are talking with him."

Evan locked his gaze into Greg's. "Let me go."

Greg looked into Evan's eyes. He drew his hands gradually off Evan's shoulders as if the slow movement would keep him from bolting through the door. It didn't.

Evan flung the door open and stopped. Relief like he'd never felt before stole his strength, and for an instant, he thought he was going to collapse, but he found himself held upright by not wanting to break contact with Jesse's indigo eyes.

Jesse sat up in the hospital bed. "Ev!"

Evan dashed past a doctor, a nurse, and two detectives. He half fell, half sat on the bed, wrapping Jesse in as tight of an embrace as he dared.

Jesse lifted his sore arms around Evan and gripped the back of his shirt in two fists. He laid his head on Evan's shoulder, his face buried in his neck. The scent of Platinum Egoist instantly calmed him.

Evan risked tightening his arms around him a fraction more. "There are no words to even begin describing how happy I am to have you in my arms right now."

Jesse wiggled forward to be yet closer to him. "There're none to describe how happy I am to be held by you."

They stayed in each other's arms, Jesse clinging to Evan, Evan gently rocking him. From behind, someone loudly cleared their throat.

"Sir?" the doctor began. "I'm sorry, but we're not allowing visitors to see him at this moment."

Evan glared at the doctor. "I'm a little more than a visitor. I'm his partner. If you want me to leave, then you'd better call up a few more cops because it's going to take more than these two to get me away from him."

Standing at the door, Brandon and Greg wore the same stunned expressions, through Brandon's softened as a slow smile crept onto his lips.

Evan looked back at Jesse. His gaze moved to the deep purple bruise on Jesse's left cheek. He summoned a smile for him and combed his fingers through Jesse's hair. "I'm not leaving your side, gorgeous. I promise."

Jesse's face lit with a smile. He fell forward into Evan's arms once again.

The doctor tapped the nurse's arm and the two turned to leave. As they stepped out, Brandon and Greg followed. The two detectives remained in the room, one shifting his stance from one foot to the other in a display of discomfort. The taller and more senior of the two followed the doctor's example and cleared his throat to get Jesse's and Evan's attention.

"Mr. Alexander, we'd like to finish taking your statement, if we could."

Jesse stayed in Evan's arms. "I told you to call me Jesse, and go ahead."

"Can you give us a description of the three men who assaulted you and Mr. Cooper, anything at all that would distinguish them?"

Reluctantly, Evan drew back so Jesse could concentrate on answering the detective's questions and moved his position to sitting beside him.

Jesse leaned against him and took Evan's hand. "They were all wearing ski masks, two in black, one in dark blue. They were all taller than me, but," a fragile smile graced his lips, "everyone is."

"And how tall are you?"

"Five-seven." Jesse paused, his expression revealing he was searching his memory. "But, it was the one in the blue mask who had the knife."

"Knife!" Evan blurted out. "No one said anything about you being attacked with a knife!"

"It wasn't much of an attack. I used Kenny's guitar case as a weapon and knocked it from the guy's hand." Jesse looked into Evan's eyes, his face, his voice, turned mournful. "They slashed my tires, Ev."

Evan placed a soft kiss on Jesse's forehead. "We'll get you new tires."

His pen to his notebook, the detective interrupted asking, "Can you describe the events as they happened?"

Jesse took as deep a breath as he could before the pain in his ribs stopped him and relayed all that happened from the time he and Kenny entered the parking garage. He felt Evan tense when he mentioned getting punched, thrown to the ground and kicked, and sought to comfort him by rubbing one hand up and down his back.

"Can you think of anyone who holds bad feelings against you or would have a reason for wanting to see you harmed?" the detective asked.

"Well, recently my band and I got into it with another band," Jesse said, describing the fight with Swiller.

When he finished, Evan added, "And don't forget Kyler."

"I really doubt it was Kyler. If he wanted to come after me, he'd do it face to face. I even doubt it was the Swiller boys since there're four of them and we were attacked by three guys."

"I don't know if that makes much of a difference," Evan said. "And as far as Kyler goes, he might act bold, but you never know what's going on in another person's mind. What could it hurt to have these guys talk to him?"

"I guess." Jesse told some of the details as to why Kyler could have an issue with him, though he didn't mention Evan's past with him since Kyler wasn't out to the public on being a bi boy. He only said they viewed each other as musical rivals. When he came to the end of the interview, for all the talking he did, he felt as though he'd given the detectives nothing.

"Well," said the senior detective, flipping his notebook closed, "we'll see what we can do. If they were all wearing gloves like you said then the chances of getting any fingerprints is low. Hopefully, the team at the parking garage will recover the knife and then maybe we'll have something."

"What about the security camera in the garage?" Evan asked.

"We have tape leading up to about eight-thirty tonight, then nothing," the younger detective replied. "The tape was pulled and never replaced."

"And you're going to work on tracking down the guard who was supposed to be on duty, right?" Evan asked.

"We'll do our best," the senior detective said. "Considering he vanished during his shift without informing anyone, my guess is he got paid or coerced to take off. He might be difficult to find if that's the case."

The detectives thanked Jesse and departed.

Evan let out a disgusted snort. "They were helpful."

"They're only doing what they can." Jesse squeezed Evan's hand. "I heard the doctor saying he might want to keep me here overnight for observation. Don't let him. I want to go home."

Evan pulled Jesse into his arms again. "Don't worry. They won't keep you."

Jesse strengthened his hold on Evan. "Brandon said there are a ton of reporters outside."

"There's a few, but don't worry about them. There're lots of police to keep them back."

"It's just…I look like shit right now. I really don't want them to get shots of me like this."

Despite himself, Evan couldn't help but chuckle. "I can't believe your worst concern is not looking good for the cameras."

Jesse raised his head, a small smile on his lips. "Well, I do have a reputation to uphold of always looking wicked hot."

"You're always a hundred times more wicked hot than any other man in the world."

Jesse stared into Evan's azure eyes, cherishing their color. He leaned a little more forward, tipping his lips up. Evan bowed his head and touched his lips to Jesse's. The kiss came to a slow end, though they stayed close, resting their foreheads together.

"Let's get you out of here," Evan said softly.

Jesse nodded, though he made no attempt to move, content to remain in Evan's arms a few moments longer.

CHAPTER TWENTY-EIGHT

With one hand resting lightly on the middle of Jesse's back to help steady him, Evan stood on the step below him and reached around to open the access door. It was only when he and Jesse were coming down the private road that he realized he hadn't closed the gates to the driveway, the garage doors, or armed the security system. Now as he followed Jesse inside, he stopped at the keypad and made certain everything was locked and armed since he had a feeling some paparazzi had tailed them.

Not that it mattered. They already knew Jesse left the hospital under his care. It took an army of cops to keep the reporters back while he helped Jesse into the Cayenne, making for some high cash photos, he was sure. Even if some did follow them home, their access stopped at the private road and the house couldn't be seen from the public road as it curved away from the estate. If there was one thing he didn't play games with, it was his and Jesse's privacy and security. If only Phoenix shared his mentality. He told Greg they needed to get better security at the studio, and while Greg agreed, getting approval for the extra expense held up the process. He already decided he'd contact the private security company who they worked with when on the road to see about having guards brought in.

Jesse sat on the floor in front of him, his arms around Achilles. "I'm so glad I didn't have him with me today. Who knows what they would've done to him."

"It might've been better if you had. He's a big dog. They might've thought twice about attacking you with him at your side."

"Yeah, right. It takes someone about two seconds of looking at him from a distance to figure out he's harmless." Jesse looked back at Evan. "Remember when I said we should get him a friend? Maybe we should look into a trained guard dog, like a German Shepherd or Rottweiler."

Evan stepped up behind him and brushed his fingers through the top of Jesse's hair. "We can do that."

Jesse closed his eyes at Evan's touch and leaned back against his legs. "I've taken for granted how good it feels to come home."

"Are you hungry? I can heat you up something."

Jesse shook his head. "Right now, all I want is to get a shower and crawl into bed." He made an attempt to stand. Pain laced through his body. He rested back on the floor. "Or, maybe I'll just stay here."

Evan moved in front of him and bent at the waist, holding his arms out to him. "Grab my arms."

Jesse gripped the lower half of Evan's biceps and, with the aid of Evan's strength, rose to his feet. He shuffled down the short hall into the entrance room, his right leg throbbing with each movement. He stopped at the foot of the stairs and looked up their height as though they were as formidable as Mount Everest.

Evan slid in on his right side and wrapped his arm around Jesse's waist. "Lean on me, gorgeous."

"I'm not feeling very gorgeous right now," Jesse mumbled, allowing much of his weight to rest on Evan when he had to lift his right leg.

"Whether you feel it or not, you are." Evan gave him a warm smile. "And you always will be to me."

His flattery earned him a grin. Gradually, they made their way to the bedroom. Jesse aimed for the bed and sat down heavily, his breath coming quick. Evan's heart wrenched seeing him fatigued from the simple act of climbing the stairs when normally Jesse could run three miles and hardly become winded. To hide his own emotional pain, Evan dropped to his knees in front of him and began untying Jesse's shoes.

Jesse stared down at him in surprise. "You don't have to do that."

"I want to." Evan carefully pulled one Nike off Jesse's foot. He did the same with the other, then rolled his socks off. He stood and moved his hands lightly under Jesse's T-shirt. Jesse struggled to raise his arms high enough on his own, since he had no strength left and his muscles were so sore. Evan gently lifted his arms for him, setting them on his own shoulders as he removed Jesse's shirt. He placed Jesse's hands back on his lap and looked down at him.

A thick pad wrapped around Jesse's torso to help protect his ribs from being jarred. Peeking out from under the pad, purple splotches marred his ivory skin and more bruises darkened his forearms. Evan moved his gaze to Jesse's, but Jesse looked away.

His voice a trembling whisper, Jesse said, "You must think I'm so pathetic."

Evan startled at his words. "Why would you say something like that?"

"Because I couldn't defend myself."

Evan gripped him gently by the chin, forcing Jesse to look at him. "I don't think you're pathetic. I could never think that of you." He let out a long breath, weariness took over his stance, remorse his expression. He sank down to his knees again, laying his hands on the sides of Jesse's thighs. "If anything, I'm the one to blame for this. Instead of coming home after I wrapped up with the orchestra, I should've gone to the studio to be with you, to take you to dinner, to not let you work so late. But I didn't, and because I wasn't there to protect you, I almost lost you."

"Ev." Jesse cupped Evan's face in both hands and lifted his head to meet his gaze. "This isn't your fault. You had to come home to take care of 'Chilles, and I'm sorry for saying this, but I'm glad you weren't with me tonight. There's no way of knowing that you could've protected me. You could've gotten stabbed, maybe even killed. And where would I be if I lost you? Most likely, right behind you, because I wouldn't be able to face this world without you."

"Then you know how I feel." Evan's voice shook with rising tears. He laid his head on Jesse's lap and embraced him around his waist. "When Brad called, when he said you'd been hurt, I've never known such fear. You said you've taken for granted how good it feels to come home. Well now I know I've taken for granted having you with me every day. If I ever lost you, Jess, I know I'd forsake my life to come after you in whatever lies beyond this existence."

Jesse felt, and saw, Evan's shoulders shaking. He heard a sob, muffled from Evan's face buried against his lap. He knew then how much the experience had frightened Evan. He bent over him as much as he could, holding him with one arm around his shoulders, rubbing his other hand up and down Evan's back. "I'd never leave you without fighting for my life, because my life belongs to you and I know I have to take good care of it to keep you happy. Your happiness is the only thing in the world that matters to me."

A choked sob came from Evan; he tightened his arms around Jesse. Jesse continued to hold and caress him. After a few long moments, Evan calmed. He stayed kneeling before him, keeping his head on Jesse's lap, and allowed himself to slowly relax as Jesse's soothing touch coursed through his hair, over his shoulders, down his back. He sat on his heels, wiping his eyes with his hand.

The sight of Evan's beautiful eyes red at the edges and so strained broke Jesse's heart. He sat forward, cupped Evan's face again, and kissed him tenderly on the lips. "I love you, Evan. There's nothing in the world that means more to me than you."

"I love you too, Jesse. So very much."

Jesse brushed Evan's hair back from his forehead and smiled. "And now that I'm feeling your snot seeping through my jeans, I'm really ready to get a shower."

Rough chuckles sounded deep in Evan's throat. "Let me help you."

He stood and offered his hands to him. Jesse took them and borrowed Evan's strength once again to get to his feet.

Evan stepped closer to him and reached down, unfastening the button of Jesse's jeans. "This is the first time I've ever undressed you without the intention of doing naughty things to you."

Jesse laughed softly. "This is the first time you've ever undressed me where I don't have the energy for you to do naughty things to me."

Evan smiled and bent to guide Jesse's jeans and boxers off. His gaze came in contact with Jesse's right leg, the thigh and shin blotched with bruises, the knee swollen. Emotion rose in Evan's throat again, but he forced it down. He eased Jesse's pants off the rest of the way with Jesse bracing one hand on his shoulder as he lifted each foot.

Evan straightened, and taking a deep breath to prepare himself, pulled at the Velcro straps holding the chest padding in place. It fell away. Evan stood dumbstruck. From a few inches below his collarbone to the top of his abdomen, Jesse's torso was discolored with bruising. Evan gently laid his hands on Jesse's shoulders and guided him to turn around. His saw the same horror, the smooth white skin of Jesse's back painted with bruises.

"How…how are you not hurt worse?" Evan stammered.

"I guess I'm more durable than I look." Jesse grinned at him. Evan's expression vanquished the grin from his lips. He looked forward, his head lowered. "You still think I'm gorgeous?" he asked softly.

Evan wrapped his arms carefully around him. "Yes, I do."

"Will you help me in the shower?"

"You don't even have to ask."

Evan released him, only to take his hand and lead him into the bathroom. Jesse sat down on the closed toilet lid while Evan went to the shower and turned the water on. While it got up to temperature, he lifted his shirt over his head.

Jesse watched Evan's muscles stretch with the movement. Warmth swirled deep between his legs, and despite his body being battered, his cock stirred. Evan brought his jeans down, and Jesse saw he was half up. His own organ responded and filled faster.

Evan looked at Jesse's hard cock, then down to his own that had finished rising, and back to Jesse. "They just respond to each other, don't they?"

"Yeah. If only they'd get in touch with the rest of our bodies."

He started to push himself up and Evan was instantly at his side, helping him the rest of the way. Evan tested the water temperature again, then allowed Jesse to step in first. Jesse moved directly under the water and tipped his head back, relishing in the heat soothing his knotted muscles and inflamed flesh. He brought his head forward and stood unmoving while his hair became saturated. From behind, he felt Evan's warm, strong presence, then Evan's hands were in his hair, gently working the water through. He almost whimpered when Evan's touch left him, but it returned quickly with shampoo.

Other than his body swaying slightly, Jesse remained motionless while Evan washed and conditioned his hair. When Evan finished, he stepped out from under the water and turned to face him. Evan squeezed body wash over a blue loofa sponge and moved it lightly over him, then handed Jesse a bar of soap. Jesse took it, knowing Evan wanted to let him clean his more intimate areas to keep from getting carried away.

While he washed, Evan moved under the flow. Jesse watched his chestnut hair become darker with moisture, the gold and copper highlights streaking even brighter through it. Water rolled over Evan's flawless back, the rivulets traveling in curving paths around the muscles. Jesse's eyes followed the water's path to Evan's ass, mesmerized by a stream flowing down his tailbone along his crack.

"Are you ready to rinse off?" Evan asked.

Jesse didn't answer.

Evan glanced back at him. Jesse stood leaning one shoulder against the wall, a sudsy hand gripping his erect shaft, though not moving, as if he had fallen into a trance halfway through washing. He noticed where Jesse's eyes were focused and chuckled under his breath. He held his hand out to him. "C'mon. We need to get you rinsed, dried, and in bed."

Jesse moved toward him. "I'm feeling a little better."

"No, you're feeling a little horny." Evan wrapped his arms around Jesse's waist. "The doctor said to keep you quiet and not to let you get excited. What kind of nurse would I be if I didn't follow his orders?"

Jesse's lips curved in a mischievous smirk. "A compassionate one."

"Get rinsed off."

Jesse stepped under the flow. "You're a mean nurse."

"I'll be nice when my patient is less difficult."

"Your patient is less difficult after he comes."

"Then I guess I'll have to keep being mean because he's not getting that tonight."

Once done rinsing, Evan turned off the water, cracked open the glass shower door, and grabbed the plush towel off the rack outside. With great care, he dried Jesse's body and hair, then wrapped the towel around him. He hastily dried himself with a second towel and walked with Jesse from the shower.

As they reached the bed, Evan flung the royal blue and gold trimmed comforter back along with the white silk top sheet. Shedding his towel, Jesse eased down on his back, letting out a long groan as he did.

Evan tucked the covers up around Jesse's neck. "I'm going to run 'Chilles out, then I'll be back up."

Jesse nodded and closed his eyes. Though his mind felt sluggish, he couldn't help but relive the events of that night. He pictured each of his attackers, heard their mumbling voices, saw again the flash of the knife. Scenarios raced through his mind of how things could've turned out; Kenny getting stabbed, himself getting stabbed, his face kicked in, a fractured skull, internal bleeding, damaged organs, death.

Evan walked in the bedroom and flicked off the light. Jesse listened to him remove his pants, and a moment later, the mattress dipped as he climbed into bed beside him.

Evan leaned over him and pressed his lips to his forehead. He paused, then leaned back and laid his hand on Jesse's forehead. He touched the back of it to Jesse's cheek, moving next to his neck. He sat up and looked down at him. "Jess, you're sweating. Are you alright? What's wrong?"

"I was just thinking about everything, how things could've turned out. I'm okay, though."

Evan gently stroked his hair. "It's alright to admit you were afraid. There's no shame in that."

"Yeah well, that's the thing. I wasn't afraid at the time." He let out a couple anxious chuckles. "That's really pathetic, isn't it? To be freaked out now over things that didn't happen."

"No, it's not," Evan said softly. "Your mind is just now starting to catch up to what happened. You have to let yourself feel these things. And I'll be here, right beside you, if you need to talk, or cry, or yell about any of it."

"Right now, I think I just want you to hold me."

Evan lay down on his side and moved close to him. Jesse lifted his head, and Evan slid his right arm under it. He placed his left hand on Jesse's chest, feeling his heartbeat under his palm.

"Are you comfortable?" he asked.

Jesse inched toward him. "Yeah."

Evan kissed him on the temple. Even when Jesse's breathing deepened with sleep, Evan remained awake, listening to him breath and feeling his heart beat.

Chapter Twenty-nine

Jesse sat at the black grand piano in the live room, his ribs aching, his head pounding. A full week had passed since the attack. During that time, Evan refused to allow him to come to the studio and stayed home to take care of him until Thursday, when with having an entire orchestra waiting on him, he had no choice but to return. He dropped him off at Shunichi's home and dojo to spend the day with Brandon, who told Jesse they were living together now.

He was glad for the distractions from the studio, but it also left him edgy, as if delaying it made his anxiety worse. Evan was reluctant at the idea of him coming today, but under gentle coaxing, relented.

What he couldn't believe were the paparazzi camped outside the gates to the private road the whole time. At the sight of the SUV, they sprang from their own vehicles frantically snapping pictures. Even though the Escalade's windows were tinted dark, he was sure it was discernable there were two figures in the SUV. His attack was all over the media and Internet, and with it, images of Evan throwing the reporter to the ground, then a couple hours later, guiding him tenderly to the Cayenne. Since reporters now knew where the entrance to their home was, it was also known he went in with Evan and hadn't come back out. Greg issued a statement saying because of his injuries and their close friendship, Evan was caring for him. It wasn't a lie per say, but the media read between the lines almost as soon as they were spoken.

When they arrived at the studio that morning, more reporters waited outside. The security was increased, but even with the additional staff, as he and Evan walked in, a reporter stretched a camera through the guards to get a shot of them. Evan shoved the camera back at the guy with such force the man dropped his valuable tool. For his entire career, Evan was always congenial with the paparazzi, allowing them to get good shots of him when he was in public promoting, often taking a moment to chat with them. He felt the best way to keep them off his back was to not make a spectacle of himself. This new fiercely protective side of him sent the paparazzi into a frenzy, and also solidified their belief in the depth of their relationship.

Jesse couldn't deny internally he rejoiced at this, hoping it could mean he and Evan would soon come out together, though Evan hadn't said anything to such an effect. Outwardly, he remained silent and walked past the reporters as if they weren't there.

Yet out of everything, one thing weighed the heaviest on his emotions; since the attack, he and Evan had yet to make love. Evan doted on him, leaping to take care of his slightest need, he was tender and affectionate, but when he tried to encourage Evan's affections to move to a deeper level, Evan withdrew from him. Poisonous doubts whispered in his mind that despite what Evan said, he really did think less of him for not being able to defend himself, and because of that, his attraction toward him had diminished. Nothing brought more fear to his heart than that thought.

A hand settled on his shoulder, breaking his thoughts. Jesse looked up. His left eye still bruised, now more green than purple, Kenny sat heavily on the piano bench beside him. Jesse learned of Evan's accusations against Kenny at the hospital, though he hadn't questioned Evan on it, wanting to see how he and Kenny would interact the next time they saw each other. When they did, it seemed no grudges were held, both understanding the intense emotions dominating everyone that night.

"How ya feelin'?" Kenny asked.

"A little tired." Jesse expected when he arrived at the studio to be filled with nervous anxiety. Instead, he found himself comfortable and relieved to be back, even if they hadn't gotten much done other than working on instrumentals. He found it difficult to sing with his chest so sore, not able to take the deep breaths he needed, and regulating his air and voice from his diaphragm exhausted him like never before.

"Maybe we should call it a day," Kenny said.

Jesse looked down at his watch. Only two o'clock in the afternoon. He didn't want to disrupt Evan's work by calling and telling him to come get him.

"I can take you home," Kenny offered. "We can hang out and play some video games."

"That sounds good." Jesse looked back to Brad and Julian. "Do you guys care if we call it a day?"

"I can't believe you even wanted to come in today," Brad said.

"I thought it'd be a good introductory session, then I could chill over the weekend and things can get back to normal next week."

Julian's expression turned concerned. "Do you think you'll be ready to go at things normally so soon?"

Jesse smiled. "Another couple days, and I'll be golden."

A deep growl came from under the piano. Jesse looked in surprise at Achilles lying underneath it. Before the attack, the dog wanted to be friends with everyone. Now, other than Shunichi, who he took to instantly, Achilles growled and barked at people he didn't know.

The door opened. Greg walked in leading the two detectives who had spoken with Jesse at the hospital. Achilles sprang up and rushed forward, barking loud and fierce. Jesse dove for him, catching more fur than collar, and wincing in pain as the dog nearly dragged him off the bench. Kenny grabbed Achilles also, and helped Jesse reel the dog back in.

"'Chilles, enough!" Jesse bellowed, his normal patience with the dog broken by pain.

Achilles let out a final deep growl and slowly sat in front of Jesse, his tawny eyes fixed on the detectives.

Jesse stroked the dog's head with one hand and got a better grip on his collar with the other. "It's okay," he said, his voice quieter, the pain in his ribs subsiding.

Detective Harris, the senior of the two, stepped forward. "Looks like you got a better bodyguard there than any person you could hire."

"He's not usually this way. Normally he's more like Lassie and less like Cujo, but he's been a little more protective since I came home hurt."

"You look like you're doing better," said the younger detective, Daily. "How're you feeling?"

Self-conscious of the bruise on his cheek that was now deep purple in the center, yellowish-green on the edges, Jesse gingerly touched his fingertips to it. "Not horrible."

Daily gazed around the live room. "This is so cool. I've never been in a recording studio before. That first room is crazy with all the equipment."

"That's the control room. Everything we play in here gets recorded and adjusted for sound in there." Jesse's lips rose in a smile. "Though, we hit it perfect whenever and wherever we play."

"I'm a little bit more old school in my music tastes," Harris said. "Led Zeppelin, Pink Floyd, but I got into your band after hearing your CD blasting out of my daughter's bedroom every night. She's a really big fan of yours, Jesse. She's fifteen and thinks she's in love. I'm sure you've dealt with that a lot."

"Yeah, I've heard I've been a lot of girls' first love since we came on the scene. So, if you guys are here, I hope it means you've got new information on who attacked us."

The smiles faded from the detectives' faces. Harris cleared his throat. "I'm sorry, Jesse, but as of right now, we've got nothing. The knife you said one of the perpetrators had wasn't recovered. Maybe during all the commotion one of the assailants picked it up again, and there weren't any fingerprints on your car."

"What about the garage security guard?" Greg asked. "We gave you his most recent address."

"And we went there, but apparently he hasn't returned since the assault."

"We're holding his final paycheck," Greg said. "I guess the best we can hope for is he comes in to get it."

Harris nodded and turned his attention back to Jesse. "We also talked with the band members of Black Heart Down, with special attention to Kyler Christenson, but all had alibis."

Brad grumbled, "Depending on who Kyler's alibi was, I wouldn't put much faith in that."

Harris looked back at him. "It was Robbie Russo, the guitar player."

"I don't think Robbie would lie to cover Kyler's ass," Kenny said.

"Man, he's his best friend," Brad cut in. "He'll do anything Kyler tells him to."

Julian spoke up, "Did you also question the band members of Swiller?"

"We communicated with their manager and it appears the band's been in L.A. for a little more than a week. He said he sent them home for a while to let them cool down and relax from the stress of recording." Detective Harris shook his head, giving Jesse a sympathetic expression. "I'm sorry, Jesse. Unless something else turns up, we've got no other leads. For all we know, it could've been a random gang attack. A lot of gangs do things like this as initiations for new members."

"Yeah," Jesse said softly. "Some things are beyond anyone's control."

The detectives said their farewells and left.

Silence filled the room. Jesse stared blankly at floor, his mind holding no thoughts other than disappointment.

Greg walked over to him and placed a gentle hand on Jesse's shoulder. "Go home and get some more rest, son. The music will wait for you."

Jesse laid one hand over Greg's and lifted his head. "Thanks." He stood and patted his leg for Achilles to follow him. "Well guys, let's call it a day."

Kenny fell into stride beside him, Brad and Julian behind, knowing they were invited to come to his house without the invitation vocalized.

Jesse sighed at seeing the reporters outside the doors. The group of security guards hanging out in the lobby stood at his approach, prepared to escort him. Before walking out, he paused to call Evan and let him know he was going home. He left him a message, then taking a deep breath, walked out to the flashing cameras and shouting voices.

CHAPTER THIRTY

His mood soured by paparazzi lurking outside the Symphony Center, Evan headed out wearing silver-trimmed sunglasses with black lenses to not accommodate them in getting good shots. Security guards formed a ring around him as he turned up the sidewalk toward the Cayenne, ignoring the reporters yelling questions and waving their cameras. One of the reporters, his voice a high pitched whine, repeatedly called his name. Evan glanced at him out the corner of his eye, seeing the short, light brown haired young man hopping and pushing against other reporters.

"Evan! Evan! If I could talk to you for a moment! Evan! Evan!"

Evan rolled his eyes behind his sunglasses and kept walking.

"Evan! I have something I think you'd be interested in!"

Evan let out a doubtful snort no one could hear over their own shouting.

"Evan, please! Just a moment of your time!" The young man paused, then said softer as if it would keep the other paparazzi from hearing, "It's about what happened to Jesse."

Evan slammed to a halt, his attention focused on the young reporter. With a flick of Evan's hand, one of the guards took the paparazzo by the arm and pulled him around another reporter. The circle of guards closed behind him, leaving the younger man face to face with Evan. He stood silent, staring in awe at Evan.

Having no patience, Evan prompted with, "You have something to show me."

The paparazzo blinked himself out of being star-struck and nodded. "Yeah, but," he glanced around with suspicion at the other reporters, "I think we should find somewhere more private to talk."

Evan stood silent. The young man shifted in place, visibly uncomfortable by Evan's scrutinizing gaze. Evan started walked again. The guards hastened to mimic his pace and left the paparazzo no choice but to be swept along.

Evan lowered his voice. "You'd better not be wasting my time."

The young man edged closer to Evan's side. "Considering the cops don't have any leads on who attacked Jesse, I think you'll be pleased with what I have to show you, Evan."

Evan placed a hand on the reporter's shoulder and pushed him to create greater distance between them. They reached the Cayenne, and he came to a halt, turning to the young man. "You can follow me. There's a bar up the street and around the corner we can go to."

"Oh, well…I don't have a car…"

Evan took another long moment to stare at him. There was no way he was going to let some strange paparazzo ride in his car. He began walking, guards following. "Whatever you have better be good."

He didn't have to look at the reporter to sense his jittery nerves or know how tense he walked, clutching a digital video camera to his chest. They came upon the Irish inspired pub and Evan stepped inside, leaving the guards at the door to keep the other paparazzi out. He walked over the dark hardwood floor, past the mahogany bar lined with a thick brass railing, to a small round table near a corner and sat down.

"What's your name?"

The young man hastily pulled out a chair beside him. "I'm sorry. It's Paul. Paul McClain."

"You haven't been a paparazzo for long, have you, Paul?"

"About three months."

Evan nodded. This guy had no experience whatsoever in dealing with celebrities or the world of show business. He was timid, shy, nowhere near cutthroat or bold enough to make it in the career he was shooting for. He really doubted what Paul had was worth taking the time to hear him, but after speaking with Jesse earlier that afternoon and learning the cops had nothing, he was willing to look at any possibilities. If the police couldn't find out who hurt Jesse, then he sure as hell would.

Evan glanced up at the waitress as she approached their table. "Guinness, please."

She stared at him. "Are...are you Evan Ar—"

"No. I get that all the time." He looked at Paul. "What're you having?"

"I'll have the same."

The waitress gave Paul a suspicious look, and after carding him, retreated to get their drinks.

Evan leaned back in his chair, having yet to remove his sunglasses despite the dim lighting of the bar. "Do you work for anyone in particular?"

Paul shook his head. "I'm freelance."

"Score anything big yet?"

Paul held up the small camcorder. "I have with what's in this."

"If you think you've got such a big score, then why are you here showing it to me and not selling it to the highest bidder?"

"Because I figured you have as much money as they do and this would be more valuable to you than anyone else."

A smirk lifted one corner of Evan's lips. Maybe the guy was savvier than he thought. "So you're looking to gain some cash from me."

"You didn't expect me to give it to you for nothing, did you?"

"Well, I had thought maybe I stumbled upon the one paparazzo with a heart." Evan saw the waitress returning and waited until she left again before talking again. "So, show me what you got."

Paul paused with his glass to his lips. "I think we should settle on a price first."

Evan took a long drink from his beer. "We can't settle on a price until I see what you've got and determine what its value is to me."

Paul sat quietly, then nodded. He hit a few buttons on the camcorder and passed it to him. Evan hit play. As soon as the scenes began to play out, his casual demeanor disappeared. He sat forward and lifted his sunglasses, holding the screen closer to his eyes.

The camera moved slowly over Jesse's F430, the tires not yet flat. The camera jerked and pointed to the ground, the concrete racing by making it clear that Paul had taken off running. He ducked behind Julian's Audi and the camera peeked out from behind a back tire to film three ski masked men, two in black, one in dark blue, approaching Jesse's car. The two in black watched while the one in blue knelt by the right back tire, a flash of steel betrayed the knife. Within seconds, the Ferrari was sinking toward the ground. The threesome turned to leave, but as they neared the garage exit, the sound of laughter sent them diving for cover.

Even at the muted volume of the recorder, Evan recognized the laugh. His heart clenched knowing what was to follow. Helplessness rose in him as Jesse and Kenny entered the garage. He saw how Jesse stopped, realizing something was wrong. When the three emerged, Evan leaned closer to the screen. He studied their movements, their postures, their height, and body size. He smiled at Jesse's brazenness, then the fight began.

He watched unblinking. Pride rose as he saw how Jesse fought to protect Kenny, but when he went down, he physically winced himself. Tears welled in his eyes, and he had to force himself to continue watching. When Brad, Julian, and Jeremy ran into the garage, sending the three attackers fleeing, Evan paused the camera. He stared down at his beer, the images flashing through his head. Those three needed more than masks to hide from him.

Slowly, Paul pulled the camera from Evan's fingers. For a long moment, he allowed Evan to absorb what he had seen, then quietly said, "You really care for him, don't you?"

"What do you think?" Evan snapped. He raised his sharp blue eyes to Paul. "You watched the whole thing. You watched him get beaten, nearly killed, and did nothing."

"I'm not a brave person, Evan."

"You've made that pretty fucking clear. Why the hell were you there to begin with?"

"To get shots of Jesse's car to sell to mags. No one's gotten good pictures of it yet, so when I saw the garage wasn't guarded, I took my chance and went in. Luck just came to me that I happened to be in the right place at the right time."

Evan gnashed his teeth at Paul's words. "Luck?"

"Yeah. So, how much is it worth to you to keep this video under wraps and not sold to Showbiz Tonight?"

"Not a goddamn thing." Evan picked up his beer, tipped his head back, and drained his nearly full glass of Guinness.

Paul's eyes rounded. "W-what?"

"I've seen what I needed to see." Evan stood up and pulled his money clip from his front pocket.

"But we had a deal."

"Did we? I was under the impression we'd set a price after I saw the video and decided how much it was worth to me. I've decided it's not worth anything."

"Then I'll sell it and it'll be all over every entertainment show on TV!"

"And you think I care? The whole world already knows what happened to him. Seeing it isn't going to make any difference. If anything, it'll gain more sympathy and support for him. And what's more, by you selling it, it'll allow the police to see it, then maybe they can learn something new from the footage."

He clapped his hand down on Paul's shoulder. "But let me give you a word of advice. If you want to make it in this business, never, under any circumstances, show all of your hand to anyone, no matter how much you believe you can trust them, until the cash is on the table in front you." He tossed a fifty down on the table. "Have another beer on me and take a cab home. Good luck to you, Paul."

Without a backward glance at the stunned young man, Evan walked from the bar.

CHAPTER THIRTY-ONE

At the sound of the security system beeping as it was disarmed, Jesse hopped up from the couch in the family room and walked quickly into the kitchen. He couldn't decide if he was more hungry or horny, but knew Evan's coming home signaled an end to both since Evan picked up dinner and he was determined to get Evan naked, hard, and inside him before the night was over.

Kenny, Julian, and Brad had left an hour before, and with them gone, he had nothing to do but think about Evan and get himself worked up. He nearly took care of things on his own when he showered, but collected his willpower and focused on preparing his body for Evan.

The access door opened and closed, the security system beeped once more as it was rearmed. Jesse leaned one hip against the kitchen counter, watching the doorway anxiously. He heard Evan's footsteps moving with a dancer's lightness across the hardwood floor.

Evan walked into the kitchen, a paper bag filled with Chinese food under one arm, and smiled at Jesse. "Hey, gorgeous."

"Hey," Jesse replied on an exhale.

Evan looked more divine than he remembered from the morning. He wore a powder blue button down shirt with faint, thin gray stripes running vertical that hugged his body. His legs were clad in black dress pants, and Jesse stared at how they conformed to his slender hips. As he envisioned those hips pumping between his thighs, he decided he was definitely more horny than hungry.

Jesse met Evan's gaze. "You look incredible."

A husky chuckle rumbled in Evan's throat. He stepped toward him and angled his lips close to Jesse's. "I look the same as I did this morning."

Jesse paused when he thought he caught the scent of alcohol on Evan's breath under the minty scent of chewing gum. He leaned closer to kiss him. "Which was incredible."

Evan kissed him, but before Jesse could send the signal from his brain to his mouth to open, Evan retreated from him. He stood in shock for a moment, trying to figure out if he had really felt the light brush of Evan's lips on his. He turned and saw Evan tossing his gum in the trash, then yank open the refrigerator. Evan grabbed a bottle of Guinness, popped the top off, and took a long drink.

Jesse clenched his teeth to bite down his irritation. He took a deep breath and fueled his determination. He moved close to his side, pressing his chest against Evan's arm. Jesse drew his right hand up Evan's torso to the top of his shirt where a few buttons were undone and slipped his hand inside, rubbing Evan's collarbone and the top of his chest. He willed his voice to come out deeper, more sensual. "How was your day?"

"Fine," Evan said, his voice tight.

Jesse nuzzled into Evan's hair near his temple. He pulled one of the buttons free on Evan's shirt. "Then let's wrap it up in a way so you'll say it was an amazing day."

Jesse felt Evan take a breath to protest. Before he could, Jesse grabbed a fistful of Evan's hair, forcibly turned his head, and claimed his lips. He gave Evan's hair a sharp yank. Evan's lips parted in a gasp, and he pushed his tongue into Evan's mouth. Evan gripped his arms, and for a second, Jesse thought he was going to shove him away. Instead, Evan held him, returning the kiss with equal passion.

Jesse pressed against him. Evan fell back against the refrigerator. Jesse pinned him between it and his body, shifting his hips to feel if Evan was hard, and nearly broke the kiss with a huge smile at finding Evan's solid cock. He slowly ground his own hard cock against it. Despite the desire he felt coming from Evan, he also felt tension, and decided to amp things up even more.

Jesse brought his lips to Evan's neck, licking, sucking, kissing the tender skin. "Let's go upstairs. Make love to me, fuck me, make me come. I need to have it, Ev. I need you inside me."

A soft moan came from Evan. Jesse thrust against him harder. Evan's hands moved, trembling, from Jesse's arms to his hips. He took a firm hold of them and stopped Jesse's motions.

"Jess, please…I…I'm really tired, and…"

At Evan's protestations, Jesse's lust turned to heated rage. "The hell you are!" He backed up from Evan, his gaze going up and down him. Evan breathed fast, his cheeks were flushed, his pants jutted outward with his erection. "Look at yourself! You're so hot, you're ready to blow right now! I know you want it just as bad as I do!"

Evan averted his gaze. "You don't understand. It's just that I—"

"No, I get it." Jesse's eyes narrowed in accusation. "You want it, just not from me."

"What the hell are you talking about?"

"You think I haven't noticed the difference in you since I got my ass beat?" Jesse's rage rapidly deflated as he spoke what he feared. His throat tightened, his eyes burned with pain filled tears that he refused to shed in front of Evan. "I'm not a strong enough man for you to be attracted to anymore."

Evan stood in stunned silence, his lips parted in shock. Never had he heard Jesse speak anything so far from the truth. How could he feel such a thing after seeing the fight for himself? But Jesse didn't know he'd seen the video. He didn't know the pain, the pride, the desire that had gone through him watching Jesse so valiantly defend himself and Kenny.

Jesse lowered his head, his voice softened. "You've been taking wonderful care of me, but you haven't touched me in *that* way. And when I've tried to initiate things, you've denied me, again and again. Our two year anniversary is in a couple weeks, and I thought it'd be like it was last year, that we'd celebrate in each other's bodies for days before and days after, but now I'm wondering if you'll ever want to make love to me again."

Evan took two quick steps toward him and reached for him. "Jess, that's not true. The things you've said, they're not at all how I feel. Not a day has passed since then that I haven't looked at you with admiration for being so strong and standing up for yourself and Kenny."

"Then why won't you make love to me?"

Evan rested his hands gently on Jesse's shoulders, looking into his eyes. "Because I haven't wanted to hurt you. I haven't wanted you to strain yourself. I've been waiting for you to heal more, because I knew when we were going to be together, I wouldn't be able to control myself. I wanted to be sure you could handle it." A warm smile graced his lips, and he brought his head closer to Jesse's. "As it is, haven't you noticed my showers have been longer lately? I'm doing all I can just to take the edge off because I want you so badly."

Jesse gazed into Evan's eyes. "I wish you would've said that sooner, because you pushing me away has hurt worse than what anyone could ever do to me."

Jesse's words caused a jolt of pain to shock Evan's chest. He pulled Jesse into his arms. "I'm so sorry, gorgeous."

Jesse squeezed Evan in his arms. "Don't apologize. Just be with me. I can't fully get back to myself until we're together."

Evan leaned his head back just enough to find Jesse's lips. Jesse opened his mouth, and at the feel of Evan's soft tongue gliding over his own, he melted against him. He knew he needed this deep of affection from Evan, but with finally receiving it, he felt lightheaded with joy, desire, and relief.

Evan moved his lips to Jesse's throat. Jesse let his head fall back on his shoulders, exposing every inch of it to him. As Evan licked his way down, his hand moved to Jesse's chest and lightly teased one nipple from outside his shirt. Jesse took Evan's hand. He drew it down his body and pressed it to his erection, sighing loudly in pleasure as he did.

Evan rubbed him through his jeans, then slowly pulled back. "Let's go upstairs."

Jesse nodded. He held Evan's hand in both of his and let him lead the way to their bedroom. Evan brought him to the edge of the bed and slipped his hands under Jesse's shirt, caressing him as much as lifting the material free from him. Jesse worked the buttons loose on Evan's shirt. At the same moment, each pushed the other's pants off his hips, but found themselves halting in their movements once their cocks were fully bared. As if being pulled together by an unseen force, they couldn't stop themselves from bringing their cocks together.

The feel of silken skin sliding against silken skin caused both Jesse and Evan to pass soft sighs into each other's mouths. Evan drew Jesse's tongue deep into his own mouth. Jesse stood motionless in his arms, savoring the heat of Evan's hard organ against his own. When Evan released his tongue, he took his lips down Jesse's neck, then progressed lower, placing fluttering kisses over his chest and abdomen, then guided him to turn around and did the same to his back. Jesse realized Evan was kissing each of his bruises in his own private act of healing.

At a gentle touch from Evan, Jesse sat on the edge of the bed. Evan kneeled before him and drew his jeans off the rest of the way. He followed their progress down Jesse's legs by showering his right leg with whisper soft kisses. With Jesse fully undressed, Evan stood up. He turned Jesse's head to the right and placed the most tender of kisses on his bruised cheek.

His skin tingling from Evan's ritual, his mind floating with sensation, Jesse slid back toward the center of the bed and lay down with his head on the pillows.

Evan retrieved the lube and finished removing his clothes. He climbed onto the bed with him, and Jesse spread his legs wider. Evan kneeled between them. He gazed at Jesse's supine form laid in offering before him. Jesse's swollen cock stretched up toward his navel, his sac rested heavy between his legs, and just below, his small, tight hole. He moved his gaze higher, drinking in Jesse's slender body. He reached his face, Jesse's dark, twilight blue eyes, his black hair fanned on the white pillow.

"You're so gorgeous," Evan whispered.

A soft smile touched Jesse's lips. "And you're the most beautiful man to ever exist."

Jesse moved his gaze over Evan's body of powerful muscle. He looked at Evan's cock, long, thick, the slit glistening, and felt a pulse around his rim with the desire to be stretched, a yearning in his channel to be filled. He lifted his gaze to Evan's face, to his eyes that even in the darkness were still the brightest blue he'd ever seen.

Evan took hold of Jesse's cock near the base. He bowed his head and swallowed it down his throat. Jesse gasped loudly and arched his hips. Evan placed his free hand on one of Jesse's hips and forced him back to the bed. Jesse nearly let out a giddy laugh over the sheer joy of Evan taking control. He ran his fingers through Evan's hair and gave it a light pull. Evan groaned loud. The reverberation of his voice heightened Jesse's pleasure.

Jesse's body trembled, the exquisiteness of Evan's warm, wet mouth sending his mind spiraling with euphoria. Heat rolled in his groin, and he knew it wouldn't be long before he climaxed. He choked out Evan's name to tell him he was getting close. Evan continued his oral assault and stretched for the lube. Jesse handed it to him. Evan coated his fingers, tickled the outside of his hole in warning, then pushed two fingers inside him. Jesse let out a high moan as Evan's touch opened him.

Evan felt Jesse's muscle constrict. He savored the pre-cum Jesse's cock leaked. He felt torn between wanting to taste all of him or feeling him climax when inside him, then decided he wanted the latter more. He wanted to be connected fully with him. He released him from his mouth and brought his body over Jesse, gazing down at him, panting and flushed. Without giving him a moment's respite, Evan quickly slathered lube over his own cock and pressed it against Jesse's hole.

Jesse let his legs drop to Evan's shoulders and gripped Evan's biceps, his body at a point of desperation. As Evan entered him, he sank his fingers into Evan's arms. Evan kept his weight braced above him, pumping into him quick and deep. Jesse moaned long and low; Evan's cock milked his gland on every thrust. Evan added more speed, more force, and it set him off. He heaved up against Evan as his orgasm claimed him. Evan slammed into him; a hard groan escaped his throat. Jesse felt Evan's cock throb inside him, his cum filling him to the point where some seeped out.

Fighting for breath, Evan carefully brought Jesse's legs down from his shoulders. He sank down, angling his body on one elbow to keep his weight off Jesse's torso. He placed his other hand on the side of Jesse's face. "We can't ever go that long again."

Jesse laughed softly. "You're telling me this?"

Evan grinned and hovered his lips above Jesse's. "Guess what?"

Jesse wrapped his arms around Evan's neck. "What?"

"I'm not done yet."

"I kind of figured that out by your still very hard cock resting inside me. But now you guess what?"

"What?"

Jesse raised his hips and rubbed his erect organ against Evan's stomach. "Neither am I."

Evan gently kissed him and slowly started thrusting into him again.

❊   ❊   ❊

Jesse stirred in bed. His body's clock told him it wasn't time to wake up, yet something had roused him. As he became more conscious, he felt the pleasant ache around his rim from his and Evan's vigorous love making and moisture between his ass cheeks from Evan's fluid leaking out of him while he slept.

He reached for Evan. His hand moved over the cold sheets, and though their bed was big, when his arm was fully stretched and he still hadn't touched him, he realized he wasn't in bed. Jesse opened his eyes and focused on the digital alarm clock on Evan's nightstand. Seeing it was just past three-thirty in the morning, he sat up to check if Evan was in the bathroom, then saw him through the closed French doors standing out on the balcony wearing only his black running pants. A breeze lifted his hair, and it was the only movement that came from him as he stared over Lake Michigan.

Concern rose in Jesse's chest. He slid from the bed, pulling off a blanket folded at the foot and wrapped it around his shoulders and body. He silently opened one of the doors. A blast of cool night air sent a shiver through him. He took a step out onto the balcony. "Ev? What are you doing out here? Is everything okay?"

Evan's head turned slightly. "Everything's fine. I just couldn't sleep."

Jesse moved behind him and embraced Evan around the chest, enclosing him in the blanket and pressing his body against his back. "Are you sure everything's okay? Whenever you're upset or worried, you always stare at the lake."

"Do I?"

Jesse nodded and laid his head against the back of Evan's head. "If something's bothering you, talk to me. We'll figure out how to fix it together."

Evan placed one hand over Jesse's. He remained silent.

Jesse gave him time, understanding he was trying to find a way to speak, but was having trouble choosing his words. He could feel it in how heavily Evan's heart beat beneath his palm. Evan's chest expanded as he took a slow, deep breath.

"This past week has forced me to think about a lot of things, and it's brought me to some realizations that I should've come to a long time ago." Evan turned in Jesse's arms to meet his eyes. "I could've lost you last week. I can't tell you how many times that thought has come to me, and with it, suffocating fear. During those moments when I'm trying to breathe, my mind continues to race, and of all the thoughts I've had, the most disturbing is I could've lost you without ever giving our love all it deserves."

Jesse found himself barely breathing, so focused on every word Evan spoke. Evan lowered his gaze to his left hand. Jesse followed with his gaze, noticing for the first time the small black velvet box he held.

"I don't want the world to look at me as a single man anymore," Evan continued. "I don't want to keep pretending you're nothing more than a friend to me." He met Jesse's gaze. "I don't want to hide my love for you."

He placed his other hand on the box's lid and slowly opened it.

Jesse's lips parted, though no breath or sound came out. He stared down at the matching pair of men's titanium wedding bands. The edges of the rings were grooved and a thinner strip of yellow gold wrapped around the center of the bands.

Evan spoke, uncertainty in his tone. "I was going to show these to you on our anniversary, but I couldn't even wait until then. I know we can't get married in Illinois, but I thought maybe we could go to Massachusetts or Vermont. Even though it wouldn't be recognized here, I still want to marry you. I want that bond." He paused, then cleared his throat. "But, if you're not ready, I understand. I just thought, maybe, with how you've spoken in the past, that you might want to..." his voice trailed off as if not knowing what else to say.

Having stared at the rings while Evan spoke, Jesse looked up at him. He flung his arms around Evan's neck, dropping the blanket. "Yes! Let's go this week!"

Evan choked out a shocked cough. "Are you serious?"

Jesse pulled back enough to look at him. "Of course I am! We could charter a private jet and fly to Vermont. Well, I suppose we could go to Massachusetts, but the chances of us getting tagged by the paparazzi would be lower in Vermont. We could apply for a marriage license and by the time we get it and set up an appointment at a courthouse, we could get married on our anniversary. Wouldn't that be perfect?"

"It would be perfect." Evan shook his head slightly, as if he disbelieved Jesse had accepted, that they were going to take this step in their lives. A slow smile shone over his lips. He lifted one hand to Jesse's cheek. "All the things I've accomplished in my life, all the things I have, seem so trivial compared to you agreeing to marry me."

Jesse laid his hand over Evan's, which rested on his cheek. "And since I first met you, all the things I've wanted for my future were just means to get to this point with you."

Evan drew in a deep breath, and chuckled anxiously. "Of course, now we have to tell the guys. I'm more nervous about that than coming out to the world."

"Maybe it'd be better if we just went off and did it without telling them. Then once it's done, there won't be any changing it."

"Yeah, but they're our family, the most important people in our lives besides each other and Brandon."

Jesse lowered his gaze to the rings and stood silent for a moment. "I just don't want any negativity surrounding this."

"I don't either, but I think we have to tell them."

Jesse smiled. "You're right. But now we have a bigger problem."

"What?"

"Deciding where to go on our honeymoon! I'd kind of like to go to Greece again since I didn't get to see much when we stopped there on your tour. What do you think?"

Evan couldn't help but laugh. "Greece is fine. I think we could both swing taking a couple weeks off from recording. This could be a mini-honeymoon, then after you finish your tour, we'll go on a longer one."

Jesse's smile broadened still more. "We're really going to do it, aren't we?"

"Yeah," Evan said softly. "We are."

Jesse's arms went around Evan's neck, Evan's around Jesse's waist as they brought their smiling lips together.

CHAPTER THIRTY-TWO

Jesse stopped a few feet from the chill-out room. He drew in a deep breath to help steady his racing heartbeat and turned to Evan. "Are you ready?"

A couple hesitant chuckles left Evan's throat. "You know, now that we're about to do this, I'm starting to think we should just elope."

Jesse took Evan's hand. "But like you said, they're family. It'd be wrong to do this without telling them."

"Well, considering between the two of us, we only have two relatives we're on speaking terms with, and on my end I don't even enjoy talking to my mother, pissing off our other family should be about right."

"Was that a glimmer of your horrible sense of humor coming through?"

"A little bit. And just think, when we're married, you'll really never be able to get away from it."

Jesse smiled. "Then I'll have everything I've ever dreamed of."

Evan kissed him gently, and as he slowly drew back, looked toward the room. "I'm ready whenever you are."

Jesse nodded once. "Let's do it."

Hand in hand, they walked in to Kenny, Julian, Brad, and Greg. Greg being there was unexpected, but just as well Jesse thought. There was nothing wrong with fighting all the battles on the same day.

Greg glanced at them, his gaze settling on their joined hands. He fixed a scowl on them. "Please tell me you two weren't skipping down the hall holding hands."

"Of course not," Jesse said.

Greg's expression relaxed slightly.

"I'm way too sore from our weekend of constant lovemaking to skip."

Evan couldn't catch the laugh before it slipped out. Julian grinned at Jesse. Brad hid his smirk behind his hand.

Kenny rolled his eyes. "Can't you just say hi like a normal person?"

Jesse looked at him. "Well, you'll have to forgive me if I'm a little overly exuberant today since the whole reason Ev and I were making love as close to nonstop as humanly possible all weekend is because he asked me to marry him."

Not even a breath could be heard in the room. Jesse waited for a reaction and got it when Julian sucked in a sharp breath.

"Are you serious?" Julian asked.

"I am. We're going to Montpelier this week. We've already got a private jet booked."

Julian sprang to his feet and hastened toward them. "What wonderful news! Congratulations!" He wrapped Jesse in an embrace, then Evan next.

Brad laughed and stood up, shaking his head at Evan. "I'm surprised, and at the same time, I'm not. It's totally your style to lay something like this on us out of nowhere." He pulled Evan into a rough hug. "Congrats, Prince Pretty."

Evan chuckled. "Thanks."

Brad turned to Jesse next. He caught him by the front of the shirt and yanked him into his arms. "And you, good work on getting his wild ass to settle down."

"Well, it *is* all my good work *on* his wild ass that's settled him down."

Evan, Brad, and Julian burst out with laughter.

Chuckling with them, Jesse looked at Kenny and Greg. To his surprise, Greg looked more shocked than angry. He aimed his gaze at Kenny, and at his stoic expression, his light mood turned leaden.

"Why are you doing this?" Kenny asked.

"I think that's obvious," Jesse said. "Because I love him. And I'm guessing from your reaction, you don't agree."

"Whether I agree or not isn't going to make a damn bit of difference, will it? You'll still just go ahead and do whatever the hell you want."

Jesse willed his voice to remain calm. "It's not like you didn't know this was coming."

"Yeah, but you've always led us to believe it was a long way away. What about our careers? What you do affects all of us. Are you even thinking of us and our futures? How goddamn selfish can you be?"

Jesse's calm façade crumbled. "How goddamn selfish am I? Why don't you ask yourself the same fucking question! Have you ever stopped to think for a moment how hard things are for me and Evan?"

Kenny pushed off the couch to get on equal standing with Jesse. "It's not like you guys don't get to see each other! For Christ's sake, you live together! But that's not enough for you, is it? Nothing ever is! Whenever you get one thing, you want more and more and more, and damn to hell anyone who tries to get in your way!"

"You're damn right! No one is going to stand in my way of marrying him!"

"I don't even understand why you want to do this! What's the freakin' point? It's not even recognized here! It's a meaningless thing to do!"

Jesse's voice rose to a deafening roar. "What you call meaningless is the most important thing I plan to do in my life! And it doesn't matter who recognizes it! There are only two people in the world who are important in recognizing our marriage, and that's me and Evan!"

Never had Evan seen such fury in Jesse, and fearing the situation was getting out of control, he gently but firmly grasped

Jesse's upper arm. He laid his other hand on Jesse's shoulder and willed his voice to be soft and soothing. "Jess, calm down. We can't work this out if everyone's shouting."

Jesse turned a sharp look on him.

Evan nodded, acknowledging Jesse's unspoken thought. "I know. Usually you're the one trying to calm me down from throwing someone into a wall, but this is different. This is Kenny. He's been at your side since you were six years old. You don't want to do something you'll regret later."

Jesse looked back to Kenny. "It's because he's been at my side since I was six years old that I would expect him to understand and support me."

Kenny straightened his posture, annoyance filled his countenance. "All I've ever done is support you, even when you kicked people out of the band without talking to me about it. Yeah, I'd bitch at you about it, but I always stood by whatever you wanted. But now you've taken it too far. It was one thing when we were playing little shitty clubs not making any money. Now we're a world known band and it's millions you're throwing away!"

"So that's what this is about?" Jesse spat. "Money?"

"Yeah, money! You might think it's no big deal because you've got him to fall back on," Kenny pointed at Evan, "but the rest of us need to live on our own!"

Jesse lunged toward Kenny, his movement so fast Evan nearly lost his hold on him, but managed to pull him back.

Julian leaped between Jesse and Kenny, standing with his arms widespread, one hand on Jesse's chest, the other directed at Kenny as if to hold him back, though Kenny made no attempt to move toward Jesse. "Enough! Both of you!" He turned to Jesse. "I can understand how hurtful Kenny's words are to you, Jess, but the two of you have gone through too much together to argue like this." He looked at Kenny. "And you, shame on you for saying such things to him. A wedding is a time to rejoice. *Union* is the entire point of a marriage, and not just for those who are wedding each other, but for all the participants in the ceremony."

Brad faced Kenny. "He's right, man. No one's going to have it harder than these two when they come out. They don't need shitty attitudes going into this."

"My attitude is shitty?" Kenny screeched.

"Yes, Kenny, it is."

Everyone turned at the sound of Greg's voice. Jesse had forgotten he was there with how quiet he was.

Greg rose from his chair and walked toward them. "You should be more supportive, Kenny. With everything that's happened over the past couple years, with the rumors about Jesse and Evan that threatened your careers early on, Jesse never once faltered in doing everything he could in seeing to Conquest's success, and I don't think he would've fought so hard then only to let it all go now."

"Greg," Evan said softly.

Greg held up one hand. "I know, I know. I'm going against everything I've always said to you both, but this is different. If this is what you want and you're ready to make this commitment to each other, to hold you back wouldn't just be wrong, it'd be the worst type of cruelty." He laid his hand on Evan's shoulder, giving it a squeeze. "There was a time when I once told you to forsake love to protect Jesse's career. Now I'm telling you grab it with both hands and don't let go. Money, music, what the hell does any of it mean if you have to live in misery? And if there's one thing I've seen from you two, it's you could be sharing a cardboard box in the dead of winter with one blanket between you, but you'd both be happy because you would be together."

He raised his hand to Evan's cheek. "I'm proud of you, son. Congratulations."

Jesse smiled as he looked at Evan. Evan's eyes shone with dampness. So often Evan only allowed others to see two emotions from him, happiness and anger. To give everyone a glimpse at his vulnerability made a burst of pride surge through Jesse.

Evan stepped forward and wrapped Greg in his arms. He spoke, his voice soft. "Will you be my best man?"

"I'd be honored," Greg said.

Evan lingered in Greg's arms for a few moments, then pulled back. He took a deep breath, and Jesse saw he was collecting his composure once again.

Evan turned to Kenny. "I understand your concerns about money and your career, but do you honestly think you'll have to stop playing just because he and I are going to come out? You guys have made your mark, the world already knows you. Even if you lose a few fans because they can't stand the idea of enjoying music created by an openly gay singer, don't you think just as many will turn to your music for the same thing?

"We're not going at this stupidly, Kenny. When we publicly announce our relationship, it's going to start a bidding war between tabloids and entertainment shows to get the exclusives on us. Our relationship, our story is going to be everywhere, and do you know what that means? More publicity for Conquest than you've ever dreamed. You guys are going to sell singles and albums just from people trying to satisfy their curiosity on who Jesse is and what his music sounds like if they've never heard of Conquest before, which means more new fans. Can't you see how it could all snowball into bringing you guys greater success?"

Kenny snorted and glanced away. "It sounds like it could work in theory."

"In theory my ass," Jesse blurted out. "Kenny, you can think I'm selfish as much as you want, but what you don't see is all I've sacrificed for everyone else's happiness and success. If it was up to me, from the very first day I stepped before the cameras I would've been open about who I am and who I love. But I listened to what everyone else wanted to get us to where we are today and even more so, to make sure I wouldn't hurt Ev's career. But now he's retiring and we're a multi-Platinum band, so it's my turn to be happy and be myself wherever I go. What you need to do is think about what it'd be like for you if you had to hide being straight, and if you found a woman you loved, what it'd be like to hide it from everyone but a handful of people."

"It'd suck," Kenny mumbled.

"To put it mildly." Jesse's voice softened. "I know how this can make you guys nervous over what it could mean for our careers, but you have to know I wouldn't let them end. Even if at the worst we lose most of our fans and Evan's fans go against me, so long as there is one person out there willing to listen, then I'll keep singing. But that's not how it'll be. It's true we won't stay at the level of popularity we are now, because we're going to rise above. I won't be defeated."

Minutes ticked by before Kenny's barely audible voice broke the silence. "I'm sorry I said you guys getting married was pointless."

Jesse fixed him with a stare. Kenny looked at him, and when Jesse said nothing, flicked his gaze away.

Julian took Jesse's hand, raising his voice to be cheerful as if to distract from the tension. "You said you're going to Montpelier. I've been there and to Vermont several times, it's lovely. What are your plans so far and are we invited?"

"Of course you're invited." Jesse's gaze moved to Kenny. "All of you."

Kenny visibly relaxed at Jesse's words.

Jesse flicked his head toward the door. "Let's go down to the studio and I'll fill you guys in on what we have planned so far while we get ready to work."

Evan moved to Jesse's side, Brad, Julian, and Greg followed after him, Kenny trailing further behind them.

They entered Studio B, and Evan caught Jesse's hand. He leaned forward to kiss him on the cheek and whispered, "Are you okay?"

Jesse summoned a smile for him. "Yeah."

Evan raised Jesse's hand to his lips and placed a kiss in his palm. Jesse led everyone to the live room, chatting about their plans as they readied the instruments for the day of recording. Evan watched how neither Jesse nor Kenny looked at each other and hoped things would calm between them.

Chapter Thirty-three

At the judge's cue, Brandon offered Evan's wedding band to Jesse, Greg held Jesse's match toward Evan. On Jesse's side of the aisle, standing next to Brandon, was Kenny, and after him, Julian. On Evan's side, Greg, JJ, and Brad formed a line. Each man was dressed in a black Armani tux. Shunichi sat on a bench, recording the ceremony, and next to him was Greg's wife, Crystal, Greg's daughter, Krista, who had grown up following Evan around to his concerts and who he looked at as a younger sister, and next to Krista, was JJ's wife, Rebecca.

Jesse rested his hand lightly under Evan's and slid the titanium and gold band onto his left ring finger. Evan took Jesse's hand next and glided the ring into place on Jesse's.

The judge, who at first was stunned to see the two famed singers come before her, smiled at them. "By the power invested in me by the State of Vermont, I now pronounce you legally wed."

For a brief instant, Jesse's head spun. Were the words real? Was it true? Or was this just a dream? Though he doubted his status as awake, the proof embraced his left ring finger, and even more so, stood before him. The warmth of Evan's hands in his could be nothing more than reality, and his eyes were too brilliant of a blue to be conjured by even a dream. Jesse gazed at the smile on Evan's lips, and at the same moment as Evan, he leaned forward, meeting him in a tender kiss.

His lips still on Evan's, Jesse whispered, "I love you, Ev."

Evan drew Jesse's breath into his body. "I love you too, Jess."

They eased back, though their gazes remained on each other. Slowly they turned to the judge, giving her their sincere thank you. Everyone took turns embracing them, Kenny jostled Jesse and they both laughed, their fight days before forgotten. Hand in hand with the group behind them, Jesse and Evan followed a security guard to a back exit of the courthouse. They walked out to two white limousines waiting for them, Jesse, Evan, Brandon, and Shunichi going to the front one, while the others jumped in the second.

Shunichi laid his arm around Brandon's shoulders, gazing at Jesse and Evan seated across from them with Jesse tucked against Evan's side, and Evan holding him close. "That was one of the most beautiful things I've ever witnessed."

Jesse grinned at him. "It's your turn next."

Shunichi looked at Brandon. An unspoken agreement passed between them through their gazes.

Brandon reluctantly broke his gaze with Shunichi to bring it to Jesse. "He's still learning all my flaws. Once he knows them and still isn't scared away, then it'll be our turn. Maybe even Illinois will allow it by then."

Shunichi laughed. "Just how many flaws do you have it'll take me that long to learn them?"

They joined Shunichi's laughter.

Brandon spoke through his chuckling. "I know you guys wanted to take off right away, and I know it was a little risky, but we got you a cake. You just can't have a wedding without cake. We had it sent to our suite at the hotel. I wish you guys didn't have to be so incognito. There are going to be a lot of disappointed people that you didn't do a big ceremony."

Jesse sighed. "I know. But this wasn't about pleasing other people. It was about us, and for once doing what we wanted. And all the most important people in our lives are here. We couldn't ask for more than that. If we would've come out before getting married, our wedding would've turned into a media circus, and we didn't want that. By staying quiet, we actually get to enjoy each other and our day."

His eyes damp, Brandon gave him a warm smile. "I'm so proud of you. Of your strength, of all the things you've accomplished, of who you've chosen to spend your life with." He let out a couple rough chuckles. "And maybe I'm mourning too, because now I really don't have to worry about you so much and I don't know what I'll do with all the extra time that'll leave me."

Jesse leaned across the space between them and pulled Brandon into a hug. "I'm sure I'll still find plenty of ways to make you worry about me."

Brandon nodded, allowing joyous tears to fall as he embraced Jesse.

The limo slowed to a halt outside a lavish hotel. The group hastened inside, their strides carrying them past the few curious onlookers in the lobby quicker than people could recognize them and pull out their camera phones. The elevator took them to the top floor and Brandon and Shunichi's suite.

Brandon walked across the expansive living room to the kitchen and went to the refrigerator. He lifted out a circular three-tier cake covered in white frosting resting on a silver platter. He carried it to the living room and set it on an ornate cherry table.

Jesse gazed at the cake, each tier edged in white and pink roses made of frosting. Atop it, two fine porcelain white swans faced each other, their beaks touching, their necks arched to form a heart, and two men's gold wedding bands laid over their necks to rest on their bodies. He looked up at Brandon. "It's beautiful. But you shouldn't have been so extravagant with just the few of us."

Brandon shrugged and handed him a silver cake cutter. "You're only going to get married once…hopefully."

"Absolutely!" Jesse retorted, then paused. "Well, I should rephrase that. I might get married twice, but always to the same man. If Illinois ever allows same-sex marriage, we'll do it again there." He looked to Evan. "Then we'll throw a huge ceremony, won't we?"

Evan smiled and laid his hand over Jesse's on the cake cutter. "Yeah, we will."

Jesse positioned the cutter on the cake, and together, he and Evan cut into it. Shunichi stood back with the camcorder focused on them. Kenny snapped shots with a digital camera. Jesse slid the first slice onto a plate of china and scooped some upon a fork. Evan also gathered a bite on a fork, and they fed each other, their gazes never wavering from the other's, their lips never losing their smiles.

Brandon went to a stereo and hit play.

Jesse recognized the first notes sounded by gentle violins as Pachelbel's Canon. "You remembered our song."

"Of course I did. You can't have a wedding without at least one dance, too."

Jesse turned to Evan. Evan took his hand and led him to the open space of the living room. As Evan's arms slid around his lower back, Jesse stepped as close to him as possible and wrapped his arms around Evan's waist. He laid his chin on Evan's shoulder and closed his eyes, letting Evan guide him in slow, shuffling movements.

Shunichi propped the camcorder so it stayed recording where they danced, then reached for Brandon's hand. Brandon took it and walked with him to dance beside his little brother and new brother-in-law.

Brad turned to Julian and offered his hand. "Would you give a straight boy a dance?"

Julian chuckled softly as he dried his moist eyes with a silk kerchief. "Of course."

As Brad and Julian joined the others, Greg glanced at Kenny out the corner of his eye. "You know I like you, Kenny, but don't even bother asking."

Kenny snapped another picture. "Don't worry, Greg. I like you, too, but not that much."

Crystal cleared her throat. "You could think about asking your wife."

Greg grinned at her. "I was just trying to avoid getting yelled at if I stepped on your Manolo Blahniks like at the last wedding we went to."

She gave him a playful swat and took his hand as they moved out with the others, JJ and Rebecca following.

Kenny threw a tentative glance at Krista. "I don't suppose you would, maybe, like to dance with me?"

Krista offered her hand to him. "I'd love to, Kenny."

Jesse smiled at seeing everyone dancing around him, all sharing in the glow of their happiness. He realized everything he ever dreamed to achieve with his career was nothing compared to this moment.

The song came to a soft conclusion, though Evan and Jesse remained embraced. Evan took in a slow, deep breath and raised his head as if coming out of a trance. He glanced at the clock in the room, then back to Jesse. "I don't want to end this, but we should probably get changed so we can go."

Jesse nodded, then with everyone following, left for his and Evan's suite up the hall. After changing from their tuxes into more comfortable clothing for the long flight to Greece, Jesse turned to the group. "Thank you, guys, for all you've done."

"Thank you for letting us share this day with you," Julian said.

One by one, Jesse and Evan took turns embracing everyone.

Jesse wrapped his arms around Shunichi. "I can't tell you how happy I am to have my brother's soul-mate at my wedding."

Shunichi smiled at him. "Well, I'm feeling a little privileged that I'm one of the few witnesses to the marriage of the decade."

Jesse chuckled. "I don't know about decade, but maybe of the year. You have at the very least a couple million cash sitting in that camcorder right now."

Shunichi's eyes widened. "Tabloids don't pay that much, do they?"

Evan let out a disgusted huff. "When they know they'll earn it back plus gain a profit, they'll pay even more."

Shunichi glanced at the camera in his hands and sighed. "It's a shame I like you guys as much as I do. My damn sense of loyalty won't let me sell it."

Jesse laughed and went at last to Brandon. His voice hushed. "And I need to thank you more than anyone. It's because of you, how you always put me before yourself, that I'm where I am today and I've gotten the chance to find the man of my dreams."

His voice tight with emotion, Brandon said, "Don't thank me, Jess. I'm just so happy that I got to be here for you." He gave Jesse a teasing smirk. "Actually, I'm just happy that I was able to get you to this day at all with how you were sometimes."

"I wasn't always easy for you, was I?" Jesse pulled on his Chicago Bears baseball cap, bringing the bill down over his eyes. He picked up a pair of black lens sunglasses and slid them on, then glanced at Evan. "Shall we?"

"I'm ready." Evan also put on a pair of dark sunglasses and his New York Yankees cap.

He hefted up two of their bags. Jesse lifted the third and followed him to the door. After everyone said their farewells, wishes for safe travels, and final congratulations, Jesse and Evan headed to the elevator. Evan had already checked them out, and they exited to one limo ready to take them to the private jet that would whisk them to Greece.

In the limo, Evan laid his arm across the back of the seat, his fingers going automatically to Jesse's hair, playing with it. "It looks like we've made a clean getaway so far. I'm glad we kept things quiet for now, but for the first time in my life, I can't wait to stand before the cameras." He licked up the outside edge of Jesse's left ear to the silver hoop earring in the cartilage, then back down to suck on the silver hoops in Jesse's earlobe. "I may even go hunting the paparazzi down myself."

Jesse chuckled. "That'd freak them out, a celebrity hounding and stalking them for a change."

Evan brought his lips to Jesse's. Jesse groaned softly as Evan's tongue entered his mouth. He felt Evan press against him more firmly, and before he realized it, he was on his back on the plush leather seat. Evan eased on top of him, settling his hips between Jesse's thighs.

Jesse smiled through the kiss. "We're not going to make it to Greece before consummating our marriage, are we?"

"We might not even make it to the airport." Evan's lips moved to Jesse's throat, he spoke between the tender kisses. "I never realized how badly I wanted this, to have you one hundred percent mine."

Jesse weaved his fingers through Evan's hair. "I've always been one hundred percent yours."

"I know, but it feels different somehow." A playful smirk rose to Evan's lips. "You're really trapped by me now. It'll be a lot harder for you to get away."

"I'll never try to."

Jesse tightened his hand in a fist around Evan's hair and pulled him back down to his lips. Evan rolled his hips against him, pressing their erections together. Jesse slid both hands under Evan's shirt, savoring his warm, soft skin, yet how powerful and firm his body was beneath it. He drifted his touch lower, over Evan's hips, and stretched to reach his ass, taking each cheek in a clenching grip.

A rumbling groan left Evan. His head lifted, and Jesse raised up to lick and suck at his throat.

The sound of roaring plane engines leaked through the windows.

Evan fought to clear his head from the desire filling him. "I think we're nearly there."

"Maybe you are, but I'm not even close."

Evan laughed and pushed himself off Jesse. "I never want to hear you criticize my bad sense of humor again."

Jesse sat up. "Well, they do say married couples start to act alike after a while."

Evan gave him an affectionate bump on the shoulder with his shoulder, then looked to see the limo heading back to the hangers where the private planes were kept. With the help of the driver, they hauled their bags onto the luxury jet while the pilot and co-pilot disappeared into the cockpit.

Jesse moved to take a seat, but Evan caught his hand. He turned to him, noticing his Chicago Bears duffel bag over Evan's shoulder.

Evan walked backward up the aisle toward the back of the plane. "Now I know you haven't forgotten this jet has sleeping quarters."

"I remember when you were on the phone chartering it you checked that fact three times, but didn't bother asking anything about maintenance or pilot credentials."

"I just figured if we're going to crash, we might as well have a good time on the way down."

Jesse shook his head, chuckling as Evan led him into the sleeping quarters where a queen-sized bed took up almost the entire space.

Evan closed and locked the door. He retrieved lube from the duffel bag and tossed it on the bed. He turned to Jesse and stepped close enough for their bodies to touch. He rubbed his hands down Jesse's sides to his hips and lifted his shirt.

Jesse raised his arms to accommodate him. "Shouldn't we at least wait until takeoff? They always say to keep your seatbelts fastened and I'm not seeing any on that bed."

Evan tugged the button free on Jesse's jeans. "I think we'll be fine lying down, but if you want straps on the bed, I can tie some to it."

Jesse moved his hands under Evan's shirt. He put his lips to Evan's neck, kissing under his jaw while his hands floated up to his chest. "Not for this session."

Jesse pulled Evan's shirt over his head. Wrapping one arm around Evan's lower back, he pressed Evan against him and met his lips in a passion filled kiss. He caressed down Evan's sides to his waist and opened Evan's jeans. As Jesse's fingers hooked over the tops, Evan copied the movement, and together they shoved their pants down.

Jesse brought his hips closer, sliding his cock along Evan's. A soft sigh passed over Evan's lips, his eyes closed, his movements halted. Jesse pulled his hips back, then eased forward again, letting his cock glide over Evan's in excruciatingly slow movements. Evan's head fell back on his shoulders, his lips parted to allow a hushed rumble of pleasure to escape his throat. Jesse dipped his head low and traced Evan's neck with his tongue, going up to where it met his jaw and nipped the tender spot. Evan's throat trembled as he drew in a sharp intake of shaking breath.

Jesse nudged him toward the bed. Evan dropped down upon it and kicked off his shoes while pushing his jeans down his thighs. Jesse quickly removed his remaining clothing, grabbed the bottoms of Evan's jeans, and tugged them off for him.

Evan went to his back in the bed's center, pulling his legs up so his feet were flat on the mattress, his knees bent. He let his legs fall to the sides, leaving himself spread wide. Evan ran his right hand down his abdomen to his cock and gripped the solid shaft in a tight fist. He raised his left hand to his mouth. He inserted his index and middle fingers, and as he withdrew them, they shone with saliva. Evan brought his left hand down below his sac and touched his wet fingers to his hole. He rubbed small circular motions over it, moistening the outside, all the while his gaze stayed on Jesse.

Jesse knew Evan looked at him, yet he couldn't meet his gaze. He drank in the vision of Evan's right hand, strong and veined, moving in slow strokes up and down his shaft, his swollen cock head peeking above his grip. He gazed at Evan's hole, wet with saliva. But what captured his attention most was the titanium and gold band on Evan's left ring finger.

He looked up at Evan, and what he saw in Evan's eyes overpowered him more than physical desire. He had grown accustomed to seeing love and warmth in his azure eyes, but now it was different, deeper, and he knew they had entered a new stage of their life together.

Jesse climbed onto the bed. Evan wrapped Jesse in his arms. Jesse gently laid over him and brought his lips to Evan's, sending his love, devotion, joy, and desire through the kiss. As the long kiss ended, Jesse kept his lips touching Evan's and reached for the lube. He brought his slicked fingers to Evan's hole and tenderly stretched him. After only a few short moments, Evan said his name in a pleading whisper. Jesse pressed his cock head to Evan's entrance and pushed inside him.

Evan rolled his head to the side, all his breath rushing from him. He drew in another only to release it in a long, low groan as Jesse sank deeper inside him. Embracing Jesse with his arms and legs, Evan pressed their bodies together still more.

Jesse slowly thrust into him. He covered Evan's face and hair in gentle kisses, and pushed one arm beneath Evan's shoulders to hold him tighter. Through the PA, the pilot's voice sounded, though Jesse didn't comprehend the words. Minutes later, the jet lurched forward, lightly bumping down the runway. Jesse's instincts felt the speed of the jet increase, and his own pace quickened with it. The front of the jet tipped up as it left the ground, and for an instant, it seemed to him as if their bodies had surpassed gravity.

The jet surged skyward. Beneath him, Jesse felt Evan's body tense, his breath blew quicker against his neck. Evan's fingers clenched onto his back, the internal muscles in his tight channel clamped around his cock.

"Jess…Jesse," Evan panted between fast breaths. "I love you. I love you so much. I love you. I love you. I love you…" his last word ended with a deep shout. His body bucked up to Jesse's, his hips working as his cum pulsed out between them.

As Evan's climax left him, Jesse managed to thrust into him a few more times before his body surrendered to his own orgasm for several sweet seconds. He rested on Evan, soft moans leaving him on each fast exhale. He felt lightheaded, his mind continued to swim in the pleasure he'd just experienced. His senses slowly returned, and he nuzzled into Evan's hair.

"I love you, too," he lifted his head and looked into Evan's eyes, "my husband."

Evan squeezed Jesse to him, letting him feel his smile against his skin.

CHAPTER THIRTY-FOUR

Jesse gazed at the studio from the passenger seat of the ebony Aston Martin DBS as Evan steered toward the parking garage. His heart drummed a nervous cadence. They'd returned to Chicago two days prior, but wanting to linger in the afterglow of their honeymoon for a while longer, they'd stayed home. In his mind, he played out every scenario imaginable, and even some unimaginable, for how his fans, Evan's fans, the public in general, would react to the news of their relationship. The suspicions from long ago had never fully left people's minds, and with what happened to him, they resurfaced fresh, so maybe things would go smoothly...he hoped.

Jesse lowered his gaze to his left hand, clasped tightly with Evan's right and adorned with his rings; the first Evan had given him of white and yellow gold with its sparkling diamonds and never ending pattern of the Greek meander, and the second behind it, the titanium and gold band, simple in its beauty and powerful in its meaning.

Evan squeezed his hand. "Ready?"

Jesse flashed him a bright smile. "Let's do it."

Their hands parted to allow them to depart the car, then immediately joined again as Evan came to his side. Hand in hand, they walked from the parking garage. Jesse noticed one plus of having disappeared for nearly three weeks, only a handful of paparazzi loitered outside the studio. Many left two weeks prior for L.A. when a young actress started going through a very public, very embarrassing, and, for the photographers, very cash earning mental breakdown. It all made the suspicion of his and Evan's relationship rather bland. Though, he knew in a few short moments, it wouldn't stay that way.

The paparazzi stood almost calmly as he and Evan approached, until they caught sight of their clasped hands. Like hungry sharks having scented blood, they leaped into a frenzy, shouting questions, snapping photos with defying speed. Security wrangled them back and created a path for Jesse and Evan to reach the doors.

As they passed, one reporter called, "Hey, you guys keep walking around holding hands and we'll be calling you a couple again."

"Which is fine since you'd actually be hitting on the truth for once," Evan retorted.

Jesse smirked. And just like that, it was known. He never realized paparazzi were capable of being so quiet. For a split-second, it was almost as if they weren't there. But only for a split-second, as they recovered quickly and the questions flew.

Jesse and Evan stood with their backs to the studio doors, facing the reporters and encircled by security.

Evan held up his hand and signaled for silence. "We'll answer a few questions, but we can't answer what we can't hear, and you can't get your answers if you can't hear us. That said, I'll answer most of your questions now. Yes, I'm gay. Yes, I have been gay my whole life. No, none of the women I was ever connected with were my lovers. And yes, Jesse and are I in a monogamous relationship, and furthermore, we celebrated our two year anniversary on May seventh by getting married in Montpelier, Vermont."

Jesse's lips curved with mischief. "And in case his answers left any doubt, I'm gay, too."

For a second time, silence took hold of the paparazzi. One finally managed to stammer out, "M-married? How? How did you do it with no one finding out?"

A sly grin spread over Evan's lips. "During the years that I took my extended hiatus from music, no one could track me down. You didn't really think I couldn't do that again, did you?"

More questions bombarded them, asking the history of their relationship, how they met, how long they had lived together, and many more. They let most of the questions go unanswered so as to leave enough mystery around them to be valuable for a publication or show to want the exclusive on them. From the midst of the reporters, Evan saw a light brown head pushing toward the front. He recognized the young paparazzo, Paul McClain, and gestured to him to ask the next question.

"Why now? Why didn't you do it back when the rumors first began?"

Jesse's gaze settled on Paul. "Because my career was so young, and it still is, but when we first met, I hadn't even broken onto the music scene yet. Evan was concerned our relationship could hinder my success, because let's face it, there are a lot of people who aren't comfortable with homosexuality, much less a man being brazen about it like how I can be. And at that time, Ev was planning a comeback. On my part, I feared hurting his career. So we stayed silent and loved each other in secret. But we don't want to keep our relationship a secret any longer. We love each other too much to hide it."

Another reporter yelled out, "Does your timing have anything to do with the attack on you, Jesse?"

"Partially. We were planning on confessing our relationship in the near future, but what happened to me did play a role in moving it up. We want to be able to be close to each other without worrying what people think."

"Jesse, were you attacked because someone discovered you're gay?"

"Since we don't know who jumped me and Kenny, we can't say for sure what their motivation was, but it's doubtful. More than likely it was just punks bored on a Friday night since it started out with my tires being slashed."

Evan added, "That doesn't mean we're not anticipating hostile backlash from our speaking publicly about our relationship. I'm well aware that in the eleven years I've been a known performer, I've put up the front of being straight and now coming out could anger, upset, and confuse a lot of my fans. I've hurt them by my charade, and for that, I deeply apologize. And even though I know I have no right to ask anything of them, I beg that they try to understand. Tonight, I'll be posting a letter on my official website in an attempt to explain more clearly, as Jesse will also on the Conquest official website, though," he turned a playful smirk on Jesse, "his will probably be shorter because I don't think anyone ever really bought he was straight."

Jesse burst out laughing with the media joining him.

More questions came, but Evan held up his hand. "I'm sorry, guys. We didn't mean for this session to last as long as it has. We just wanted to let people know we're a couple and answer the most immediate questions. Now, I've got to get him working since I'm Conquest's new manager."

Jesse grinned at Evan's evilness for dropping another juicy tidbit that sent the reporters into hysterics, then not answering their questions, making it clear Evan was toying with them.

They turned to enter the studio, and Paul yelled, "At least give us a kiss before you go! Show how sincere you are!"

Evan looked to Jesse. They turned toward each other. Jesse slid his arms around Evan's back. Evan wrapped one arm around Jesse's waist and buried the fingers of his other hand in Jesse's hair. Each brought his head forward, and when their lips were a fraction apart, they parted them and glided their tongues over each other before their mouths closed together.

Through the passion of the kiss, Jesse heard cheers go up from the paparazzi, more because they were rejoicing in the dollars this would bring than celebrating their coming out. As the kiss drew to a close, Evan tipped his head down and laid another tender kiss on Jesse's neck.

"That seemed genuine enough!" joked one reporter.

"It should," Evan said, "because I love him."

Jesse smiled, his gaze unwavering from Evan's. "And I love him."

Jesse took Evan's hand again, and waving to the reporters, led him into the studio. Having seen their cars in the garage, Jesse knew his band members were inside. They came upon Studio A, saw the door open and the studio empty. He hadn't seen or talked to anyone in BHD since his attack, though Robbie called Kenny to ask if they both were okay and Kenny told him Robbie felt horrible for what happened.

He heard voices drifting out the open door of Studio B. They swung in the control room to find his band and Jeremy chatting with Kyler and Robbie.

Kenny looked up as they walked in. "Dude, you're twenty minutes late. I would've thought you could at least make it on time today since you've been doing nothing but lounging around the past two weeks."

Julian hopped up and greeted Jesse with a hug. "You look wonderful. Playing in Greece did you good."

"And I'm guessing you don't have any tan lines," Brad teased.

"Not a one," Jesse said. "And I'm sorry we're late. We got tied up making out in front of the paparazzi."

A large smile glowed over Julian's face. "Then you did it?"

Evan wrapped his arms around Jesse's shoulders from behind. "We did. And it felt so damn good!"

Kyler stared at them. "What did you do? What are you guys talking about?"

Evan turned a smirk on him. "We just informed the media that we're a married couple." He took Jesse's left hand and stretched it toward Kyler, who was sitting on the couch beside Robbie. Evan stuck his left hand beside Jesse's.

Kyler and Robbie both gaped at their hands.

Jesse barely managed to keep from bursting out in laughter. He'd never seen Kyler look so utterly stunned, and it seemed he was proven wrong in believing Kyler couldn't be speechless.

Robbie snapped his gaze up to them. "You're serious? You guys really got married? You really came out just now?"

Jesse nodded once. "Yep. It's probably shooting across the Internet and around the world that Evan and I belong to each other."

Robbie sprang up. "That's awesome!" He pulled Jesse into a hug. "Your courage..." he shook his head, "you guys are amazing. Congratulations."

"Thanks," Jesse said, releasing Robbie as he went next to hug Evan.

Kyler slowly stood. "Well, I guess now with all the publicity that'll be around you, it'll be damn hard to keep up with you guys on the charts."

Robbie whipped his head around to him. "That's all you can say? They express ultimate commitment to each other, and you think of album sales?" He let out a huff. "And for some reason I'm surprised. I should've guessed your reaction."

"I'm sorry," Kyler said softly.

For some reason, Jesse felt he was apologizing more to Robbie than to him or Evan.

Kyler faced Jesse. "I'm happy for you guys, I really am. It took balls to do what you did. I admire that." He shot a glance at Evan while pointing at Jesse. "Is it alright if I give him a congratulatory hug? You're not going to try and beat my ass if I touch him, are you?"

Evan gave him a smile that held no warmth. "Just this once and keep your hands above his waist."

Kyler rolled his eyes and turned back to Jesse, opening his arms wide. "Congrats, Jess."

Jesse stepped into his arms. "Thank you."

Kyler released him and looked at Evan. Jesse could feel the tension between them, neither seeming thrilled at the idea of hugging the other. Evan extended his hand, ending the pretense for an embrace. Kyler took it, offering his congrats to Evan as well.

As he released Evan's hand, Kyler took a deep breath and faced Robbie, presenting his brightest smile to him. "Hey, why don't we head out to an early lunch?"

"It's not even eleven o'clock," Robbie said.

"Okay, then it'll be brunch, or a snack, or something. Whatever you want."

Robbie gazed at him for a moment. He shook his head, a soft smile on his lips. "Alright. Let's go." He looked to Jesse and Evan once more. "Congratulations again, guys. I'm so happy for you."

Jesse nodded to Robbie. "Thanks." When Kyler and Robbie left, he spun toward Evan. "I'm too pumped up to concentrate on music now! We should all go out, too!"

Evan laid a slap on Jesse's ass. "Get your butt in there and start singing. Now more than ever you need to push out a great album. We'll all go out tonight."

Jesse let out an exaggerated sigh and turned away from him. "You're no fun."

Evan tackled him from behind, sending Jesse into instant laughter as he placed playful kisses on his neck. "This is what I get for not asking more about a job before I take it, a pushy brat for an artist."

Jesse broke from his hold and pointed at him while walking into the live room. "And for a husband. Don't forget that."

A loving smile touched Evan's lips. "I never will."

CHAPTER THIRTY-FIVE

Standing in the control room, Jesse wrapped his arms around Evan's neck as Evan clasped him loosely around the waist. In the two weeks since openly declaring their relationship, things exploded. For their part, he and Evan agreed to have Greg act as their agent and handle things for them, which equated into Greg selling exclusive rights to their first official interview for a sum that made even their jaws drop. They were booked for three photo shoots together, they had a meeting for a joint website, which went live three days after their chat with the paparazzi, and numerous other interviews with magazines and TV were set up.

Jesse couldn't deny his nervousness that being in the public eye so much would burn people out on them, but every tidbit tossed out about them was eagerly gobbled up, so maybe his nervousness was unfounded. They were dubbed a "gay power couple" and "gay royalty," both tags making him laugh hysterically when he heard them. The media was nothing if not extravagant. There was a burst of paparazzi around the studio and the entrance to their home, but with the exclusives already sold, most moved on to more profitable fodder.

For the most part things went far better than he imagined, though there certainly was backlash. Just as his and Evan's website went up, numerous others spoke out against them. He disregarded them as crackpots who when they spoke their narrow-minded bigotry made themselves look foolish. He saw some televangelist on the news preaching how people like him and Evan were the source of society's moral degradation. As much as he would've liked to take claim to such a thing, not even he could accomplish such a grand feat. He knew more challenges were to come, but so far, reactions were more positive than negative; it was just the naysayers whined the loudest.

The biggest plus was that his motivation soared to new heights for putting out Conquest's best work. His energy transferred to his band members, and now the album was three-quarters finished. With how they were rolling, the album would be complete, pressed and packaged with the first single ready to hit in August, the full album, *No Fear,* out in September. For their first single, they were going to rock the world with "Twisted Destiny." He decided to hold "No Fear" back to be the second single since there would be no guesswork behind the song's meaning now and he didn't want people to think he was marketing off his and Evan's relationship.

Only one dark spot marred his happiness. The police never discovered who attacked him and Kenny. Since coming out with Evan, most people drew the conclusion that his sexuality made him a target, despite him saying he didn't believe that to be the case. What shocked him was when a video emerged showing every detail of the fight. With people now having the visual imagery, sympathy for him doubled.

Jesse gazed into Evan's eyes. None of it really mattered. What mattered most stood before him, looking at him with love. Even if the people behind his and Kenny's attack were never caught, he'd always feel strong and safe with Evan at his side.

"I wish you were going to lunch with us." Jesse said.

"I know, gorgeous, but I've got to talk to Greg about some of the publicity stuff I'm planning for you, and he needs to go over the interviews he's scheduled for us together."

"I could go with you."

"I don't think there's any reason for both of us to suffer. Besides," Evan grinned and moved his lips closer to Jesse's, "I *am* your manager. It's my responsibility to handle the boring stuff."

"And what a good manager you are." Jesse brought their lips together.

Kenny blurted out, "Are we gonna go, or are you gonna play kissy face all day?"

His romantic thoughts interrupted, Jesse turned an unappreciative glance on Kenny. "I'm coming. Chill your ass."

He looked back to Evan. "Make sure you eat something. I know how you and Greg get when you're talking business."

"I'll grab something on my way to his office." Evan placed another kiss on Jesse's lips.

Jesse headed out of the control room, smiling over his shoulder. "I love you."

"I love you too, gorgeous."

Evan sat back against the control desk, mentally timing Jesse's departure. When he felt certain Jesse had left the studio, he pushed off the desk and walked from the room, turning left toward Studio A. He knocked on the closed door, then opened it without waiting for someone to admit him.

The members of Black Heart Down sat in the control room, discussing one of their songs with Jeremy. They all looked at Evan. Evan's gaze rested on Kyler.

Kyler rose and started for the door. "I'll be back in a little bit, guys."

Robbie looked from Evan to Kyler. "Is everything alright?"

Kyler smiled at him. "Everything's perfect."

He closed the door and fell in beside Evan as he turned toward the depths of the studio. For a few strides, they walked in silence.

Evan drew a deep breath. "Thanks for doing this."

"Are you kidding? I've been dying for this since you came to me. But on a separate topic, I have to warn you, I'm going to be *accidentally* losing one of my sex tapes to the media soon to keep up with the publicity that Conquest is getting from the Jesse and Evan Love Fest."

Evan chuckled. "You do whatever you think you have to."

They rounded a corner toward Studio C. Laughter leaked through the cracked open door. Evan stepped through with Kyler behind him, who shut the door tight and flicked the lock into place. The laughter in the room ended. Three pairs of hostile eyes focused on Evan, a fourth nervous set darted about.

Evan strode further into the room. "It's been a while, boys." His gaze moved over the members of Swiller, pausing at length on Trent, Matt, and Joey. His eyes skimmed over Eric, but Evan already determined he wasn't a target unless he made himself one. He saw their looks bouncing from him to Kyler and watched as realization entered their expressions.

"You know," Evan continued, "I've been wondering something these past few weeks. How did it feel jumping a guy three to one? Did it make you feel like big men?"

"It wasn't three to one!" Joey blurted out.

Trent whipped his head toward Joey. "Shut the fuck up, moron!"

Kyler moved to Evan's side. "Come on now. There's no need to be shy and hide what happened. You guys already spilled everything to me, and I'm sure even you guys are able to figure out I've told him. But since I might have missed a detail or two, why don't you tell him in your own words?"

"We ain't gotta tell that fag shit!" Trent snapped.

Kyler shrugged. "I guess we'll just go straight to the ass beating then."

Trent, Matt, and Joey stayed motionless.

"What's the matter?" Evan mocked. "You can't fight without your masks on, or are you waiting until you've finished pissing yourselves?"

"Fuck you!" Matt lunged for Evan.

Knowing Evan's main target, Kyler leaped forward and drove his fist into Matt's stomach. Air rushed from Matt's body through his mouth.

Joey and Trent launched their attack a split second after Matt. Evan swept to the side, allowing Joey's momentum to carry him by, and as he passed, Evan swung his cocked elbow around and impacted hard with the back of the stocky drummer's head. The hit made Joey stumble, his feet tangled together, and he went face down to the floor.

Evan whirled around to see Trent's fist blazing toward his face. He ducked his head to the side, and at the same moment, grabbed Trent's stretched out arm and jerked him forward, drawing up his knee and slamming it into Trent's stomach. Trent doubled over. Evan clenched a fistful of his long hair, ripped his head back, and slammed his fist twice into Trent's face. Trent remained standing only by the grip Evan had on his hair. Evan released him, and Trent dropped to the ground.

Evan turned to see how Kyler fared. Matt and Joey lay rolling at his feet, Kyler shaking out his right hand.

Kyler lightly kicked Joey's arm. "Little fucker's got the hardest jaw I ever hit."

Evan looked at Eric. "Not a scrapper, boy? I noticed you weren't on the video."

Eric slunk back toward the control desk. "I was sick that night."

"More likely a bolt of sense hit you," Kyler said. "Well, this was fun, but I really should get back to work—"

"Fucking liar," Trent groaned, spitting blood onto the floor. "That's what he is."

Evan turned a lethal glare on Trent and squatted down at his head. "If you have something to say, say it."

"He let me believe he was straight. Then we saw you two, all gropin' and flirtin' on each other. He fucking lied to me. I just wanted to be his friend, and he lied to me from the moment I met him."

Evan's rage rose again. "And if he would've told you the first day you met him that he was gay, would it have changed anything? And when you found out about us, if you wanted to be his friend so badly, why didn't you talk to him about it?"

Trent looked away from him, his lips clamped shut.

Evan stood and looked back to Kyler. "Let's go."

Kyler unlocked the door. They walked out, both stopping in mid-stride at the sight of Jesse and Robbie rounding the corner.

Evan watched as shock, suspicion, and hurt flashed over Jesse's features.

Knowing his index and middle knuckles were red from the fight, Evan tucked his hands behind his back and smiled at Jesse. "Hey, I thought you took off already."

"We got all the way to Kenny's truck before he realized he left his keys in the control room." Jesse stopped before them. "We came back in and ran into Robbie and the guys. He said you two took off together down this way." He attempted to look around Evan's shoulder to Studio C. "What's going on?"

Evan's mind worked frantically to find words, any words, but it stayed horribly blank.

Seeing Evan was speechless, Jesse darted around him toward the control room. "What the hell happened?" He disappeared inside. Robbie shot after him.

Kyler called Robbie's name in a pleading voice that he ignored. He sighed and turned to Evan. "I told you we should've done this somewhere else."

Already rushing after Jesse, Evan didn't respond.

Jesse and Robbie stood in the middle of the control room, their gazes moving with equal slowness over Trent, Matt, and Joey. Eric had managed to help Joey sit up, Matt clambered into a chair. Trent had worked himself as far as sitting up, though was hunched forward. He pressed the bottom of his shirt to his mouth in an attempt to staunch the blood flowing from his split lip, though more soaked his shirt from his bleeding nose.

Jesse hastened toward Trent and extended his hand toward him. "Here, I'll help you up."

Trent slapped his hand away. "I don't need your fucking help!"

"Jess," Evan stepped up behind him and laid his hand on his shoulder, "it was these three who jumped you and Kenny."

Jesse spun toward him. "How do you know that?"

"It's a long story." Evan lightly tugged Jesse's shoulder. "Just leave them alone and come with me."

Jesse remained in place. He looked around the room at the battered bodies, Robbie shouting at Kyler, "I can't believe you! You always do shit like this! Do you want to end up with your ass beat or killed? Is that what you want?"

Jesse looked away from Kyler's reprimand to focus on Trent. He stepped away from Evan and grabbed Trent by his upper arm. "Get up."

Trent weakly attempted to shake Jesse's arm off. "Leave me alone!"

"You can't stay on the floor." Jesse half hauled Trent to his feet. "Now get your ass up."

Unable to resist Jesse's greater strength, Trent scrambled to his feet. "You're a liar. You told me you had been with girls. You let me think you were straight."

Jesse steered him toward a chair. "I let you think what you wanted about me, and I don't recall ever specifically saying I've been with girls, but just for the record, I have."

Trent snapped his head toward him.

Jesse gave him a wry smile. "But also for the record, it was before I accepted that I preferred guys, which was when I was a teenager, so it's been a while."

Trent collapsed down in the chair Jesse directed him to.

Jesse took a deep breath and sighed loudly. "Trent, you and I, we haven't gotten along since day one. A lot of it was because of your prejudices, but a lot of it was because of my lack of patience with you. But I realized after we had our first fight, you're just immature and ignorant, and I'm guessing I'm probably the first gay guy you've ever actually talked to."

Trent's gaze quickly lifted to him, then slowly lowered again, letting Jesse know the truth of his statement.

"That doesn't excuse you," Jesse continued. "And it doesn't mean I wouldn't love to punch you in your face right now for what you did to me, but even though you won the battle that night, I want you to understand fully and clearly, you did *not* win the war against me. That victory became mine the day I walked in front of the cameras holding Evan's hand and telling the world we belong to each other. Your attack on me didn't weaken me. It made me stronger."

Trent lifted his stunned gaze to him.

Jesse turned around and faced Evan.

Evan summoned a tentative smile. "Jess…"

Jesse silenced him with a glare and stormed past him. Robbie exited with Jesse, leaving Kyler and Evan to trail after them. As they came upon the chill-out room, Robbie broke away to go inside, calling, "Later, Jess."

Jesse flicked his head in acknowledgement and kept his direction to leave the studio. From the single set of footsteps behind him, he knew Kyler had diverted to follow Robbie.

"Jess, wait," Evan said.

Jesse kept walking. As he came upon Studio A, he saw his band members lingering outside the door with Adam and Kevin of Black Heart Down. He marched by them and their confused faces without a word.

"Hey," Kenny yelled after him, "what's going on?"

"Nothing," Jesse replied without looking back. "Go to lunch without me."

He reached the doors leading outside and slammed them open.

From behind, he heard Evan say, "Jess, will you please stop."

Jesse continued into the parking garage. He reached his F430 and spun toward Evan. "How could you do this to me?"

Evan shook his head in confusion. "I did it to protect you, to make sure they'd never try something like that again."

"I don't need your goddamn protection!" Jesse's voice echoed through the garage. Pain filled him to the point where he could hardly stand, could hardly breathe. "You lied to me! And not only that, you went to Kyler for help! You should've come to me!"

"There's no way I would've gotten you involved in this. I needed his help because he was the only one who could get close to them without making them suspicious." Evan sighed, knowing his words made no sense to Jesse, and reached for him. "Just let me explain."

Jesse jerked his arm away from Evan's outreached hand. He tore open the car door and climbed inside. As he fired it up, Evan opened the door.

"Jess, get out. We're not done talking."

"Yes, we are." He put the car in reverse and tried to close the door. Evan pulled against him. Jesse looked up at him. "Let go of the door and back away before you get hurt."

"No. I know you would never hurt me."

"I wish I could say the same thing about you."

Pain at Jesse's words loosened Evan's grip on the door. Jesse slammed it closed. Evan stumbled back from the Ferrari. Jesse whipped it out of the parking space and shot from the garage. Evan stood helpless, watching him vanish from sight.

CHAPTER THIRTY-SIX

Jesse stopped the F430 at a stop sign, wondering how exactly he ended up in Lincoln Park. He hadn't noticed the turns he took, yet it seemed his subconscious knew where he needed to go and guided him to Brandon.

Jesse looked at his cell phone on the passenger seat. Two missed calls. He knew they were from Evan. He had seen his name flash on the screen the first time, but the sound of Evan's voice singing the chorus to his ballad "One More Time" on his ringtone upset him with such force, he grabbed the phone and turned the sound off. Now he reached for it. Instead of calling Evan, he hit the number three to speed dial Brandon's cell. By the fifth ring, he decided his brother wasn't going to answer when right as the sixth started, Brandon's voice came through saying a breathless, "Hey."

"Do I even want to ask why you're out of breath?"

"I'm mowing the lawn, smart ass. It's a lot of freakin' work."

"You're...mowing the lawn?" Jesse said, his voice betraying his disbelief.

"Yeah. Shun's so busy giving lessons six days a week, the only time he has to do stuff like this is on his one day off, and even though I have to practically tie him down to make him sit still, I want to lighten his load as much as possible so he can rest."

Jesse snickered. "Yeah, like you tying him down will make him rest. I'm sure it does lighten his load, though."

Brandon laughed. "Shut up, pervert."

"I just can't believe my theatre freak brother is mowing a lawn."

"I used to mow all the time when I was living with mom and dad. Your prima donna ass sure as hell never did." Brandon took a deep breath, exhaled, and his voice became less breathless. "So what's going on?"

"You're not going to believe all the bullshit that went down. I was thinking about stopping over to talk, but if you're busy…"

"No, come on over. I need a break, anyway."

"Thanks. I'll be right there. I'm about five minutes away."

Jesse hung up and continued his route toward his brother and Shunichi's home. The dojo and house were impossible to miss for two reasons. The first, though all the buildings in the area had a suburban feel with lawns and trees, it had more yard space than the others and was elegantly landscaped. The second, its design made it look like it had been lifted from seventeenth century Japan and dropped in Lincoln Park.

The dojo, more visible from the road than the house, was made entirely of wood. The roof curved in a graceful downward sweep to the eaves, and rather than shingles, was covered in rounded black tiles. A wooden veranda wrapped around the dojo's perimeter. In front, stalks of leafy bamboo grew tall, mixed with rhododendrons.

Jesse turned the Ferrari into the gravel driveway. From the number of cars in the small parking lot, he assumed a lesson was going on, and when he coasted past the front, he saw through the large picture window white uniformed shadows moving inside. He continued down the right side of the dojo, past the tall privacy fence that hid the Japanese garden, and finally came upon the house, which mimicked the dojo's architecture.

Shunichi's white Tundra and Brandon's motorcycle were parked in the driveway since the two-and-a-half-car garage was full with Shunichi's Mustang and Brandon's Mercedes. As Jesse parked, an amused snort rattled from his nose at seeing his brother pushing a rickety, well-used and much-aged lawn mower down the side lawn. He climbed out, watching him for another moment before walking toward him.

Brandon looked up and turned the mower off. Unable to help himself, Jesse broke into laughter at the sight of his perpetually perfectly groomed older brother with a streak of dirt across his face, his hair disheveled, and grass sticking to his sweaty skin.

Brandon glowered at him. "I'm glad you're getting a good laugh out of this."

"It's just…you're so dirty!" Jesse choked out between laughs.

Brandon chuckled with him. "Well, it'd be easier if this thing wasn't older than me. I think this weekend Shun and I have to go looking for a new one. If I'm going to take this on as one of my chores, I need better equipment."

"Don't go buy one. We have a brand new riding mower sitting in the garage. Ev bought it the first summer in the house saying if you have a lawn, you should have a lawn mower, but he's never used it because we have the gardeners. Now he does nothing but complain about it taking up space. We'll give it to you guys."

"That'd be awesome." Brandon abandoned the mower and turned for the house. "Let's head in."

Jesse followed him up the steps to the veranda and went inside. As Brandon did, he removed his shoes in the sunken foyer, set them in a wooden rack, then stepped up the single stair to the living room. The interior was a mix of Japanese and Western flavor, and several of Brandon's possessions had found a home there, including the large stone Buddha, who watched over the house with his serene gaze. Jesse spied the jolly little Hotei smiling down from the fireplace mantel, and Brandon's tall shelves lined another wall filled with his DVDs.

Jesse looked at the shelves, shaking his head. "He must really love you to put up with your obsession."

"He likes watching movies as much as I do and gets just as excited as me when a new DVD comes in the mail. We can sit on the computer for hours browsing movies to buy on Amazon and CDJapan."

"You guys are scary perfect for each other."

"I know," Brandon said, wearing a wide smile. He turned toward the hall that led to the bedrooms. "I'm going to wash up real quick. Go ahead and get yourself something to drink."

On his way to the kitchen, Jesse glanced out the sliding glass door to the garden. He went to the refrigerator and pulled out a can of Pepsi, then took a seat at the oval oak kitchen table.

Brandon entered, his hair brushed, face washed, and a clean light blue tank top on. He grabbed a Pepsi for himself, then took a seat across from Jesse. "So what was the bullshit that went down? It must've been something pretty big if it kept you from the studio and you don't have Evan with you."

"That's because he was the cause of it!" Jesse launched into his story, though as he told it, he realized he really had no details other than what he personally witnessed. He didn't know how Evan discovered it was Swiller who jumped him and Kenny, and he didn't know how Evan came to enlist Kyler's help.

His chest constricted as he spoke. He felt so hurt by Evan lying to him about his plans, so betrayed, his emotions overcame him and he hadn't stopped long enough to hear Evan out. And he also couldn't deny the jealousy mixed in with it, as if Evan believed Kyler was more capable than him. Then guilt rose in him with the mental image of Evan in the parking garage, pleading with him to talk. Throughout his telling the story, his emotions continued spiraling wildly, leaving him not knowing what to feel.

"And so I left him there," Jesse finished softly, staring down at the table.

Brandon sat quiet. He cleared his throat after a long moment. "Well, I understand how pissed and hurt you must've been finding out what he did behind your back, but I'm not sure leaving him there was the right thing to do."

Jesse snapped his head up. "Even if it wasn't, what else was I supposed to do? Give him a hug and a pat on the back and tell him it was fine? Because it wasn't! What he did was wrong!"

"Settle down, spaz. I agree what he did was wrong. All I'm saying is that maybe you should've tried talking to him before running off. Of course, had you stayed, you may have ended up in an even bigger fight. I don't know, but what's done is done, so all there is to do now is move forward. You need to figure out what your next move is going to be, and you only have two choices, leave him, or forgive him."

"I'll never leave him! I love him!"

"Then you only have one choice."

Jesse stared at his brother. Leave it to Brandon to put it in the simplest, yet truest terms. Jesse heard the sliding door in the living room open and close again.

A few seconds later, Shunichi entered wearing his white karate uniform and black belt. He smiled at Jesse. "Hey, I've got a bone to pick with you. Your beautiful car rolling down the driveway broke all my students' concentration and it took me five minutes to get them focused again because they kept hounding me as to who I knew that drove such a hot car."

Jesse summoned a smile for him. "Sorry."

Shunichi bent and hugged him. He drew back, cocking his head while giving him a thoughtful look. "What's wrong?"

Surprised by Shunichi's astuteness, Jesse quickly retold the events. Shunichi sipped on a bottle of water, listening. When Jesse finished, like Brandon, Shunichi sat silent for a long pause.

"Well," Shunichi began, "I agree his methods weren't the most appropriate, but his intentions were good. I know I'm still getting to know him, but I think I'm right in saying that since the attack on you, Evan's blamed himself for not being with you. And I don't think I'd be wrong saying Evan's the type of person who when he loves someone, there's nothing he won't do for them and he takes it on himself to take care of them in every way possible. When you got hurt, I'm sure he felt he failed in that responsibility and was willing to do anything to set it right, even if it meant not being honest, and also swallowing his pride and going to someone he doesn't like for help."

Jesse nodded slowly, the truth of Shunichi's words hitting hard. Evan had battled the foe of his father's cancer, going to the extreme of selling himself into the music business to gain money. But for all he did, for how hard he fought, ultimately he lost to death. He now saw that Evan, most likely unknowingly, looked at the attack on him in the same way, and once again he rose to fight, determined to not lose this battle. Remorse for Evan closed his throat to where he could barely breathe. Guilt won out over anger.

"I know one thing, though," Shunichi said softly. "The thought of hurting you never entered his mind."

Jesse's throat opened enough to allow a pained whimper to escape.

Shunichi laid his hand over Jesse's. "I'm sorry for upsetting you even more."

Jesse shook his head. "No, you and Brandon just said what needed to be said. I was too close, too emotional, to see clearly. But still," his hand went to his chest, his fingers gripped his shirt in a fist over his heart, "I feel so…betrayed. I just wish he would've been honest with me."

Having no words left, Jesse stayed silent. The silence broke as Brandon's cell phone rang, singing a catchy Japanese pop song.

Brandon pulled his phone from his pocket. "It's Evan. He must be trying to figure out where you are." He rose from the chair, answering his phone as he walked to the living room.

Shunichi leaned toward him. "Jess, I understand how you could feel betrayed about Evan not being honest about his intentions, but I think it's pretty clear why he wasn't. I'm sure he thought lying to you would be the lesser evil rather than risking you getting physical hurt. You know, he has a way of seeing through people as if they were made of glass." He smiled. "I think the only person who baffles and truly challenges him is you."

Jesse nodded. "He's always been good at seeing people for what they are. He knew my former drummer, Trish, had a thing for me when no one else saw it. He told me to stay away from the Swiller boys as if he knew how dangerous they could be. He reads our producer, Greg, like a book. I just can't believe I didn't understand this about *him*."

"Well, relationships are a never ending learning process. Mistakes are made, misunderstandings happen, and hopefully, forgiveness always follows. I know you've already forgiven him. You just have to decide when and how to tell him."

"Yeah." Jesse looked up as Brandon entered the kitchen.

"Evan told me to tell you he's at home waiting for you and even though it won't feel as meaningful coming through me, he's sorry, and he'll apologize better when you come home."

Jesse sighed. "He has a remarkable way of making me feel guilty when I shouldn't."

Shunichi laughed softly. "I'm sure that's not his intention, either." He stood up and stretched his arms over his head. "I hate to leave you like this, but I've got to get ready for my next class."

Brandon stepped in front of him and slid his arms around Shunichi's waist. "We were all talking so much you didn't eat lunch. How about while you're doing this lesson, I'll go to the deli up the street and get you a sandwich?"

Shunichi lowered his arms around Brandon's neck. "I'm getting too used to you spoiling me."

Brandon tipped his head to the side, angling his lips toward Shunichi's. "You know you like it."

"I love it," Shunichi said, bringing his lips to Brandon's.

Jesse smiled, watching them, then glanced away to give them a moment of privacy.

The kiss drew to an end, and Shunichi looked toward Jesse. "Have you eaten? If not, you should join us."

"Of course he'll join us," Brandon said. "Especially since I'll be taking his car."

Jesse laughed. "The hell you will!"

Shunichi drifted one hand down Brandon's back and gave his ass a light slap before walking toward the door. "Alright boys, some of us have real jobs that don't let us slack off whenever we want to."

Jesse snorted. "Yeah, like playing Captain Karate all day is a real job."

Shunichi winked at him. "It's harder than yours."

"Well, I'll give you that."

Brandon watched Shunichi walk away, then turned to Jesse. "You want to come with me, or stay here?"

"I'll come with you." Jesse rose from his chair. "But as soon as we finish eating, I'm going to head home and talk things out with Ev."

CHAPTER THIRTY-SEVEN

Evan walked into the entrance room and stopped, his gaze on Jesse, who smiled and talked to Achilles while the dog pranced circles around him. Jesse looked up at him. Evan lowered his gaze.

Jesse could see the uncertainty in Evan's stance, his wracked nerves betrayed in how he twisted his father's eagle ring on his index finger. Jesse let out a loud sigh and shook his head at him. "What am I going to do with you?"

Evan chanced a glance at him. "Love me?"

"Well yeah, that's a given. But all the love in the world isn't going to turn you into a civil human being."

Feeling encouraged by Jesse's calm voice and humor, Evan decided to hazard another suggestion. "You could try exhausting me with sex. Maybe then I'd be too tired to raise my fists."

A warm smile graced Jesse's lips. "That was already my strategy."

The apprehensiveness left Evan's eyes, his posture straightened. "Jess."

Jesse walked across the entrance room; Evan hastened to meet him. At the foot of the stairs, Evan slammed against him in a rough embrace, squeezing Jesse to him.

"I'm so sorry, Jess. I'm sorry for not coming to you right away when I realized who was behind the attack. I'm sorry for going to Kyler for help. I'm sorry for betraying you about my intentions today. I'm so sorry for everything."

Jesse rubbed one hand up and down Evan's back. "It's alright, Ev. I forgive you. And I'm sorry too, for not giving you a chance to explain earlier." Keeping his arms around Evan's waist, he leaned back. "But I don't want you to think you're off the hook. I still need to hear the whole story of how this all came about."

"I'll tell you everything."

Jesse took Evan's hand and stepped up the first stair.

Evan looked at him, confused. "Why are we going upstairs?"

"Because after you finish your story, I'm going with my strategy of wearing you out with sex to keep you from being a bad boy."

Evan climbed the stairs with him. "We're going to have to practice this strategy daily, maybe even more. Who knows what I'll do if we miss a day."

"I know. That's why it's good I'm fully devoted to this strategy."

"But can I still be a bad boy sometimes?"

Jesse grinned at him. "If you do it in a way I like."

Evan lifted Jesse's hand to his lips and laid a tender kiss on the back of it.

They entered the bedroom, and Jesse released his hand to climb onto the bed. He lay down on his back, folding his arms behind his head on a pillow.

Evan crawled onto the bed and faced him as he recounted his meeting with the paparazzo, Paul McClain. "When I was watching the video, I studied the three figures, how they moved, how they stood, their height, their weight. Two stood hunched like Trent and Matt, the one wearing the blue mask more so like Trent. The heights were right for them both, and the shorter one had a stocky build like the drummer. Even masked I noticed the way Trent and Matt moved, always loosely swinging their arms and bobbing their heads, and the third moved with the rigid stiffness the drummer carries himself with."

Jesse stared at Evan, stunned, and a little impressed by his deductions. A thought struck him. "But the cops said they returned to L.A."

"They *were* in L.A., but it was after they jumped you. I had Greg check and the only time the Phoenix jet has left for L.A.

recently was the day after you got jumped. I have a feeling their manager knew what happened and sent them out of town until things cooled off, and the cops took his word for it that they left earlier."

Jesse allowed himself to absorb Evan's words before asking the question he dreaded. "And how did Kyler get involved?"

Evan laid a hand on Jesse's thigh. "Let me say first that nothing happened between us, not even a handshake. I swear on my love for you."

Jesse placed his hand over Evan's. "I know, but you have to understand how much it hurt me to see you with him. It was like you believed he would be greater help to you than me."

Evan squeezed Jesse's hand. "That's not what I believed. I didn't come to you because I didn't want you to be a part of more violence, and even more, I didn't want to risk you getting hurt. I came close enough to losing you, I wasn't going to purposely put you in danger. Do you really think I would've cared if Kyler got the shit beat out of him? If he got hurt, I could've shrugged at him lying on the floor, then walked away pondering what to get for lunch."

"That's a little cold."

"It might be, but it's also the truth."

"What confuses the hell out of me is why Kyler helped you. I realized a long time ago, he's disgusted with you for retiring. I just hope he hasn't gotten over that and he's trying to move in on you again." Jesse spoke his last words through clenched teeth, instantly angered at the thought.

"Trust me, him having an interest in me is *not* why he helped. You know whose number one in his life. And even though they have the most fucked up relationship I've ever seen, they can't seem to break away from each other."

"So why did he help you?"

Evan looked directly into his eyes. "He did it for you."

Jesse shook his head slightly. "I don't understand."

"Believe it or not, he really likes you and respects you. When I first approached him, he didn't even want to talk to me. It wasn't until I said I needed to talk about what happened to you that he gave me his full attention. I told him about the video and my suspicions as to who it was. Since I knew he could get closer to them than I could, I asked if he would try to get the truth out of them, and he did.

"While we were on our honeymoon, the Swiller boys came back, and Kyler and Robbie conned them into going to some strip clubs with them. Well, it wasn't much of a con. Kyler told them he could get them into the best clubs regardless of them being underage, and all they heard was boobs and beer. Between supplying them with a constant flow of alcohol and having some of the women distract them, Kyler said all it took was some gentle coaxing to get the story out. He also said he nearly beat their asses as soon as he heard the truth, but for once he managed to practice restraint and decided to wait until he talked to me.

"He told me after we came back and asked what I was planning to do. When I told him, he said he wanted in, and I decided even though I felt like I could take on all three, in reality I couldn't." Evan averted his gaze from Jesse. "It wasn't easy for me, going to him for help. It took a few tries before I could swallow my pride enough to talk to him, but I did it because it was for you. I had to know who hurt you. I had to know so I could stop it from happening again."

Jesse sat up and wrapped his arms around him, his voice soft. "It's alright, Ev. I understand why you did it." He cupped Evan's face in both hands. "But do you know what upset me most with what you did?"

Evan shook his head.

"Fear. Fear at what could've happened to you. Don't you understand your life isn't your own anymore? That it's mine? If I ever lost you, I'd be crushed, I'd be lost, I'd shatter. Just as you said you didn't want to put me in danger, I don't want you to do the same with yourself."

Evan laid his head on Jesse's shoulder. "The thought of something happening to me never entered my mind, but I know what you mean. I wouldn't want you to do something like what I did. If you did," he raised his head and smiled, "I'd develop a strategy to exhaust you daily with sex."

Jesse laughed softly. "That's right."

He placed his fingertips under Evan's chin, and with his gentle touch guiding him, brought Evan to his lips. A soft groan rumbled from Evan's throat. He pushed against him, and Jesse eased to his back. Evan lay over him, settling his hard cock atop Jesse's. He pressed down harder. Jesse responded by tightening his hand in a fist around Evan's hair.

Evan broke the kiss with a shaking breath. Jesse gripped his hair firmer and pulled him to his lips again. A whimper of need sounded in Evan's throat. Jesse slipped his free hand under Evan's shirt, caressing his back. Evan's touch moved up Jesse's shirt, petting the smooth, taut flesh over the wiry muscle of his torso. For several moments they lay enjoying the simple pleasure of kissing and cherishing the feel of the other's body.

Jesse placed one hand on Evan's shoulder and heaved his body upward. Evan rolled in harmony with him, putting Jesse on top of him. Jesse claimed his mouth once more, his kiss fiercer, hungrier. Evan wrapped both arms around him. He slung his legs over Jesse's lower body, holding him to him. Jesse moved his hips in the smallest of motions, creating friction between their hard cocks.

After a few short moments, Jesse slowly drew back and rose to his knees. He pulled his shirt over his head and flung it, then extended both hands to Evan. Evan took them, and with a strong tug from Jesse, found himself sitting upright. Jesse lifted Evan's shirt, tossed it away, and moved his fingers to his own jeans. Anxious to feel Jesse's bare skin on his, Evan fell to his back again and worked his own jeans off.

Kneeling on the bed, bared of his clothes, Jesse smiled at Evan's ready desire. He beckoned him with his index finger. Evan sat up. He brought his knees under himself and moved toward him. Jesse pulled Evan against him, bringing their chests, their hips, together. The sides of their cocks slid against each other. As Jesse exhaled, Evan breathed in his expelled breath. In unison, they touched their lips together.

Their cocks pinned between their bodies, Jesse rocked his hips toward him. Evan matched his movements. Moisture dampened their stomachs, a mix of pre-cum and sweat. Jesse dipped his head, laying a line of firm kisses down Evan's neck. He licked at the curve, then covered it with his lips, sucking hard.

Evan hooked his fingers into Jesse's lower back, realizing Jesse was marking him, and for the first time in their relationship, in a place where others could easily see it.

Jesse drifted his lips higher, his tongue teasing the two gold hoops in Evan's left ear. "I want to watch you prepare yourself for me."

Unable to find his voice, Evan nodded. He could feel it from him, the inner strength Jesse possessed, his unconquerable spirit, his dominance.

Jesse stretched for the lube on the nightstand. He placed it within easy reach for Evan, then lay down on his back, his head resting on the plush pillows, and guided Evan to straddle his hips. His gaze coasted over Evan's body. Evan knelt over him, his thighs wide apart. The cords of his quads stood out against his skin, the muscles in his abdomen tense, his chest expanded with quick breaths. His entire body looked tight, as if in desperate need for release.

Jesse brought his gaze to Evan's, a mischievous smirk lighting his lips. "You're already breathless and flushed. You're going to lose it the second I get in you."

Evan laughed softly. "I may." He bent over Jesse, going to all fours. "But all that means is we'll have to keep going, for the rest of the day and night until neither of us has anything left."

Jesse grazed his lips over Evan's. "Turn around."

Evan couldn't help the smile that came to his lips. He loved it when Jesse got into these naughtier moods, but it showed Jesse had let go of all negative feelings from earlier. That's how his Jesse was. He never held grudges against him, he always forgave him. He placed a light kiss on Jesse's lips, then moved to do as he asked. He swung his left leg across Jesse's body, spun on his knees to face the foot of the bed, and brought his right leg over him to straddle him again. He could feel Jesse's heated gaze on his ass and bent forward further than he needed to reach the lube.

Jesse rubbed Evan's ass cheeks. "You may be retiring from being a great showman on stage, but I'm not sure that part of your personality will ever die."

"Of course it won't. Not with the beautiful duets we'll do like this for the rest of our lives."

Jesse sat up, kissed Evan's right ass cheek, and fell back to the pillows.

Evan placed his left hand on the bed beside Jesse's knee, and with the slicked fingers of his right, he reached back, massaging the outside of his hole. He pushed his middle finger inside himself. As Evan slowly thrust it in and out, he felt Jesse's fingers clamp onto his calves and knew his control was cracking. He decided to push it to its limit.

Evan drew his middle finger nearly out of himself and entered again with his index joining it. As both fingers stretched him, he groaned long and low. Below him, his saw Jesse's cock twitch, the slit moistened. He scissored his fingers, spreading, stretching his hole for him, then Jesse's hands left his calves.

Jesse grabbed the lube off the bed. He brought slick fingers to Evan's hole. As Evan pulled his fingers back, Jesse joined his index with Evan's other two, pushing into him as Evan thrust forward again.

Evan groaned, the sound hard. For an instant, his internal muscles clenched around their three fingers, then slackened. He stopped his thrusting motions, Jesse halted as well. He needed to savor how amazing it felt to have his and Jesse's fingers sheathed inside his body together. When he moved again, Jesse moved with him, both pumping with equal speed and force.

Jesse felt warm drops drip onto his stomach from Evan's leaking cock. He pulled Evan's hand away from. He pushed himself back to slide out from under him and knelt behind him. Jesse held his own cock by the shaft and rubbed the tip against Evan's hole, letting him feel it, but denying him every time Evan pushed back to take it. Mere moments passed before Evan dropped down to his elbows, his head sagged between his arms, and he whimpered Jesse's name in a voice that sounded near tears. Deciding he'd tormented him enough, Jesse gripped one of Evan's hips and thrust forward.

A loud, trembling groan left Evan's throat as Jesse's cock pushed in. Jesse eased it in further, feeling more and more heat as Evan's soft flesh encased him. He willed his body to remain calm, but he wanted to slam Evan down on his full length. Evan, seeming to know his desire, pushed back, taking him in hard and fast.

A high moan escaped Jesse's throat. His fingers hooked into Evan's hips as he jerked his own forward in deep thrusts. Evan met him on each one. Jesse leaned over Evan's back. He slipped his right arm underneath Evan and around his chest. He sank his left hand into Evan's hair. In one forceful movement, he hauled Evan back by his torso and hair, then hurled them both to their right sides on the bed.

Evan gasped as he landed hard. He gripped the edge of the bed. Jesse pushed his left arm under Evan's left thigh, lifting it up and bending it, the movement allowing him to go deeper. Each thrust grew in urgency. With his right arm still across Evan's chest, he moved his hand to Evan's left nipple and pinched it.

A sharp, high moan broke from Evan's throat. He felt his orgasm burn in growing strength. He grabbed his cock in a tight fist, having no need to stroke it as Jesse's thrusts pumped it into his hand for him. But more than he wanted his own pleasure to be satiated, he needed to feel Jesse come deep inside him.

Jesse's body tensed and trembled behind him, and he knew he was nearly there.

A heartbeat later, Jesse cried out. The first pulse of Jesse's orgasm, the heat of his cum filling him, trigged Evan's release. He rocked back on Jesse, shouting in passion as he came.

Gradually, Jesse loosened his hold on him. After several moments, he sat up enough to nuzzle into Evan's hair and placed a gentle kiss on his cheek. "Thank you for what you did, Ev. Thank you for protecting me."

Evan turned his head toward him. "I always will. But from now on, I'll work to protect myself also, for you."

"And I'll help you with that, forever." Jesse bowed his head to him, claiming Evan's lips in a love filled kiss.

CHAPTER THIRTY-EIGHT

Three months later

Sitting on a couch in the chill-out room, papers scattered across the table in front of him detailing upcoming publicity gigs and tour dates, Jesse looked over the list of bands that would be their opening acts for the *No Fear World Tour*. Only a third of the shows were booked so far, but since Swiller got pulled from the tour, they decided they'd have bands local to the cities they played in open for them. He came up with the idea, thinking it might be a nice way for Phoenix to find new talent and to help other musicians get a shot at their dream, and the label already had scouts out at their tour destinations scouring the clubs.

The sound of Brad laughing broke Jesse's concentration and he caught Kenny telling Brad of his adventure the evening before in attempting to win over twins, that he somehow failed miserably, despite Conquest being the most recognized band in the country.

Julian leaned over to Jesse, whispering, "Poor, poor straight boy. Having to work so hard just trying to get a blowjob, then forced to walk away with nothing."

Jesse snickered. "I don't think it's an issue of being straight. He's a dork, that's his problem."

Kenny whipped his head toward Jesse. "Did you say something?"

"Yeah, I said maybe if you weren't the biggest dork to ever play in a rock band, you might have more luck getting laid." Jesse looked up as Evan entered the room. His gaze moved to the two figures prancing at Evan's side. He clapped his hands, pitching his voice high as he called, "Achilles, Iris! Here, babies!"

Achilles sprang to gallop the short distance to Jesse, and at his side, running on large paws not yet fitting her body, charged a four-month-old black and tan German Shepherd. Achilles leaped at Jesse, landing half on his lap. Iris scrambled to do the same. Jesse wrapped one arm around them both, roughing up their fur and laughing.

Kenny shook his head. "Are you ever going to have a dog that you name something normal?"

Jesse talked to the puppy in a baby voice. "But you're a little bringer of happiness, aren't you? And Iris was a Greek messenger goddess, wasn't she?"

Kenny rolled his eyes. "I can't believe you guys drove all the way to Michigan to get a personal protection dog and that's what you come home with."

Jesse flicked his head toward Evan. "They fell in love. I couldn't say no when she looked up at me with her big brown eyes and he looked at me with his beautiful blue ones."

Evan sat beside Jesse and the puppy promptly jumped on him. He wrapped one arm around her and stretched his other arm behind Jesse, his fingers toying with Jesse's hair. "She was the last puppy from their spring litters and she was in a kennel all by herself. When we walked by, she started crying her little head off. I felt so bad for her. Then when one of the handlers went to calm her, she slipped away and ran to us."

"Ran to you." Jesse looked toward the others. "If I spill water on his jeans, he's ready to cry. But a puppy jumps on him with paws covered in mud and who knows what else, and he thought it was cute."

"It was cute," Evan said.

Achilles, having managed to wiggle the rest of his bulk onto the couch, lay across Jesse's lap. Jesse hugged him around the neck with both arms. "I really didn't care what we got so long as 'Chilles was happy and they hit it off right away." His tone shifted once again to baby talk. "Now you have a playmate, don't you? It's not so lonely when you're left at home, is it?"

Kenny leaned toward Brad. "He really thinks the dog's going to answer him one of these days."

Jesse aimed a teasing glare at Kenny. "He might. I know he's smarter than you."

Before Kenny could respond, Jesse's attention moved off him to the doorway as Greg entered. They had waited for him so they could all go down to the United Center to rehearse for their upcoming kick-off concert, but where Greg should have looked excited at the flow of money coming in from the start of Conquest's tour, instead he looked somber.

Jesse's voice lifted in concern. "Greg? Is everything okay?"

Greg sat heavily in a chair. He closed his eyes and rubbed them. "It could be better."

"What's going on?" Evan asked.

"I just got the reports on the sales of *No Fear*. Conquest…" Greg paused, as if getting the words out caused him physical pain. "Jesse, Swiller and Black Heart Down are above Conquest. As it stands now, they've beaten you guys."

Jesse froze, mentally and bodily. After a long moment of no one daring to speak, a pained gasp left Jesse. "That's not possible. 'Twisted Destiny' is the Number One single in the country. In the world! *No Fear* can't be below their albums! It can't be!"

Greg slowly raised his head, looking at Jesse for the first time. A smile sprang to his lips. "You're right. It's not. It debuted in the top spot, iTunes almost froze up from so many people downloading it, and it's already gone multi-Platinum. Swiller's album isn't even in the top twenty-five, but BHD is holding tight to the two spot. At the pace *No Fear* is going, it'll outsell your total album sales for *Conquest* by the end of the week, though the sales for *Conquest* have been up too, but they have been ever since you and Evan came out. Congratulations, guys. You've done it again."

"I knew it!" Jesse sprang to his feet, forcing Achilles to jump down, and punched the air with a triumphant fist. "I knew we'd kick their asses!" He whirled around, slapping a hard high five to each of his band members and Evan. He spun toward Greg and halted, his eyes narrowed in accusation. "I can't believe you. Since when do you have a sense of humor?"

"Since you and Evan have given me numerous close calls with heart attacks during your careers, I thought it's about time you got a taste of what one felt like." Greg stood up and pulled Jesse into an embrace. "Congratulations, son."

"Thanks," Jesse said softly. When Greg released him, he turned to Evan, a warm smile on his lips. "And thank you, manager."

Evan smirked at him. "I deserve more than just a thank you after busting my ass to keep you focused and get this album done and out."

Jesse leaned down to him, gently blocking Iris from getting between them, and put his lips close to Evan's. "You'll get a lot more than a thank you later on."

Evan's lips brushed Jesse's. "You know, since you're my boss, this is sexual harassment."

"It's only harassment if you don't like it."

"It's harassment that we have to watch it!" Kenny blurted out.

Jesse ignored Kenny's words and pressed his lips to Evan's in a long kiss. He drew back, a smile still on his lips. "You're next, you know."

Evan nodded. "After we wrap up this tour, I'll hit the studio with the orchestra again to get *Finale* finished." He took Jesse's hand in his and met his gaze. "Then I can finally live a life where I'm focused on what's most important to me."

Jesse caressed Evan's cheek. "And I'll work to make sure every day of your new life is one filled with happiness." He slowly turned his gaze to the others. "Now, let's head down to the United Center and get ready to launch a tour that will leave everyone who sees us stunned for days afterward."

Evan clipped Iris's powder blue leash to her matching collar, and handed Jesse Achilles' paw prints and crossbones leash. He moved to Jesse's side and took his hand as they walked from the room. They exited the studio, and Jesse turned his head to the sound of a deep rumbling car engine, recognizing Shunichi's Mustang rolling toward them. The car glided to a halt and the passenger window lowered. Jesse peeked in at Brandon, seeing his brother's hand resting over Shunichi's on the shifter.

"Hey," Brandon said. "We were on our way to the arena to watch you guys rehearse and thought we'd stop by to see if you were still here. Looks like we just caught you."

"We're heading over there now." Jesse looked past his brother to Shunichi in the driver's seat. "You ready to see how it all goes down?"

"I've been excited all day," Shunichi said. "I've always wanted to see how a big concert is put on."

"Just wait until you guys come with us to Japan and you're hanging with us twenty-four/seven. Then you'll really see what a good time is."

Brandon turned an exasperated look to Shunichi. "Now you'll *really* get to see his ego in full glory."

Jesse reprimanded him with a light shove on the shoulder. "Let's get going."

Brandon grabbed Jesse's hand before he could turn away. He tugged him closer to the car, and Jesse bent near the window.

"Congratulations," Brandon said softly. "And not just on the album, on everything. On not being defeated from getting jumped, on staying strong and doing what you love, but mostly, on coming out with Evan publicly. You told the world who you are, who you love, and you did it with pride and bravery. I'm so proud of you, Jess."

Jesse laid his other hand over Brandon's. "Thanks."

Shunichi leaned over Brandon's lap. "Hey Evan, what car are you driving?"

"Since we got the dogs, we brought the Escalade. Why?"

"Because I would've raced you down there if you were driving one of your overpriced wrecks and embarrassed you when I got there first."

"Is that so?" Evan laughed. "It's on tomorrow! I'll even let you pick which overpriced wreck you want to try and embarrass."

Jesse turned to Evan. "You will not be street racing! I can finally do whatever I want to you in public, I'm not going to have you killed in a car accident!"

Brandon turned on Shunichi. "And I've spent my whole life trying to find my other half, and now you want to put yourself in danger!"

Evan and Shunichi allowed a chastised expression to fall on their faces for a brief instant before glancing at each other with conspiratorial grins.

Jesse huffed and pulled Evan's hand, heading toward the parking garage. "We'll meet you guys down there."

Once in the garage, everyone broke apart to their vehicles. With the dogs loaded in the back of the Escalade, Evan went to the driver's side, Jesse to the passenger.

Before firing up the SUV, Evan took Jesse's hand and reached toward him with the other, gently combing his fingers through Jesse's hair. "You did it, gorgeous. This time, you really have conquered the world. You've led your band to victory and you did it with the world knowing exactly who you are."

Jesse squeezed Evan's hand. "I couldn't have done it without you at my side. You're my strength, Ev. You're my heart, my soul, the love of my life. So long as I have you, I'll always fight to be victorious in all I do. I love you."

"I love you too, Jess. So very much."

Evan leaned toward him. Their arms slipped around each other as their breath mingled before their mouths closed together. Evan tightened his hold on Jesse, and Jesse strengthened his on Evan's, their kiss holding the promise of love beyond eternity.

ABOUT THE AUTHOR

S.J. FROST resides on a mini-ranch in Ohio with her husband and son, as well as a kind-hearted German Shepherd, a Collie who is the anti-Lassie, a few kooky cats, and some very special horses. She enjoys experimenting with her writing and dabbling in different genres, though it's guaranteed that no matter what she writes there will be hot erotic action appearing somewhere in the story. She's a romantic at heart, which is reflected in her writing. The majority of her work is m/m, though she's had the occasional m/f piece published too. Her short stories have been featured in several erotic and romance anthologies including, Best Gay Romance 2007 Edition, Girls on Top, and Surfer Boys, all published by Cleis Press, Ultimate Gay Erotica 2008 and Best Gay Love Stories: Summer Flings, both published by Alyson Books, and Honey Flava published by Atria Books.

You can find out more about the author and upcoming works at: http://www.sjfrost.com/

SERVICEMEMBERS LEGAL DEFENSE NETWORK

Servicemembers Legal Defense Network is a nonpartisan, nonprofit, legal services, watchdog and policy organization dedicated to ending discrimination against and harassment of military personnel affected by "Don't Ask, Don't Tell" (DADT). The SLDN provides free, confidential legal services to all those impacted by DADT and related discrimination. Since 1993, its inhouse legal team has responded to more than 9,000 requests for assistance. In Congress, it leads the fight to repeal DADT and replace it with a law that ensures equal treatment for every servicemember, regardless of sexual orientation. In the courts, it works to challenge the constitutionality of DADT.

SLDN
PO Box 65301
Washington DC 20035-5301
On the Web: http://sldn.org/

Call: (202) 328-3244
or (202) 328-FAIR
e-mail: sldn@sldn.org

THE GLBT NATIONAL HELP CENTER

The GLBT National Help Center is a nonprofit, tax-exempt organization that is dedicated to meeting the needs of the gay, lesbian, bisexual and transgender community and those questioning their sexual orientation and gender identity. It is an outgrowth of the Gay & Lesbian National Hotline, which began in 1996 and now is a primary program of The GLBT National Help Center. It offers several different programs including two national hotlines that help members of the GLBT community talk about the important issues that they are facing in their lives. It helps end the isolation that many people feel, by providing a safe environment on the phone or via the internet to discuss issues that people can't talk about anywhere else. The GLBT National Help Center also helps other organizations build the infrastructure they need to provide strong support to our community at the local level.

National Hotline: 1-888-THE-GLNH (1-888-843-4564)
National Youth Talkline 1-800-246-PRIDE (1-800-246-7743)
On the Web: http://www.glnh.org/
e-mail: info@glbtnationalhelpcenter.org

If you're a GLBT and questioning student heading off to university, should know that there are resources on campus for you. Here's just a sample:

US Local GLBT college campus organizations
        http://dv-8.com/resources/us/local/campus.html
GLBT Scholarship Resources
        http://tinyurl.com/6fx9v6
Syracuse University
        http://lgbt.syr.edu/
Texas A&M
        http://glbt.tamu.edu/
Tulane University
        http://www.oma.tulane.edu/LGBT/Default.htm
University of Alaska
        http://www.uaf.edu/agla/
University of California, Davis
        http://lgbtrc.ucdavis.edu/
University of California, San Francisco
        http://lgbt.ucsf.edu/
University of Colorado
        http://www.colorado.edu/glbtrc/
University of Florida
        http://www.dso.ufl.edu/multicultural/lgbt/
University of Hawai'i, Mānoa
        http://manoa.hawaii.edu/lgbt/
University of Utah
        http://www.sa.utah.edu/lgbt/
University of Virginia
        http://www.virginia.edu/deanofstudents/lgbt/
Vanderbilt University
        http://www.vanderbilt.edu/lgbtqi/

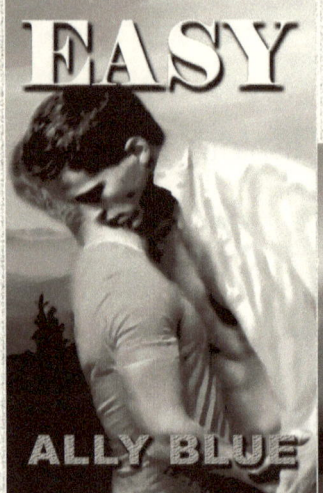

www.ingramcontent.com/pod-product-compliance
Lightning Source LLC
Chambersburg PA
CBHW050912250626
47155CB00001B/201

* 9 7 8 1 6 0 8 2 0 1 3 6 5 *